Wild Side OF THE HEART

A FINDING FAITH ROMANCE NOVEL

JESSICA ALYSE

ACKNOWLEDGEMENTS

Thanks to my family. Without you, I wouldn't have become a reader-turned-writer. A special thanks to my mom, who has patiently listened to hours upon hours of my passion for fiction and storytelling. You've always been front row when I'm shining my brightest.

Thank you to Dana McCall Michael, who, after reading my second novel, encouraged me to write a story about "sweet Peyton." God used you to help this story come to light in a way I didn't expect.

Thank you to Alexis A. Goring, who has been my go-to author for countless ideas, advice, and second opinions. Your kindness and dedication are priceless.

And last but certainly not least, thank you to Taylor Greenhouse for her time, devotion, and expertise in editing—and for letting God use her to wrap up the final pieces of this ten-year-long series. You are the representation of God's perfect timing.

I couldn't have done it without any of you.

DEDICATION

This book is dedicated to Jesus.
To my Father, my King, my Healer.
I am undone by the love in Your gaze.
In the compassion of Your voice, I melt.
Your mercy and majesty captivate my identity.
All that I am fades away in the light of Your glory.
All that I'm called to be is forever drawn to Your presence.

Secondly, to every inner child who is begging to be released from the pain of someone else's actions. To the unhealed hearts who yearn to be seen, heard, held, and gifted the grace to be and become. May you find freedom in the wild side of Christ's heart—where Love dared to step away from the law of death, to break unbreakable chains, to redeem an irredeemable bride, and to honor an impossible covenant. We do not serve a God who is limited by rules, restrictions, and regulations. His love for us is wild and free. Hope, restoration, and abundance are yours to take from His hand.

"From the end of the earth will I cry unto thee,
When my heart is overwhelmed:
Lead me to the rock that is higher than I."
Psalm 61:2

WILD SIDE OF THE HEART

AUSTIN, TEXAS

Nothing on earth could compare to the joy inside a room crowded with family. The chatter, the laughter, the squeals of kids playing tag.

Too bad Peyton Brooks couldn't make it reach his soul.

In the whirlwind of happy chaos packed within the walls of his brother's home, there was a void in his heart he'd been trying to put a name to for a while. It was like everyone around him was aware of some incredible work of art that Peyton couldn't see. He pretended like he could, just so nobody asked questions. Mainly because he didn't have any answers to give them.

The shrill cry of a two-year-old pierced the celebration noise and chased away his thoughts. Peyton pushed himself out of the armchair and started for the hallway.

"Uncle Peyt, could you see to them?" Natalie, his sister-in-law, yelled from the kitchen.

"I'm on it," he called over his shoulder as he reached the last room on the right where a slice of darkness peeked through the cracked door. He gave it a gentle push and it creaked open to the sound of soft kiddie music playing naptime lullabies. The flip of the switch doused the room in light and revealed the pouts of his twin nephews sitting in the middle of their own racecar beds. "What's up, fellas?"

Those pouts were replaced with smiles once they realized who was standing in the doorway.

Pushing their blankets aside, they stood on tottering legs to reach him. Peyton met them halfway, easing down on the carpeted floor and leaning back against the dresser as the two tykes descended on him. He wrapped an arm around each one of their middles and tickled their sides. Noah squealed. Or maybe that was Dakota? He still had trouble telling them apart. "Which one of you guy's is Noah?"

They pointed toward the squealer.

"Thought so." He tickled them again, this time until they were a heap of squirming, breathless giggles. Both boys spitting images of their mom with their straight, blond hair and sky-blue eyes. And she hadn't forgotten to pass down her tenacity to them, either.

Noah rushed over to a tub of toys and started rifling inside while Dakota went back to his bed and pulled a sippy cup from under the covers. Peyton waited patiently for each of them to return. He much preferred the stillness and quiet of this room to the pure pandemonium in the living room.

It wasn't all that bad. He just wasn't in the mood to party. He'd never voice that to Austin and Natalie, though. It was his brother and sister-in-law's anniversary. Their eighth. And everyone had come out to celebrate.

Everyone.

The footsteps of a small army thundered outside the twins' room and Peyton braced himself. The boys' older sister, Riley, flew through the doorway and straight into his arms with five other girls on her heels.

"Uncle Peyt, come play with us!" She hung from one arm hooked around his neck. She, unlike her brothers, took on the likeness of their dad with her sandy brown hair and green eyes. She got her relentless energy from him, too.

"Under one condition," he said, and she nodded once as if it were a done deal. "We have to play hide-and-seek."

Without so much as a negotiation, the little troop of girls left the same way they'd come, shrieking as they went in urgent search of a hiding spot. Peyton chuckled under his breath. That'd buy him about five minutes.

But he was a man of his word. So, a minute later he pushed himself off the ground, gathered the munchkins in each arm, and delivered them to the living room.

"There they are!" Peyton's mom and dad, Jenny and Jake, swooped in like hawks and stole the boys from him.

Peyton pushed the fallen sleeve of his button down up to his elbow. "Aw, Mom, I remember when you used to look at me like that."

"Don't worry, Peyt. They'll make time for you again." Austin grinned as he stepped out of the kitchen and disappeared through the open patio doors at the back of the living room. His Great Dane, AJ, shadowing his every step.

"Peyton." From the couch, Avery Reed waved a hand through the air. "Did you ever go out with that girl—what was her name?"

"Claire?" He stepped aside as two of Avery's boys jetted for the hallway behind him.

"I thought her name was Clarissa?" Natalie said as she lowered herself into the loveseat with her rounded belly tipping toward nine months.

"Clarissa," he corrected himself. It didn't matter what her name was because she didn't exist. It was just the name he'd given Avery the last time she'd tried to hook him up with one of her friends from Houston. "She's, uh, seeing someone else."

"Aww, too bad," Avery cooed and then sucked in a breath as quickly. "I met a girl at church this morning about your age and I'm pretty sure she's single, too."

Bad idea. His imaginary girlfriend was about two seconds away from breaking up with her non-existent boyfriend. "Uh, yeah..." Through the front window overlooking the porch, Marcus Williams, Austin's co-worker, and Liam, Avery's husband, talked near the railing. Maybe Peyton could use them for cover. "I'll give her a call."

He swung the front door open, and his grandparents filled the empty space.

"Peyt! Boy, give your Nan a hug!" She waved him forward with both hands, the cherry-red tips of her short, gray hair brushing her shoulders. "Did you get taller?"

At twenty-five? Unlikely. "A half inch since the last time you saw me."

"I thought so." She patted his stomach as she moved to hug Sierra Aguilar, the wife of one of Austin's friends.

Pop stopped short of Peyton and looked him square in the eye, a sun-tanned wrinkle between his furry, gray brows. "You married yet?"

Peyton fought back a laugh that turned into a snort. "No, sir. Still looking for that special lady with a retirement plan."

Pop huffed under his breath as he moved to shake the hand of Sierra's husband, Gavin. That was as close to a chuckle as they were gonna see from Pop this afternoon.

Liam and Marcus followed behind Nan and Pop. So much for using them to escape Avery's matchmaking schemes. He'd have to find somewhere else to duck and cover. He stepped at the back of the line moving at a slug's pace toward the kitchen. They were all like salmon trying to get upstream. He got as close to the kitchen island as he could and snatched a warm brownie from a decorative plate.

"Hannah baked those." Cassandra, Marcus's wife, held their newborn daughter against her shoulder and nodded toward Hannah Reed sitting at the island. The girl dipped her chin and smiled, peeking up at him with one blue eye and one brown eye.

He took one bite and savored the sweetness with a hum. "As a dessert connoisseur, I can say with confidence that these are the best brownies I've ever tasted." He lowered his voice and winked. "Just don't tell Aunt Nattie I said that."

She giggled and leaned against one of the Aguilar girls whose name was lost on him at the moment. He made his way over to the one empty space at the edge of the kitchen counter, next to a bowl of fruit that was long forgotten in the wake of the feast Natalie had cooked up.

Two pots of chili, towers of sandwiches, mounds of chicken nuggets and fish sticks for the kids—Peyton, too, if he could sneak a few—mac and cheese, potato salad, and casserole. And then there were pies, cakes, cupcakes, brownies, and cookies spread across a piece of brown parchment paper that covered the island.

Peyton's stomach growled. Not that he could hear it. Or anything else for that matter, over the chorus of voices fighting to be the loudest. He snatched an apple from the bowl of disregarded fruit and rubbed the shiny red peel against his shirt.

Austin strolled back inside, and Nan threw her hands in the air. "You call this a party?" She shook her hips with such finesse that any salsa dancer would be jealous. "Where's the music at?"

"What? You can't break a hip to *Floppy and Friends*?" Austin gestured to the cartoons playing on the TV over the fireplace. He wrapped Nan in a hug and pulled her off the ground. It was supposed to be a secret that Austin was Nan's favorite grandkid, but Peyton knew it. Had known for years.

Not that she treated him differently or loved him less. But Austin was ten years older than him, and the two of them shared a decade's worth of memories from before Peyton was born. There was a connection with Austin that Peyton didn't have with his grandparents. Or with anyone else for that matter.

But he was cool with that. Life was good. He couldn't complain. Even if there was an endless drive to question life at the end of every day.

"While we've got everyone here," Austin called out and a hush fell over the room. "We'll start with the speeches—Marcus, you wanna kick things off?"

Everyone turned and Marcus's eyes widened. "I'd like to start by saying this is very unexpected and I have nothing prepared."

Sudden laughter filled the room.

"Seriously though. We're just happy to have everyone here today," Austin said, sharing a smile with Natalie as her friend, Jo Palmer, helped her from the couch. A giant circle started to form against the walls as everyone gathered shoulder-to-shoulder. "Natalie and I want to thank everybody for being here for us today, and for the other three-hundred-sixty-four days, too, for that matter."

As everyone laughed again, Peyton bit into the apple.

"I'll start with prayer, then I'll bless the food, and we can dig in," Austin said, waving for the kids playing on the patio to join them. All seventeen of them—save five little girls.

Peyton almost choked on the bite. He tossed the apple on the counter and swallowed what was in his mouth as he shouldered his way out of the circle. "Uh, Austin, if you can stall...I'm, uh, in the middle of an intense game of hide-and-seek right now." He backed through the open patio doors as laughter followed him.

Intense was the key word if he couldn't find these kids in the next thirty seconds. In the crisp January sunshine he scanned the trim, green lawn. The space was no bigger than half an acre and mostly fence anyway. Besides the jungle gym in the middle of the yard and the giant dog sleeping upside down with four legs in the air, there weren't many places for five girls to hide.

Then his brother's art studio came into view, sitting catty corner beside the house. They weren't supposed to play in there, but if anyone was gonna test the boundaries of a rule it would be Riley. He swung the door open and skimmed the messy building with its colorful canvases, stained countertops, and random supplies scattered over every surface. The smell of paint and stale coffee mixed with the breeze that blew through the place and pushed against the drop cloths covering the windows. Or maybe it wasn't a breeze.

Peyton crossed his arms and leaned one shoulder against the doorjamb. The drop cloth moved again, this time without the help of the wind. And then there was subtle giggling. The tip of someone's pink shoe peeked out from under the dusty, beige material.

Well, at least he won this time.

He made his way over and yanked back one edge of the makeshift curtain. Screams split the air all at once, like a bunch of sorority sisters inside a haunted house. Giant eyes fearing for their lives watched his every move. Peyton couldn't help the chuckle that started deep in his chest. Something joyful sparked, but he couldn't make it stay.

It never stayed.

"Last one to the house is a zombie for the rest of the day." He gestured to the path that would lead them there.

The girls took off at once, four-year-old Riley bringing up the rear. He dawdled, giving them enough time to be collected by their parents. AJ joined them, plopping down in a pile of black and white fur in the middle of the circle like the celebration was for him.

"Uncle Peyt's the zombie!" Riley, perched on Austin's side, pointed as he stepped through the doorway.

"Do zombies still get to eat?" That drew a few chuckles as everyone bowed their heads.

"Lord, thank You for letting us gather together today." Austin started the prayer. "Everywhere we look, we see traces of Your love..."

Against better judgement, Peyton took advantage of the moment to scan the faces of his family and friends who loved like family. To his left, Mom and Dad stood holding hands. It didn't matter how old he got—he never tired of seeing them together. He'd spent ten years under the roofs of a single mom and a weekend dad before they got remarried, and he didn't care to ever revisit that part of his life again.

To his right, Hannah stood with one of the Aguilar girls, both surrounded by siblings. Seven Reeds and six Aguilars. Beside them was Nan, swaying back and forth and bobbing her head to the prayer with all the vigor of a church lady agreeing with the Sunday sermon. Pop stood stock-still beside her, hands clasped, eyes closed. Memories of fishing with Pop and eating at Nan's kitchen table made Peyton smile.

To their right was Gavin and Sierra, bumping shoulders as each one of them leaned toward the other. A pastor by profession, he'd only come into their fold four years ago when he tracked Austin down to thank him for saving his life when he was younger. A story Peyton still wasn't a hundred percent clear on.

And then there was Jo who worked at the soup kitchen with Natalie and had earned herself the title of honorary grandma to the three and a half Brooks kids. She held Noah like he belonged to her, even as the kid tugged on her glasses. At her side was Liam and Avery, who had been close friends to Austin from way back in the day when he'd moved to Houston for a while. Liam and Austin had been partners on the beat when they were cops. Now Liam worked as a detective and Austin an art teacher. Life had taken them in two different directions, but they were still best friends.

Toward the end of the circle was Cassandra, Marcus, and their baby. Marcus taught at the same school Austin did. The couple had gotten married sometime around two years ago and Cassandra had shared a trimester with Natalie before she gave birth a few months ago. The baby squirmed in her hands, and she bounced the bundle a little quicker.

The prayer was coming to an end. He could hear it in his brother's voice. So, his thoughts moved to Austin and—

Peyton stood a little straighter when he found Natalie already looking at him. He gave her a crooked grin, just to let her know that he'd been caught red-handed lollygagging during prayer. But she didn't flinch. Not even so much as a smile. Her blue eyes watched him like she was reading his soul and translating all his questions about life. If she was, maybe she could help him make sense of a few.

"In Jesus' name, amen," Austin said, and the room echoed.

As a chilly day turned into a cold night, everyone else made their way inside the warmth of the house, and Peyton found himself alone on the patio. The once bright lawn now a shadowy blue yard cluttered with kids toys and forgotten dishes. The clean night air filled his lungs, and he leaned his head back against the chair.

The door creaked open behind him, and he figured Riley was about to ask him to play dolls with her again. Well, she played with dolls—Peyton had hijacked a cowboy from the twins' room and made him do odd jobs around Riley's pretty pink castle while her doll got a makeover.

"Out here contemplating the purpose of life?" It was Natalie's voice instead of Riley's.

He glanced up at his sister-in-law who glowed with all the joy of a new mom. "I know the purpose of life. It's flat earth that I can't wrap my mind around."

"Clever," she said as she eased down into the chair beside him. "I saw you looking around during the prayer earlier."

He figured she'd have something to say about that. "I can explain. You see, I was casing the place because Austin said he bought a leaf blower last week and I could really use one."

Her lack of amusement told him she wasn't in the mood for jokes. "It looked to me like you were trying to memorize everyone's faces."

The muscles in his chest tightened. She knew. Everyone else had been distracted, but Natalie was a bit too keen.

"I'm leaving." Everything inside him relaxed with those two words, confirming what he'd already known. This was the right decision.

"I was afraid of that."

Peyton pushed himself to the edge of his seat and rested his elbows on his knees. "You've got an eye for detail, Natalie. I should have known I couldn't pull one over on the Brooks' Family Manager."

"Family Manager. I like that. I should get that printed on a nameplate for my desk." A thoughtful frown crossed her face, then faded. "Have you told Austin yet?"

That was easier said than done. "You're the first person to get it out of me."

"Let me ask you a question—and you be honest—is it something we did? The teasing? The matchmaking? Did we ever make you feel uncomfortable here?"

Peyton pushed himself out of the chair. "As much as I'd love to tell you about all the ways Austin has messed up my life..." He shot her a grin as he walked over to the corner post and leaned his back against it. "No. It's not anything anyone did. It's just time."

"So, this is something you've been planning?"

Planning insinuated that he knew what he was doing. "Dreaming is probably a better word."

She nodded softly, her set jaw telling him she wasn't happy with his news, but her silence meant she was willing to let him speak.

"I figure I'll wait 'till after the baby's born. Maybe clock in a few more hours as a new uncle again."

"And then?"

"No idea." Probably wasn't the best answer to give someone who was full of ideas.

"What about your job? Your house? Your family? Where are you going? Where will you live? How will you eat?"

He couldn't help the smile that tugged at his lips. "I'm thinking I could live under a bridge for a while, maybe sleep in my truck, eat fast food, binge watch the entire 2001 baseball season on my phone."

"You're telling me not to worry, aren't you?" She raised an eyebrow. "You're too much like your brother."

It was the truth. He and Austin had been partners in crime for most of his life. He was bound to pick up a mannerism or two.

"You should tell him," she said.

Peyton nodded as the door creaked open again and Austin stepped out. "Perfect timing."

Austin dropped into the now-empty chair. "What? Talking about me behind my back again? I thought you grew out of that last year?"

Peyton was still playing cowboys and princesses on weekends surrounded by sippy cups and cartoons. He had a

19

lot to grow out of.

"I think I'll head inside," Natalie said, struggling to scoot to the edge of her chair. "It's getting too cold out here for me."

Peyton moved to take one of Natalie's arms while Austin took the other. She blew a strand of hair out of her face and smiled, tightening her grip on Peyton's arm before she shuffled inside the house.

"Either I'm crazy or my wife just sent us some kind of signal that you and I need to have a talk," Austin said, stuffing his hands in his pockets as he watched the door with a faraway gaze.

"You're not crazy." Peyton huffed a laugh that came out sounding more like he was being strangled. He shoved his fingers through his hair. This was easier with Natalie filling in the gaps of conversation. Austin was his brother, the best friend he'd ever had. Telling him wasn't an easy thing to do.

"What's up, man?"

He took a deep breath and dropped his hand to his side. "I'm skippin' town."

"Like, you're in trouble?"

"Like, I'm moving away."

Austin's eyebrows raised. Then he blew out a long breath. "I kinda figured that day was coming."

Peyton walked over to Natalie's chair and sat. "I've got to get away for a bit. Clear my head. Figure some things out." He looked over at his brother as Austin sunk into his seat. "Kinda like you did when we were kids. A little less rebellious though. A little more God-fearing."

Austin shook his head. "I was angry back then. I chose a hard road. And while I don't regret a single second of it..." Austin looked right at him. "I wouldn't wish it on my worst enemy."

Peyton had heard the stories. Even their parents and grandparents had testified of how lost Austin had felt for most of his life. Until he was eighteen and finally left it all behind. Then eight years later, he returned home ten times the man he left as.

Peyton was hoping for a similar story. Maybe not quite as long, though. He couldn't stay away from these people for more than a year, if that. "I was born and raised in this city.

Graduated high school here. Got the first job I could get my hands on after college. A five-minute commute with two coffee shops on the way. I think a lot of people would call this life perfect."

"But something's missing." Austin had taken the words right out of his mouth.

Peyton nodded. "I need to know what that is. And I need to stop dating and chasing girls, hoping a wife'll change that."

Austin sighed. "Any idea where you're going?"

"Not a clue."

"Well, be sure you don't take four lefts or else it'll be a short trip."

A short chuckle bubbled from Peyton's chest and blended into Austin's laugh. They shared more than just a mannerism or two.

"The Lord will show you, Peyt. Seek Him in every moment and He'll show you."

That was the part he was struggling with. How was he supposed to know where God was leading him when Peyton thought he'd already been seeking Him all his life?

The door creaked open, and AJ came trotting out, followed by a small daycare of screaming kids hyped up on cookies and fruit punch.

"No!" Avery yelled as she raced out behind them, stopping at the edge of the dark lawn. "I said AJ could go outside. Only AJ! It's too cold to play in the yard this time of night."

Too late. The little group had already conquered the jungle gym and were running circles around it.

"It won't hurt to run off a little energy, Mom," Austin offered. "The house gets stuffy with all those bodies in there."

She huffed a breath and spun around. Tucking a strand of hair behind her ear, her eyes lit up when she looked at Peyton. "You know, I was just thinking. There's this girl who works behind the desk at the teen center where Liam and I volunteer. She's super sweet and really smart. I could get her number for you."

Oh, boy.

"Actually," Austin said, chair creaking as he stood. He

walked over to Avery and turned to stand at her side. Then he put on a smirk. The same smirk he used to wear as a teenager when he was up to no good. Peyton could only imagine what his brother was about to pull out of his sleeve. "Peyton has an announcement to make."

CHAPTER ONE

There was something about a Texas sunset that made Peyton Brooks feel like he wasn't dead. Since he'd left his hometown in Austin a month ago, he'd made it his mission to check out the sunset in every city he could.

It was easy to lose himself in the beauty stretched across the horizon, a hazy blend of yellow, orange, and pink clinging to the bottom of gray clouds. The bold sun making its exit for the day captivated his attention without fail. No two skies were the same and he forever looked forward to seeing what tomorrow's held.

On the western outskirts of Hill Country, in a town called Heavenly, Texas, he'd found the perfect hill to park his truck on, drop the tailgate, and watch the day fade into dusk. Back settled against the rear panel of his truck bed, head resting against the glass, Peyton let the warm spring air soak into his lungs. In his hand he held a 1992 Samuel "Ace" Wooledge baseball card, flipping it through his fingers the way his dad had taught him when he was six and went through a magician phase. He paused the routine to grab a piece of beef jerky, the nearly empty bag crinkling in protest.

Beside him, his phone lay with its screen black. The message inside letting him know his job interview had been canceled. A mid-level research position for a tech company outside of Albuquerque that apparently couldn't wait until Monday morning after all.

Bad news, bud. Promoted from within. Sorry about the mix up. A former-co-worker-turned-middleman had texted. One who had called Peyton a shoo-in not two days ago.

It was easy not to get his hopes up when hope seemed lifeless to begin with. It didn't matter one way or another to

Peyton if he got the job or had to find another one. All he knew was that his savings were being siphoned into this trip and he'd have to start thinking about a paycheck pretty soon.

It wasn't so bad, living out on the open road solo—after he'd ended his lease, sold his furniture, and dropped a box of sentimental possessions off at his parent's house on the way out of town. Every sentimental possession except for this one. He lifted the baseball card. This one had lived in his wallet since the year he'd gotten his driver's license and suddenly had a reason to carry one.

This and the Bible at his side.

What hope he did have ached for something to materialize from that Book like a smoke signal pointing him in the right direction. Nothing ever did. But little did he care. The words inside were enough. And these wide prairies dusted with golden sunshine could make him forget the questions and doubts just long enough to catch his breath.

Reminiscent of his grandparent's place in New Mexico, where he'd spent many a boyhood summer barefoot, tan, and full of energy, he took it all in, reliving the carefree days where chores were the worst burden he'd carried and two skinned knees were the worst ache he'd fall asleep with at night. These days were a little different. An endless loop of bills and a heart that burned with loneliness were his latest afflictions.

He flipped the card in his hand and made it vanish. Where had his spark gone? He couldn't even write down the year he thought he might've lost it. It had simply disappeared. And he'd been cool with that for a while through high school and college. But now the emptiness seemed to swallow him whole. Adulthood wasn't all it was cracked up to be. With the flick of a wrist, he made the card reappear.

"Lord, lead me where You want me," he whispered into the breeze that ruffled the front of his T-shirt.

Since he'd left his home, he'd expected to lose this hopelessness in one of the small Texas towns he'd drifted through. But it was still here, sitting somewhere inside his chest, keeping his heart in poor company.

"I just want to be with You."

He knew better than to believe God didn't hear him. He

was sure the Lord was well-acquainted with his prayers and pleas. But for some reason, God wasn't talking to him. And if He was, then Peyton was doing a sorry job of listening. Even when his words felt futile, he still said them. Maybe one day he'd say the right thing and God would answer back.

As the last rays of sun fell behind the horizon, Peyton scraped together his daily resolve. He still had a few cities to put behind him before he clocked out for the day. As gratified as he'd feel dropping into a warm bed and doomscrolling on social media until he fell asleep, he was on a mission that required his undivided attention. If the Lord spoke, he wasn't gonna miss it this time.

And if He didn't speak...

Peyton closed his eyes. "When my heart is overwhelmed, lead me to the rock that is higher than I."

Psalm sixty-one had been a morsel for his hungry soul too many times for him to stop coming back for more. It was etched into his heart and seared into his thoughts. He'd seen it plenty. He prayed to one day taste it.

By the time he opened his eyes, the sun was gone, taking the array of colors with it. Only gray clouds were left behind, taunting Peyton with dreary reflections of his soul. Wind pushed through, promising a chill to match. With the warm welcome long gone, he picked up his wallet and slid the baseball card back inside.

Then he made it to his feet and tucked the wallet in his pocket. He grabbed the jerky, his phone, and his Bible. At the edge of the tailgate, he spared one last glance at the sunset, then he stepped off the edge. He gave the tailgate a solid shove and it clicked shut. Before he climbed behind the wheel to put in his last hours of service today, he opened the rear door, set his belongings on the seat, and pulled a plaid button down from his bag.

As he looked out over hills once more, he pushed his arms through the sleeves, fixed the collar at the back of his neck, and said goodbye to Heavenly, Texas.

Olivia Whitmore didn't mind the dark when she was on her family's farm, watching the stars from her little brother's treehouse. But sitting at a blacked-out gas station off the highway alone was a different story. The abandoned building with its murky shadows was the stuff of nightmares.

She'd driven by this building a thousand times in the daytime, but just after last light when obsidian cloaked the beautiful Texas landscape, it was enough to drive a chill down her spine. Every nerve ending in her body stood at attention as she pressed the phone against her ear, the ringback tone echoing endlessly as her eyes strained to decrypt what might be hiding in the darkness tucked around her truck.

"Hey there, darlin'," Dad answered.

"Hey, Dad," she offered in a singsong voice.

"How was the wedding?"

"Uh...it was good. I'm on my way home and—"

"What's wrong?" He could see right through her.

"It's nothing, really. I've got a flat tire. At Red's Gas Station. I think I'm okay, though. I can change it—I was just letting you know where I was before I..." *Disappeared* was on the tip of her tongue. Olivia pinched her eyes shut and shook the word from her head. "Got out."

"All right." Dad sounded like he was walking at a high rate of speed. "You've got your gun on you?"

"About to." The locked console under her right elbow kept it tucked away safely until moments like this. "I'll call you back if I have any problems."

"Stay safe and don't take any chances. I'll be there in about fifteen minutes. Love you."

"Love you," Olivia echoed and ended the call. Fifteen minutes meant he planned to put pedal to the metal. Their farm was all of thirty minutes away, on the other side of town.

She wouldn't expect any less from the man who would spare no expense to keep her safe. Even if she got the tire changed without a hitch, knowing Dad was closer and closer every minute helped soothe her frazzled nerves.

She unlocked the console and pulled her rose gold firearm out of its case. A quick sideways glance assured her it was set to safety. She slid it inside its holster, stepped out into the chilly night air, and pushed aside the thin material of her long cardigan. "Lord, I could really use Your mightiest angel right now." The holster slid into its place inside the waistband of her jeans at the small of her back. "Here goes nothin'."

Cell phone in hand, she put a stream light over the tire in front of the driver's side door. Shredded rubber wrapped around itself. Good thing she didn't push the rim too much further. It could still be salvaged, she was sure. Rocky terrain crunching beneath her high-heel boots taunted her with every step as she made her way to the other side of the truck. Under the back passenger seat, she found the jack and wrench laying side by side.

She dropped the supplies with a clatter against the pavement near the tire and reached inside the truck for her key fob. At the tailgate, she slid the key from the fob and pressed it into the keyhole to access the—

Whining brakes cut through her thoughts as a white van slowed down and pulled over on the stretch of road in front of her truck. Her heartbeat jumped into her throat, making it hard to swallow as she stared at a pair of glowing red brake lights through the swirling dust. Alarms sounded in her head. There were very few upsides concerning white vans and every one of them had to do with ice cream. She was pretty sure this one wasn't handing out chocolate-dipped cones tonight. Tire forgotten, she palmed her key and went to the driver's side door, pausing with her fingers on the handle.

Nobody got out. Olivia's lungs tightened. She only had seconds to decide if they were a threat or a solution. But as those seconds dragged out, her heart banged harder against her collarbone, begging to be set free from this uncertainty. The muscles in her arm tightened as she prepared to pull the handle.

Then a second vehicle approached.

At the red light, a green truck turned in her direction, taking up four lanes to make a U-turn and interject itself into the situation, directly between her truck and the white van. Relief poured through her that she wasn't alone. But some reprieve that was. Two strangers were no more promising than one. And if they both decided to team up against her, then...

Olivia swallowed.

A man stepped out of the truck. His door clicked shut and he stood completely still, his attention on the white van. Was he noticing the same lack of ice-cream-truck-music that she was? Or were they part of the same group? Were they here to take her away from her family? Had her heart ever beat faster?

Just past him, the red brake lights dimmed, and the white van pulled onto the road, headed east. Something about that made her breathe a little easier. Though her predicament hadn't changed all that much. As long as he kept his distance, she wouldn't have to use this stainless steel pressing hard against her back.

His gait was long and easy, like a man who wasn't much in a rush to get anywhere. In the glow of her headlights, the wind tussled his clothes as he rolled one sleeve up to his elbow. "I guess they're out of ice cream."

Olivia would have laughed if the muscles in her face weren't tight with worry right now. She swallowed every normal response that she probably would have given in the daylight. "I appreciate it if you're here to help me, but I want to let you know right off the bat that I'm packin'."

His smirk lifted a little more on one side and his eyebrows piqued for a split second. He rolled up the other sleeve as he stopped far enough away that she didn't feel the need to practice her quick draw. "This is Texas. Aren't we all packin'?"

Olivia lifted her chin a little higher, unsure if she was impressed with his quick-wittedness or alarmed by the fact that he admitted he was carrying like she was. Her attention dropped down to the waist of his jeans, but his shirt covered every place he might be hiding a holster.

"You don't use yours and I won't use mine." Her voice dipped lower than she'd meant for it to. This time he gave her a better glimpse of his smile—it was nonchalant. Seemingly permanent. Like he probably wore it a lot and he wasn't just smiling because he got a kick out of her plight.

"Deal." He tipped his chin toward the tire. "Want some help with that?"

"I can get it. Thanks."

He reached up and rubbed the back of his neck, the truck

lights behind him creating a silhouette of the man. "I don't doubt it. But the faster you get that tire changed, the faster you can get home."

He had a point there. And her heart wasn't beating at the same rate with this man as it had with the van. Something about his persona promised reliability, reminded her of Dad. "Spare's in the back."

He bent at the waist and picked up the wrench. Olivia stepped away far enough to put him in her sights if she had to. But he walked to the rear of her truck without incident. To the north, she hoped to see headlights flying in her direction, but the road was empty.

"My dad should be here any minute." Maybe he'd stay on his p's and q's if he knew she wasn't gonna be alone for long.

"Just between you and me," he said, the pull of his voice indicating that he was spinning the wrench to lower the spare. "I would've kept driving, but I didn't like the look of that van."

"You got that feeling, too?" Olivia glanced at the black stretch of highway. A shiver crossed her shoulders. She didn't even know where the van had come from. Had it been following her? Was the flat a coincidence? Had someone tampered with her tire back at the wedding?

"My mom warned me about big, white vans offering kids free candy, so I thought it was worth pulling over for." He dropped the tire with a bounce beside her truck. "Thought maybe I'd get a few pieces of that candy."

A soft giggle bubbled out of her quicker than she could stop it. She chided her amusement with a quick shake of her head. This was a stranger. She still wasn't sure she was completely safe. Even if he *could* pull a laugh out of her with ease.

He kneeled beside the flat and started working on the lug nuts at a steady pace that backed up his previous statement. Olivia raised one eyebrow and crossed her arms. "Were you insinuating that I can't change a tire as fast as you?"

A quiet chuckle spilled out of him, and he gave her a quick glance over his shoulder. "I think I've got a little more brawn than you do, so...yeah."

Well, he wasn't wrong.

"But even if you could," he said as he pocketed the lug

nuts. "You shouldn't have to. I don't have anything better to do right now. And between me and the white van, I'd rather be the one keeping you safe."

Keeping her safe? Her smirk melted away. He might be a stranger, but he was doing a solid job of making her feel like she didn't have to go up against the world alone. "Who are you?"

He pushed himself off the ground with ease, brushed his hands against his jeans, and reached out for her. "Peyton Brooks."

Peyton did everything in his power to put the girl at ease from the moment he saw her standing beside her truck like a stray cat ready to bolt. He'd used every opportunity to make her laugh, and still she stood in the shadows watching him as if he could turn on her at any given moment. He blamed the world they lived in.

She inched forward until she was close enough to stretch out one long arm and shake his hand. "Olivia Whitmore."

The subtle glow from the headlights crossed her features and he caught sight of a wide, black mark on the right side of her face, reaching up to her eye. His first thought was pity. His second thought was of his brother, Austin, who hated pity. So, Peyton pasted on a smirk and thought of her as family. "You do this often?"

The edge of her mouth curved upward and this time she didn't shrink back into the night. "Break down on the side of the road?"

Grinning, he kneeled to the ground again and shuffled the jack against the concrete, under the truck. "It's just that you handled yourself well when I first walked up. Seems like you might've been through this once or twice."

Arms crossed, she tilted her head to the side as if she were sizing up his intentions behind every statement. "No, I don't do this often. My parents just did a very good job of teaching me how to keep myself from getting dragged off in the middle of the night."

"Sounds like you have good parents."

"I do." There was a breath of silence as he pumped the

handle of the jack. "Are you a cop?"

"What makes you think I'm a cop?"

"I don't know. You kinda talk like one. You said you were keeping me safe. I was wondering if you had the credentials to back it up."

Peyton huffed a laugh. "I work in logistics. I'm not sure how far those credentials will get us out here, though. But my brother was a cop, if that helps."

"I'm sorry to hear that."

Peyton slowed the jack handle. "He's not gone. He teaches for a living now."

She pulled one hand from her crossed arms and laid it at the base of her throat. "That's good. I thought you meant that he'd passed away. I was heartbroken there for a second."

Heartbroken? She didn't even know him. She must be a peach to have that kind of compassion.

"Are y'all from around here?" she asked.

"No, ma'am." Peyton shimmied the tire away from the truck. "My family's back in Austin. I'm making my way up to New Mexico."

"You're not homeless, are you?"

That was a long story. "Let's just say I'm between houses."

"Sounds like something a homeless person would say."

Peyton chuckled as he set the spare in place. He got a kick out of the way she quizzed him. There was a mixture of interrogation and innocence in her voice. Like she'd probably be a lot of fun to hang around if her circumstances weren't so stressful.

"What about you? What do you do for a living? If that's not too personal a question."

Arms relaxed at her sides, her stance was no longer defensive as she kicked a rock out of her way and took a couple steps closer. She was incredibly tall. And curvier than a lot of the girls he knew. She wasn't petite by any means, but there was a softness about her that seemed uniquely feminine. "I'm a baker."

"Do you like it?" He lowered the jack and set the truck back on the ground.

"Oh, yeah. It's one of my dream jobs."

One of? "You have more than one dream job?"

She lifted a shoulder and dropped her focus to the ground. But not before he caught a glimpse of a smile.

He jerked his chin up once. "What else you wanna do?"

"Silly things, really."

He'd be willing to bet they weren't. There was something in the way she carried herself that told him she was too smart to waste her time on silly things. Peyton spun each lug nut in place, tightening the last one as a pair of headlights pulled onto the shoulder beside her truck. The aggressive speed and crunching gravel gave Peyton the impression that this was the dad they were waiting for.

Peyton stood, dusting off his hands.

The door opened and a man about his height stepped out, focus pinned on Peyton. He pulled his daughter into a hug that implied he hadn't seen her in a while. "You bring back somethin' from the wedding?"

That would explain why she was all fancied up.

"Dad," she complained. "He stopped to help change the tire." She pressed her hands across her face like she was trying to wipe away embarrassment. "A strange van stopped over there and when Peyton showed up, they left."

The man sized him up with one eyebrow raised. Then reached out his hand. "Peyton?"

Peyton shook it. "Brooks. Not to be confused with the quarterback."

"Daniel Whitmore. Olivia's dad. Thanks for keeping my girl safe. I know she can handle her own, but it doesn't hurt to have some extra security around."

"It was no trouble, sir." Peyton lifted the flat tire, carried it to the bed of her truck, and closed the tailgate with a shove. As her dad picked up the tools, Peyton reached out to shake her hand again. "It was nice to meet you."

"You, too." Her touch was warm. "Thank you for keeping me safe." She blinked slow and dipped her chin once, as if his words had meant something to her.

He mirrored her nod and made his way back to his truck.

"Goodnight, sir." He tipped his head toward the man as he set a hand on the handle of his door, and—for reasons he couldn't answer for—spared one more glance at Olivia, even though she was nothing more than a silhouette in the glare of her dad's headlights.

"Uh, Peyton." The man held one hand up.

Peyton turned, concrete crunching under his shoes. "Yes, sir?"

He lifted his chin, as if he were considering his next words. "You got somewhere you need to be right now?"

In his truck, chasing tomorrow's sunset. But he had a little less than twenty-four hours until the next one and that was time enough to get where he needed to be. "Headed west."

"You need a homecooked meal and a place to stay tonight?"

He'd empty his wallet for a homecooked meal right now. But then he'd need that money for a hotel. "Nah, I'll get a place in the next town."

Daniel looked in the same direction Peyton should be traveling right now. "You're still an hour out from the next town. Most of the food joints are closed this time'a night and there's no guarantee you'll get a room."

The man knew how to deliver good news, didn't he? "I don't mind driving through the night if I have to. Less traffic that way."

Daniel exhaled with a grunt. "I wish you wouldn't do that, son. It'd make me feel a lot better if you had a place to stay for the night."

"Your safety matters to us, too, Peyton," Olivia said.

Why'd she have to say it like that? He'd been out on the road alone so long, just that simple statement took the starch out of his drive. He took a deep breath and let it puff through his cheeks. He didn't care to impose and cared even less to make himself a burden. But what was one night out of his comfort zone? It didn't mean he'd have to spend a lifetime here.

"I can spare the time."

CHAPTER TWO

Daniel Whitmore watched his daughter's headlights in his rearview mirror, catching glimpses of the boy's truck behind her as they headed home. He stroked one hand over his mustache and down the short, graying beard covering his chin. He couldn't help the smirk that tugged at his lips.

He could only imagine how terrified Olivia had been when she realized she'd have to change a tire on the side of the road on her own at dark—and the persuasion it took for the stranger to talk her into letting him change it. Daniel had rushed to his daughter's aid with a prayer for her safety and was met with an odd sense of reassurance in his spirit. The words God had laid there had bewildered Daniel ten minutes ago.

Now they made sense.

His phone rang, pulling his attention to the screen on the dashboard. Olivia.

He tapped a button on the steering wheel. "What's on your mind, darlin'?"

"It took you fifteen minutes to get here from the farm," she greeted in return. "Why are you driving so slow right now?"

"I'm just giving the boy a fair chance. He doesn't know how we rip up and down these back roads."

"I'm sure he's a fast learner—I'm starving."

Daniel pressed a little harder on the gas pedal, and his daughter kept up. To his surprise, so did the boy. "You okay with me inviting him to stay the night?"

"I don't think we can really disinvite him at this point."

"We can take a sharp right up here and lose him through the huntin' lease."

She snorted. "I've got a gut feeling the Lord put it on your heart to ask him to stay, so I can't see you doing that."

She was right. His daughter knew him well. "Something like that. He say where he's from?"

"Austin. He might be homeless. Sounds like he doesn't have a place to live."

Maybe God wanted Daniel to help the young man get on his feet?

"And for the record, he carries a gun."

Every fatherly instinct Daniel had accumulated over the last twenty-two years piqued and pressed down on the brake pedal. "You saw a gun?"

"No, not at all. He just made a comment about having one. But in his defense, I told him I was carrying one first."

Daniel chuckled and set his foot back on the gas pedal. Of course, his daughter would make sure everyone within the vicinity knew she was capable of defending herself.

"He doesn't strike me as the dangerous type, so I don't think one night can hurt."

Daniel had the same feeling. Everyone on the farm was either carrying a gun or knew where the closest one was located. It wasn't a concern for now.

His headlights flashed across a small clearing occupied by a handful of deer. He tapped the brakes. "On the right."

"I see 'em."

They made it through without a darting stag wreaking havoc on their night. "How was the wedding in Eastridge?"

"Long," she drawled. "I don't think Sophie planned for the reception to last that long, but nobody would leave. I practically had to sneak out."

Daniel smiled. "Did you dance with anyone?"

"Sophie's cousin and someone's brother."

"Did they ask you out?"

"Dad," she snarled under her breath. "Why are you trying to get rid of me?"

"You know better than that."

"And *you* know that I have no immediate or future plans to settle down with *anyone*."

"So, you've said." Since his daughter was twelve, she'd sworn marriage wasn't for her—and she'd chosen a lifestyle to back it up. She'd opened her bakery and opted to move into the cottage through the woods. Paid all her own bills, bought all her own necessities, and paved her own way in their community. His daughter was as independent as they came.

Just short of changing her own tire in the dark.

Truth was he didn't mind it too much. It did a father's heart good to know he didn't have to worry about a man sweeping his daughter off to a different state where he couldn't keep an eye on her heart. Despite her own criticism over her birthmark, he knew she was beautiful inside and out. But it took a lot of worry off his shoulders where future boyfriends were concerned. As long as she was happy single, he wasn't complaining.

"What did Momma make for supper?" she asked.

"Roast is what I smelled before I left."

"Mmm." He could imagine his sweet girl smiling at the sound of that. "Sophie's a vegan so if I wanted any meat at the reception, I had to go hunt it myself."

"And I believe you would have." Daniel chuckled again as their driveway came into view. "I'mma let you go."

"Love you, Dad. Thanks for coming to help me."

"Anytime you need it, Sweetheart." He flipped on his blinker and pressed the button on the steering wheel to end the call.

Headlights flashed across their new farm sign sitting a dozen yards away, but moved too quickly to admire the recent installment. Twin cattle guards separating the main road from their livestock rumbled under the tires. Still a half mile away from home, Daniel took his time, watching for any playful calves that might dart out in front of him.

A group of black angus cows bedded down beside a patch of woods. A pair of jackrabbits froze at the edge of the gravel driveway and sprinted into the trees as the trio of trucks drew near. He kept his eyes peeled for a horned owl that might be perched on a low branch. By the time the trees parted, and the cabin appeared, he'd spotted three.

Two of their home security systems laid in lazy heaps of snow-white fur on the front porch beneath the golden glow of the light. Birdie and Boone, both Great Pyrenees with a knack for sleeping during the day and patrolling the yard at the dead of night, didn't bother moving until the third truck pulled into the circle drive. Then both, with a shrill howl that was as good as any alarm, started chomping at the air. Hopefully their guest didn't have a fear of dogs.

Daniel set his truck in park and turned off the engine, giving the other two time to do the same before he hopped out.

"Birdie, Boone, go lay down," he said as he stepped out. Both dogs obeyed, looping in a circle and returning to where they'd been laying.

"I'm gonna go on in," Olivia said as she crossed paths with him.

"Right behind you, sweetheart." He touched her elbow.

By the time he reached the boy's olive-green truck, Peyton was already pulling a bag from his back seat.

"If you have any items in there that might be considered illegal in fourteen countries, then I suggest you leave 'em in your truck 'til mornin'."

The boy chuckled, a deep but quick sound that rang with authenticity. "She tell you I had a gun?"

Daniel nodded.

"I told her that thinking she'd feel safer if we both had something to protect ourselves with. But I think it scared her more than anything." He pushed the door, and it fell shut with a click. "I didn't mean for that to happen. It's locked under my front seat. You have my word I won't be shooting any clay pigeons through the night."

"Olivia doesn't scare easy. But she is cautious. Worst case scenario, it might take her a little more time to let her guard down with you," Daniel said as he led the way across the stone path to the porch.

"I'll be out of her hair by sunrise, so she won't have to worry about me for long."

Birdie let out a low growl as they moved toward the door, and Peyton's brow wrinkled. Daniel lifted a shoulder. "She's Olivia's."

High-heeled boots abandoned beside the front door, Olivia shuffled through the house in socked feet, following the smell of supper that coaxed a growl from the pit of her stomach. Past the living room bright with chandelier light, she found Momma in the kitchen, standing at the stove with a wooden spoon in hand. The dimpled smile that reached her eyes was as warm as any hug she'd ever given.

"Heard you had some car troubles. Glad everything panned out."

"I had help," Olivia said as she descended on a pot of green beans cooking in bacon grease and garlic salt. "A weird van stopped near where I was parked and then some guy came out of nowhere and the van left. Then he changed my tire."

"What now?" Olivia didn't miss the piercing glare Momma gave her. A few more details would have made the story less sketchy. Fighting back a grin, she shoveled a scoop of green beans into her mouth, blowing through O-shaped lips to cool her burning tongue.

"Peyton, this is my wife, Gianna," Dad said behind them, suddenly in the kitchen and standing beside the stranger who had a black backpack hanging from one shoulder. "Gianna, this is our guest for the night, Peyton Brooks."

Cheeks filled with green beans, Olivia spun around to face the patio doors at the back of the kitchen while she fought to swallow. Could their timing be any worse? Even while her stomach screamed, 'People gotta eat!' her pride demanded that she compose herself. Once she downed the tasty appetizer, she turned to face them again.

"Mrs. Whitmore," Peyton said as Momma skirted the counter.

He was...much younger than she'd assumed.

An amused smirk tugged at the edge of his smooth mouth and his focus danced between her and Momma. Brown hair was cut very short and parted at one side, like he worked a corporate job and respected its dress code. Sideburns faded into a sharp, clean-shaven jawline. Dark brows arched over eyes that sported youthful lines, as if he'd found a lot to be amused by over the course of his life.

While changing her tire there had been a chord in his voice that made her think he had an old soul, but under the lights of her momma's kitchen he seemed a little closer to her age.

"Please, call me Gianna." She shook his hand.

"Thank you for having me."

"Now, what is this about a weird van and some guy? I haven't been filled in on the details yet..." Momma said as she peeked over her shoulder with a raised eyebrow. "I'm assuming you're the "some guy.""

"Yes, ma'am. I wouldn't worry about it." A laugh hung in his voice as he met Olivia's gaze. "It was probably just an ice cream truck that lost track of its route."

Was he trying to make her laugh? Olivia dropped her attention to the burner knobs in front of her. The mashed potatoes looked like they were finished cooking, so she did Momma the favor of turning them off.

"Well, since you stopped and gave my daughter a hand, I'd say you've earned yourself a treat. And lucky for you..." She spun around, her big blonde locks bouncing around her shoulders, and scooped up a pair of oven mitts. She reached into one of the double ovens built into the wall and, like a magic trick, pulled out a steaming hot dish. "I've also got fresh cherry crumble waiting."

One eyebrow rose and his smile broadened a smidgen more. "And lucky for you, I inherited my grandpa's sweet tooth."

Mom's giggle mingled with Dad's chuckle. "I'm glad to hear that."

What was happening? In the sixty seconds he'd been here he'd already charmed both of her parents? Olivia hadn't seen them this giddy since they'd adopted her brother eight years ago. If she didn't keep a close eye on them, they might try to adopt this one, too.

"I'll show Peyton to the guest room," Dad said, leading the way to the wide staircase jutting out between the kitchen and the dining room.

While he spared Momma a courteous smile, he nodded when he looked at Olivia. She circled sharply to the right until he was out of sight, then she leaned back against the counter.

Their footfalls faded away and Mom lifted a roast out of the second oven. "Well, he seems nice."

"He seems it."

"Sweetie, would you go find your brother?"

Olivia pulled herself away from the counter and left the

same way she'd come in, passing through the empty living room. Outside the door of the study she stopped at a massive painting of Jesus walking on water that lay behind a piece of glass. The dark ocean waves transformed into a mirror when Olivia turned her head at an angle and let the light catch her birthmark just right.

On a normal day, she could see her auburn waves that spilled down to her waist, or her thin but long eyelashes that stretched over her brown eyes, or the smile that—although framed by thin lips—was her favorite feature.

But right now, all she could see was the black mark covering her right cheek, crawling up the side of her nose, and fading to brown at the base of her eyebrow. She lifted her fingers to the tiny hairs that tainted her soft skin. They were dark, so they blended in, and most people never looked at her long enough to see them.

Any makeup she'd put on for the wedding had worn off, otherwise she could pretend like the birthmark didn't exist for a few more hours. But between the Texas heat and the long day, she was now at the mercy of whatever the beastly stain wanted.

Her family and friends were used to it. She'd grown content with the way strangers looked at it. And she'd learned to live a happy life despite it. But it never failed to remind her that she wasn't beautiful. Not the way other women were beautiful.

Not the way a man craved beauty.

Olivia ran her fingers through her hair, fluffing the locks until they were big enough to hide behind. Then she swallowed her insecurities and pivoted away from her marred reflection.

Peyton trotted down the wooden staircase that was as wide as his childhood bedroom, he was pretty sure. The kitchen and dining room combined could fit his parent's entire trailer. Cedar walls wore wooden knots the same deep shade of brown as the trim. Oak beams held up high ceilings with black iron chandeliers. Tall windows at the front of the house mirrored the ones at the back.

"Y'all have a beautiful place. I didn't think homes like this existed outside of magazines and daydreams."

"Thank you," Daniel said, pulling a stack of plates from a china cabinet tucked against the dining room wall. "We built it ourselves about twenty-five years ago, give or take. Back before we adopted Olivia and still had some of the older generation with us. But a lot have passed away and now it's just us and the farmhands."

"Oh, yeah?" That was pretty interesting. "Olivia's adopted?"

"She is." Daniel nodded, a fallen piece of black hair above his brow bouncing with the motion as he set the plates on the table. "Gianna and I couldn't have children of our own, so we decided to foster with the goal of adopting. After a few years we couldn't take the heartbreak anymore, so we let the Lord close the door on that chapter of our life. Then we got a call. She was only eight months old and as sweet as pie."

Daniel chuckled deeply. As if the memory stirred a place of elation in him. "The adoption was quick and went through without a hitch. We thank God for that every day."

"At any point in the process," Gianna said as she went to the icebox that was twice the size of any he'd ever seen. "The state could have taken her out of our home. Needless to say, Heaven heard plenty from us that year."

So, these were godly people? Something about that made sense. There was a peacefulness here that he'd rarely experienced outside of his family.

Peyton walked over to the china cabinet. "Can I help?"

Daniel handed him two glasses. "God answered those prayers in more ways than we could ever count. We begged Him not to take her from us, and He was faithful. We thought that part of our lives was truly behind us. And roughly eight years ago we were approached by the same lawyer who'd worked Olivia's adoption. They had a little boy who hadn't been born yet, and the mother was looking for parents in lieu of an abortion."

The hair on the back of Peyton's neck stood up as he set a glass down on the table.

"Even with fear in our hearts," Gianna added. "We took one look at each other and knew we had to do it. The entire process was in God's hands, and we trusted Him with all of it—even if it meant making us the middleman."

"Took a little longer than Olivia's adoption, but the heartache was worth every moment to bring our family full circle."

Peyton scanned the space for any signs that an eight-year-old boy lived here. "How is he now?"

Like he'd been summoned, a kid half Peyton's size slid into the kitchen in socks, a pair of grass-stained jeans, and a T-shirt with deer on it.

"Ask him yourself," Daniel said.

The boy spun around and looked up at Peyton with wide eyes. "Whoa, who are you?"

Peyton set the last glass on the table and made his way over to the kid who was baffled by the unexpected company in his kitchen. "Peyton Brooks." He stuck out his hand. "Put 'er there."

The kid shook it with enthusiasm. "Joshua Whitmore."

"Hey, that's my middle name."

"Cool! My friends call me Josh." He galloped over to the right of where his dad had seated himself at the head of the table, and pulled a chair out, legs screeching against the floor. "Are you eating with us?"

"Sure am." Peyton reached out for the bowl of potatoes and gravy boat that Gianna carried, and she relinquished both with a sweet smile framed by deep dimples. Peyton set the dishes on the table and pulled out the chair next to Josh. "Am I takin' anybody's seat if I sit here?"

"Mine," Josh said with a shrug as he leaned his elbows against the table, knees in his seat. "But that's only because I'm in Pepaw's chair. But he won't care because he already went to bed."

Peyton took a seat. "Pepaw?"

"Our grandfather, Vernon," a familiar voice chimed behind him as Olivia walked into the room. "Everybody else calls him Vern. He's mom's dad." She made her way around the table and took the seat directly across from him. She was missing the long sweater thing she'd been wearing earlier, and her hair was different. The dark reddish-brown locks thicker, wavier.

"Hey, Olivia! Did ya meet Peyton?" Josh blurted out. "We have the same name!"

Olivia lifted her eyes just enough to meet his gaze. There was a sparkle of amusement resting there as she scooted her chair closer to the table. "So now your name's Peyton?"

Daniel and Gianna laughed softly. Peyton couldn't help but join in.

"No," Josh growled. "Joshua is his middle name and it's my name, too."

"I'll say the blessing," Daniel offered with a chuckle as Gianna set two more bowls on the table and took the seat to his left. He reached out and took her hand, a look of respect passing between them. "Heavenly Father, we thank You for the family that surrounds us today, the company You've provided, and the meal You've supplied. We ask for Your blessing on the food, that it nourish our hearts, minds, and bodies. In Jesus' name."

Everyone echoed an amen, and without hesitation, reached for the utensils sticking out of the dishes. Peyton held back, not wanting to appear as hungry as his stomach told him he was.

"Please make yourself at home, Peyton," Daniel said as he sliced a knife through the roast. "We pass no judgement in this house, especially when it comes to food."

"Since you put it that way." Peyton took a helping of green beans. "That might be a dangerous invitation. I've been known to put away my fair share of groceries."

"We've got plenty, so eat up," Gianna said as she filled a glass with tea and passed it to him.

"Tell us about yourself, Peyton." Daniel lifted the gravy boat and poured a steaming drizzle over his plate.

Where did he start? His birth, his bachelor's degree, or the gaping hole in his life that pushed him to leave behind everything he knew to find out who he really was? "I'm a research analyst by day and an uncle by night."

"You have nieces and nephews?" Gianna's smile broadened a bit.

"Yes, ma'am. Four now. Riley's the oldest girl. Noah and Dakota are twins. And my brother and his wife had their second girl in February. Reese Noelle."

Their voices chimed together in congratulations and compliments.

Peyton dipped his head. "If she's anything like her big

sister, she's gonna give her parents a run for their money."

"You don't have any children of your own?" Gianna asked before taking a bite.

"No, ma'am. I'm not married. But I have been thinking about getting a dog if that counts."

Josh leaned his seat back as he wiggled against the table. "What kinda dog? We've got two Great Pyrenees-es, and a mutt named Mutt."

"That's not his name." Olivia laughed—a sound that started chest-deep but came out in soft tones. She peeked up at her brother. "That's just what he is." Her hair hung in bouncy waves over the side of her face where her beauty mark was.

So that's what she'd done with it—made it bigger so she could hide behind it?

Josh shrugged. "Pepaw calls him Mutt, so I been callin' him Mutt."

Daniel chuckled. "Mutt is a stray who came out of nowhere a few days ago and our Pyrs didn't put him on the run, so I guess you could say he's an honorary member of the family now."

"*Peers*?" Peyton echoed.

"The Pyrenees. You met them out front."

Ah. Peyton paused before he took a bite. "And left a good impression with any luck."

"So far, so good." Daniel wore a smirk. "We got 'em about a month ago after we were burglarized."

"You were burglarized? Your place isn't exactly easy to find. How'd that happen?"

Daniel and Gianna shared a pointed look, and Gianna raised one eyebrow. "We aren't sure. All we know is that we had contractors in the house about that same time. By the time we realized the money was missing, they were long gone and the police had nothing to go on."

"You never got it back?"

Daniel shook his head. "It's still being investigated, but we've got no leads."

"I'm sorry to hear that. Maybe they'll make some headway soon."

"We hope so. Ten thousand dollars is a lot of money."

Whoa. Peyton let out a low whistle. How rich were these

people that they kept ten thousand dollars cash on hand?

"We've ramped up our home security since then. New alarm system, guard dogs, surveillance. Needless to say, it won't be happenin' again."

Peyton took a drink of tea and set the glass down. "What do y'all do for a living?"

"Farm. Among other things. We dabble here and there," Daniel said as he cut another slice of roast.

"We've got a phone tower on the north side, too. It's *huge*," Josh drawled.

"How much land do you have to own to be able to call it the north side?"

"Plenty," Daniel said before he took a bite, his grin poorly hidden behind his fork.

Peyton got the feeling there was more to that answer. But if they weren't offering then he wasn't prying.

"What about you, Josh? What's your occupation?" Peyton said. Across from him, Olivia snickered.

"Farm." He raised both eyebrows and nodded. "And I go to school. But since it's summer now, I can hang out in my treehouse all I want to." He shoveled a bite into his mouth. "Have you ever been in a treehouse, Peyton?"

"As a matter of fact, I have. My brother and I built one before my—" He stopped short. "—well, back when I was seven. We found a stack of old pallets behind a hardware store and drug 'em home. Worked through the night and slept in by morning."

"You paused," Olivia said, her eyes pinched with curiosity. "Is it a bad memory?"

Peyton picked up his tea and took another drink to clear his throat. He'd have to make a mental note that Olivia was a woman unafraid to say what was on her mind.

"Not at all," he huffed a laugh. "It was an amazing day. One of the best for a seven-year-old kid. But, uh..." He shook his head at the half-empty plate in front of him. "It was the year my parents split and that's usually how I tell time in my life. Before and after the divorce, if that makes any sense."

"I'm so sorry to hear that," Gianna said, her hand falling through the air briefly as if she wanted to reach out to him.

"It's actually a very short story because ten years later they remarried each other. So, it's all good."

"That's great," Olivia said, the happy spark returning to her eyes. "It's just you and your brother?"

Peyton nodded, taking the time to swallow another savory bite. "That's right. He's ten years older than me. He was always my hero even though he's the wildest person I know."

Gianna reached for her glass. "How's that?"

A dozen stories resurrected in Peyton's thoughts, like a filing cabinet drawer had slid open and revealed his memories. "He's just different from most people I know. He's adventurous and fearless and doesn't back away from...anything, really. He's the first person to tell a good joke and the last person to leave a good party. You could find him at church volunteering for something and later that day he'll be spraying graffiti on the side of brick businesses."

Daniel, Gianna, and Olivia looked at him.

"He's an artist. Commissioned."

Like it suddenly made sense they all nodded with hums of realization as they went back to eating.

"As a kid, I hung onto his every word. Whatever Austin told me was the truth, even if someone else tried to make me believe otherwise. I always wanted to be like him. Still do, actually. That's what led me to go on this trip. Get something out of my system on the way to Albuquerque."

"What's in Albuquerque?" Daniel tipped his chin.

"Supposed to be a job interview. But that fell through a few hours ago."

"What're your plans now?"

Peyton pulled in a deep breath and let it out slowly. "Stay the course. My grandparents live near there anyway, so I'll go ahead to meet them and find my way from there."

Daniel nodded in a way that reminded him of his dad. As if he were granting approval of a good idea. Peyton found himself mirroring the nod, appreciation whirling in his chest. Maybe this was God's way of signing off on Peyton's plan to venture into New Mexico.

He got a good feeling.

"So, you're *not* homeless?" A smirk pulled up the edge of Olivia's mouth. An amusing glint rested in her eyes.

He matched her levity. "Homeless, no. Without a home, yes."

She tipped her head to the side as if she expected more of his story.

"My brother, uh, disappeared when he was eighteen. He went on a...journey, I guess you could call it, and found the Lord." Peyton didn't miss the quick look that Daniel and Gianna exchanged. "I'm a little older than he was back then, but I thought what could it hurt to try?"

Daniel leaned forward until his elbows were braced on the tabletop. He laced his fingers together and rested his chin on them. "You're searching for the Lord, Peyton?"

"Not entirely. I believe in Him. I've seen Him move in other people's life. In my family's lives."

"But?" Olivia asked, her fork hovering beside her plate where her hand rested.

But he'd rather be talking about Josh's treehouse than this. "I just feel like I don't know Him as well as I want to, if that makes any sense."

She jerked her head in one swift motion so that her hair wasn't much in her face anymore—he was sure she didn't realize she did it. "We've all been there before."

Peyton dipped his chin to her. It was good to be reminded that he wasn't alone. But he'd already known that. A lot of Christians talked about how hard it was to hear God speak. But he wasn't looking for sympathy. He was looking for an answer. A reason. A clear path to show him what life was really about and what he was supposed to do with it.

But he didn't want to bother these people with his problems tonight. He didn't even want to bother himself with it most days, but the questions constantly ate at him. Especially when it was dark and he was alone.

"I pray you're able to know Him better soon, Peyton," Daniel said. "It'll rock your world when you do."

Something in his chest swelled with those words. Hope, maybe? He wasn't sure. Happiness was something he'd learned to manufacture, and hope seemed like a luxury he couldn't afford. "Thank you, sir."

As supper got swapped for the dessert Gianna had touted earlier, they covered all the small talk about their hometowns, the drought that Texas was experiencing, and current events. By the time Peyton's plate was clean, Josh had fallen asleep with his cheek on his hands, and Olivia had forgotten to hide behind her curtain of hair.

Gianna rose, the clank of dishes colliding as she stacked her dessert plate atop her supper plate. Peyton followed her example, rising the same time Olivia did, and stacking his own plates.

"Leave it," she said across from him. "You're our guest. We got this."

"Your dad told me to make myself at home, so..." He lifted a shoulder and offered her a smirk.

She giggled so gently that he didn't hear it but saw it in the way her shoulders moved. In the kitchen she set her dishes beside an apron front sink, and he did the same, gently clacking them against the gray stone countertop.

"For obvious reasons, we didn't have a normal supper tonight," Daniel said, setting his dishes beside Peyton's. "We usually eat a little earlier than this—with Vern, of course. Then we have dessert outside around the patio fire and fellowship some. Worship the Lord with a song or two."

"Sounds like a lot of fun." Peyton leaned back against the counter, crossing his arms.

"Sometimes the kid's friends will stop by, maybe a farmhand or two with their families." Gianna lifted Josh's head to pull his plate out from under his laced fingers. "We might do s'mores or campfire cones. Daniel gets out his guitar and Olivia sings."

Olivia stood at the island across from him, scooping green beans into a plastic bowl. Hiding her beauty mark behind her hair again, she looked up at him with a guilty grin.

"Too bad I missed it." Peyton turned to face her and lifted his chin in one quick motion. "Is that one of your dream jobs?"

Eyes wide, she scanned her parent's reactions and then schooled her features. "I do love to sing, but surprisingly it's not one of my dream jobs."

The subject was obviously one she hadn't shared with her parents. So why divulge it to a stranger she met in the dark on the side of the road? Nerves? Vulnerability, maybe? Trust? Whichever the answer was he wished he had a little more time to try to pry one, maybe two, of those dream out of her.

"You've done it again with supper, Momma." Daniel set his hands on his wife's shoulders and kissed her cheek. "I'm stuffed."

Peyton gently cleared his throat at the intimate act and took steps to distance himself from the kitchen. He'd not lost his ability to read the room. "Thank y'all again for having me." He shoved his hands in his pockets and inched closer to the foot of the stairs. "Supper was amazing, I second Daniel—but, uh, without the goodnight kiss." As soon as the words left his mouth, he wished he could stuff them back in.

Olivia's smiling eyes followed him closer to the stairs, her shoulders giving away her laughter again. He made another mental note—she was easy to make laugh. Which worked out well since he was funny on occasion.

"I'm glad you liked it." Gianna said, pulling open the dishwasher. "Have a goodnight, Peyton."

"'Night, Peyton. If you need anything, we're down the hall," Daniel added.

"I appreciate it." He tipped his head toward Olivia. "Goodnight."

"Peyton," Olivia said. His name sounded warm and sweet in the tone of her voice. "I won't be here in the morning when you leave, so I wanted to make sure you knew that for me you were a hero tonight. Things could have gone differently if it weren't for you."

He couldn't help the slow smile that tugged at his lips. He assumed she was talking about how he referred to his brother earlier. It was enough to draw him a step back toward the kitchen. "It was my pleasure. It's not every day I get to stand guard for a beautiful woman."

Her modest smile fell. Her eyes widened.

With a grin, he started up the stairs.

CHAPTER THREE

With the flip of a switch, light washed over *Slice of Heaven* bakery and brought it out of a deep sleep. Faux marble floors covered the short walk to a display counter that would be filled with tasty breakfast pastries in four quick hours. White tables with pink chairs filled the space in between.

Olivia set her bag on the counter beside the point-of-sale system and took a sip of the coffee she'd brought from home. Which paled in comparison to Emma's coffee at the *Cozy Cactus Cafe* next door, opposite of *Wilson's Donuts* located on the other side of Olivia's building.

She, Emma, and Wilson had made pacts as each one moved onto the Main Street block over the years—leave the coffee to Emma and the donuts to Wilson, and Olivia could corner the pastry market. Everything else was up for grabs. Going four years strong, she and her best-friend-turned-business-partner, Caroline Coleman, had established a prosperous routine.

Olivia plucked her rose-pink apron from its hook beside the kitchen door and tossed the loop over her head. Where the front of the shop was bright, soft, and cheery, the kitchen area was a stark contrast with its concrete floors, wooden countertops, and gray walls. It wasn't a huge space, but it was big enough to bake for the eleven thousand residents of Heavenly.

A tall shelf packed with baking supplies and flattened display boxes met her first. To her right, the ovens, two long islands, a stove, sink, and commercial refrigerator. To the left, a set of double doors that led to the alleyway behind the cafe and a single door that led to the storage room at the back of her building. Immediately to her left was a storage fridge with a glass front for the cakes she'd be delivering later today.

Olivia took one more sip of coffee, letting the caffeine work its way into her system. Later, when Caroline would show up for her shift at eight, she'd deliver whatever mouthwatering flavor of the day Emma would surprise her with. "Bless Caroline and Emma, would You, Lord?"

Coffee tucked away on the counter beside the fridge, she tightened the rolled sleeve of her white button up shirt around her elbow and reached for the bucket she kept beside the sink. A minute later, a wave of hot, soapy water splashed across the metal surface of the island, rinsing away any dust that had settled there through the night. A rag in hand, she wiped it clean and then reached for a dry one.

As she waited for the sanitizer to do its magic, she cranked up the ovens with the push of a few buttons and stopped in front of the planner that lay open from the day before. Friday's specials would be—she hovered a clean fingertip over the list—apple strudels and blackberry turnovers. Her mouth watered at the thought of them.

Bread would need time to rise, so she started with dough. After gathering the ingredients, taking the time to knead it all together, and setting it aside to rise, she stole another sip of coffee. Muffins, kolaches, and cinnamon rolls were the most popular breakfast items on her menu, so those were next. She prepped enough to carry the early crowd and slid them into the oven. As she hummed a worship hymn, indigo morning light peeked through the small square windows of the double doors. She was right on pace.

Olivia's Baby Face cookies that were so big they were always compared to a baby's head, and her War and Peace brownies that were as thick as the book itself. Those were her everyday treats. Not the most popular, but always the most requested when a sugar craving was in full swing.

She took sweet time mixing in the chocolate chunks with each goodie and got them into their own pans. Safely inside the oven, she started working on the smaller, quicker cookies next. Peanut butter, hazelnut, and oatmeal were the easiest to make.

Lastly was the cake family—cakes, cupcakes, and

cheesecakes. As the first wave of cupcake batter dripped into its pan, the kitchen door flew open with a long creak and Caroline appeared, a large paper cup in each hand. "Blueberry-Butterscotch is Emma's flavor of the day."

Head cocked slightly to the side as she watched the cupcake pans fill one by one, Olivia raised one eyebrow.

Caroline closed her eyes and shook her head as if she knew what Olivia was thinking. She set one cup on the counter beside Olivia's planner. "It's better than it sounds."

Caroline left the kitchen just as quickly as she'd come flying in, only to re-enter a moment later without her coffee. She was holding the rose-pink twin to Olivia's apron instead.

"Wow, you're on time for once." Olivia smiled, letting her eyes dance between the second pan of cupcakes she poured and her childhood best friend.

"I skipped putting in my extensions today," she said as she tossed the apron over her head.

True to her word, Caroline's silky, dirty blonde ponytail was a tad bit shorter than it typically was, dangling against the collar of a sky-blue blouse that matched her eyes. Her hands fidgeted with one earing as she descended on the island where pans of muffins and cinnamon rolls waited to be transported to the displays in the front.

"I'm starving." She picked up a cinnamon roll and sunk her teeth into it. "Oh my goodness," she mumbled through a mouthful. "How do you do it?"

Olivia carried the cupcakes to the one available oven and slid them inside. "The real question is how do you manage to keep your figure with as much as you eat?"

Her head tilted to the side as she savored a second bite. Her eyes rolled behind her fake eyelashes as if the taste were more important than the question. "For what it's worth, I would give up my figure to be able to bake like this."

Olivia made a quick curtsy, gesturing to her apron. "I guess that was the deal I made with God at some point."

Caroline rolled her eyes as she took another bite. Olivia snickered as she went to the storage room for cheesecake supplies.

While Caroline always had a slim, athletic figure, Olivia's weight had gone up and down throughout high school. Sometime after graduation, she'd plateaued at a nice, curvy figure that always made her feel like a big, fat dumpling next to Caroline. She'd never envied her friend, but she would admit that there was a day or two that she wished she could trade bodies with the ever-glowing Caroline only once. Just to see what it felt like to not have to squeeze into a pair of jeans, wear a blouse that was a size too big to hide her tummy, or count calories when she taste-tested her creations.

"How was the wedding last night?" Caroline called out from the kitchen.

"It was nice. Sophie had a ton of bridesmaids. The food was so-so," she called back.

"Meet any cute guys?" Caroline asked and it was Olivia's turn to roll her eyes.

"Plenty that you would have enjoyed flirting with." With both arms full of cheesecake ingredients, Olivia stepped into the kitchen and returned to the island. "There was one at my parent's cabin last night."

Like Olivia had just spouted the nuclear codes, Caroline spun around and pinned her with a look, a half-eaten muffin in one hand. "What's that now?" Caroline and her fluttering lashes that could put any hummingbird to shame. "You're telling me a cute guy—like an actual living and breathing man—stopped by your parents' place last night?"

Olivia bit back a laugh. "He did a lot more than that." She snorted. "He even stayed the night."

Caroline's jaw fell, her sparkling white teeth on full display. "And you didn't call me? Wait—how cute was this guy? Was he, like, attractive-on-the-inside-where-it-counts kind of cute, or was he hot enough to take to the Fourth of July dance and make all the other girls jealous?"

Olivia pulled the counter mixer from under the island. It was no big secret that Caroline was a careless flirt and twirled her hair at any eligible bachelor that passed through Heavenly. And since she'd never be seeing the man again, Olivia didn't mind getting Carolines hackles raised. "Oh, he was gorgeous."

Caroline leaned against the island, holding herself by her forearms, muffin crumbs falling around her. "How gorgeous?"

Olivia mimicked Caroline's posture, leaning against the

opposite side of the island. "I would have ran away with this man if he'd have asked me to."

As if the metal beneath her caught fire, Caroline shoved herself away from the island. "You're lying."

Olivia straightened and held one hand to her chest. "Cross my heart. He's real. About six-foot tall, olive skin, dark brown hair that curled just a bit at his nape."

Caroline stuffed the rest of the muffin in her mouth and started untying her apron. "Is he still there?" she asked with her mouth full.

"What?" Olivia screeched. "You're willing to leave me here to run the front *and* back of the bakery by myself while you chase some out-of-towner?"

As if the ridiculousness of her actions dawned on her, Caroline's shoulders slumped, and she started retying her apron. "Of course not. But you should have called me, Olivia. I could have been at your parents' in less than ten minutes."

Olivia barked a laugh as she went to the fridge. "To do what? Peep through the windows?"

Nose wrinkled, Caroline bounced on her heels like a cranky toddler. "We already know all the guys in town. It's nice to meet someone new every once in a while." She perked up a bit, one eyebrow raised. "How long does he plan to stay?"

The foil packaging crinkled as she ripped open cream cheese. "He was just passing through and Dad offered him a place to stay. He's probably long gone by now."

"Wait—your parent's cabin is a half mile off the road— what do you mean he was passing through?"

"It was on the outskirts of town. I had a flat tire on the way home from the wedding and he helped me change it."

Caroline spilled herself over the island again, propping up her chin with one fist. "Leave. Out. Nothing."

In the time it took her to prep the cheesecake crust and its filling, Olivia rehashed the details that mattered. "You see, there's nothing to it. He stopped, the van left, and we talked while he changed my tire until dad got there."

Eyebrows knitted together, Caroline frowned. "There's nothing to it? Olivia, people write romance novels that aren't even that captivating."

Olivia held up one finger to stop her friend in her tracks.

54

"There was zero romance."

Caroline's shoulders slumped. "None? Not even a little?"

"Let's just say there was as much chemistry between us as there is between you and my pepaw."

"Olivia! Why would you say that? Do you know how long it's gonna take to get *that* image out of my head?"

Olivia laughed. "Then you get the picture."

"How am I supposed to look Pepaw Vern in the eyes when I come for supper tonight?" Caroline finally picked up a tray of baked goods and backed through the kitchen door with them. A second later, she returned to the kitchen as if she didn't have a job to bother with. "One more question. What's his name and where's he from?"

Lucky for her, Olivia knew those answers. She looked up from the glass pan where she packed graham cracker crumbs with her fingertips. "Peyton. He's from Austin."

"A city boy," she said breathlessly as she started to leave again. "I could have been swept off my feet by a city boy."

Even as she smiled, Olivia groaned. "You have a problem, you know that?"

Unending silence drew Peyton from the dark abyss of sleep. Somewhere in central Texas he was laying on a bed that wasn't his, in a room he didn't remember paying for. As morsels of reality collected in his dreamless thoughts, a memory of friendly voices and smiling faces surfaced. Laughing, silverware tapping against plates, the taste of tart cherry and brown sugar.

Peyton opened his eyes.

Cheek pressed against the pillow he stared at the cabin wall in the black of night. Although, the glowing numbers on the nightstand clock said it was five forty-nine in the morning. He hadn't bothered setting an alarm. His body was used to a pre-dawn routine that let him catch the sunrise and a quick workout most mornings. Looks like today would be no different.

Wrestling his way from under the warm quilts, he turned and sat up, facing a door he couldn't see. The flip of the switch on the lamp beside him was enough to wake the room as much as it woke him. Elbows resting on bent knees, he scrubbed his hands across his face and through his hair. He really needed to get on the road soon.

These people had done enough for him. He couldn't imagine imposing on them for another few hours or a second meal. If he could manage to pack his bag and find his way back to his truck before anyone even knew he was awake, he'd prefer it.

One chapter of Exodus later, Peyton laid his Bible on the nightstand and reached for the baseball card and his phone. While he flipped the card in one hand, he checked his messages with the other. Only one waited for him. From his grandma.

I know you told us not to worry about you, but I'm just checking in. How are things? Are you safe? Do you eat three solid meals a day? Call me when you have the time. Missing my boy.

Peyton chuckled. Nan had a sweet spirit. She didn't mean any harm. Even if he *had* specifically told everyone not to constantly prod him for updates. He needed this time on his own—unmonitored by his well-meaning family. But in her defense, she knew he was headed her way. He couldn't blame her for being excited.

This adventure was coming to a swift close, and though he wasn't ready for it to end, he knew the next chapter in his life was a necessary one. Even if he didn't know what that chapter held for him.

"Lord, lead me to the rock that is higher than I," he whispered.

Resigned to whatever this day would bring, Peyton left the card and his phone on the nightstand. He stepped off the bed and shuffled to the bathroom, grabbing his backpack as he passed it on the dresser.

Ten minutes later, he stood in front of the mirror, brushing his teeth, and staring at a pair of sad, blue eyes. Did other people see the sadness when they looked at him? He needed to do something about that. Feign joy a little better.

In the room, he dropped his bag in the same place he'd left it last night and set his Bible inside, the zipper loud in the quiet room. He pocketed his phone and wallet, eyes drawn to the sliver of first light cutting through the curtains. He'd find dawn beyond the window, he knew that much, but he had a gut feeling there was more.

He pushed the curtains aside and his breath hitched in his chest. "Whoa."

Miles and miles of hills stretched for as far as the eye could see, gilded in morning sunlight and veiled by early fog. Wooded areas lined the valleys and climbed up the peaks of hills. On the green, rolling pastures nearest to the cabin were scores of perfectly aligned Christmas trees. To the left, more hills dotted with the same trees. It was enough to stir the Christmas spirit in him, even in June.

"Farm," he breathed. That's what Daniel had told him last night. But he didn't specify what kind. "An actual, real life Christmas tree farm."

There were animals, too, he noticed near a barn with a monitor roof that had short, rectangle windows. Cows surrounded it, like the ones he'd seen on the drive up yesterday. There was a bull, tossing his head as a couple walked near his wooden fence. A family of pigs stood inside a pen, dripping with mud. Sheep with tattered wool coats and goats with long horns had fields of their own. Chickens scratched and pecked around a building that looked like a miniature house.

In the pasture at the bottom of the hill, a massive garden sat beside a greenhouse and a pond that looked like it had seen better days. Tall grasses took on a beige hue in this sunlight and waved in the breeze, mixing with wildflowers and a few leftover bluebonnets that led to a giant oak tree that held a treehouse—Josh's treehouse, he assumed.

No wonder Daniel had kept quiet about what they do to make a living. There were no words to express what he was looking at. In all of its grandeur and glory, calling it by any singular aspect would be an injustice. It was a farm in every sense of the word.

Peyton left the window and snatched up his shoes from beside the door. He slid them on, tightened the laces, and shouldered his bag without so much as a look back. At the end of the hallway, he trotted down the stairs where the scent of breakfast met him halfway.

"I thought the smell of bacon might wake you up,"

Gianna said with a dimpled smile as she flipped thick, golden slabs in a cast iron pan.

"I'm not so sure about that. Still feels like I'm dreaming." His stomach let out a well-timed growl as he dropped his bag into the seat at the end of the dining table.

"Make yourself at home, Peyton. Everyone else has already eaten except for Josh, who's still asleep upstairs, milking his summer break for all it's worth."

The kitchen island was covered in bowls, plates, and trays filled with three types of eggs, hashbrowns, toast, chorizo, tortilla shells, cheese, pico de gallo, fruit, and bacon— Gianna added more slices on top.

"What do you typically eat for breakfast?" she asked.

"Lately beef jerky and black coffee."

"Coffee drinker? Right over there." She pointed toward a nook beside the staircase that held an espresso machine with a coffee pot attached to the side. Beside it, a rack of colorful, flavored syrups. "Cups are in the cabinet."

So much for trying to sneak off without anybody knowing. He found himself pouring coffee into a porcelain mug and adding a couple scoops of sugar just to change things up. He took a long sip and leaned back against the counter. Even the coffee here tasted better. "What is this place?"

Joy creased the edges of her eyes as she poured bacon grease from the cast iron skillet into a tin canister. "I like to call it Heaven on earth, but I might be a little biased."

He lifted his cup. "From an outsider's perspective, I'd say your judgement is spot on." He took another sip. "I've spent the last month carving my way through Hill Country, and I haven't seen any place more beautiful than this one."

"This place took a lot of hard work to build." A few drops of grease fell from the edge of her pan.

"I imagine a few generations of guts and grit."

She laughed softly as she pulled a paper towel from its roll. "Something like that."

Daniel stepped into the kitchen, his damp hair neatly parted at one side. His booted steps were heavy against the hardwood floor with all the vigor of a man on a mission. "You're awake. Good. I have something I want to talk to you about after breakfast." He stopped beside Peyton and filled a cup with coffee, the carafe tapping the machine as he returned it. "Once you finish here meet me on the patio."

With that, he left through the glass door at the back of the kitchen.

Torn between taking his time to taste test breakfast and hearing what Daniel had to say, Peyton looked between the feast and the door.

"Allow me." As if she could see the battle he fought, Gianna opened a drawer, pulled out a sheet of brown parchment paper, and set it on the countertop. She dropped a huge tortilla shell on it, scooped a healthy portion of scrambled eggs, chorizo, cheese, and pico into it, and then rolled it so perfectly that she would give any professional burrito roller a run for his money. She snatched another paper towel and pushed both items into his hand as he passed her. "Can't talk business on an empty stomach."

Business?

The dewy morning air filled his lungs, and he was sure healed some part of his soul. The view was even more electrifying when he wasn't standing behind glass. It was hard to pull his attention away and follow the curved sidewalk to a covered area that jutted off the corner of the house. Unable to be seen from inside, it sat at an angle that made the walk from the kitchen to the patio a short one.

On the furthest corner there was a brick smoker with a built-in grill. On the opposite side, near the walkway, a skinny bar with tall stools. At the back, a horseshoe-shaped booth that could easily seat a half dozen people. In the center of the patio, a rectangle fire table with green glass rocks framed by four Adirondack chairs painted to match. At the front corner, Daniel stood with his arms crossed over his chest beside a porch swing that faced the view.

Peyton set his breakfast on the table, the cup clinking gently against the surface. Daniel glanced over his shoulder.

Between the fire table and a pair of chairs, Peyton went to join the man. "The Lord sure set you in a breathtaking place."

Daniel huffed a laugh, as if he agreed but was too humble to admit it.

Peyton leaned one shoulder against a column. "I gotta tell you, when you said y'all farm, this was not what I imagined."

Daniel's eyes lit with good humor. "We do farm. We've got a vegetable farm, a sheep farm, a cow farm, a chicken farm."

"A Christmas tree farm," Peyton added.

Daniel nodded, his focus scanning the horizon. "It was only supposed to be a hobby. Something...*fun* to take our minds off the infertility. Gianna and I married at nineteen and thought by the time we were twenty-five we'd have a house full of kids. We ended up with no kids and a yard full of Christmas trees."

The sadness in Daniel's voice put Peyton on a lonely farm where a younger version of the couple celebrated Christmas mornings without the warmth of children's laughter.

Daniel slowly turned and made his way to the booth at the back of the patio. He sat on the edge of the seat where he rested his elbows on his knees. "We started with a couple acres just beyond those trees." He tipped his head to the woods that sat at the very bottom of a knoll and dipped behind a hill. "Somewhere out of sight because we didn't really know what we were doing. We studied up, learned good lessons the hard way, and gained a few friends over those years.

"Our first harvest was meager but healthy. We cut down enough to fill up two trucks, set up on the outskirts of town, and sold out before lunch." He stroked one hand down his goatee and chuckled. "We waited too close to Christmas and set our prices much lower than we should have. But we enjoyed every minute of it. Meeting people and hearing their stories about how they celebrate Christmas and how the trees remind them of some part of their childhood...It's priceless. On the ride home, we both agreed to do it again, but bigger."

Peyton could imagine falling in love with a hobby like that.

"We started clearing land by the acres and planted until it was too dark to see. By that spring we had a thousand seedlings in the ground and hearts that felt like we'd found our purpose." He took a deep breath and let it out slow. "Shortly after that, we started fostering. We were open to adopting every child who passed through our home. We would have kept them all if we could have." He chuckled, but the sound was strained. As if there was a deep sadness penetrating the memory of those days. "But year after year, the children kept leaving our home until we couldn't do it anymore."

Peyton cleared his throat and took a few steps closer, hands tucked in his pockets. "I'm sure you planted a seed of love in those kids' hearts that God's gonna use throughout their lives. No pun intended," he said as he looked over his shoulder at the hill of Christmas trees.

Daniel chuckled and nodded. "I think you're right. God does nothing without a purpose."

"And He led you to Olivia."

"That, He did." Daniel cleared his throat. "We didn't foster the year we got the phone call. It was purely an act of God. The caseworker we'd worked with back then had caught wind of a baby girl out of Oklahoma whose chances for adoption were slim to none because of her birthmark. She would require medical attention for the better half of her childhood and most parents saw that as a liability."

Peyton stood a little straighter, pulling his hands from his pockets and crossing his arms as he listened.

"Doctors would have to monitor it over the years to be sure it didn't develop into melanoma. For most foster families, all they heard were 'medical bills.'" Daniel frowned and shook his head. "Didn't matter to us. We wanted her, no matter the cost. The next day we drove up and got to meet her. She was the chunkiest little baby I'd ever seen, and she had the biggest smile, as if she knew just who we were. And when they put her in our arms—" Daniel's voice broke, and he bumped his fisted hand on the knee of his jeans with a quiet chuckle.

Peyton's chest tightened as he looked off into the distance. He forced himself to swallow the brick in his throat.

"She was perfect. Every ounce of her. We couldn't thank God enough. For every day of her life. Every step in the adoption process that we cleared. Every doctor's visit that let us leave with a clean bill of health."

Peyton looked back at the man. "Is she still at risk?"

"Oh, no. She's been cleared for years. The doctors don't see anything that would cause them concern." Daniel lifted his chin and looked right at him, his eyes glossy from the show of emotion. "They told us we could have had parts of the birthmark removed surgically, but it would leave her with a scar. Laser treatment wasn't an option since it's so close to her eye. But Gianna and I, we were content with the way God made her. As far as we're concerned, there's nothing we can add or take away from that girl to make her any more beautiful."

A smile tugged at Peyton's lips.

"And you already know about Josh's adoption. He was the miracle we didn't know we needed. Olivia was the song that made our house joyful, and Josh was the spark that made it vibrant. Don't get me wrong, if the caseworker called today with another child, I have no doubt that Gianna would want me to speak on her behalf when I say we would accept in a heartbeat. But..."

His voice trailed off, and Peyton got the gist.

Daniel cleared his throat and sat a little straighter. "Have a sit, Peyton. There's something I'd like to talk to you about."

Peyton obliged, taking the seat on the other end of the round booth and pulling the breakfast burrito from its wrapper. He took one big bite and savored the warm flavors with a groan. "Your wife deserves some kind of award for the way she cooks."

Daniel raised an eyebrow. "Don't worry. They're hangin' in the office."

Peyton smiled as he picked up his coffee cup.

"We've got a little more than fifteen hundred acres here. Some of the best views in Hill Country. When the seasons are kind, you won't find a better quality of life anywhere on earth. Hard years are tiresome, but the longsuffering is worth it."

Peyton stopped mid-sip and lowered his cup. Something in Daniel's tone seemed rehearsed. Like he was about to try to sell Peyton something he didn't need.

"We live on the crops we grow, the milk we get from the cows, and the eggs from the hens. We raise pigs and cattle to put in our freezer and our neighbors' freezers. The horses have their fair share of maintenance. And the trees, though they're a labor of love, take up a bulk of our time, especially when it comes Christmas season. And when we're not working, we're on the water, in the woods, or out here on the patio—looking for something to hunt, fish, or eat. In short, we work hard so we can play harder."

Peyton didn't doubt him. This lifestyle required no less than a lifetime contract signed with blood, sweat, and tears.

But what did that have to do with him? "Why are you telling me this?"

Daniel lifted his chin and pinned him with the look of a father giving life advice to his kid. "I'd like you to stay on through the summer."

There it was.

The thing Peyton didn't need. He'd already relied on the kindness of this family longer than he should have. Time was slipping away from him the longer he drug his feet here. And kicking around dead-end ideas about spending a summer in a place like this was a cruel and unusual punishment.

The Whitmores were likely built on generations of farmers that loved the Lord and lived off the land. He was one generation past a broken marriage out of a trailer park. Peyton leaned away from his breakfast, and a frustrated sigh broke free before he could stop it.

"Last night when I drove up on you and Olivia, I was nervous." Daniel said. "Even though I knew my daughter could handle herself with a stranger, I never want my kids to be left in a dangerous situation. But, uh..." He paused long enough to draw Peyton's undivided attention. "Before I got there—before I knew you were there—the Lord told me, 'Don't worry. He'll stay.'"

Peyton looked down at the table between them. Staying wasn't an option. Why would the Lord tell Daniel it was?

"I know this must sound strange. Sounded strange to me, too. I didn't know what it meant or even if it was Him talking to me. And then I saw you there, changing her tire. And I knew. That's when I invited you to stay for supper, to stay in our guest room."

Fair enough.

"But those words have been rattling around in my head

this morning."

Peyton huffed a laugh that was void of amusement. So, his invitation to supper was stretching into a summer job?

Somewhere in the distance a rooster crowed. Wind blew through the trees, across the surface of the pond, and over the crops in the garden. Like an invisible person walking through the rows, brushing the tops of the plants with one hand.

What would it be like to spend a few months losing himself here? Working with his hands instead of just his head for a change? Finding the same purpose that Daniel and his wife had found here? "Can I ask you something?"

"Go ahead." Daniel turned and braced both elbows on the table.

"You said you felt like the Lord told you that?" Peyton paused and Daniel nodded. "Why didn't God speak to me, too? Why didn't He tell me you were gonna ask me to stay?"

Daniel's shoulders raised as he took in a deep breath and let it out slowly, eyes trained on a faraway place. "I don't know the answer to that."

Too bad. Peyton picked up his burrito and took a bite. He hadn't really been expecting an answer. It was the one that seemed most elusive in his life right now. His hopes hadn't been high. But he still had to ask.

"I do know this, though. The Lord works in ways we don't understand. He has to. Because a god that can be understood by mortal man is not God at all."

A smirk tugged at the edge of Peyton's mouth as he chewed. That was a really good way to look at it. Nevertheless..."I was raised in the city. I don't know anything about this kind of life."

Daniel dipped his head once, as if he were open to negotiations. "I've had farmhands come from the city, and by the end of the month they're at home in the saddle."

Peyton couldn't help but chuckle. He attempted to hide it behind his hand as he rubbed his chin. "I'm not a farmhand. I'm not...anything right now." The road was calling his name, begging him to find out exactly what he was. "I'm sorry, Daniel. The offer is mind-blowing, to say the least, and I'm probably crazy to pass up an opportunity like this. But I'm pretty sure I'd cause more trouble here than y'all deserve."

Daniel nodded gently, as if he made peace with Peyton's answer.

"And I think if I were supposed to stay at a place like this then the Lord would tell me somehow. Like He told you."

A thoughtful frown pulled at his mouth. "I respect that."

"Thank you. For everything." He'd felt more at home here in the last twelve hours than he ever had at his rental in Austin. "This life, it's truly a dream."

But that was where it would end for Peyton. Just a dream.

He stuck the last bit of breakfast in his mouth and stood, crumpling the greasy paper. Daniel followed suit, standing and stretching out one hand. "Thank *you*, Peyton. For being there for my daughter."

Peyton shook his hand and nodded once. Not trusting his voice to hold firm to his decision, he picked up the coffee cup and downed the rest on his way back to the kitchen. Inside, he found Gianna at the stove, stirring something in a huge pot that smelled a lot like strawberries. She had a line of different sized jars standing along the counter like little soldiers awaiting orders. Her smiling blue eyes found him the moment he walked in.

"Breakfast was life-changing." He tossed the paper in the trash can on his way to the sink.

Her smile broadened and her dimples appeared.

"Seriously, I'm not the same man I was a half hour ago."

"I'm glad you liked it." She turned back to the stove. "What's the verdict on where you're spending your summer?"

The porcelain cup clinked against the bottom of the sink as Peyton froze. So, Daniel had brought his wife in on the pitch, too? He cleared his throat and turned on the faucet just long enough to keep the coffee residue from sticking to the bottom. "It's a generous offer, ma'am, but I can't stay."

He had too much to lose if he dedicated himself to a place like this. Focus. Isolation. Long miles where he could talk to himself about all the things that didn't make sense.

She nodded, her thick, blonde curls bouncing around the tops of her shoulders. "We really enjoyed having you around here, Peyton." She turned and picked up a brown paper bag from the edge of the island. "I won't lie. I was hoping to unpack this after your talk with Daniel." She held it out to him. "It's last night's leftovers. For the road. You can probably warm them up at a truck stop somewhere."

Crying shame. Peyton was getting weaker by the minute. The bag crackled as he took it from her. "Thank you, ma'am. I appreciate it more than you know."

At the head of the dining room table, he lifted his backpack out of the seat and tossed it over his shoulder. Sights set on the opening that led to his exit, he stopped short of the threshold. "Is, uh, Olivia nearby?"

Gianna looked up at him, her smile fading a smidgen. "I'm afraid not. She goes in to work at four in the morning."

She'd told him that she wouldn't be here when he left, didn't she? And then she'd sent him to bed with a compliment that he wouldn't soon forget. "Would you tell her—and Josh—bye for me?"

Her dimples reappeared. "Absolutely, I will."

With a nod, Peyton walked out. On the porch where two guard dogs were waiting, he held the paper sack higher. "I've got nothing on my person except for roast."

Which he'd gladly trade for his life if need be. With lazy eyes and panting tongues, they watched him walk across the porch and down the stairs. His truck was still parked where he'd left it last night. Olivia's and Daniel's were gone, giving him the space he needed to pull out of the circle driveway. He tossed his backpack in the passenger seat and set his lunch beside it.

It smelled more like brunch to him.

Behind the wheel, he gave the cabin one last look as he pulled the strap of his seatbelt. This place really was something else. Peyton had grown up in a trailer park, running up and down abandoned train tracks, and throwing rocks in Lady Bird Lake for fun. He didn't even have enough money to dream of a place like this. He was lucky to have even encountered it. And the kind family inside.

But he still had some bets to settle with himself. Demons to face down. Skeletons to dust off.

On the driveway that seemed more like a road than an entry, he passed the cattle they'd talked about. A group of deer stood near a cluster of trees, watching him as if they knew he was no harm. In the daylight, the fifteen hundred acres was more visible. Some of it was nothing but fields, but most of what he drove past were thick woods. All of it, a hill or a valley. At some point down the way, he caught glimpses of a river—or maybe a creek—snaking through the brush.

The kid in him wondered what it would have felt like to explore that creek. To check and see if there were any fish he could catch, or rocks he could toss, or logs he could walk across to the other side. His chuckle echoed in the empty cab.

At the end of the driveway where gravel met asphalt Peyton checked the traffic to the right—the way they'd driven in last night. Which reminded him, he'd need a GPS to find his way out of here. He tapped the dashboard screen and set the address to his grandparent's Las Vegas, New Mexico, oasis. Then he turned and checked for traffic on his left.

The breath in his lungs was suddenly held hostage.

Not more than a dozen yards away was a sign hanging between two logs and held up by chains, pointing a welcome for anyone looking for the tree farm. The words staring back at him echoed the cry of his heart.

Higher Rock Ranch

CHAPTER FOUR

Feet cemented to the ground where he'd shaken Peyton's hand, Daniel looked out over his land, frustration clawing at his thoughts as seconds stretched into minutes. What had he missed?

"Lord, I know what You said," he whispered.

Or maybe Daniel had misunderstood. Maybe he'd read too much into it. Maybe the words didn't have anything to do with Peyton at all. In any case, the kid had wiped the Higher Rock dust from his shoes and headed west. Something in his gut told him that the boy needed this place as much as it needed him. If even for the summer.

Or maybe Daniel was falling back into old habits of trying to control an outcome that was only meant for the Lord's hands.

Whatever the answer was, he let the matter drop and followed the walkway to the kitchen where Gianna spooned ruby-red jam into jars. She spared a look over her shoulder at him and smiled before she turned to her task again. Daniel leaned one elbow on the countertop beside her, pulled a finger along the warm edge of the pot, and sampled the rich preservative. "Mmm. Just when I think I've tasted the best of your food, you go and prove me wrong again."

She laughed gently, a sound that would forever soothe his soul. Her joy drew a smile to his own face and, as it always did, pulled him to her like a moth to a flame. She leaned forward with expectation and shared a quick kiss with him. Paperwork called his name from the office, so he reluctantly pushed himself away from the counter and headed out.

"You're right," Gianna said before he could clear the doorway. "The jam does taste good."

Chest warm with an ever-evolving sense of love for her, Daniel chuckled. He backed through the opening, not wanting to break away from the trance her sparkling blue eyes steeped him in. When the wall broke it for him, he spun around and headed for the office down the hall. Birdie and Boone sounded the alarms from the porch and turned Daniel around. He grabbed the knob and swung the door wide as the young man outside reached for the doorbell.

Peyton stopped short and dropped his hand to his side. His shoulders rose and fell where he pulled in a breath and let it out slowly. "I'll stay."

Now that made more sense.

"Glad to hear it," Daniel said as Birdie and Boone went back to their resting spots on the porch. "I'll grab my truck, and you can follow me to the homestead."

A short drive through the woods near the cabin, down a well-worn dirt path where low-hanging branches and overgrown shrubs reached for any vehicle that dare traverse the single lane, Daniel was met with a familiar nostalgia. Nestled in the shade of towering oaks and mighty elms was the house where he'd grown up in his early days. The one his grandpa had built before his dad had built the cottage, and before Daniel had built the cabin.

The metal roof with a single gabled dormer window in the front held more rust than his grandpa's old toolchest ever had. Gray shiplap siding was still intact but could use a good washing. Same for the windows framing each side of the wooden door. The covered porch looked like it was in good spirits, but his weight would tell the tale here in a few minutes.

Their truck doors shut in unison as Daniel made his way toward the little home that had sat hungry for company for the last several decades. Dead leaves crunching under his steps, Daniel stopped at the foot of the stairs as Peyton joined him. "This was my grandpa and grandma's place. Lived here until I was ten and my parents were able to get on their feet."

A breath of fresh air filled Daniel's lungs. "This house taught me everything I needed to know about being a boy. Playing with toy soldiers on the windowsills. Lining up empty cans in the backyard for shooting practice with my

BB gun. Learning how to read by the light of the fireplace."

Over his shoulder he found Peyton studying the house. He was surprised by the look of appreciation in the lift of his chin. "Sounds like every boy's dream."

"Not these kids lately," Daniel sighed. "If this place doesn't have Wi-Fi and A/C then they're buggin' out."

"Times are different now, I guess. These kids don't have to make do with what we had to."

We? Fifty had met Daniel back in January. "If you don't mind me asking, how old are you, Peyton?"

His eyes left the house for a split second. "Twenty-six."

He would have guessed younger. Something about this kid seemed...naive. He had an air of innocence about him. Could be his friendly nature or the way he wore a hint of a smirk at all times, as if he were ready to tell a good joke at any given moment.

"It's livable and sturdy. I've been meaning to come up here and give it some TLC, so you might have to evict a mouse or two. But it's clean for the most part. Still got power. Indoor plumbing. A coffee maker."

Peyton huffed a laugh, and Daniel led the way up the stairs. They creaked and whined but held strong. He pulled a key from his pocket and held the knob to insert it.

But the knob twisted.

Daniel hesitated. This door shouldn't be unlocked. Nobody had access to it besides his family. Maybe he'd ask Vern about it later.

Inside, the smell of musky curtains and dirt filled his nostrils. Specks of dust floated in the rays of sunshine falling through the windows. There was a small loveseat, a recliner, a coffee table, and a dining table for two surrounded by boxes of storage they'd relocated here over the years.

Daniel pointed to the door on the right. "Kitchen and mud room are that way. You'll find the washer and dryer out there, too. Bedroom and bathroom are to the left. There's not much more than what you see here. You'll have a bed, a stove, and a roof." Daniel pointed to the narrow stairway behind the recliner where he'd ridden the banister many a morning. "There's a half story with a couple more beds, but I figure you won't need all those."

"Not unless Goldilocks stops by."

Daniel couldn't help but chuckle. "If this works for you then I'll leave you to it. We also have some bunks at the top of the barn for some of the farmhands who stay overnight if you'd prefer that."

Peyton shook his head as he wondered a few steps into the room. "Not at all. This is perfect."

"Good. I'll have Gianna make you up some foodstuffs to keep you tied over for a while."

Peyton turned slowly. "That's not necessary, sir. I can find a grocery store or dollar store, if y'all have something like that around."

"'Bout twenty minutes east of here. But I know Gianna will want to fix something for you, so expect it." Daniel nodded. "Once you're settled down a bit, meet me back at the barn and I'll put you to work."

Peyton reached out his hand. "Thank you, sir. You don't know how much I appreciate this opportunity."

Daniel shook it. "I look forward to working with you, Peyton."

With that, Daniel started out. Over the threshold, he paused, turning just enough to look at the kid once more. "Peyton, can I ask you something?"

"Shoot."

"What made you decide to stay?"

The boy's smirk broadened a little. "Your sign at the end of the driveway. I guess I missed it when I drove in last night. *Higher Rock Ranch and Christmas Tree Farm.*" He tilted his head to the side, kicking at something on the floor. "That scripture has been heavy on my heart during this trip. I figured that had to be God trying to tell me something."

"I'll be," Daniel muttered. Perfect timing.

Once Peyton unpacked his meek belongings at the place Daniel had called "the homestead," he'd found his way back through the trees and to the trail where dust filled his rearview. As it would turn out, the barn was as nice as the cabin.

What was he doing here? This place was better than anything Peyton had to offer it.

"Lead me to the rock that is higher than I," he whispered to the empty cab of his truck as he spun the wheel and turned into a parking space at the end of a long line of trucks.

He killed the engine and straightened his baseball cap in the mirror. A heavy sigh rushed from his chest. This was crazy. But he knew he'd regret it for the rest of his life if he would've made it to New Mexico. He'd been praying for a sign, and, boy, did God deliver.

Keys jangling against the steering column, Peyton stepped out into the Texas heat. He was positive nobody within the vicinity would be interested in committing grand theft auto. Gravel crunched under his tennis shoes as he made his way to the barn doors, drowning in that first-day-of-high-school energy. He had no experience, no expectations, and no right to be here in this stunning place.

Just short of the door he paused. The view of the wide, green hills dotted with cattle and Christmas trees still hadn't settled in yet. To the east, midmorning sun hid behind a brilliant explosion of white clouds. And to the west, pastures of high grass, wind blowing in waves against the tops and painting works of art across the range.

Peyton finally stepped inside. Concrete floors beneath him and tall wooden ceilings above made up a long corridor with a tractor sitting at the other end. The smell of manure mingled with the scent of hay. Voices grew louder as he made his way down the lane of stall doors. Midway, at the back of the barn, he found an alcove with two sets of stairs tracing parallel walls. A table sat squarely below the landing where they met. Sconces hung from the walls and a faded cowskin rug covered the floor beneath a group of men.

"Stu, Wyatt, Grady, you'll come with me to the east fields. Leon, see if you can get that mower runnin' again." Daniel paused when Peyton stopped at the edge of the crowd. "Boys, this is our new hire, Peyton Brooks. He'll be staying at the homestead and working with us through the summer."

Eight men turned, most with wide stances and crossed arms, and looked him over. Peyton tapped the brim of his cap. Two reached out and shook his hand. Another looked down at his tennis shoes. That's when he realized they were wearing boots—all of them. Dust-covered, well-worn leather boots. And most held cowboy hats in their hands. Peyton dipped his chin and chewed on the inside of his cheek.

He was in over his head.

"Jordan, Hunner, Charlie, and Simon—start vaccinations on the cattle in the south pasture," Daniel said as he gestured to each man.

Down the breezeway, an older guy stepped out of a stall, Josh quick on his heels. Though he was bowed at the shoulders, his walk was strong and steady. Behind them, a little dog trotted to keep up, his tongue hanging out of his panting mouth. No more than a foot tall, it looked more like a bear cub with its shaggy, caramel-colored snout and fuzzy eyebrows. Must be the one they called Mutt.

Josh's eyes widened when they landed on Peyton. His mouth dropped open and snapped shut just as quickly, like he was afraid to interrupt the meeting.

The older cowboy, however, had no qualms about it. "How tall is everybody?" he asked with a gruff voice. "I need someone who isn't hunched like me."

The group of men remained planted. As if they had no obligation to volunteer.

Peyton leaned up on the tips of his shoes and rock back on his heels. "I'm six-three on a fishin' day."

Quiet bursts of chuckles echoed through the group. The old cowboy's eyes found Peyton and the wrinkles around them smoothed for a brief second as his mouth curved into a smirk. "Good 'nuff. Come with me."

"What's that mean?" Josh asked, thin eyebrows scrunched. "What's so funny?"

"Means men tend to stretch the truth when they catch a fish they aren't proud of," the old cowboy chomped out.

"Vern, this is Peyton," Daniel said with a laugh hanging in his voice. "He's the one you'll be working with today."

The old cowboy looked him over again, this time without a smirk. "You ever worked on a farm before?"

He cleared his throat and shook his head. There was no point in trying to hide the truth. "Nope."

The snorts from the men didn't escape his notice.

"When you're finished up here, come find me. I'll make a farmer out of you." He turned and hustled back to the stall he'd come from, Josh and the little bear cub not far behind.

"All right," Daniel said, folding a sheet of paper in his hands. "It's gonna be a long, hot day. Stay cool, men."

Some set their hats on their head and started for the door at the end of the barn. Some stayed behind, looking at Peyton as if he were an artifact Daniel had drug out of the woods somewhere.

"Which big city are you from?" one asked with a smirk.

It was no secret that he hadn't spent a lot of time in rural Texas. But he wasn't sure which part of his person tipped them off. "The one with lots of traffic and people who don't make eye contact."

"That could be any of 'em." Another cowboy laughed and walked away.

Three were left standing. One extended his hand. "Grady Clark."

Peyton shook it and then reached for the next two. "Good to meet y'all."

"I'm Wyatt Shaw," the second one said, then jabbed a thumb at the guy in the middle. "This is Stu Wallace."

"I look forward to working with y'all."

"We'll see," Stu said as he stepped around Peyton. The other two followed.

Peyton watched over his shoulder as they made their way outside.

"They're gonna give you a hard time," Daniel said, fiddling with the folded paper as he approached. "They want to see if you're tough enough to hold up under the pressure. Can't trust you if you tuck tail and run. Not good for morale."

"I wouldn't expect any different." Nothing they could say to him would be worse than the hazing he went through in college. "I'll make sure they find me trustworthy."

Daniel pointed with the paper in the direction the men had gone. "We have a venue east of here—an event hall for celebrations and weddings and such. It's where we sell the trees during Christmas. That's where our east fields are located. Those are the trees we let families walk through and pick from at Christmastime. These fields you see out here," he said as tipped his head. "Those are the fields we cut from to ship trees to our vendors in the city. We have a tent located in Austin. Your family might've even bought a tree from us at some point."

Not in this lifetime. "We actually never had a real tree. Mom bought a fake one before my brother was born and it's still going strong. Missing some needles and spunk but still covers the presents."

Daniel huffed a laugh as he nodded. "Well, make sure you tell her these trees were taken care of by her son this year. She might want one."

He wasn't wrong. Mom would be ecstatic about buying a tree she thought her son might have grown himself—even if he never had anything to do with the growing process—and she'd want to show it off to everyone, like putting his artwork on the fridge when he was five. In fact, he could see his whole family wanting in on it. Austin and Natalie. Even Nan and Pop would want to celebrate.

Which reminded him, he'd meant to call Nan once he was on the road again.

"Today we're spraying the east fields with pesticides and checking for damaged or sick trees. The others are working with the livestock. I'll let you get used to the place first before I throw you into one of those chores." Daniel walked past Peyton and turned to face him. "Though, I can't say the same for Vern. He may very well have you building a house from toothpicks."

Peyton chuckled. "I look forward to it."

With a nod, Daniel walked out into the sun and Peyton turned back to search out the old cowboy. He was in a stall, holding a pitchfork—Josh and his dog nowhere in sight. He paused raking the hay beneath his boots and shoved the wooden handle toward the corner of the stall. "Pull that hay net down for me."

Hanging from a nail, the dingy blue netting was tattered and twisted. Peyton walked over and gave it a tug. The thing held tight, so he took a second to work the knot from the nail. It wasn't too tall for Peyton to reach—or this old cowboy back in his prime. He might've stood as tall as Peyton if the years hadn't weighed on his shoulders. Peyton handed the net over and the man they called Vern shuffled toward the door. "Tried knocking it down with this fork, but some wise guy thought it was a good idea to tie a knot in the darn thing..."

He stepped out of the stall and his words went with him. Peyton stroked his jaw, covering his smile. Today would be a long and very interesting day, for su—

"You comin', greenhorn?" Vern yelled.

Oh, boy.

Peyton stood resolute with a pitchfork and no clue. In an enclosure that wasn't as clean as the first one, he watched Vern walk over and pull the empty net from the wall with no mercy.

"Ever mucked a stall before?"

Peyton leaned in and propped both hands on top of the handle. "I cleaned a bathroom one time when I was twelve."

Vern, with his harsh brows, sent him a look that would have banished Peyton from earth if it could have.

"Scoop all them yard apples up and dump 'em into this wheelbarrow." He lifted the arms and wheeled it closer to the door. "Then you'll push the clean hay to the back wall, come out here, get a fold of new hay, and cover the ground with it. Then you'll rake the old hay over it, again. Too hard for ya?"

Peyton's focus followed each direction Vern gestured to. "Just one question. What's a fold?"

The tanned veins in the old cowboy's temples bulged and his jaw ticked beneath his thin, white beard. Babysitting the rookie was probably the last thing Vern wanted to do today. "It's a slice of hay. A cut. A section. You'll see once you pick it up."

With that, the old man headed out, bootheels echoing down the corridor and fading into the distance. Peyton still wasn't clear on what a fold was, but if Vern trusted him enough to figure it out then how hard could it be?

He did as he was told and scooped up the yard apples. Peyton laughed under his breath as he turned and tossed them into the half-full wheelbarrow. Then he pushed the hay against the back wall, as instructed. Now, for the fun part. In the empty corridor, he walked over to the tractor that pulled a trailer with square bales of hay behind it. Orange pieces of twine lay on the ground. Like Vern had said, he picked up one end of the hay and it separated with ease, like sheets of paper falling away from the next.

"A fold of hay," he filed away for future reference.

He spread the hay on the concrete floor, shaking two folds in each hand until he had decent covera—

A mouse ran across the floor in front of his shoes. Peyton croaked and backed into the wall behind him with a thud. As quickly as it had appeared the tiny thing left, and Peyton checked to be sure none of his co-workers were standing watch outside the stall. If there was any reason to give him a hard time for the rest of the summer, it would be because of the noise he just made.

He took one step and a tug on his sleeve gave him pause. A rogue nail ripped right through the material at his bicep. He snatched it away and finished raking the hay back over the floor.

Where Vern had disappeared to was anyone's guess. So, Peyton picked up his tools and moved the wheelbarrow to the next stall. Scoop the yard apples, rake the hay, spread a fold. By the time he reached the fourth stall, he'd established a steady routine.

Vern appeared in the doorway, two bold wrinkles between his brows that surveyed Peyton's work.

"I was worried you got lost somewhere," Peyton said as he pulled the hay net off its hook. "Thought about coming to find you but I figured I'd be even more lost."

"One thing about working on a farm, boy, is that you'll find yerself doin' ten tasks while you're in the middle of one." Vern tilted his head to the stalls behind him. "You already finished these?"

"I didn't want to stand around wondering, so I figured I'd keep going." Peyton stopped in front of a new hay bale, and picked it up by its tight, orange strings. "Do I untie these knots or is there a loop I'm supposed to pull to set the folds free?"

Vern looked over his shoulder at him with a frown so deep it was no wonder he had so many wrinkles. "Use yer pocketknife."

"Uh..." Peyton froze, the hefty bale resting against his knees. "Pocket knife wasn't on the school supply list."

Vern unveiled a knife from his waistband and flipped the

blade out as he came closer. He sliced through the two cords between Peyton's hands, and they fell loose, hay spilling over his feet. Then Vern looked up at him with one furry eyebrow raised, the blade gesturing toward Peyton's chest. "What kind of grown man don't own a knife?"

Right now, staring the old cowboy in his cold, stormy gray eyes, he didn't feel very much like a grown man at all. And now was regretting the school comment.

Vern turned and walked away. "Get one. And get yerself some boots, too. Them sneakers won't last a week out here."

Peyton stepped out of the pile of hay and grabbed a few slices before he followed Vern inside the stall. "These are pretty sturdy. I wear 'em to the gym three times a week and they've held up so far."

"Tell me how they hold up when a horse steps on you or you get too close to a truck tire." Vern took the hay that Peyton held out and started spreading it around. "Steel-toed boots is the only thing that'll keep yer digits safe, boy. Unless you don't care how many you lose."

Point taken. Peyton held out the last bit of hay. "Anything else I need to buy to keep my personal anatomy safe while I'm here?"

Vern stalked up to him and snatched the last bit of hay, pausing to look straight into Peyton's soul. "Y'know, we probably wouldn't have to skip supper if we didn't tag team a one-man job."

Peyton leaned away, fighting the laugh that stuck to the back of his throat. Vern was quick on his feet, so to speak. Peyton prayed he'd be as sharp when he was Vern's age. "Got it."

In the breezeway, he picked up the pitchfork and started on the next stall. "How many of these do we have left?"

Vern grunted. "Gettin' bored already, kid?"

"Not a chance, sir," Peyton chuckled. "I was curious about how many of these I get to look forward to every day."

"Nine."

"Nine including these, or nine more—"

"Altogether," Vern chomped out.

"And then what?"

"Then we work on the rest of the farm." An unamused sigh came from the other side of the wall.

Peyton couldn't help but smile. Maybe he shouldn't be bugging the old cowboy so much. By the sound of it, Peyton would need him close if he wanted to stay safe for the time being. It was probably best if he found a way to get on his good side.

After the stalls were mucked, the feed inventoried, and the equipment checked—for which Peyton felt more like a kid holding a flashlight for his dad than a functioning member of the farm—Vern had him move sheet metal from a pile at the edge of the woods to the same trailer that had held hay that morning. Vern had moved the tractor to the pile, and Peyton had ridden on a small step, holding on for dear life as he'd watched the huge tires turn over and over again, bouncing across the terrain.

The sun-heated metal warmed straight through the gloves Vern had tossed him a few minutes ago. Another item he'd have to remember to buy. The rusty, gray metal had seen better days with its scrapes, scratches, and jagged holes that kept snagging his shirt as he carried it to the trailer and tossed it on top with a loud bang.

Vern sat perched on the tractor in the shaded part of the yard, hard eyes following Peyton's every move like a buzzard waiting for a carcass to decompose. A smirk curled the edge of his mouth. Why did he get the feeling that Vern was enjoying this chore?

"You'll want to be careful with those sheets, boy. One slice is enough to ruin yer day and we're a good twenty minutes from the nearest clinic."

Chest heaving from the motion of lifting and throwing more than a dozen times, Peyton took advantage of the moment to rest his muscles. "Duly noted."

Vern's smile grew a bit wider when he heard Peyton fighting for his life. Where was a bottle of water when a man needed it? Or a stream? Or an ice-cold shower?

If someone were to ask him to rate how in-shape he was, yesterday he would have said a ten. But four-plate deadlifts and thirty-minute battle ropes had nothing on this. He was a five, at best. Pushing his hat up with the back of his glove, he wiped the sweat from his forehead with his sleeve and gestured with his other hand toward the cabin sitting at the top of the hill. "You never get tired of this view, do you?"

Vern looked over his shoulder at it, staring for a long second. "When you worked yer whole life behind a desk, you don't."

Peyton tipped his chin. "What'd you do?"

Vern stayed stock-still, only his eyes moved from the cabin to Peyton. "I was an accountant."

So, the old cowboy used to be white-collar like himself. "How'd you get here?"

Peyton appreciated the break, but silence stretched on for so long that he thought Vern might not answer. In the distance, cows bellowed, grasshoppers chirped, and wind rattled the leaves on the trees.

"My dad always watched them ole western movies after he got home from work. And, uh, I always...dreamed of being a cowboy. And then Gianna married up with Daniel and he moved her out here. After they adopted Olivia, they asked me to come out here with 'em. The rest is history."

That girl had done more for this family than anything Peyton had ever known how to do for his own. "So, she's kinda like the glue that holds everyone together?"

He thought he saw a softness iron out the old cowboy's wrinkles, but he couldn't be sure from all the way over here.

"Daniel and Gianna needed her more than she'll ever know. This place wouldn't be nothin' without their family comin' together like it did."

Peyton swiped his sleeve across his forehead again, nodding as something akin to anticipation sparked in his chest. "You're telling me here's hope for guys like us?"

The harsh lines returned to Vern's mouth, and he grunted. "There's hope."

Good to know. Peyton had more questions, but he figured he'd burned enough time. He grabbed another piece of metal and sent it to the top of the pile. It ricocheted and teetered off the edge, sliding to the dirt—Peyton reached out to steady it and felt a prick against his forearm, just below his elbow. A guilty sheet of metal stuck out from under the pile at an angle, the corner devastatingly close to where Peyton had rushed to catch the other piece. The prick turned into a red-hot papercut and a drop of blood trickled down his skin.

He was sure to get sent to the principal's office after that.

Vern had warned him. Daring to look up, he found the old cowboy watching him with a line between his brows. "Yer lucky, kid. It ain't usually so merciful."

Biting his glove with his teeth, Peyton pulled it off and wadded his shirt against the spot, enjoying the breeze that snaked around his back and cooled the sweat collecting there.

"It's not gonna stop anytime soon," Vern said as he grabbed the steering wheel and climbed off the tractor. "You're too hot. Blood's pumpin' too hard."

Peyton must have skipped that day of biology class. Vern had probably learned the hard way.

Gloveless, Vern picked up a sheet of metal and tossed it on the trailer. Peyton lifted the fallen sheet, carefully this time, and fixed it on the pile. He slid his hand back into the glove, dabbing the wound against his jeans every few minutes.

He reached for one of the last scraps on the ground, laying against the dead, dry grass. Sunlight spilled across the browned area, and a black rope with a distinctive hiss had Peyton dropping the piece in his hand. "Whoa—that's a snake."

Vern made his way over and fearlessly lifted the piece, with Peyton standing a little further away in what he would call the safety zone. At least he could outrun a snake.

Maybe.

"Just a little Texas garter snake." Bent at the waist with his elbow resting on his knee, Vern studied the animal. "You see that orange stripe on his back and the yellow ones on his sides?"

Time to man up. Peyton left his safety zone and came closer, letting Vern be a human shield in case the snake took an issue with him. The thing had to be a foot and a half long. If that was considered little, then Peyton wasn't interested in waiting around for its parents.

Sure enough, it had the colorful markings Vern mentioned. "Yeah."

As if he could sense Peyton's tension, Vern turned to look at him. "You ain't never seen a snake before, boy?"

"Sure I have," Peyton said in a higher pitch than he'd meant to. He cleared his throat. "At my grandparent's place.

But we were told to run when we saw one." And ran they did—like little outlaws who'd robbed a bank.

It had been fun when he was seven, racing his brother across the field to see who could tell Pop about the discovery first. Now it felt like he was hovering over an anaconda that had a twenty-foot striking distance.

Vern shook his head and hefted the metal away from the snake, taking it to the trailer. "We don't mind garter snakes. They help keep pests out of the garden."

Peyton kept his full attention on the danger noodle as he reached for another sheet.

"A cottonmouth, now that's a different story," Vern said between blasts of colliding metal. "If you see one of those close to the livin' quarters, relocate it to Heaven. I won't have it messin' with my family."

Peyton made another mental note to buy a book on snake breeds and evacuation strategies.

With the last piece of metal on the trailer, Vern nodded to the tractor. "Let's head back to the barn and get something cold to drink."

With a sigh of relief and one last stare-off with the snake, Peyton stripped off his gloves and took his place on the step of the tractor again. As he kept his grip on the rusty paint job with one hand, he bent his other arm to check the wound. Proof that Vern was right, it still bled. He wiped it across his jeans again as a trio of horses sprinted across the field closest to them.

Two were pale yellow and one was solid black except for a white star on its head. "I have to warn you. I've never ridden a horse before."

"You won't be on a horse. You're stuck with me for the time bein', and I don't ride no horse."

That was good news. He wasn't looking forward to taming a bronco. At least not yet. Maybe when he got finished feeling like a rookie. "What about construction? You do any of that? I've spent a little time swinging a hammer and putting up walls in my day. I've worked on a few—"

"You know you talk about as much as my grandson? What's it gonna take to get you to stop yappin'?"

"I just wanted to get the inside scoop on becoming a

cowboy." Peyton bit back a grin.

Vern grunted, glancing in his direction. The tractor hit a bump and Peyton held on a little tighter. Vern wouldn't be happy until he was under one of those tires, Peyton was sure.

By the time they took a break for water, dried the sweat out of their clothes, and caught their breath, Vern had managed to prep mineral and salt blocks for the cattle, fix a leaking faucet on the outside of the barn, and replace a gate that had fallen from its hinges. All of which he'd talked Peyton through in great detail.

By the time Vern was finished with him, Peyton would know how to start a farm from scratch.

CHAPTER FIVE

Daniel gripped the leather reins of his black Friesian, Dagger, and steered the horse west. Five o'clock sun hung low in the distance, hovering above the trees in the direction that Vern had Peyton replacing a section of barbed wire. In a matter of seconds Dagger crossed the few hundred yards, slowing to a trot as they came closer to the men.

While Vern worked a clamp onto a T-post, Peyton drank from a bottle of water, his focus on the setting sun.

"It's startin' to look like a real farm," Daniel quipped as he swung down from his saddle and let Dagger wander.

Peyton turned his way, sweat dripping from the ends of his hair at the back of his hat. "Do y'all ever get any clouds out here?"

"Only on the days we work inside," he said, noticing the small cuts on Peyton's arms—most likely where he'd learned that barbed wire wasn't made of foam. Daniel walked over to the side-by-side and propped one bootheel against the bumper, bracing both arms against his knee. "I noticed the chicken coop finally got a new roof. Looks good."

Peyton dropped his water bottle in the grass near their tools and produced a handful of clips for Vern at the next post. "I can't take too much credit. Vern helped me out quite a bit."

"What credit, boy?" Vern snapped back. "We both know you handed me supplies the whole time. All that talk about being good with a hammer and you didn't even know how to offset a shingle."

Though Vern couldn't see it from where he stood, Daniel saw Peyton's grin, as if he knew he was getting under Vern's skin. The kid was brave. The other farmhands rarely dared to make eye contact with Vern for fear he'd put them to work on one of the many menial tasks around the farm. Ribbing him was downright unthinkable.

Peyton tipped his chin. "Vern said I'd make a real fine cowboy in no time."

"I said no such thing, tenderfoot, and don't go puttin' words in my mouth. I've got an old wellhouse on the north pasture that needs to be taken down if that's what you want to do tomorrow."

"We can't do that on a rainy day?"

"Ain't rained here in two months," Vern mumbled.

"That's my point."

Vern snapped a look over his shoulder at the kid and Peyton looked off into the distance as if lasers might shoot from Vern's eyes.

Daniel shook his head at the two of them. "When you're done here, Peyton, come see me in the barn."

"We're about ten minutes out, son." Vern nodded toward the last post that waited for wire.

Daniel returned to Dagger, gathering his reigns, and stepping into the stirrup as the sun ducked a little lower. In the barn, he let Stu, who was one of a few men to stay after the end of the workday, take Dagger to his stall to be unsaddled.

True to his word, Vern drove the side-by-side into the barn a few minutes later. The kid took the grab bar with great care and pulled himself to his feet. With a sleeve that had a tear in it and jeans that sported dried blood, he had the walk of a man well-acquainted with exhaustion.

"Tired?"

"Not even a little." His eyes followed Vern as he drove out of the other end of the barn, then he leaned one shoulder against the wall. "I wouldn't share this with Vern, but I think I discovered new muscle groups today that science doesn't know about."

Daniel chuckled. "Long day?"

With one eyebrow raised, the kid looked off into the distance. "I'm still trying to figure out how a fifty-pound bale of hay is heavier than a four-hundred-pound deadlift."

"Farm work will mess with everything you ever thought you believed about life."

"That's what I'm looking for," Peyton said.

Before Daniel could ask what he meant, Stu stepped out of Dagger's stall, dusting off his hands. "All done, boss. I'll head over to replace the gate on the pig pen."

Peyton shook his head. "Already done."

Stu raised one eyebrow, a wrinkle in between. "Then I'll..." He hesitated. "Check the water pumps in the pasture."

"No need."

Daniel smirked, scuffing his boot through a bit of fallen hay on the ground. He'd figured Vern would throw every task he had at Peyton. What he hadn't anticipated was Peyton rising to the occasion. "We'll call it a day, Stu. Tomorrow we'll start shearing trees, so next week is gonna be a long one. Go ahead and take off."

Stu touched the brim of his hat and turned to leave, but not before he spared a hardened glance at Peyton.

Once Stu curved out of sight of the barn door, Daniel tipped his head. "Stu and Olivia went to school together. She says he was an angry kid, but he's been with me for three years and I've seen nothing but hard work out of him." Until now. Though he didn't voice it. "If he gives you any trouble let me know and I'll talk to him."

Frowning, Peyton shook his head one quick time, as if that wasn't even a consideration.

Daniel respected him for it. "Most days I let the men get home in time to have supper with their families, but some weeks keep us working until well after sundown. Since you'll be staying here with us, you'll see that the work doesn't truly end for farmers. Vern, Gianna, and I still have plenty to do. So, you know, I won't be asking for you to pitch in after the others go home. You'll work the same hours they do, and the rest of the time is yours to spend as you please."

"I appreciate that, sir. But if there's anything I can do to help out, count me in. Giving me a place to work and sleep is more than I could ask. This opportunity means more to me than you know."

Daniel appreciated the kid's spirit, but he wouldn't be taking him up on his offer. He deserved to see the parts of the farm that didn't include sweat and sacrifice.

A high-pitched bark echoed down the breezeway at his back. Daniel looked over his shoulder as Josh and his dog came running up, sweaty hair plastered against his forehead. Propping both elbows against the stall door behind him, Daniel waited for what his son had to say.

"Mom said you were staying the summer. That true?"

"That's right," Peyton said.

"Cool. That means we can go fishin', and huntin', and we can hike in the woods and find arrowheads and bugs, and hey, do ya wanna come see my treehouse?"

Daniel cleared his throat. "Josh, I'm sure Peyton would prefer to get cleaned up and rest a bit first."

His disappointment was obvious, but short-lived. "But you promise you'll come after?"

Peyton smiled. "I promise."

Content with that answer, Josh turned around and ran back through the barn with his dog in quick pursuit.

Peyton pulled himself away from the wall and downed the rest of his water. With the posture of a man about to head out, Daniel tipped his chin. "Supper's at seven."

He twisted the cap onto the bottle and kicked at the concrete under his feet. "I appreciate that, sir. But I can't impose on y'all twice. I know you asked me to stay on, but I don't want to take advantage of your kindness while I'm here."

"That's noble," Daniel nodded thoughtfully. "But needing to eat isn't taking advantage of anything."

Peyton huffed a laugh as he swatted at a mosquito.

"If it helps, some of the other farmhands stay for supper every once in a while."

He heaved in a deep breath and sighed.

"Gianna is making enchiladas with chili con carne."

"That actually does help."

Daniel chuckled. "Good deal."

Peyton turned to leave, sweeping his hat off as he did.

"Before you go," Daniel called out, reaching for his wallet. He pulled an Ace Wooledge baseball card out and held it between two fingers. "This yours?"

His hand went absently to his back pocket as he retraced his steps. "It is. Where'd you find it?"

"Gianna found it on the nightstand in the room you stayed in last night." Daniel handed it over. "Good thing you decided to stay."

He studied it like Daniel had just handed him a ten-thousand-dollar check. "Sentimental?"

Peyton lifted it with halfhearted effort. "Something like that."

It was a five-minute walk from the homestead to the cabin, Peyton realized when he caught glimpses of the home through the trees up ahead. He had no regrets about leaving his truck parked and making the hike—until he realized he'd be walking back in the dark. Another lesson he'd have to learn the hard way today.

The path was clear, the air rich, and the wildlife abundant. Mulch crunched under his shoes, wind tossed low branches around as he passed them, and the deep hoot of an owl echoed somewhere through the woods. The yard came into view, and the rolling hills behind it. Sunlight hugged the tops of Christmas trees and dusted everything in a rusty orange haze.

As he crossed the freshly-mowed lawn on the way to the cabin, he caught sight of Josh's treehouse in the backyard, peeking out of the giant oak where a tire swing hung from a branch. The grass was a little higher around the oak, brushing the shins of a fresh pair of jeans he'd thrown on with a clean T-shirt.

Peyton hadn't been sure about the family's dinner attire—he hadn't paid attention last night. Truth was, it hadn't mattered because he'd never expected to see these people again. But a lot had changed in the last twenty-four hours.

A lot.

He paused on the outskirts of the enormous tree's shade, staring up at the most magnificent treehouse Peyton had ever laid eyes on. A balcony stretched across the front, branching off into a full-blown porch on the right side. The middle portion was the thick of the house with a door, canopy, and two windows. To the left was a small room that stood a half story above the rest, which meant there must be stairs inside there somewhere. The whole thing was covered in aged wood the color of burnt charcoal and promised every adventure a boy could hope for. Peyton's inner child roared with triumph.

"Anyone home?"

Josh's little dog let out a howl from the other side of the tree, popping his head out of the tall grass. Satisfied that Peyton was no threat, the howling stopped. But it didn't dissuade the little mix-breed from coming to sniff on his shoes.

"Peyton!" Josh stuck his head through one of the windows that opened to the outside. "Come on up!"

Though the ladder looked solid, he wasn't sure any of it was made with a grown man in mind. "I don't think that thing's gonna hold me, Josh."

"It will! Olivia comes up here all the time."

Peyton couldn't help but smile. "But Olivia is smaller than I am."

"Sure, but it never creaks or nothin'. Dad built it!"

Peyton didn't know Daniel too well yet, but if there was anything he'd learned today, it was that the man didn't do things halfway. If he was gonna build his kids a treehouse, it would probably put Peyton's childhood pallet treehouse to shame.

"Here goes nothing." He grabbed onto the wood and climbed up. About three steps in, he discovered a twinge in his shoulder blades that felt suspiciously like soreness. He would have thought his time spent in the gym would grant him a free pass from the ache of new work, but untrained muscles were introducing themselves already.

At the top, he stood and dusted his hands against his jeans. The place was a little bigger than it looked from the ground. The door swung open and out stepped Josh, wearing a pair of night vision goggles and holding a gun loaded with foam bullets. "In here."

Peyton had to duck to fit through the door, but the roof inside was cathedral-style, leaving enough space for him to stand comfortably. The walls were loaded with old toys, rusted signs, crooked sticks, arrowheads, and sheets of paper with drawings on them. There was a bench tucked beneath the back window beside a shelf with books and toy planes. The entire solar system hung from small slips of string attached to the highest peak of the roof. There was a table to the right, cluttered with polished rocks, toy soldiers, tin boxes, and comic books.

If he didn't know any better, he would have thought he'd stepped through a portal into his childhood bedroom.

"Look at this place," he said as he eased himself down to the floor, legs bent, and his forearms balanced on his knees. "Just out of curiosity, how do your parents feel about video games, Josh?"

The kid slipped his goggles off and tossed them on the table beside the gun. "They say video games make your brain rot and leak out your ears."

"I had a feeling they might think that way."

Josh shrugged. "But I still play them sometimes. Olivia lets me use her computer to play *Mutant Firestorm Conquest.*"

Peyton huffed a laugh.

"You wanna see my bug collection?" Josh asked, dropping to his knees in front of the bookshelf.

"Josh, buddy, you have to *lead* with the bug collection."

A grin split his face, and he pulled a tin box from the bottom shelf. As he made his way over, Peyton noticed the three stairs that led to the other room. It was smaller, but still big enough to hold plenty. The roof was flat over that portion, and it held a circular skylight. Boy, this place was a palace compared to the one he and Austin had built when they were kids. Well...when *he* was a kid. Austin was ten years older, but still as fun to hang out with as any kid his own age.

Until he was eight and his brother left.

"This is my favorite." Josh held up a huge dragon fly with iridescent blue wings. "I caught him when I was six!"

While Peyton had imagined insects pinned to a cork board, Josh's collection consisted of a bunch of dried bugs resting on piles of napkins in the bottom of the tin. He bit back a smile and carefully took the bug that Josh handed him.

"And look at this guy!" He held up a giant grasshopper that filled his entire hand.

"Whoa, where'd you get him?"

"Down by the pond. Olivia helped me catch that one."

Somehow the vision of the girl he'd met last night diving

into the weeds to catch a giant grasshopper didn't fit with his perception of her. "Does your sister catch bugs with you a lot?"

His eyebrows arched high as he nodded. "Yup! Sometimes we catch other things, too. Like minnows and lizards and snakes."

"With a net?"

"Sometimes. And our hands."

He did a lot of crazy stuff with his brother when they were young, but picking up snakes wasn't a hobby they'd practiced.

He handed the bugs back to Josh. The kid placed them gently inside the box and snapped the lid shut. "Wanna see my baseball cards?"

"Would I ever?"

Josh rushed over to the bench under the window and pulled a milk crate from beneath it. As he shuffled through it and unveiled yet another tin box, Peyton fished out his wallet and produced his own card.

Josh dumped a pile of cards out on the wooden floor between them. They were as worn as Peyton's—corners folded, edges tattered, ink faded from years of handling. "These are my favorites."

Peyton took the stack Josh passed him. There was a Babe Ruth card among a couple of players he didn't recognize. One card had a crease down the middle where it had been folded—probably from a show-and-tell excursion.

"Here's my favorite card." Peyton passed him his Ace Wooledge card and the kid's eyes lit up.

"You collect cards, too?"

Peyton shifted through the stack Josh called his favorite. "Not really. I just like that one."

"Where'd you get it?"

Peyton's smile faded. He hadn't thought about that day in a while. The details were hazy, the memories like a radio with static. "A gas station, I think. It came out of one of those packs wrapped in foil."

"Awesome!" Josh returned the card and Peyton did the same with his stack.

"Wanna see something cool?" Peyton held the card up for the kid to see. Then, with an easy move, he made it vanish.

Josh's eyes widened. "Hey! How'd you do that?"

He made the card reappear. "Something my dad taught me when I was a boy."

"Will you teach me?"

Peyton had all summer. "Sure. Why not?"

Josh picked up the milk crate and took it to the shelf where he'd gotten it. Before Peyton tucked his card into his wallet, he held it for a moment, flipping it in his hand. Front, back, front, back, front—

"You ever talked to a girl before?"

The card nearly slipped from his fingers. "What's that?"

Josh kept his back to him, his hands fidgeting with the edge of the shelf. As if he gained an ounce of invisible courage, he nodded once and turned around, dropping to his knees across from Peyton. "You ever talked to a girl before? One that you took a likin' to?"

Peyton tucked the card in his wallet, leaned to the side, and stuck it in his pocket, all while searching for the right words. "Sure, I have."

"What'd you say to her?"

"You mean, how'd I ask her out?"

Josh's focus dropped down to the floor, brows wrinkled as if he were strongly considering the question. "No. I mean, how did you tell her you liked her?"

Peyton pulled in a deep breath and let it out slow. "I think I probably said, 'I like your hair. Will you play hide-n-seek with me?'"

"You still play hide-n-seek, even as an adult?"

Peyton couldn't help but chuckle. "No, actually I haven't played since the second grade. I assume you're asking for a more adult response, then?"

Josh nodded.

"First you have to—" Peyton squinted up at the kid. "Josh, have you asked your dad or Vern this question yet?"

"Not yet. That's only because I just started likin' her today."

Peyton rubbed the day-old stubble around his mouth to smother a smile.

"Remi and her gramma stopped by to see Mom earlier and while we were playin' out in the backyard, I kinda started likin' havin' her around."

"Girls do tend to have that effect on us." He cleared his voice. "Alright, here's what you do—the next time you see Remi tell her, 'I really liked playing with you in my backyard the other day, and if you're okay with it, I'd like you to be my best friend.'"

"Best friend?" Josh's nose wrinkled.

"Absolutely. Best friends are the perfect thing to be with a girl you like. Because it means you get to see a side of her that the other boys don't get to see."

"Really?" Josh leaned forward with intrigue. "Like what?"

"Like when she trusts you enough to be herself around you, and not, like, the fancied-up version of herself." Surely that wasn't too hard for a boy to understand.

His eyes widened and he nodded slowly. "Like she'll wear her regular clothes instead of her church clothes when we play together!"

"Okay." Peyton could work with that. "And she'll be able to rely on you to always be there for her because she doesn't have to worry about you finding a new best friend."

"Yeah! I could do that." As if Peyton had fully answered his question, he pushed off his knees. "Hey, you wanna go up to the house and steal a few cookies when Mom's not looking?"

"I'll leave the cookie-snatching up to you, but I could go for a water."

Josh nodded and went for the door. Peyton pushed himself off the ground—mindful of the soreness in his legs—and hustled to keep up with the kid who was halfway down the ladder. Together they set off across the field for the cabin, the little dog leading the way.

In all of his seven years on the planet, Peyton had never had a better day. His parents had taken him and Austin to play mini golf and ride go-karts, and they'd even went to eat pizza and play arcade games at the GameOver Grill. Even the few rain drops that fell against the backseat window of his parent's car and the sun disappearing behind dark clouds couldn't dull his happiness.

"I understand, Mrs. McKinney," Mom said on the phone as Dad came out of the gas station with a plastic bag full of goodies and Peyton wiggled in his seat. "Thank you for calling me. We'll talk to him. Yes, ma'am, I understand. This can't keep happening. Thank you for calling. Bye."

"I hope Dad got my baseball cards," he told Austin who was shaking his leg and fidgeting with his hands in his lap. "Wouldn't it be so cool if we found an Ace Wooledge card today. That would be so cool!" He couldn't contain his joy even as his brother made a growling noise that kinda sounded a little excited.

They'd been looking for that card for years—Austin had said it would be neat to find one because he'd never seen one in person before. It had to be the rarest card out there if even Austin hadn't seen one. And today would be the coolest day ever if he could play mini golf and ride go-karts and eat pizza at the arcade and find his brother's favorite baseball card.

The front door opened, and Dad got in the car, handing the bag to Mom. Peyton pulled the seatbelt away from his chest, leaning forward as much as he could. He hoped Dad hadn't forgotten about him.

Mom dug through the bag with a sigh. "We got another call from Principal McKinney."

Peyton grabbed the bag of chips Mom held out to him as Dad turned and looked at Austin who was looking outside his window.

"What'd she say?" Dad asked.

Peyton kept his arm outstretched, waiting to see the shiny pack of cards Dad always got him when he went in the store.

Mom's hands rested on the bag. "Austin was suspended for fighting again."

"Mom," Peyton called out.

Mom shook her head and reached into the bag again, this time pulling out a drink that she handed to Austin. He took it and set it in the cupholder.

Dad pulled on his seatbelt and drove the car back onto the road that went to their house. "When's this fighting gonna stop, Austin?"

"I had a good reason for it," his brother said.

Dad laughed—but not in the fun kind of way. It was the way he laughed when he didn't find things funny at all. "A good reason for getting suspended? That's real smart, son. How good will your reason be for getting expelled altogether? Huh? You think you're gonna be able to hold down a job if you don't have a degree?"

"Jake," Mom said.

The tips of his tennis shoes pressed against the floor, Peyton leaned as close as his seatbelt would let him. He needed those cards.

"You said you were gonna talk to him last time, Jenny. And here we are again. How many talks do you have left in you before we have a son that's living on the streets and joining gangs—"

"Jake!"

Peyton huffed a breath as he reached out again. Maybe if Mom would let him have the bag...

"We'll just have to keep praying and working together."

"Working together?" Dad snorted. "We haven't worked together in years."

Mom reached inside the bag. "Whose fault is that?"

"Here we go again," Dad said. "I'm the bad guy in all of this and you're the innocent bystander?"

Mom pulled her hand out of the bag, holding the packet of cards. "You're not the bad guy, Jake. But you always rush to punish Austin and that's clearly not working."

"Mom," Peyton said as he reached out.

She looked at the pack in her hand and handed them over. "Sorry, honey."

He sighed, happy to finally rip into them. With the stack clamped tightly between his fingers and his palm, he went through each card, looking for only one as thunder rumbled above the car.

"I haven't seen you successful with him either, Jenny."

He accidentally dropped a couple, and they slid to the floor.

"I don't hear you coming up with ideas that are helpful, Jake."

Peyton swiped through the deck, one after another, after another, after—

There it was. He held his breath. Samuel "Ace"

Wooledge. Pitcher for the Chicago Comets.

"Austin," he whispered, unable to talk over his excitement. His brother was slouched down with his head pressed back against the gray seat. "Austin!"

Austin didn't look his way. So, he shoved the card in front of his face. "Look, it's Ace Wooledge!"

"That's neat, kid." He reached out and messed up Peyton's hair. "Gotta hang on to that one."

As Dad turned onto the road of their trailer park, Peyton held the card to his chest and hopped up and down in his seat. The other cards fell, but he didn't care. He found a real Ace Wooledge card! This was the best day of his life.

The car came to a stop and Mom and Dad both got out, slamming their doors extra harder than normal. But Peyton didn't care. He had found his brother's favorite baseball card, the one they'd been looking for forever. He'd never forget this moment, no matter what.

"Let's go, Peyt," Austin said as he leaned over and unbuttoned Peyton's seatbelt. He pushed the card into his pocket, so the rain didn't get on it. Then he jumped out of the car and ran as fast as he could to get inside the trailer.

Nothing could ruin this day—not even Mom and Dad going to their own bedrooms

CHAPTER SIX

Orange rays of evening sunshine beamed around each side of her parents' cabin as Olivia hopped out of her truck and made her way to the porch. Golden hour was her favorite part of a long day. It meant she was moments away from sitting in the breeze on the patio with a glass of sweet tea and her family.

She gave Birdie and Boone a quick head scratch before she went in, as per the routine they'd created since the dogs had become part of the farm. Birdie sat back on her hind legs and stacked two perfectly manicured paws on Olivia's arm. Both dogs panted, making their mouths look like smiles. "Chase any bad guys today?"

In the foyer, she kicked off her tennis shoes and pulled her hair up in a messy bun on top of her head as the smell of chili con carne greeted her. She followed the scent into the kitchen. "Something smells yummy."

Josh stood near the patio doors with a root beer in one hand and a stack of cookies in the other. Mom shuffled through the open fridge.

"I'm starving. I worked through lunch today. We had a bus full of kids from the summer camp stop by. And then I had to make another batch of snickerdoodles for the nursing home, and I accidentally dropped a pan of—" Olivia gasped when the fridge fell shut.

It wasn't Mom—it was the stranger from last night standing in front of her ice box, cracking open a bottle of water as he watched her with a smirk. He wore jeans and a gray T-shirt that gave him a comfortable demeanor. He seemed...at home.

"What are *you* doing here?" She hadn't meant to throw

the words at him.

He shrugged. "Your parents are thinking about adopting one more."

"Wow!" Josh yelled as he jumped and threw a fist through the air, cookie crumbs falling to the floor. "Wouldn't that be awesome? I've always wanted a brother!"

She heard the words, but she couldn't comprehend them for the panic weaving its way through her thoughts. "You're—you're not supposed to be here. You left this morning."

"And then I came back."

Like a python wrapping around her body, dread squeezed the air from her lungs. "But my...Caroline thinks..." Well, she couldn't publicly repeat what she'd told Caroline. She'd only been teasing her best friend about a man she knew Caroline would have found charming. A man who was never supposed to be seen again. "And you're still here."

"In the flesh." He grinned. "And I don't know what a Caroline is."

"It's her best friend," Josh drawled with a sarcastic voice as he came to stand beside Peyton. "She's annoying."

Olivia scrunched her nose. "She's not annoying. She's just...very outspoken."

Which could spell disaster for her ego come suppertime.

"And Dad says she's *boy crazy*." Josh made a gagging noise.

He wasn't wrong about that part.

"Then it's a good thing you're the only boy here, right?" Peyton reached out and ruffled Josh's hair.

Josh pushed his arm away. "Ew! No! Caroline is an old lady, and she smells like pineapples."

Peyton raised an eyebrow in Olivia's direction.

"She's..." She shook her head softly and lifted her shoulders. "Our age." She was guessing. Peyton didn't look like he could be much older than her. "And Josh doesn't like her fruity perfume."

"*Blech*," Josh groaned.

Peyton chuckled. "When will I get to meet her?"

Why did that question sound like he was staying for more than one day? Olivia swallowed. "She's coming over for supper."

"I bet that'll be fun," he said before he took another drink of water.

Fun. That was the last word on her mind. She'd pumped Caroline's head with ideas about this overly dreamy heartthrob of a man that had appeared like a mysterious wind out of nowhere. Now she was on her way over and Olivia had to produce said mystery man. Though with the way he kept that smirk in place and watched her as if he were interested in her every sentence really put the word "dreamy" into perspective.

Olivia shook her head. This was no time for silly observations. She had to intercept Caroline before she met this man and blabbed about what Olivia said this morning. Because Caroline was sure to blab. She was a blabber.

She lifted her chin toward Josh. "Where's Mom?"

Josh shrugged. "Somewhere on the farm."

"Thanks." She turned to go in search of her.

"Olivia..." Josh wore a lopsided grin. "I was just about to tell Peyton the story of the time we went to that church in Dallas and you—"

Olivia rushed toward Josh—fully prepared to slug him if need be—right before he got to the part where she'd spilled orange juice on her dress, which Josh swears to this day was pee. He jumped and skittered out the back door with a yelp before she could catch him. She stopped short of where he'd been standing. And found herself suddenly very close to their guest.

She cleared her throat and looked away, noticing the cookie Josh had left on the island to her right. "Be grateful you don't have a little brother who looks for new ways to ruin your life every day."

"I *was* the little brother who looked for ways to ruin lives every day."

Olivia couldn't help but smile. "Then the two of you will get along very well."

There was a moment of awkward silence. She kept her head turned enough so that he didn't have a front row seat to her birthmark.

He leaned forward a fraction, squinting. "You smell like cinnamon."

She snorted. "I smell like work."

"You work at a cinnamon factory?"

A laugh bubbled out of her before she could stop it. "I work at a bakery."

"That's right. You said that last night, didn't you?" He sobered a smidgen, and his eyes lazed with interest. "You know that happens to be my dream job, too."

She was very skeptical. "Oh?"

"Get paid to eat sweets all day?" He clicked his tongue against his back teeth. "Absolutely."

"I don't—" She groaned. "Okay, I do eat sweets..." If her hips were any indication. "But not all day. I do make a living occasionally."

"You'll have to tell me where you work so I can stop by sometime."

"Are you like..." She raised an eyebrow and whirled one finger around in the air. "Living in Heavenly now?"

"Something like that." He took a slow step toward the island and leaned a hip against the edge so that he was standing precisely in front of her. Only a couple feet of empty space divided them with nothing left to block his view of her birthmark. "Your dad asked me to stay on for the summer and gave me the keys to the old homestead."

"Oh." That sounded like Dad—never hesitant to lend a helping hand to somebody. Even if that somebody was basically a stranger standing in her parent's kitchen. "Why?"

Though his amused smirk never left, a faraway look flashed through his eyes for a split second. "I needed a job, and he needed someone to boss Vern around."

"Ahh." She crossed her arms over her midsection. "You spent the day with Pepaw. And you haven't put in your two weeks notice, yet?"

"Let's just say I haven't cried since I was a kid, but today I came pretty close to it."

She couldn't help the laugh that drew her head back and pulled out a string of giggles. Now that she looked at him, his skin did have a redness that spoke of a day spent in the sun. She also noticed the masculine curve of the bridge of his nose, a white scar a few centimeters long on his chin, and that his dark brows nearly met in the middle. Now that she was standing this close.

She cleared her throat, glancing across the kitchen and

spotting the lid that Josh had left off the cookie jar.

"Are you gonna tell me what your second dream job is?"

Hadn't she already told him? "Baking."

"I thought you said that was your first dream job?"

"I said it was *one* of my dream jobs." And the others were too personal to mention. Now she regretted saying anything about it at all. "I, uh, have several, and none of them are worth having this conversation right now. So, if you'll excuse me..." She gave a slight curtsey and turned to leave.

"What if I told you about my dream job?" he said.

She hesitated and then turned to face him again. "I'm sorry. Do we have some kind of a deal that says if you tell me yours then I have to tell you mine?"

"Make me a deal." The edge of his mouth twitched like he was holding back a grin. And his deep-sea blue eyes held a mischievous glimmer—like Josh's did whenever he was about to do something that would get him in trouble.

"You have a lot of audacity, don't you?"

His grin widened and she noticed the tiniest dimples—if they could even be called that—above each side of his mouth. And the smile lines reaching his eyes that made her second guess what she'd assumed about his age. "Give me your top five and I'll give you my top five."

She started to scoff. But truth was, number five wasn't too terrible to share. In fact, she'd bet he'd make it one of his dream jobs, too. Playing along with his little game, she lifted her chin and met his challenge...childish as it was. "Fine. I'd love to be an ice cream taste tester."

One eyebrow raised, he frowned thoughtfully. "Really? You mean one of those people who wear white coats and eat ice cream on little wooden spoons straight from the assembly line?"

"Basically, yes." When he didn't respond, she continued. "I love ice cream and getting to taste different kinds all day would be a dream come true for me." She nodded once. There, she'd said it. That wasn't so bad. "Now, what's yours?"

He started walking backwards, snatching the cookie from the countertop as he did. "I'll tell you tonight at dinner." He tucked the cookie between his teeth and turned, leaving the same way Josh did.

Mouth hanging open, she watched the man walk across the patio and into the yard. How dare he not hold up his end of the deal. She would put him in a corner come suppertime. His dream job better not be too embarrassing to mention in front of all the people she knew and loved.

"Hey, sweetie," Mom said as she stepped into the kitchen and went for the oven. "How was your day?"

"Why is he still here?"

Mom shot a glance over her shoulder as she snatched two potholders from where they lay on the counter. "Who? Peyton?"

Olivia looked left, then right. "Who else?"

Mom pulled a dish full of enchiladas out. The glass clinked against the island as she set it down. "Your dad wanted him to work here for the summer."

"So, it seems," Olivia said as she made her way to the cookie jar. "He thinks you're gonna adopt him, too."

"Well, I was unaware that there were any plans in the works, but you know your dad."

Olivia groaned under her breath as she pulled a cookie from the jar and replaced the lid.

"Has he done something wrong?" The genuine concern in Mom's eyes made Olivia change her tone.

"No, not at all. He seems like a good guy." She tucked the edge of the cookie in her mouth and broke off a piece—shortbread with strawberry jam melted on her tongue. "A little *too* good. I, uh, may have lied to Caroline about him today."

A wrinkle appeared between Mom's thinly manicured brows. "How so?"

She released a chest-deep sigh. This was humiliating to admit. "I may have told her that he was tall, tan, and gorgeous."

Cheese dangled from Mom's fingers over the enchiladas as she froze, giving Olivia a sideways glance. "Ooh, so you think he's gorgeous."

"No! Not me. I only told Caroline that because I knew she would go crazy over him. It was supposed to be a joke because I never thought she'd meet him." And now that she would, she had a lot of explaining to do. Specifically, about running away with the man.

Olivia pressed the inside of her wrist against her forehead.

Mom hummed long and slow, nodding as she turned and tucked the dish back in the oven. "Well, I don't see where you lied. I'm five-foot-three, so I would consider him tall. And he does seem to be quite tan. And since you think he's gorgeous—"

"Mom!" Olivia set the cookie on the countertop, appetite gone. "I don't think that. And even if I did, I can't have Caroline telling him I think that."

"Ahh," Mom nodded, slipping her oven mitts off and tossing them on the counter. She braced one hand against the edge of the counter and the other against her waist. "So, you just need to find a way to stop Caroline from talking too much?"

It was impossible now that she heard it aloud. "Yes."

The front door suddenly fell shut. "I'm here! Where is everyone?" Caroline said, sweeping into the kitchen with her purse dangling from the crook of her arm. "Smells good in here. I could use a latte. Do we have any more of that marshmallow creamer?" She stopped at the coffee maker and wiggled her eyebrows at Olivia as she reached for the portafilter. "Does Momma Gia know about your little tryst from last night?"

Mom grinned at Olivia. "Good luck with that."

Golden rays of sun fell through the barn window, shimmering on specks of evening dust as Daniel lifted a nail gun and placed it firmly to a couple slats of wood. Satisfied with the *thud-thud* of two nails securing the corner of only one of four planter boxes that Gianna requested, he straightened to work the kink out of his lower back. In the quiet of his pause, quick footfalls echoed up the staircase toward him.

Peyton stepped through the shadows, into the amber daylight.

"First day and you've already found your way to the workshop." Daniel picked up a couple more slats of wood and pieced together another corner.

The boy wandered over to the wide windows that overlooked the farm from the top of the barn. "Vern brought me up here earlier for some tools," he uttered, his undivided attention on the same sunset Daniel saw on a daily basis.

A sunset that he'd perhaps taken for granted with the way Peyton stared at it as if it held all of the answers to life's greatest mysteries.

When Daniel had the next planter corner ready to be secured, he picked up the nail gun again. "Brace yourself."

Peyton turned, his focus roving over the project and understanding dawning in the slight lift of his brows. Daniel unleashed another onslaught of nails.

"Is there something you need me to do?" Peyton tipped his head toward the table as he approached. "Something a greenhorn can handle?"

Daniel smiled, pointing with a piece of wood toward an old barstool. "Pull up a seat. We'll talk until supper's ready."

Peyton sauntered over and leaned against the edge of it. "Is this your dream?"

Daniel peeked up at him, unprepared for the question. "Building planter boxes?"

"Farming," he chuckled.

"Absolutely. Next to my family, I couldn't imagine loving anything else more." He gathered the wood for the next corner. "I grew up in the soil, lived off the land for as long as I can remember. If God asked me what else I wanted out of life, I'd draw a blank."

Peyton acknowledged him with a nod, his focus skimming over their surroundings.

Daniel pressed the nail gun against the wood and launched another barrage of nails. "Why do you ask?"

He lifted one shoulder. "Your daughter just asked me what my dream job is, so I have until supper to come up with something."

"Olivia's home?" Daniel looked up before he nailed the two halves together. Peyton nodded, and Daniel pulled the trigger, finishing the third corner.

Straightening his back again, he tipped his chin toward the kid. "What're you gonna tell her?"

His chest moved where he took in a deep breath and let it out slowly. "That I'm still looking for ideas."

Daniel thought he was joking, but there was something in his voice that hinted at emptiness. "Why's that?"

He looked up with bewildered eyes, as if he wasn't expecting Daniel to prod. Emotion flickered in the wrinkle of his brows and then faded. "I've got to figure out who's answering her question first."

"Is that what New Mexico is about? Finding yourself?"

Peyton looked down at his fidgeting hands. "Four years ago, my life was all about baseball, meeting girls, and going out with my friends. Then my brother had a baby. I blinked and everything changed."

Daniel braced his palms against the worktable and rested. The project could wait. "How so?"

Shoulders slumped forward, he dropped his head and raked one hand through his hair. "I was just a kid, having fun. And then I found myself stuck working behind the same desk every day, living in the same house every day, and doing the same thing every weekend. Don't get me wrong..." He waved one hand before he crossed his arms, gripping his bicep. "I love being an uncle, and my job was more than what a lot of graduates get right out of college, and I live where I can still see my parents on a regular basis. I've got a life that a lot of people would give anything for."

"What do *you* want, Peyton?"

He skimmed their surroundings again, like the answer might be hidden among the half-started and nearly finished projects. "I want to look for buried treasure on a deserted island."

Daniel couldn't help but chuckle. That wasn't the answer he was expecting. "Most people want happiness, wealth, or love. Those don't interest you?"

"Naturally, a deserted island could give me all three," Peyton smirked, raising a brow. "I mean, what more could I ask for but to lie in a hammock, sipping on coconuts and catching some sun. Maybe fight a few pirates for their gold, settle down with a mermaid. Build a shack and watch the sun set for the rest of my life."

"And this buried treasure..." Daniel shuffled the planks of wood mindlessly from one hand to the other. "What do you find?"

Peyton leaned back and closed his eyes. "A bottomless pit

of eclairs."

"Sounds like you found the perfect island."

He opened his eyes, grinning. "And now I really want an eclair."

The kid knew how to word a good joke to deflect from what he was really saying. The humor wasn't lost on Daniel. But neither was the picture he painted. "You want to get away from reality for a while is what you're saying."

"I thought that's what I was doing when I left the city."

Daniel nodded, a thoughtful frown pulling at his mouth. He'd been there before. And he'd always found reprieve deep in the wild surrounding his farm. Maybe Peyton needed a taste of that to help satisfy his search. "Keep that perspective in mind. God will show you where you need to be."

"What if I did too much for God to want anything to do with me?"

There were a million ways he could respond to that. *God doesn't shuck us off like that. His grace is as deep as it is enduring. There's no such thing as too much, too far, or too broken for God to handle.*

But he didn't start with any of those. "What d'you think you did?"

He looked up at Daniel, his throat shifting where he swallowed. He stood, distancing himself from the barstool, and shoving his hands in his pockets. Between the worktable and the windows, Peyton turned slowly. "I, uh..." He cleared his throat, but it didn't change the dryness in his voice. "I got into porn when I was in college."'

In the short time he'd known Peyton, he'd learned that the boy was good at dodging the point in a way that made people laugh. But not this time. This time was different. "Have you repented?"

Peyton looked up, a pinch of panic in his eyes. "Oh, yeah. It was seven years ago, give or take. I was searching for...*something* and it was just one more thing to try. It didn't last long. I gave it up and haven't looked back."

"You've asked for His forgiveness?"

He nodded. "My parents taught me to respect women. That every girl I go out with is a daughter of God before she's anything else—and that mindset always kept me on the safe side of dating." He shook his head, attention on the floor between them. "But I convinced myself it was different because they were on a screen. They weren't real or they weren't dangerous—I don't know. I didn't care. And then a buddy asked me to go to a campus ministry event with him, and you'll never guess what the sermon was on."

Daniel had a sneaking suspicion. "Lust."

Peyton dipped his chin in confirmation. "I couldn't stand myself. Asking Him to forgive me was like needing air after coming up from the water. I couldn't go without His mercy."

"Then why you still carryin' it?"

It was as if Daniel had tossed a bucket of water over the kid. Head hung low, his chest suddenly heaved. "I'm disgusted with myself. I can't shake it. If someone looked at my wife like that—" There was a tick in his jaw. "What kind of a man does that?"

"You're not that man anymore, Peyton."

"But I'm still guilty. Even if I've been forgiven, it's still part of my past. Part of my identity." He leaned forward a fraction and tapped his fingers on his chest. "What good could possibly come from my life if I was capable of doing that?"

So that's why he was searching, running from everything he'd ever known. He needed to find a new version of himself to replace the one he'd deemed too disgusting to exist. "That's not how it works, son."

Something in Peyton calmed, like a sneering wolf being coaxed to trust. The hard wrinkle between his brows smoothed and the line of his jaw relaxed.

While Daniel had never experienced porn in the modern fashion, as a teenager he'd been through his fair share of magazines that evoked enough imagination to make him guilty of the same sin Peyton was guilty of. But the life that stood around him now was testament enough of God's goodness. "You're buying into the lie that God is only looking to use people who have never sinned. Those people don't exist, Peyton. Everyone has sinned and fallen short in different ways, and no way is better or worse than the next. We are all the same—we need God."

Daniel gestured to the east where he knew his boy was probably playing in his treehouse. "Let's say you have a son one day and he walks up to you and says, 'Dad, I committed this heinous crime, and God can't use me anymore, what good am I?' Are you really gonna tell him to give up?"

Realization lightened the darkness in his eyes and Peyton shook his head.

"No, you won't. You'll look at him and you'll tell him that God knows your every sin, and the sum of them altogether can't stop Him from loving you. If God can pull someone like you—Peyton—from the pit of your own sin then He can use anybody."

His throat shifted where he swallowed again.

Daniel pulled in a deep breath, his heart racing with the hope he knew God had supplied him with tenfold since his youth, and he prayed it would be enough to spill over into Peyton's life. "Don't rob God of His glory, son. You're not too much of *anything* for Him. He created you for a purpose and He won't stop until He sees it through."

Daniel must have said something right, because the boy's shoulders didn't seem to bear so much weight.

"You want to be some good, Peyton? God is in the business of being good. Let Him have you."

In the reflection of dark waves beneath Jesus' feet, Olivia pulled the hair tie from her mass of wavy locks and let them fall around her shoulders. She raked her fingers through the strands, begging them to give her just a few more hours of volume to hide the birthmark. After that she would be whoever—and look like whatever—she wanted to in the comfort of her own home. But until then, she needed this thing to make like Houdini and disappear so she could focus on tiptoeing through the minefield of Caroline's gab during supper. And anything else that might transpire between her best friend and the guest.

Olivia chewed on the edge of her bottom lip.

"Supper smells so good we could practically taste it all the way from the barn." The sound of Peyton's voice sent dread spiraling through her gut.

Mentally urging Caroline not to repeat anything Olivia had said this morning, she rushed back to the kitchen, clearing her throat to chase away the nerves.

While Dad was at the sink, rubbing soapy hands together, Peyton stood in front of the patio doors where a dusky pink sky filled the windows behind him. Caroline moved with the elegance of a princess meeting a potential groom, hand outstretched and manicured nails leading the way.

"You *must* be Peyton," she drawled in the overly sweet, southern accent that she greeted every eligible bachelor with. "You're even dreamier than Olivia said you were."

His eyes darted to Olivia for a split second before he returned his focus to Caroline's waiting hand and took it in his. He bowed gently—a show of chivalry that was sure to earn him points. "And you must be Caroline."

Flicking her hair over her shoulder, she sent Olivia a sparkling smile. "And how did Olivia describe me to you?"

A shadow of uncertainty passed over his face in less time than it took Olivia to blink. "She said you were very articulate, dedicated, and sweet-smelling."

With a bark of a laugh that put her stunning teeth on full display, she withdrew her hand. "Oh, you're very charming. That doesn't sound like Olivia at all. But you're off to a good start, so I won't argue."

As Caroline swooped alongside Peyton and laced her arm through his, Olivia intercepted the bowls of pico de gallo and guacamole that Mom carried and took them to the dining table herself.

"Now, Peyton. How long do you think you'll be staying in Heavenly, and would you like for someone to show you around town?" Caroline asked as he escorted her—or he could have been dragged against his will, Olivia couldn't tell—to the table and pulled out a chair. Caroline slid her phone from her pocket and glided like a flower petal into the seat, fluttering her long lashes as a token of her gratitude.

Olivia busied herself with a bowl of lettuce at the island, unable to bear witness to the moment when all good men fell to Caroline's charisma and essentially asked her out on a date.

"Actually, Caroline," his gravelly voice raked over her name as if it were his favorite word. "I'll be in Heavenly through the summer and...Vern has already offered to show me around town."

Pepaw stood at the sink, a wrinkle between his brows and dark eyes pinning Peyton with a look of denial. His focus dropped to Caroline and the wrinkle disappeared. "That's right. First thing after Sunday service we're takin' a ride 'round town. Can't send a greenhorn out to get feed and he don't know his east from his west."

Peyton nodded adamantly as he passed Olivia on his way to join Pepaw at the sink, pumping a dollop of soap into his hands. She bit back a smile as she took the lettuce to the table and slid into the seat between Caroline and the empty chair where Mom would sit. Whatever unspoken truce had passed between the two men was a welcomed mystery to her. Pepaw wasn't one to play games, but whatever reason he had for speaking up for Peyton just now was priceless.

"Well, that's okay, Pepaw Vern." Caroline unrolled her cloth napkin and placed it uncharacteristically over her lap. Olivia bit into her smile. Since when did Caroline care about etiquette? "If Peyton's gonna be here all summer then I'll have plenty of time to steal him away at some point."

The way Peyton's hands froze under the running water went unnoticed by Caroline, but not by Olivia. He didn't say another word as he ripped off a paper towel, dried his hands, and tossed it in the trash on his way to the seat that sat directly across from Olivia—the one Josh usually sat in. But Josh was the last one to the table, as always, and didn't make a peep when he climbed into the chair across from Caroline.

Shifting restlessly on his knees, he raised his chin, spying out each dish lining the middle of the table. Once the chairs were filled with her family, plus their guest, Dad said the blessing and Olivia waited while Josh made a mad dash for the Mexican street corn. He dropped a portion on one side of his plate, tongue sticking from the edge of his mouth. Olivia resisted the urge to snicker, her focus drifting to Peyton who also waited, watching with a smile as Josh went back for a second scoop.

"So, Peyton," Caroline said, accent still in place. "What is your go-to coffee order?"

Peyton lifted a spoonful of red rice and hesitated before he added it to his plate. "I'm not really a big coffee drinker. I prefer chocolate milk, fruit punch."

Josh's sudden giggle rang out over the clatter of

silverware against dishes.

Olivia smiled at her plate as she laid a helping of enchiladas across it. "I'm sure Emma can make chocolate milk at the cafe."

Peyton stopped short, peeking up at her wide-eyed, as if he was worried she'd taken him too seriously. She pursed her lips to the side to let him know she hadn't. He lifted his chin slowly, a smile teasing his lips.

Caroline wrinkled her nose but never lost her zeal. "Do you like to dance?"

"Only the macarena," he said, followed by another round of Josh's giggles.

Caroline waved her fork through the air. "I ask because the Fourth of July dance is a month away and since you're new in town you probably don't have anybody to go with."

"Actually, Vern has invited me to go with him to that as well." He nudged Pepaw with his elbow. Pepaw launched into a coughing fit.

Mom laughed quietly at Olivia's side and Dad cleared his throat. "Peyton, whaddya say tomorrow you work on the trees with me? I hear you passed your first day with flying colors, so I think you'll do just fine in the fields."

Peyton nodded, taking a long drink of tea. Olivia smiled as she took a bite.

Halfway through the meal, after Pepaw and Dad had plotted tomorrow's work plans with Peyton eavesdropping, and Caroline had attempted to stir up a conversation with him about flower preferences on a first date, and Josh had made an appointment with Olivia's computer on Sunday to play his favorite game, Olivia took full advantage of a moment of silence.

"Peyton, have you given anymore thought to your dream job?" She took a small bite and chewed patiently.

A slow smile pulled at one edge of his mouth. "You didn't think I'd really forget, did you?"

"Not a chance. You obviously have a very good memory."

He took a bite, and she thought he might not have an answer. Maybe it wasn't fair of her to put him on the spot like that in front of everyone. Just because she had a running list of dream jobs she'd been collecting since childhood didn't mean he had his own life figured out as well.

But then he swallowed. "Fighter pilot."

"Oh, very exciting," Caroline cooed as she leaned her shoulder against Olivia's. "I can see why you wanted to run away with him."

Heat shot across Olivia's face as she pinned Caroline with a look.

"What's that?" Peyton asked, brows wrinkled.

Olivia opened her mouth to explain, but Caroline rushed in, fluttering her lashes again. "Are there any fighter-pilot-plans in the works?"

He shook his head. "I've only gotten as far as the aviator shades."

"I'm embarrassed to admit this," Caroline said, but Olivia doubted it. "I've always had a weakness for men in aviator shades ever since that one movie came out." She nodded, looking around the table as if everyone else agreed.

"Do you have a second one?" Olivia reacquired the conversation.

Peyton lifted his chin a notch. "A second what?"

"Dream job. I shared two of mine with you. Wasn't that the deal?"

He never missed a bite. "Of course."

She raised both eyebrows, waiting.

His dark blue eyes didn't leave hers, and his crooked smirk didn't falter. But she could tell he didn't have one. He must have really shuffled through his thoughts to pull one out of thin air. "Professional baseball player."

"Ahh," she hummed more for the fact that he'd been a lot quicker with it than she'd anticipated. "What position?"

"Pitcher." His fork clinked against his plate as he laid it down and leaned forward, resting crossed arms on the edge of the table as if he'd gained two steps ahead of her and knew it. "I was a pitcher in college, and I would have loved going pro. But that wasn't God's plan for me."

While Pepaw shared a shrug with her mom and dad, and Josh drank from his glass so quickly that it was spilling down his cheek, Caroline gasped. "I *love* baseball players. They by-far have the cutest uniforms than any other sport. You went to college in Austin?"

He nodded once, sparing her only a glance. Caroline lifted her phone front and center, thumbs tapping on the screen frantically.

There was an unspoken question in the way he tilted his head to the left slightly. Content that he'd lived up to his end of the deal—even with a confused audience—Olivia nodded and tucked another bite in her mouth.

"Wow," Caroline croaked, her sweet southern drawl suddenly gone. "You were hot!"

"Thanks—were?" Peyton frowned.

Caroline stuck the phone in front of Olivia. There was a picture of a college baseball team on the screen, a younger, thinner, brighter version of the man sitting across from her now standing on the left side of the team, dressed in white and orange pants and a jersey. He was easy to spot for some reason. Among the sea of dozens of players and coaches, he seemed the happiest to be there. Two of Caroline's pink almond-shaped thumbnails swiped across the screen and suddenly Peyton's young face was closer—and something about it drew heat to Olivia's face. Why would she want to see his college picture? She could care less.

"Eleven," Mom said as if his team number held some kind of importance, her shoulder pressed against Olivia's as she tried to spy the picture as well.

Caroline moved the phone so Dad and Vern could see, stopping in front of Peyton and Josh last.

"That was four years ago. My senior year. Won state that season," he said with a smirk.

Senior? That meant he'd been about her age in that picture. If he graduated four years ago, that made him twenty-six. Olivia tucked the last bite of enchilada in her mouth. She'd never done math so quick in her life.

Exaggerated accent nowhere to be found, Caroline returned her phone to the table and splayed her hands on each side of her plate. "Okay, if Olivia's not gonna do it then I will—if for no other reason than the fact that I've always dreamed of dating a professional athlete and you may be the closest I ever get to it—" She took in a long breath. "Will you go out with me?"

Peyton tossed his head back and looked at the ceiling as if she'd shot him with a dart.

Olivia took a drink of her tea, bracing herself just in case Caroline's attempts actually wore him down. She was beautiful, daring, and in many of her ex-boyfriend's opinions, irresistible. It would only make sense that a man like Peyton would want to spend time with someone as stunning as Caroline for one summer that would fade into the oblivion of their young lives.

"You're flattering, Caroline," he finally said. "But I'm not looking to date anyone for a while. At least not until I get my heart straight with God."

"Oh," Mom squeaked. Clearly nobody at the table really expected Peyton to turn Caroline down—it was unheard of. Dad nodded approvingly. Vern huffed a laugh. Josh yawned. Olivia felt a wave of relief splash over her.

There was something reassuring about that. Not that she cared who he dated, but knowing he'd be spending the summer chasing God rather than chasing Caroline—or anyone else for that matter—made her breathe easy.

"*Ick,*" Caroline said, rolling her eyes and tilting her head toward Olivia. "You're like *her*. She's sworn off dating, too. What is wrong with y'all? Life's boring without someone to go to the movies with."

Even though heat spread up her neck with the sudden spotlight on Olivia's life choice, she didn't care. She didn't have to worry about another newcomer getting swept up in Caroline's love life. She didn't have to worry about being a third wheel once again. And she didn't have to worry about the emptiness she usually got in the pit of her stomach when she was around an available guy who couldn't even look her in the eyes for fear he would stare at her birthmark and gag.

But with the way Peyton was looking at her right now, there was no fear. No hesitation. And absolutely no clue what Caroline was going on about.

CHAPTER SEVEN

The thunderstruck way Olivia looked at him made Peyton want to ask her point blank why she would swear off dating at the age of twenty-two. He had a gut feeling it had everything to do with the beauty mark under her right eye, hiding behind a wave of auburn hair right now. Something about that made his gut twist. Who had made her feel like she had to hide?

He couldn't imagine anyone at this table stoking those insecurities in her. She was a sweet girl, unafraid to speak her mind, and obviously happy with her life. Surrounded by people who clearly loved her, she had no reason to conceal herself that he could see.

Not that it mattered to him.

"Good supper," Vern huffed, standing and taking his plate with him. "I'll be outside."

The clink of the dish in the sink, followed by a splash of water, and the shuffle of the old cowboy's footsteps out of the kitchen were the only sounds around them until he was gone.

Taking advantage of the empty chair beside him, Peyton stretched his arm out along the back. "Pepaw Vern could make a mountain lion run away scared, couldn't he?"

Echoes of laughter filled the room, as if they'd not expected the silence to be broken with a joke.

"He's a character, for sure," Daniel said.

"Believe it or not, he's a lot nicer now than he used to be," Gianna said.

Ouch. "I'm glad I waited before I came for a visit."

Daniel, Gianna, and Olivia chuckled. Josh was trying to balance a spoon on his nose. Caroline was slumped low against her chair, texting, all traces of the coquettish southern belle gone. Peyton was glad. There was something pure and fair about her, despite her desperate attempts to gain his attention. The way she looked at and talked with Olivia spoke of an unwavering friendship—maybe even a sisterhood. That set well with him.

"That is..." Daniel said as if a thought occurred to him. "He's only nice when his grandchildren aren't up to their shenanigans."

Olivia snorted a laugh and Josh burst into a series of giggles that made Peyton chuckle.

"Like that one time we put a lizard in his water bottle," Josh said, his smile wide.

"Or when we super glued his wrench to the worktable," Olivia recounted, eyes lighting up with the same mischief that her brother's did.

"Or when you put bouillon cubes in his showerhead," Caroline mumbled, eyes still pinned to her phone.

Olivia and Josh shared a laugh, their deep, rhythmic cadences syncing up. They might be adopted, but their personalities were one in the same.

They were as bad as he and Austin had been as kids. They hadn't given trouble a chance to find them, they went in search of it. Peyton crossed his arms and leaned both elbows against the edge of the table. "What's next on the agenda?"

Olivia jerked her head to the side, tossing her hair out of her face—the same way she'd done last night without realizing it—and her beauty mark came into full view. "I've got a few ideas."

"Olivia Rose," Gianna muttered.

Peyton couldn't help but smile. That name fit her. A mixture of pretty and promises to be unique. "Did your names come from your birth parents or from your mom and dad?" Peyton held his breath. "If that's not too personal to ask."

"Mom and Dad," Josh and Olivia answered at the same time.

"Neither one of us had a legal name until we were adopted," Olivia said, question filling her eyes as she looked at her parents. "I think my foster family called me Angel, right?"

They both nodded.

"You know why, don't you?" Peyton asked, stretching his back against the chair until his shoulder blades popped.

Her brows lifted and she tilted her head, as if challenging his knowledge of her personal history. "Why?"

He tipped his chin. "Because that's an angel's kiss."

Her eyes widened and she looked down at her plate, hair falling across her cheek like a curtain.

That's when Caroline straightened in her seat and set her phone down with gusto. "That's what I've always told her! See, I'm not the only one who calls it that."

Olivia's nose wrinkled. "It's not that. Angel's kisses are pink and...*cute.*"

Peyton let his smirk turn into a grin.

She cleared her throat and fidgeted with her glass. "Anyway—that's one of the questions I'd love to ask my birth parents if I ever get to meet them. Not that I don't like my name. I adore it. But I'm curious about what they called me."

"You've never met them?"

She shook her head. "The adoption agency redacted their information, so there's no paper trail I can follow back to them—I mean there is, but it'll take a judge to unseal the records. I just haven't put that much effort into it yet. Mom and Dad think I should wait a little longer."

Peyton was sure Olivia missed the subtle look her parents gave each other. Whether she suspected it or not, there was more to her story. Peyton nodded, respecting whatever Daniel and Gianna wanted to keep a mystery to their family. He had to believe it was for her good, though he knew enough about the girl to trust her judgement. "I pray you find everything you're looking for."

A smirk quirked the edges of her mouth as she slowly looked up at him. "Thank you."

"I met mine!" Josh announced.

Peyton leaned back and crossed his arms. "Really?"

He lifted one shoulder. "Well, only my birth mom. She's still looking for my birth dad. I hope she finds him, that way I can meet them both together."

Chest aching with the realization of what had transpired to make sure Josh was with them today, Peyton set his hand on the back of the boy's neck. "Then I pray the same for your birth mom, Josh."

The gentle hum of Daniel clearing his throat—probably of the same emotion Peyton felt—had everyone turning. "What d'yall say we take this out to the patio?"

"Yeah!" Josh roared and was out of his seat before anyone else, racing through the kitchen.

"Plate! Josh, don't forget your..." Gianna's words faded when she saw Peyton reach for it and set it over his own. A warm smile touched her lips, and she nodded once.

When the table was cleared, dishes stacked neatly beside the sink, he turned to make his way toward the twilight beyond the patio doors when a thought hit him. "What time is it?"

Caroline checked her phone as she passed him. "Nine-twelve."

Which meant it was still early where his grandparents lived and now was a good time to drop some exciting news on them that they would find depressing. "Daniel, do you have a phone I can use to make a call? I left mine at the homestead."

"Sure." He pointed toward the nook beside the stairs, which triggered a hazy memory from this morning of a home phone sitting between the coffee maker and the ovens.

He nodded thanks and made his way over, grabbing the phone from its base while everyone shuffled outside. As he keyed in the number that his grandparents hadn't changed since his birth, movement caught his attention and shifted his focus to the walkway between the living room and foyer. Olivia stood at a large picture, fidgeting with her hair in the reflection of the glass.

So *that's* how she kept hiding behind it?

Peyton took a big step to the right, out of view, to shield himself from her secret as she turned. He held off on hitting the call button.

When her eyes found him, surprise passing over her features, he lifted the phone in his hand. "Gotta call my grandparents and let them know I might be up past curfew."

She stopped short, her hair settling around her. "Oh."

Maybe his humor was a little too dry. He sent her a wink and realization weighed in her shoulders, loosening her stance. "I should have known that about you."

"What? That I'm funny?"

"That you probably still had a curfew."

Peyton couldn't help but chuckle as he set his thumb against the button. She started on her way again.

"You, um..." Regret singed his throat the moment he opened his mouth, drawing a quiet groan from his chest. But she'd already pivoted, hiding spot forgotten as her hair shifted away from her face. "You don't have to get up early for work, do you?"

Her eyes widened just enough for him to see they were the same shade as the cinnamon she'd smelled like earlier. She pressed a splayed hand over her collarbone. "So now *I* have a curfew?"

He was an idiot for saying anything to begin with. So what if she'd have to leave? What should it matter to him? "Absolutely not," he couldn't help the laugh that rushed out with the words. "I guess I thought since you worked at a bakery then you'd have to go soon. And I'd miss the opportunity to hear you sing."

Thank God, that last thought might have saved him.

A pink tinge touched her cheeks as she turned and looked over her shoulder at the patio doors. "There probably won't be any singing tonight. Dad didn't bring out his guitar, so you might have to wait." Relief colored her voice.

"Fair enough." He nodded gently and then lifted a shoulder. "Good thing I'll be here all summer."

She wrinkled her nose in that way of hers, as if letting him know she saw his game. "And for the record, I open the bakery when I want to. If I want to sleep in 'till five AM on a Saturday, then I will."

The defensiveness in her reprimand humbled him. Smile agape, he nodded mindlessly. "You own the bakery."

"I do," she said and then giggled softly, gesturing outside. "When I graduated from high school, Mom and Dad gave me the option to use my savings for college or start a business." She lifted her shoulders, twisting gently as if she were pretty proud of herself. "I chose to start a business."

And that smirk told him it was a successful business.

"The same deal will go for Josh when he graduates," she tacked on.

"We really need to talk to your parents about adopting

me, too."

She grinned, scuffing something on the floor with her shoe. "Don't put too many ideas in their heads because they would one hundred percent do that."

Peyton didn't doubt it.

The patio door opened, and Daniel stepped inside. He passed his daughter, dropping one hand on her shoulder as he did. "I'm gonna grab my guitar if you're in the mood to sing."

With the way her smile tensed and her jaw lifted, she most certainly wasn't in the mood to give a performance tonight. But Peyton wouldn't talk her out of it. He chewed on his cheek to keep from grinning.

She sighed deeply and spun around, leaving through the same door her dad had come in.

Peyton finally called Nan's number and didn't have to wait long for her to answer. "Hello?"

"There's the voice of my favorite gramma."

"Boy, where are you?" Her tone was sharp enough to cut him. "I've been clutching my pearls all day and praying that you hadn't got kidnapped."

Nan didn't wear pearls. She wore inch-long fake nails that matched her inch-long fake eyelashes and was known to have a different tint of color to her blonde hair every time he saw her. "I'm six foot one, Nan, I don't think they call it kidnapping at this height."

"Tell me you're close by," she said as Daniel made his way back through the kitchen, holding his guitar by its neck.

"I'm not. And I've got even more bad news."

She gasped. "What's happened?"

"Nothing you'll have to call a crime fighter for. Put your pearls down." His smile turned into a grimace. "I'm still in Hill Country and I found a job here."

"What are you telling me, boy?" Her panic turned into an icy interrogation. Good. He could deal with her fierce side— he couldn't deal with breaking her heart.

"I'm telling you I won't be in New Mexico until the fall."

"But what about the job you were gonna get in Albuquerque?" Her voice raised to a squeak.

"They found someone else to fill the position."

She grunted under her breath. "Give me their number, I'll

have a talk with them."

"Absolutely. That would be a huge help. You've got a pen and a paper?"

A couple seconds passed. "I do now. Go ahead."

He rattled off her own phone number and promptly heard the pen being thrown against the table. He ducked as if it could somehow cross six hundred miles and collide with his head.

"Peyton Brooks, I'm gonna wring your neck the moment you get here."

"All right, but I'll hold you to it."

The soft sounds of a guitar strumming pulled Peyton's attention to the patio that he couldn't see from this angle. "Listen, tell Pops I said hi. I've got to go...check something out at my job."

She snuffed out a long breath. "Fine. But I'm not telling you I love you 'till you're here in my arms where I can hug you while I say it."

"Works for me. I'll talk to you later. Love you."

"Love you, too" she echoed, and he hung up before she could take it back.

He set the phone on its base, curiosity begging to step outside before Olivia sang only one verse and called it a night just to spite him.

He opened the door, and the atmosphere shifted around him. A gentle breeze blew through the covered patio where strands of warm lights hung over the blazing fire table and the family surrounding it. Daniel sat on a barstool, strumming his guitar. Caroline lounged on an Adirondack chair, glued to her phone. Josh ran in figure-eights through the grass on the outskirts of the lighting. Vern sat on the booth opposite of Gianna and Olivia, who was singing sweetly the church hymn he'd heard a thousand times as a kid.

"Come, thou Fount of every blessing;
Tune my heart to sing Thy grace;
Streams of mercy, never ceasing,
Call for songs of loudest praise."

Hands in his pockets, Peyton took a couple steps closer,

her bell-like voice drawing him in. Fear that his presence would end it all, he stopped where he was and fused himself to the concrete. Her tone was light, like the words were soft as clouds, but deep enough that they weren't lost to the guitar. A rasp lining the edge of her voice hinted that she was capable of doing so much more than whispering the lyrics to the wind.

Eyes closed, brows drawn together, her passion was evident. Face tilted upward, her beauty mark was exposed to those who watched from Heaven. As he'd suspected, her voice deepened and her volume rose with the next verse, driving a stake into his heart that felt a lot like conviction. He didn't know why, but the weight was unmistakable.

"Teach me some melodious sonnet,
Sung by flaming tongues above;
Praise the mount! I'm fixed upon it,
Mount of Thy redeeming love!"

Peyton swallowed hard, the picture before him more reverent than he had a right to witness. These people represented wholeness in every sense of the word. They were inseparable, respectful of one another's differences, and loving in ways that he didn't know could exist. Hope was their anthem, and he could see it in the eyes of every person he'd talked with today. He doubted even the hardships of life could shake their joy. Everything about it was...right.

And it interrupted something in his soul.

"Here I raise my Ebenezer;
Hither by Thy help I'm come;
And I hope, by Thy good pleasure,
Safely to arrive at home."

By the time Olivia reached the fourth verse, nobody was left unscathed. The family sang along tenderly, letting her lead. Even Josh had come to rest against a wooden post, one arm hooked around it. And Caroline had laid her phone to rest in her lap. Peyton managed to let the words fall from his lips in a whisper that couldn't even be heard by his own ears.

"Jesus sought me when a stranger,
Wandering from the fold of God;
He, to rescue me from danger,
Interposed His precious blood."

Her family fell silent and Olivia sang a verse he'd never heard before, her voice fading enough to signal a coming end to the song.

"Christ before me, Christ behind me,
Christ my left and Christ my right,
Christ above me, Christ below me,
Christ surrounds my every side."

He didn't belong. He had too much at risk by being here. The miles that had promised him answers were getting away from him every minute he stayed put. He couldn't figure out why God would ever ask him to work at a place like this—he'd have to think on that later. Everything about this was temporary, and it sent a rod of dread down his spine. The best things in life never lasted.

Agreeing to stay had been a mistake.

Focus fastened on the dim path that led to the homestead, Peyton searched himself for the courage to say what needed to be said. The headlights of Daniel's truck sent shadows dancing through the obscured branches as the man followed the trail. Between the two of them, Josh's little dog stood on the console, mouth hanging open in a wild pant.

Peyton hadn't been forced to make the trek back through the dark after all. Once Gianna had presented him with a couple of boxes of food and essentials, Daniel had offered to make the minute-long drive for him. He'd accepted for the sole purpose of telling Daniel that he couldn't stay. Even as supplies rattled in the seat behind him.

"It was real good having you tonight," Daniel said. "I'm glad you decided to come for supper. I haven't heard my family laugh that much in a long time."

"Thank you for having me." It was all he could say.

That laughter had felt like a balm to his soul. Olivia's singing, a gateway to the presence of God. The warm welcome from Daniel and Gianna, acceptance that he didn't know he was looking for.

But some unknown thing in the bottom of his soul kept joy from taking root. He didn't know what it was, but something batted away each threat of peace that came close. Everything about this place felt too good to be true. He'd known from the moment he pulled up to the cabin last night.

Headlights passed over the homestead and the green of his truck in the yard. Daniel pulled in behind it and parked. The little mutt that looked like a bear cub followed Peyton out of his door. In the windy heat that stuck to his skin, Peyton swung open the back door and picked up one of the boxes. Daniel did the same opposite of him.

Inside, Peyton flicked on the light that illuminated a house that was feeling a little too much like home. Even with the boxes and dust and cobwebs hanging in the corners. It screamed a satisfying greeting that Peyton wasn't in the mood to embrace at the moment. He dropped the box on the kitchen counter with a thud harder than he'd intended, jarring what was inside. He turned to take the second box from Daniel.

"You're sure you're comfortable here? I know it could use some fixin' up, so I understand if it's not convenient."

He wasn't staying. He had to tell Daniel. Right now, before the man could heap any more hot coals over his head with his kindness. Peyton let his eyes rove across the small home with its shiplap walls and whitewashed stone fireplace and the floor-to-ceiling shelves of family heirlooms.

"It's perfect," he found himself saying instead. "After I left the city, I spent a couple of nights sleeping behind the wheel, so this is a resort compared to waking up with a sore neck."

Daniel huffed a laugh.

Peyton took a few, long steps across a floor that creaked and stopped in front of the fireplace. Decades worth of dust covered the trinkets and picture frames across the mantel. Some untouched. Some with fingerprints. Closest to him was a red tin box with smudges where it had been handled recently.

"I was serious earlier when I told you I'd have you working on the trees tomorrow," Daniel said. "I wasn't just trying to deflect Caroline's...attack."

Peyton smiled as he picked up the tin. He shook it slightly, something bumping against the walls inside. "Honestly, I wasn't sure. She seems like a good person, but I take it she does that often. Attack?"

With his hands tucked in his pockets Daniel walked toward the door with a long sigh. "Oh, yeah. She's been trying to get the attention of every boy who's ever crossed her path since she was a kid. And Olivia is her polar opposite."

Peyton looked past the tin to the floor where dust indicated that boxes had been moved away from the fireplace not long ago. "Is she?"

Daniel hummed. "I don't fight her on it, of course—makes my job as a dad easier. But she swears having a boyfriend will hold her back in life. Stop her from traveling, seeing the world, going on adventures."

Peyton turned and looked over his shoulder at Daniel. "Does she do those things?"

Daniel shook his head.

Peyton huffed a laugh, his suspicions about her nearly confirmed—someone had made her feel inadequate. Like she wasn't worth being seen. It was a crying shame. She was a lot of fun to be around.

He tried to pry open the lid of the tin, but it didn't budge. On the mantel there was a clean spot where a key had been laying and was now nowhere in sight.

"Breakfast is at six. We'll head out around seven."

Peyton froze. It was now or never. He opened his mouth and pulled in a deep breath.

"We'll only work half a day. The family is planning a hike to the lake tomorrow afternoon. Do some fishing and see some wildlife. I know everyone would love it if you joined us."

And there were the hot coals. Peyton shook his head. "I can't do that, sir. I've already taken up too much of your family's time as it is. I can't keep doing that."

A wrinkle formed between Daniel's brows. "I hate that you feel that way, son. We really like havin' you around. It's no bother to us at all."

"I appreciate it, but I can't." Peyton turned to face Daniel, handing him the box. "Might be something valuable in there."

Daniel shook it, tried the lid, then shrugged, handing it back. "You can put it in the closet or upstairs, along with any of this stuff to get it out of your way."

Peyton took it, letting his focus skim over the boxes Daniel pointed to. There were more dusty smudges near the sofa and coffee table. "Yessir."

Where had his tongue gone? Why couldn't he just say it? Spit it out and be done with it. Get back on the road so he could remind himself of why this trip was important to begin with.

"You want to hear something funny? About that sign at the end of the driveway?" Daniel said, tipping his chin in that direction. "I only put it up three days ago."

Peyton stared, his heartbeat thumping against his throat. The man could read his thoughts, couldn't he?

Higher Rock. It had been the chant of his heart for so long. And now he was neck deep in the middle of an answered prayer and he wanted nothing more than to swim to land, hop in his truck, and head west for as long as he could stay awake.

But he wasn't a runner. That was his brother's curse. No, Peyton's was much worse—he was a stayer. Every page of his life had some evidence of a boy who made himself at home wherever he was.

Whether it was the treehouse that he and Austin had built and the night that had grown too cold to sleep restfully. Or his fifth-grade best friend's birthday party and he was the last one to call his mom to pick him up. Or in college, when he would study in the student lounge with friends and one-by-one they'd go their own way. He was always the last to leave.

Finding reasons to stay was easy for him. He never wanted the moment to end. He didn't want his heart to grow cold the second he walked away.

And even now, while his gut told him to run, to just trust God with the next chapter of his life, something rooted him.

"Perfect timing," Daniel finally said after the long silence

Peyton had left hanging in the air. He turned and grabbed the doorknob. "See you in the morning, Peyton."

"Goodnight, sir," Peyton said mindlessly.

He pulled the door open, and Josh's dog ran in. "Let's go, Mutt."

The bear cub came and laid at Peyton's feet, his body shaped like a burnt crescent roll. He looked up at Daniel with his strange ears pointed high but folding downward at the tips, as if challenging his owner to come and pick him up.

Peyton raised an eyebrow. "I don't mind the company if you're okay with him being in here."

Daniel lifted a shoulder. "Fine by me. Goodnight, son."

Once the door clicked shut, Peyton sighed deeply, regretting his cowardice. Or reluctance. Or whatever was to blame for not telling the man that he couldn't stay. He couldn't make his home here like he'd tried to everywhere else. With his parents. At school. College. Even his brother's house. None of those were his home. Not even the rent house he'd been in since graduation, or the job that had fed him for four years, or the gym that he'd spent every last ounce of his free time at. When he stayed, everyone else left, and with them, the sense of home.

"Let's go, Bear," he told the dog at his feet, surprised when he listened, following Peyton to the bedroom with a happy bounce in his step.

The closet door already stood open to a shallow room where he'd hung a few shirts, boxes belonging to the Whitmores lining the top shelves. Peyton set the tin on the top of one box, and heard it clatter inside. If he'd have known it didn't have a lid, he would have put it elsewhere.

He went to the mattress that squeaked under his weight. Legs hanging off one corner, sore back stretched out, he took in a long breath of musty air. Beside him, Bear landed on the cushioned quilt, turned in a circle, and laid down at the foot of the bed.

Around him, the dark abyss promised nothing but another sleepless night and more questions he couldn't answer. What was the difference between this and a hotel room? At least he could be making his way to Nan and Pop's if he were in a hotel. On his way to a place he knew he didn't have to leave at the end of the summer, where he had more control over the distractions that kept him from contemplating the emptiness in his soul.

Even if he did stay here to work—not to make himself part of the family—what was he expecting? What did he think he'd come away with? A cure for his despair? An answer? A direction?

"Here we go again," he whispered to the shadowy ceiling lurking over him. On with the never-ending questions that begged him ceaselessly to fix himself. He closed his eyes and let the challenges flow freely, each one of them a rock against a window that wouldn't break. Over and over and over.

Who am I? What's the purpose of my life? What are we all here for? Where is God in all of this? Why am I the only one He doesn't talk to? Did I do something wrong? But Daniel said I've been forgiven—God can still use me. What if this was all there was? What if God was already using him? What if God had been using him all along and this loneliness was the only result?

Peyton opened his eyes. One thought came to the front of the rest. One thought that he'd spent decades refusing to ask. It was too blasphemous, too disrespectful to ask. It wasn't even worth asking—he already knew the answer to it, and he'd pledged himself to that answer like a drowning man to a life vest.

Like the rocks were suddenly replaced by a single brick, he held the weight of it in his chest.

"When my heart is overwhelmed, lead me to the rock that is higher than I," he whispered.

Could he ask it? For only one night?

Peyton sighed.

If God had brought him here—to a place truly called Higher Rock—and had something of purpose, something of worth for Peyton to do while he was here and all Peyton left with was the same feeling of despair he'd come with...

Was God alone *truly* enough for him?

"You'll have to learn baseball facts—lots of 'em. And it wouldn't hurt to learn something about aviation, too. Just scatter it in your conversation whenever you talk to him. And bat your eyelashes when you do."

Makeup half-removed, Olivia paused with a wipe against her cheek and scoffed at the phone laying on the edge of her bathroom sink. "You're insane if you think I'm doing any of that. I already told you. There's nothing romantic happening. I barely know the guy."

Caroline whined on the other end of the phone.

She hadn't even been home for ten minutes and Caroline was already pitching her ideas on how she could pursue Peyton. Olivia rolled her eyes, regretting going to Caroline's third birthday party, even though she'd had no control over which birthday parties she went to at that age.

But that's where their friendship had started and here is where she found it, almost twenty years later—Caroline relentlessly attempting to coax Olivia into living life on the edge.

"You've sworn off dating. *He's* sworn off dating. Guess which two people I'm betting will end up dating."

Olivia's stomach hurt at the thought of dating anyone. She smoothed the wipe over her birthmark. "You'll lose. Big time."

"You're crazy to let that man walk out of your life."

She tossed the wipe in the trash and flipped on the faucet. "*You're* crazy for chasing after men. But that's who you are, and this is who I am."

Caroline's frustration was palpable over the line, drawing a smile from Olivia as she scrubbed soap against her cheeks. "The difference is that I actually have an interest in getting married. We both know why you don't."

Olivia paused, letting the suds fall from her chin. "You have no idea what you're talking about."

"Yes, I do. I've known you for all your life. You're afraid to let people see you—fully see you. And it's made a recluse out of you."

Olivia shook her head and splashed her face clean. She wasn't a recluse. She still had big dreams of getting out and seeing the world. She was young, she had plenty of time.

"Let him see you, Olivia. At least do that much. And if he never asks you out, then fine. But it won't be because you hid from him. Not this time."

She pressed a towel to her face and then reached for her moisturizer. "He can see me just fine. You're upset that he didn't fawn all over your charade tonight."

"That's only because he spent the whole night looking at *you*."

Olivia wrinkled her nose. "Goodnight, Caroline."

"Later, girl." Her voice was as sweet as the pastries they would sell tomorrow, distressed damsel nowhere to be found.

Call ended, Olivia smothered the last dollop of moisturizer into her birthmark. She let her fingertips linger over the tiny, moistened hairs and follow the inky outline that trailed up the side of her nose and ended at the edge of her right brow. She'd learned to embrace it—learned to make it her friend. It was a companion she didn't choose but wouldn't reject. Nobody could make her hate herself because of it, and nobody could convince her to hide in the shadows with it. But...

On days like this one, where she found herself face to face with a man like him, she couldn't stop the curiosity from eating her alive. Couldn't stop from asking what it would be like if she looked like everyone else. To have a kind, friendly, handsome man look at her with interest in his eyes because she was beautiful and unmarked.

"I trust Your plan for my life, Lord," she whispered.

If it wasn't in the cards, then there wasn't anything Olivia could do to change that. God created some people to remain unmarried until they reached Heaven. If that was her calling, she loved Jesus too much to fight Him on it.

Leaving her reflection, she flipped the light off, pulled her Bible from the desk sitting in the corner of her bedroom, and made her way across the braided rug to climb into the middle of her cozy bed. Surrounded by the pink and peach cabin quilt her mom had made her, she flipped open the floral cover of her Bible and let her eyes linger on the words.

Why had Peyton taken such a challenge in finding out about her dream jobs?

Not that it was important at all.

But there were only two types of people in her life: those who had already known her from a young age, and those who didn't care to know more about her. For someone to dive into her personal world where she was the only one who knew about her dreams was...different. Not unwelcomed, but also not easy for her to meet with an eager openness.

If she had known Peyton was staying longer than just the time it took to change her tire, she never would've mentioned the silly idea of dreams to begin with. But it had slipped out. And there was no taking it back. Not according to the challenge in his eyes as he drew them out of her one by one.

Olivia slid off the bed, bare feet sinking into the soft rug as she went to her desk drawer. It opened with a heavy pull, and she shuffled through a stack of notebooks to find her journal. She flipped it open and dumped out a number of folded sheets of paper—all of which held keys to her childhood. A regular sheet of notebook paper caught her attention. She gathered the rest, stuffing them inside the journal again and dropping it in the drawer that she pushed shut with her toes.

She unfolded the old, tired lines of the faded sheet of paper, pressing the frayed edges back and taking in the different types and textures of pen marks it had collected over the last decade or so. She was up to number seventy-four. Seventy-four dream jobs. Among them were "personal chef to a celebrity," "voice actress," and "conservationist in Africa."

A laugh broke through when she found one that said, "professional mermaid." Some of these needed a line drawn through them. She could no longer relate to the ten-year-old girl who had written that one down.

The list had always been a lighthearted hobby. Something that she could use to track all of her potential life experiences. A lot had changed over the years, but the desire to keep the list going was still strong. The last dream she'd written down was only a year or two old. "Cruise line director."

Her eyes followed the page to the top, where the five she'd promised to share with Peyton waited. They were five that she'd always loved the most—they were the most *her*. Baker, of course. Ice cream taste tester was number five and wasn't going anywhere soon. The two in between were just as silly as the rest, but number one...

Peyton didn't know it yet, but that was the one she wasn't sharing with him. With anybody. It was the most private, the most personal. It was *her* to her core. But he would never know about that one. Not even her family knew about it. Nor Caroline. It was hers to keep secret. She'd have to find some way to distract him from that one. While she couldn't bring herself to lie, maybe she could swap it with "professional mermaid." At least he wouldn't laugh as hard.

She thought to fold the sheet and stick it in the drawer, but there was an empty space on the wall behind her computer. So, she pulled the top drawer open where pens and paperclips slid around and grabbed the tape dispenser. She pulled off two short pieces and stuck the list to the wall. She smiled at the words that were like a time capsule of each chapter of her life, every dream capturing a different representation of her younger self.

Except for number one. That one had been her dream for as long as she could remember. Still was.

CHAPTER EIGHT

Golden morning light poured over the faraway trees lining the hill across from the cabin. On the passenger side of Daniel's truck, Peyton scrubbed the heel of his hand against his eye. Though sleep had come quicker than usual last night, thanks to Vern's tyranny, he still felt like a zombie.

"How'd Josh's little dog fair through the night?" Daniel asked, one hand on the steering wheel.

"Fine until about three AM when a possum found its way to the porch, and then Bear set off the alarm."

"Bear?" Daniel asked. "Does our mutt officially have a name?"

Peyton shrugged. "It's your call. I just thought he looked like a bear cub and went with it."

"Now that you mention it..." Daniel raised an eyebrow. "Bear it is. Josh will be over the moon that you gave 'im a name."

Speaking of Josh... "I wanted to let you know that I moved my firearm from my truck to the homestead, but it's unloaded, and the bullets are in an undisclosed location in case Josh ever happens across it."

"I appreciate that, but you won't have to worry about Josh. He won't go up there since he knows someone's living there. And he's trained in gun safety as much as we are."

Peyton nodded as Daniel drove through a wide gate that was hanging off one hinge, permanently open to the field of trees. Over a culvert that crossed a shallow ditch that was bone dry, the woods at the bottom of the hill parted ways and the Christmas trees were suddenly upon them.

Daniel parked and Peyton stepped out, the early morning

air filling his lungs.

Behind them, another truck parked and four men got out. Beyond that, the cabin sat on a hill that seemed further away than the thirty-second drive it took to get here. Sun beamed around the dark logs and through the tall windows. Peyton stopped at the bed of the truck where Daniel dropped the tailgate. He passed each man two machete-style knives, saving Peyton for last. But instead of a pair of knives, Peyton got some kind of contraption that reminded him of the equipment one of his catchers might have worn on their baseball team in college.

Daniel held up a long, durable piece of plastic fastened together with harnesses and dangling straps. "First time shearing trees, you'll need this."

Peyton took the thing. It was heavier than it looked.

"You're right-handed?"

Peyton nodded.

"Then it'll go on your right leg. This part..." He tapped the back of his knuckle on the smallest of the plastic pieces. "Goes over your knee and the rest of it covers your shin."

As the others gathered with their sword-sized knives near the first row of trees, Peyton couldn't help but feel like the kid who needed protective goggles and a nose piece while everyone else jumped straight into the pool. "Got it."

Once he had the piece strapped on, it didn't feel—or look—so bad. Though he wondered what kind of initiation he'd have to pass before he could go guardless like the others were. Daniel handed him only one knife. Peyton's shoulders fell.

"Do you know what kind of tree this is, Peyton?" Daniel said as Peyton followed him over to where the others stood.

The four-foot-tall tree had uneven, scraggly branches, but he couldn't deny the vision it evoked of being in someone's living room, covered in tinsel and candy canes. "A Christmas one?"

A couple of the men chuckled.

"It's a Virginia pine—a *Pinus virginiana*. It can grow up to twenty-four inches in a year, reaching maturity at about year four or five, depending on what our goal is for each tree."

Peyton leaned up on the tips of his shoes and fell back on

his heels, unsure of what any of this had to do with whacking away at limbs. But there was something in Daniel's voice that told him this was important. He needed to pay attention.

"It needs full sun, well-drained soil, and..." He kicked a pipe on the ground with the toe of his boot. "Irrigation."

"Since Vern's rain dances haven't been working lately."

"That's right." Daniel smirked and tilted his head toward the other men. They stepped into the trees and disappeared. "Shearing—which is what we're doing today—happens twice a year for these trees. Once in June and again in September if they need it."

He promptly swung one blade at an angle against the tree and the longest branches fell at his feet without complaint.

Peyton didn't stop the surprise from showing in his face. "That easy?"

Daniel cut a sideways look at him before swinging again. "Come back and ask me again after fifty trees."

Peyton chewed on the inside of his cheek, fighting a guilty grin. His shoulders were still sore from yesterday. Even if what they were doing looked a little like fun, he could see an ice pack and a couple painkillers in his near future.

"Stay with the natural angle of the tree," Daniel said. "You can see where it's already been sheared over the years and is starting to take that Christmas shape." He came around the other side of the tree and took one last swoop. The small branches fell to the ground in surrender, and there stood before them a perfect Christmas tree. Maybe a little shorter than what Peyton had imagined, but a Christmas tree, nonetheless.

Daniel tipped his head toward the tree next to it. "Give it a try."

Stretching his arm across his chest and feeling the bite of yesterday's work in his bicep, he walked up to the next tree with its wiry branches sticking out every direction. He sliced through the air with the same ease Daniel had demonstrated and the twigs fell to his feet. He did it again and again and again, making his way completely around, as instructed. On the last turn, one rebellious branch was left standing. Without missing a beat he raised the knife and sliced through the air, eliminating the limb. The blade came down at just the right angle to strike the hard plastic covering his leg.

He shared a wide-eyed look with Daniel. "That happens. Learned the hard way during my first shearing. After a few years you'll develop a rhythm to keep the blade away from your extremities."

A few years? Peyton huffed a laugh. He was still trying to survive today.

"Be mindful of the others around you. Don't get within their swing path and don't let them get within yours." Daniel swung his machete over the top of the tree and snapped off a wayward branch that was growing straight up.

With that, the man went to the next tree, swinging both blades in a pattern that would have been the stuff of nightmares if Peyton didn't know how nice the guy actually was. Peyton went in the opposite direction, following the row of trees across the front, closest to the cabin. He swung in easy motions, taking down unruly branches like they were outlaws rebelling against the natural order of the tree. Again and again, they surrendered in piles at his feet. He finished by swiping at the tallest branch at the top of the tree. Piece of cake.

Three hours, fifty trees, and a couple dozen accidental strikes against the guard on his leg later, the muscles in Peyton's arm screamed for relief. He'd been tempted a time or ten to switch the knife to his left hand, but he wasn't wearing a guard on that side. Nor was he left-handed. The image of the mess he'd make of himself had him clutching the knife solidly in his right hand. He swung again, tearing through the limbs.

"You're makin' good time for a greenhorn."

Peyton turned at the sound of Daniel's voice, letting his arm drop to his side. "Once you start to lose feeling in your fingers, it really becomes second nature."

Daniel rocked back on his heels, analyzing Peyton's work. "Not bad. You'll be a horticulturist before we know it."

"Gotta learn how to spell that first."

Daniel gestured to the wall of trees behind Peyton, untouched by his blade. "Let's call it a day. We'll get the rest of these on Monday."

Thank God. Peyton fell in line beside Daniel as they made

their way to the truck. Holding the blade in his left hand so the other one could get a break, Peyton admired the trees he'd sheared. Appreciation for his effort filled his chest. *Now* they looked ready for gifts and garland.

"Why trees?"

Daniel looked over at him.

"I know you said you were looking for a hobby to fill your time when you were starting a family. But what made you pick trees?"

Daniel was quiet for a moment, his focus surveying the land around them. "I was an only child and so was Gianna, so we never had anyone to spend Christmas with besides our parents, grandparents. When we met and eventually married, Christmas became our favorite holiday. Some of our best memories are from those early years when we spent Christmas together. So, when we were trying to figure out what to use the land for, it just...came to me. Grow our own Christmas trees. Haven't looked back."

"Have you ever considered starting a men's ministry out here?"

Daniel slowed for one step as if the suggestion had knocked him off-kilter. "A men's ministry?"

Peyton shrugged. "Kinda like a working ranch for men to come and do something different with their life for a weekend or two."

Daniel was quiet. Maybe it was a dumb idea. Peyton had no clue what it took to keep this place running from the inside.

All he knew is that the ranch had stirred something alive in him over the last two days. "It could be a place where they can talk about what God is up to and how they can get quiet with Him."

"Is that what you were doing while you were shearing trees?" Daniel glanced at him. "Getting quiet with God?"

"Didn't really have a choice," Peyton chuckled. "But I think it's something I needed."

At the truck Daniel dropped the tailgate. "I've never thought about it. Thanks, Peyton. I'll have to pray on that."

Peyton tossed his knife in the bed of the truck and started working on the straps of the guard. While they waited for the other men to join them, Daniel propped an elbow against the bed and stroked his goatee.

Inside the truck, Peyton didn't mind letting his back melt into the leather.

"A few of the men will stay on through the day to see to evening chores," Daniel said from behind the wheel. "You're free to help out if you want, or catch up on some sleep, or spend the afternoon checking out the town with Caroline."

Peyton turned his head slowly, catching sight of the smirk Daniel wore. "If those are my options, I don't mind mucking stalls for the rest of the day."

Daniel laughed.

At the barn, Peyton followed the men inside where Vern was already waiting with a few others in the meeting area near the staircase.

"Good work, men." Daniel took his place front and center of everyone and gestured to a tray of cookies on the table that the men were already sampling from. "Those aren't gonna eat themselves."

Nobody had to tell Peyton twice. This morning's hashbrowns and bacon had long worn off. He took two cookies that were still warm to the touch and tucked one in his mouth as he returned to where Vern was standing at the back of the group.

It melted in his mouth and pulled a groan from his chest. "Boss, what'd you do to get a woman who cooks as good as your wife to fall in love with you? I need some advice for future reference."

A few quiet chuckles spread throughout the men.

Daniel picked up a stack of papers hanging off the edge of the table. "Olivia made those," he muttered. "Men who are staying for evening chores..."

As Daniel launched into a speech, Peyton turned and paced a few steps away from the group, swallowing his pride.

"Didn't think that one through, did ya?" Vern said quietly with a sly smirk.

"No, I did not." Peyton stuffed the second cookie in his mouth.

"All right, men. See you all Monday, seven AM sharp," Daniel concluded with a single nod.

The men turned and started moving in different

directions. A few stood behind, talking. Daniel headed for the east end of the barn, and Vern disappeared into a stall. Peyton spun around and headed west where his truck was parked, opting for the afternoon of sleep Daniel had mentioned a few minutes ago.

A black horse stuck his head over the first stall, stopping Peyton in his tracks. It huffed, as if to say, 'Pet me.' So, with slow, steady movements, he reached out and ran his hand along the horse's nose. The same horse, he realized, Daniel had ridden out into the pasture yesterday evening. It stared at Peyton with eyes that told him the creature was probably a lot smarter than he was.

When was the last time he'd seen a horse up close? Had to be his ninth-grade field trip to the animal sanctuary. The animal dipped his head and nodded, as if he approved of Peyton's affection. Maybe he'd make it a point to stop by this stall more often.

Rowdy laughter echoed through the corridor from where a few of the men dawdled near the stairway. The horse stepped back, lifting his chin over the stall and out of Peyton's reach.

"Before I head out, lemme get a few more of these cookies that Lackluster Livy made," one of the cowboys said.

Like a bolt of lightning hit the ground beside him, Peyton's blood went hot. He stepped out away from the wall as the one they called Stu picked up the cookies.

"What'd you call her?"

Stu sobered, his smile fading and then returning just as quickly. He looked Peyton over from his shoes to his head. "Lackluster Livy. That's what she was called in high school." He lifted one shoulder. "What's it to you?"

"Does Daniel know you talk about his daughter that way?"

Stu's smirk disappeared altogether. "It's Daniel, is it? The rest of us call him Mr. Whitmore." He looked over Peyton again. "I guess that makes you the chosen one, doesn't it?"

The man's insult wouldn't find a place to land. Peyton stayed where he was, unwilling to start anything he'd have to finish with his fists. "Her name's Olivia."

With slow, meticulous steps, Stu closed the distance, stopping a few inches away. "Whatever you say, boss."

In the dark waves where Jesus walked, Olivia checked her reflection, hair gathered in a French twist with a claw clip. It was only her family going on the hike—she'd overheard Dad telling Josh—so she was free to wear her hair out of her face. Not that she wasn't free any other time. But if Peyton had been coming along...

In the glass, she caught sight of a man walking past the living room windows behind her. On socked feet, she spun around as the patio door opened, and Peyton stepped inside. His eyes landed on her and the upward tilt of his chin told her he'd found something he'd been looking for.

"Good morning," he said, shoving his hands in his pockets.

She pressed her lips together to keep from giggling. "Good afternoon."

"That, too." He either chuckled or cleared his throat—she couldn't tell which. "Are you going on the hike?"

"Yeah." She squinted. "Are you?"

"Yeah." He rocked back on his heels.

"Good." She wasn't sure why that was her first response.

"Good," he echoed. He turned and walked out the same way he'd come in, leaving Olivia frozen in place.

What just happened?

Why did her dad think he wasn't coming? Was Peyton doing family activities with them for the rest of the summer? Had her parents really adopted him?

She turned to the picture of Jesus and pulled a long strand of hair out of her clip, letting it hang down the right side of her face. "There."

An hour later, she held tight to the straps hanging over her shoulders, shrugging her backpack into a more comfortable position as she followed her family through evergreen woods. Dad and Pepaw guided the group, hauling fishing poles and tackle, respectively. Josh and Peyton weren't far behind, kitchen supplies and snacks in their backpacks. And Olivia walked beside Mom whose backpack carried food for a campfire supper, while Olivia's held the first aid kit, water, and basic necessities. Up ahead, leading the pack was Mutt, bat-shaped ears perked high on his little head.

Mulch and leaves crunched underfoot. Sunshine dimmed behind branches shaking with celebration that the Whitmore family had finally made time to visit. It wasn't long before they were deep enough that the birds were singing openly, the bugs flying freely, and if they were lucky, a chipmunk or two might feel comfortable enough to cross their path.

Olivia filled her lungs with a deep breath of the same air she'd walked through no less than a hundred times over the course of her twenty-two years. It was her essence, her very being. These woods were in her DNA by now. She knew this path like she knew her own heart. She'd worn out its adventure until it became a second home. Vacations were great when she could manage to get away, but nothing soothed her like Hill Country woods could.

Her eyes found Peyton up ahead, walking alongside her brother as they talked about the likeliness of finding dinosaur bones.

What was he seeing for the first time? How did these surroundings look to a newcomer? Was he noticing the different shades of green that danced in the wind as the sun glistened through the leaves? Did he see the fox trails at the edge of the path, sneaking under the shrubs? Did he catch the spiny lizard that raced up a vine as they walked by? Did he see speckled songbirds swooping over the route up ahead?

Did he care?

"Hey, what happens if we see a wild animal—like the kind that can eat us?" Peyton said, loud enough for the entire group to hear.

"Now, what kind of animal d'you think's hungry enough to eat a family of six?" Pepaw griped over his shoulder.

Family of six? Olivia snorted.

"I mean, it probably wouldn't eat all of us. It'll definitely get Josh, though." Peyton bumped Josh with his hip and Josh shoved back. "Like, are their lions and tigers and bears out here?"

Pepaw turned a smirk on Peyton. "Scared?"

"'Course not. Just wondering which ones to look out for

in case I need to outrun the group."

"One thing's for sure, Peyton," Dad called out over his shoulder. "We have eyes watching all over these woods." He pointed up ahead to a tree hollow hovering some ten feet off the ground and the racoon sitting in it. His lazy masked eyes watched their approach. Mutt noticed the little bandit, too, and let out a high-pitched howl, his legs stiff with aggression.

"Chill, Bear," Peyton said as he passed the dog. "He's got a right to be here."

"You called him Bear?" Josh asked and nodded thoughtfully. "Yeah, he kinda does look like a bear. Hey, Olivia, doesn't Mutt look like a bear?"

She looked down at the little dog who was now sniffing through a pile of leaves as she passed him. With his dark coloring and course fur and rounded snout, she could see how he might get mistaken for a bear cub. "He sure does."

"Bear, let's go." Josh tested the name out and the dog picked up the pace, racing to catch up with Josh and Peyton. "I like it!"

When the pines and oaks parted ways, a tract of overgrown Christmas trees came into view. Their elevated peaks let sunlight splash in patches across the straw-covered ground underfoot, streaming rays like waterfalls through the air where motes and insects floated. If there was any place more captivating on earth then Olivia wanted to judge it for herself, because this...

"Whoa," Peyton mumbled, mirroring the same awe that Olivia felt inside as she came to stand beside him.

"These were our first year of trees," Dad said as he brushed his hand along the low branches of a Cyprus. "We chose this location because it was out of the way, and we didn't expect to fall in love with the way the rows looked on the hills."

Peyton walked over and mimicked Dad's gesture, running his hand across the needles that Olivia knew were soft to the touch.

"Once we relocated, we decided what was left of this lot we'd let go wild and free."

"Wild and free," Peyton echoed.

Olivia turned in a slow circle, admiring the crooked rows

and soaring heights, but she could hardly pull her attention from Peyton's fascination. His smile wide, his eyes searched out the tops of the trees, like a kid discovering adventure for the first time.

Without warning, he dropped his focus and looked right at her.

"C'mon, Peyton!" Josh ran between them and disappeared inside the thicket.

Olivia followed, nervous that Peyton would read too much into her observation of him. She'd only been watching his reaction out of pure inspiration, honest. As the cypress and cedar branches reached out and brushed her shoulders, she found her way through the overgrown maze to the sprawling oak that lay at the edge of the tract.

The gnarled trunk reached out like the muscled arms of an octopus, stretching in every direction and begging to be climbed. As always, Josh was already walking along one of the lowest branches, arms balanced at his sides and his backpack discarded on the ground. Peyton passed her, dropping his beside Josh's and stepping up on the limb without hesitation. Together, they tested out the branches, scaled the higher ones, and made their way toward the trunk.

"Not going up?" Dad asked, standing near the Christmas trees with Mom and Pepaw.

"Not this time." She squinted up at the tallest branches waving in the wind.

"Can't imagine why." The sarcastic cord in Pepaw's voice sounded oddly suspicious.

The last thing she needed was for her family to think she had some kind of a complex about her dad's new employee. Who just happened to be doing every single family activity with them over the last two days. That would be insane.

Over her shoulder, she sent Pepaw a glare. He lifted his shoulders with a "humph."

Fine. She would show them. Sliding the straps of her backpack off each shoulder, she let it fall to the grass. She turned to the oak to find an outstretched hand waiting for her. Peyton stood on the lowest limb, his eyes lit with amusement.

She placed her hand in his—his touch firm but patient—

and let him aid her step up. Then withdrew the moment she gained her footing. She'd climbed this tree all her life—she was no damsel in distress. With her arms extended on either side she worked her way up the forked branches. Bark and moss fell where her shoes scuffed the tree, peppering Bear down below as he tracked the scents of critters with his nose to the ground.

Where the limbs met the trunk, Olivia pulled herself up on a higher branch and took a seat, stretching out her legs in front of her and crossing one ankle over the other. No sooner had she gone still than a blue butterfly flitted across her path and landed on the tip of her shoe. She smiled, taking in the intricate design on its pulsing wings. If not for the clip holding her hair, she'd lean back and enjoy a quick nap. She settled for closing her eyes and taking in the fresh air instead.

"Look what I found, Olivia!" Josh said, suddenly at her side.

She opened her eyes to a lizard hanging mercilessly between Josh's fingers, it's red dewlap expanding angrily.

"Would you look at him," she said, reaching out and tracing its tail with her fingertip.

"Hey, you wanna help me look for a kissin' bug for my collection?"

"What's a kissin' bug?" Peyton asked, suddenly on her other side, arms wavering as he gained his balance.

"It's a *bad* bug that bites you and gives you diseases," Josh clued him in.

Peyton's eyes shifted to Josh without moving his head. "And we want to catch one?"

Josh's head bobbed up and down. "For my collection."

"Those are nocturnal, Josh," Olivia said. "You'll have to wait 'till night."

"Hey, kids," Dad called out. "We're gonna head out to the lake. Y'all all right to catch up to us?"

Peyton leaned both arms against the section of branch where Olivia's legs rested. "Sounds good. We're gonna catch bugs."

Chuckling, the three of them started toward the path as Pepaw waved one hand in the air like he wasn't the least bit concerned about their safety.

Josh set the lizard free on a nearby branch and made a grand leap to the ground. At his backpack, he crashed to his knees and started riffling through—retrieving his killing jars, no doubt.

"I heard you're an expert bug catcher." Peyton rested his chin on his arms, peeking up at her.

Olivia rolled her eyes until they landed on her little brother who radiated joy. "Has he been sharing my secrets again?"

"A few," he said. "But he hasn't shared the one about your dream job yet."

She wrinkled her nose. "He doesn't know about that one, so it would be a miracle if you got it out of him."

"What about you? What's it gonna take to get it out of you?"

She pulled in a deep breath and considered the branches above her for a moment. "Ten million dollars."

He made a low whistle. "I'm not sure where I'm gonna get that kind of money, but I'll work on it."

She couldn't help but laugh as Josh made his way back to them, clutching a handful of small nets. "Here. I got each of us one."

Both pockets bulged with small jars packed with paper towels that were damp with acetone, meant to suffocate whatever bug caught Josh's fancy. Once he delivered their nets, he turned and hopped out of the oak, sprinting toward the woods. "Let's see if we can find a longhorn beetle!"

As Olivia turned and slid her legs off the edge of the branch, Peyton was ducking under it and balancing on the one she was about to drop down to. He tucked his net into his back pocket and held one hand out for her. She took it as she slid off the side, dislodging shards of bark on her way down. "I've been climbing trees since I was a toddler, you know."

He stepped off the limb and dropped to the ground below. "I figured," he said, squinting up at her. "And it just so happens that I've been chivalrous since I was a toddler."

She couldn't help but laugh. But it was quickly cut short when he reached up with both hands to help her down. She swallowed the concern of having him feel her middle and realize she was no dainty woman. As his grip found her waist—with a composure that wasn't surprised by her width—she braced her hands against his shoulders. He set her on the ground with unanticipated ease, as if lifting curvy women were a hobby of his. The moment her feet were on the ground, she started after Josh.

What were they looking for again? Oh, yeah. Longhorn beetles. Right.

She pushed past the soft leaves of a sumac bush and tried to focus. She knew what kind of bugs Josh liked, but she hoped she wouldn't have to make a spectacle of herself by chasing one through the wild. Bear trotted past them to catch up with Josh just as she caught sight of an inchworm hanging from a silk thread. Only a couple inches from her face, she threw on the brakes.

Peyton bumped into her, his hands suddenly on her arms.

Olivia couldn't help the nervous laugh that slipped from her as she pointed to the wiggling little thing. "Sorry. I didn't want to ruin his escape route."

He moved one hand to the small of her back and reached out past her, grabbing the thread. He slowly lifted the tiny guy until he was planted on a nearby leaf. She must have worn a look of bewilderment on her face because he winked once before he continued on.

Who was this man?

Olivia gave her head a quick shake and stepped over a fallen log.

"I'm not sure what I'm looking for," Peyton said, eyes scanning their environment. "Warn me if I cross paths with a kissin' bug, will you?"

She chewed on the inside of her cheek. "Don't worry. It's not painful—you won't even know you've been bitten."

He stopped in his tracks, falling behind as she peeked inside the hollow of a tree for any waiting insects. Empty.

"Olivia! I got one!" Josh yelled.

Up ahead, he had something pinned down with his net, Bear growling and squaring up with the bug like he was there to make sure it cooperated. She made her way over as Josh slipped the lid off one of his jars. He shimmied the net over the glass and dumped a Hercules beetle inside. Olivia crouched down to get a better look.

The little green bug landed upside down, its legs working to right itself. "Wow, that's a big one."

"*Yeah* it is!" Josh drawled as he spun the lid on the jar and tucked it back in his pocket, wasting no time returning to his hunt.

Olivia rose slowly, her eyes following him through the brush.

"He adores you," Peyton said, a step behind and a lot closer than she'd expected him to be. He was on her left, so she didn't bother to turn away.

"I adore him."

"Do you ever wish your parents had adopted more?"

She shrugged as she started walking again. "Sometimes, yeah. But at the end of the day, I know God designed our family how He wants it, so it's not something I complain about." She could sense he was close behind. "What about you? Do you wish your parents had had more kids?"

"Uh...yeah. Kinda."

Something in his voice had her checking over her shoulder at him. He rubbed the back of his neck as he looked over the ground with a careful eye.

"*Uh. Yeah. Kinda,*" she mimicked in a bored voice, drawing a smile from him. "Sounds like there's a story there."

He lifted one shoulder. "Not so much a story. Just a few lonely years when I was a kid that made me wish I had more than one sibling."

She nodded. He had a brother, she remembered. One who'd been older than him and a cop. "When your brother left for the police training?"

His eyes found her then, a look of casual surprise mixed with innocence rested there, and for a moment she regretted mocking his answer.

"No, it wasn't for training." He started looking for rogue bugs again as if a shadow of a memory hadn't just passed over his face. "He, uh...left. When he was eighteen. He was going through a lot back then and he needed to start fresh."

Eighteen? Which meant if Peyton was ten years younger...

"I spent a while playing in the treehouse by myself." His throat shifted where he swallowed. "So, it would have been nice to have another brother...or a twin." He grinned, peeking up at her.

"I get that. I was fourteen when they adopted my brother." Olivia straightened and turned. "Wait—where is Josh?"

"He's right there," Peyton moved closer and lifted the net in his hand, gesturing through the greenery to where Josh hunted something with wings, and Bear was tiptoeing behind him like a faithful gun dog.

She breathed easy. "I grew up with Caroline. We've known each other since we were babies, but he was the best friend I didn't know I needed."

Silence stretched on and Josh sprinted out of sight. Before she followed after him, she looked at Peyton to find him watching her with a smirk.

"What?"

His smirk vanished and he shook his head. "Nothing."

Okay...She took a step in Josh's direction, but Peyton's hand was on her arm, holding her in place. He pointed the net toward the treetops. "Josh isn't gonna want me to catch that one, is he?"

She followed his focus to a banana spider that was no smaller than the top of a paint can, hanging from a web at least a dozen feet in the air. Olivia shuttered. "If we don't let him see it then we won't have to find out."

Fishing line zipped through the air and plopped through the surface of the water as Daniel checked over his shoulder for the hundredth time. The path from the oak to the pond was a thick one, but his kids had taken it dozens of times on their own. There was nothing different about this time. He could stop worrying.

He told himself again.

Daniel set the line and started reeling in slowly, adding a gentle lurch every so often. It wasn't that he worried they'd get lost or that Peyton was a threat, though still a stranger to them all. But the trees around them were unpredictable and held unpredictable wildlife that he didn't want any of his kids to face alone. While Josh was a pro at handling anything that crawled, slithered, or flew, and Olivia was a crack shot up against any target, neither one of them had ever faced down a predator without him by their side.

Lions and tigers and bears. Peyton's earlier question pulled a quiet chuckle from Daniel. But Texas had its own version with mountain lions, bobcats, and black bears. Daniel sobered.

Something tugged on his line. He eased up on the reel and waited for the anticipated jolt. Behind him, laughter echoed through the trees and eased the tension in his shoulders.

Even if it did cause him to lose his catch.

He doubled his speed and reeled the rest of the line in as he looked over his shoulder again, this time to find his two kids plus Peyton stepping out into the evening sunshine. Bear sprinted past them all. "Run into any trouble?"

Peyton's eyes held wonder as he looked out across the water, sliding the backpack off his shoulders. "Just a family of anxious chipmunks."

His kids' giggles mingled with his wife's from where she fished a couple dozen yards to Daniel's right.

"Oh, wow," Peyton mumbled as he came closer.

Daniel readied his line, watching to be sure the kid didn't come too close as he let it fly again.

"Hill Country has no right to be this beautiful," he said.

Daniel scanned the water that reflected a blue sky up to the bank on the other side where towering trees climbed a hill. Nearby was a knoll that bloomed the most beautiful bluebonnets anyone could ask for during peak season. And beyond that, a patch of sandy shore that was as relaxing as any beach he'd ever visited.

"When you said y'all were hiking to the lake, I wasn't aware that you owned it," Peyton said as he raised one eyebrow.

"Technically speaking. But it's one of the smallest in the state. And I've no doubt it's been demoted to pond in this drought. See that waterline back there?" He gestured to the dusty, foot-tall ledge that met the overgrown grass. "Supposed to be the bank."

"Every part of this ranch I visit leaves me speechless."

Daniel readied his line to cast again. "Any good fishin' in

Austin?"

"I hear there is, but I've never actually fished in the city. My grandparents own a plot of land in New Mexico and my brother and I would spend summers up there. That's where we fished. Hunted. Told scary stories around the campfire."

Daniel smiled.

"That's where I was headed before I landed here."

"It's a change of pace, for sure."

Peyton walked a few steps closer to the water's edge, his shoes stopping shy of the lapping waves. "Something like that."

Silence fell for the length it took Daniel to cast again.

"Life started feeling monotonous in the city," he said with a sigh.

"That happens."

Peyton nodded. "Everything felt lifeless all of a sudden. My house. My job. The drive to my parent's place every Friday night. Even church started feeling dull."

Daniel felt a tug on the line. He fought every ancestor in his body begging him to set the hook. But he resisted, holding out instead for whatever Peyton wanted to say.

"No offense."

"Hmm?" Daniel hummed, afraid he'd missed something other than the fish.

Peyton glanced over his shoulder and shook his head. "I don't mean to sound disrespectful about church."

Oh. "None taken. Sometimes it can get that way. Going through the motions without putting your heart in it. You start to feel like there has to be something more."

Staring at the ground in front of him, he nodded. "Yes."

"Like you know God is there and He is who He said He is, but you start to question if He's enough if this is all there is to life."

He turned slowly, as if Daniel's words were a magnet pulling him in. "Exactly."

Daniel cast again, for nothing more than the appearance, the anticipation of fishing lost on him. "And you want nothing more than to move, to experience a change of scenery, hoping that maybe it's your perception tripping you up."

Peyton finally looked up at him. "I guess you've been

here, too, huh?"

"Once or twice." Or a few hundred times. He pulled in a long breath and filled his lungs with fresh air. "Peyton, I think it's time you learn about the wild side of God's heart."

The kid leaned forward a fraction. "Come again?"

Daniel nodded gently. "You heard right."

"God has a wild side?"

Daniel smirked. "What do you think wild means?"

His eyes looked left and then right. "Rebellious. Crazy. Defiant."

"Wild means free, Peyton." Daniel lifted his hook out of the water and straightened the dripping wet lure. "It means untamable, unburdened, unrelenting." He looked the kid in his confused eyes. "All aspects of God's heart."

"Wild and free," he said, echoing Daniel's earlier sentiment.

"That freedom is what makes salvation attainable. Otherwise, we're still slaves to sin and we can't get out of it on our own." The zip of the line whistled as Daniel cast again. "Praise God that He *is* wild. Imagine if you served a god who was limited to the world's rules and restrictions and regulations." Daniel huffed a laugh. "Imagine if it were possible to tame Christ's love and convince Him to avoid the cross. That's not God, son."

"I get where you're coming from." He crossed his arms, hugging one bicep, and watched the line.

"There's a talk that every dad should give his boy when he's young and learning life the hard way, about becoming a man."

Peyton swiped one hand over his mouth and massaged his chin. "My dad left when I was a kid, and he was never really...*emotionally available* back then."

Daniel had figured. "Then allow me to give it."

Peyton dipped his head.

"The wild side of the heart is where we meet God. The part that's unwilling to live inside a box, unwilling to settle for the status quo. The part that might look a little peculiar to the world."

Daniel couldn't help the grin that tugged at his lips. "The wild side is what caused Jacob to wrestle the Living God. Caused David to dance before Him with all his might. Led

Joshua to fight battles for Him that couldn't have been won under worldly circumstances. It's what made a murderer named Saul surrender his name to God Almighty.

"You see, these men had wild hearts. Hearts that weren't content to conform to a subdued and colorless world. There's nothing normal or conventional about signing up to suffer, yet they wanted to stand before God even if it cost them." He looked over at Peyton. "You can't get that kind of passion from a nine-to-five job and a thirty-year mortgage."

Peyton's throat shifted where he swallowed.

"Men are made in the wild, son. When isolation becomes the only choice and we realize there's nobody coming to save us. It's up to us to seek the Savior for the strength to survive, for the strength to carry our families. It's during those quiet, patient moments that we discover who we are and what we're made of. Until we reach that point, we're just boys with a bunch of best friends and big ideas."

Peyton nodded repeatedly as if he were letting the words settle over his thoughts.

"God's love for us is wild, Peyton. The world can't compete with it. That's why we're always looking for satisfaction. And we won't find it in the hustle. It's only found when we get quiet with God. When we get still with Him."

The kid looked out across the water again, his shoulders rising as he took in a breath. Daniel prayed his words were the right ones and would guide Peyton to whatever he was searching for.

He cleared his throat. "If I were to take a walk right now, how lost will I get?"

Daniel tipped his head to the woods. "Go ahead. We'll send up a flare if you're not back by sunset."

Smiling, Peyton shoved his hands in his pockets and started in the direction of the treeline.

Daniel reeled his line in for the last time and set the hook on the keeper.

Josh darted out in front of him. "Hey, Peyton! You wanna go look for—"

"Whoa," Daniel said as he gently tugged his son to a halt. "Why don't we give Peyton a minute to explore on his own for a bit. Sometimes a man needs to get still with the Wild."

Josh peeked over his shoulder and then looked up at Daniel with a scrunched nose. "What's that mean?"

Daniel pulled in deep breath and smiled. "Well, son. There's a talk that every dad should give his boy when he's young..."

CHAPTER NINE

An orange sunset hovered beneath a blue and pink sky beyond the faraway hills as dusk settled. Seated on the ground and leaning back against a fallen cedar, Olivia breathed in the earthy scent of lake water and relished in the crackling of the campfire behind her. Mom and Dad prepped the supplies for supper while Pepaw cleaned the fish they'd caught. Josh giggled at something Peyton said, and Bear ran along the bank in front of her, snapping at a grasshopper that kept flying out of his reach.

Olivia tipped her face up to the ever-darkening sky hanging over her. A few stars glittered as the last of the lavender clouds moved toward the horizon. She breathed deep and let the troubles of life fade away.

"Watch this, Pepaw!" Josh called out as he walked along the other end of the cedar like it was a balance beam. He passed behind Olivia and jumped off the edge into the dirt.

"Watch this, Pepaw!" Peyton echoed, stepping up on the tree and following her brother's path.

"Give 'em heck, Army," Pepaw yelled from where he sat on an old stump near the fire, arms crossed and eyes tired.

Peyton made his way across and stopped just short of Olivia. Instead of leaping through the air in grand fashion like her brother did, he dropped down beside her and took a seat on her left. Legs bent, he rested his forearms on his knees. "Wanna come catch fireflies with me and Josh later?"

Before she laughed, she checked his expression to see how serious he was. He raised one eyebrow, waiting for an answer. She snorted. He was having far too much fun for someone who was supposedly twenty-six. "Sure. Have you ever caught fireflies before?"

He leaned forward a fraction, his eyes focused squarely on her. "Not since I was seven, but it's gotta be like riding a bike, right?"

The intensity of his gaze had her turning back toward the sunset that was a few minutes away from fading. "I don't see why not. Gotta be fast, though."

"I'm fast. Didn't you see me and Josh racing earlier?"

She glanced at him, grinning at the reminder. He inched forward again—his attention entirely too riveted with her face. "What are you looking at?"

"Just trying to see your beauty mark."

"I'm not really comfortable with—" Her train of thought was suddenly derailed. "What did you call it?"

He shrugged one shoulder, his eyebrows lifting in the middle. "Beauty...mark?"

She threw her head back and let out a single laugh. "I've never heard anyone call it that before. That's a first."

"That's always what my family called it. My mom, really. A birthmark on a woman is called a beauty mark."

Her chest warmed at the sentiment. That was actually kind of...sweet. "You've got a good mom."

"I do." He nodded confidently, then gave a slow blink. "Can I see it?"

Nobody—*nobody*—had ever asked to see her birthmark up close. "Are you serious?"

"Absolutely."

"Why?" She shook her head.

"I think it's cool."

"Are you crazy? This isn't cool. This is a nightmare."

He leaned away as if her words were bullets aimed for him. She hadn't meant to sound so abrasive. This was new territory for her.

Rolling her eyes, she pushed a frustrated sigh out of her lungs. "But if you really want to, then just brace yourself because it's not pretty."

She tucked the fallen strands of hair behind her ear, twisted her head so that he had an unobstructed view, and ignored the crazy urge to run all the way back to the farm the moment he slid closer. He was inches away, staring as if she were a riddle he had to figure out before the last rays of golden sunlight disappeared behind the horizon. With her chin pressed against her shoulder, she dared not wonder if her family was watching.

At what point would he finish his observation? When he realized that the mark was covered in small, disgusting hairs? When he noticed that the skin was textured and puckered beneath the shadowy outline? When he saw how truly big it was when she wasn't hiding it behind her hair?

Would he regret looking?

She cut her eyes to his face, only to find him already looking at hers. She'd never been this close to a boy before. Not since the sixth grade—she swallowed the memory of that day. His navy blue depths held captive something inside of her that she couldn't explain. A smile teased her lips the same time a grin crawled across his.

"You can breathe now, Olivia," he whispered, his breath tickling her jaw.

A stubborn giggle spilled out as she turned back to the sunset that dipped behind the hills. She gathered herself and chewed on the inside of her cheek.

"What dream are we on?" he asked without scooting away or putting space between them.

She took it as a sign that he wasn't, nor would he ever be, disgusted by her birthmark. And something about that granted her permission to just be. "Why are you determined to get those answers out of me?"

"I've never met someone with so many dreams before. For a person like me who never really had any, I'm inspired."

Mm-hmm. She squinted sideways at him. Dream number four was harmless to share. It was truly one of her favorites. "Ride verification technician."

His eyebrows drew together in the middle. "Sounds like something you have to go to school for."

"You do—actually, it's an engineering job. Which is why it's number four, but..." She wrapped her hands around her knees and swayed forward and backward. "Ride techs get to test out all of the roller coasters at theme parks and fairs." She held one finger out. "I would only test out water coasters, though. Roller coasters are fine, but I love swimming and being in the water, so it sounds the most fun to me. If I ever got the chance, I would one hundred percent volunteer to test out a water coaster for free."

He let out a long breath of air through puffed cheeks. "I've never been a fan of roller coasters. The heights are..." He shook his head. "I'm the one you see walking around the park with cotton candy and silly straw glasses."

The image pulled a giggle from her chest. "Okay, then what would you do? What's your fourth dream job?"

"Stuntman," he said without hesitation.

She frowned thoughtfully. "Interesting. Like for the movies?"

"Movies. Broadway. Crash test dummy."

She tilted her head. "Why that one?"

"I like being active and moving and running."

She was sure there was a lot more to that job. "And what if one of your gigs wants you to jump out of a plane?"

He took on a faraway look. "On second thought, maybe I'll be a personal trainer. They keep their feet on the ground, I heard."

"I hear that, too." Olivia couldn't help but smile.

Out across the sky reflecting on the glassy sheen of the water, gentle ripples moved over the surface. "Y'know, whenever I see the wind move like that, I can't help but think that's what it must've looked like when the Bible says that the Spirit of God moved upon the face of the waters."

"Mmm," he hummed deeply as if she'd just given a sermon and it had landed in some place of importance.

She reached out and with her fingers mimicked the way the wind touched down on the water. "Like He's right there, watching us and the only thing we can see is the water reacting to Him."

Peyton nodded, appreciation reflecting in his eyes as he shared a glance with her. "Like even the water knows to reverence His presence."

"Exactly." Olivia studied him for a second. "You know what I mean?"

"I know what you mean," he whispered.

Warmth spread through her chest as she returned her gaze to the water. That was a pleasant exchange. He didn't ask her to explain herself or think her silly. He wasn't looking for a reason to change the subject or go in search of something more interesting. Comfortable silence wrapped around them and Olivia rested her shoulders against the tree behind her.

Over the lake, a bald eagle swooped low, soaring with an incredible wingspan until it's talons dipped into the water and snagged a fish. As quickly as it had come, it disappeared into the trees. She looked at Peyton, hoping he'd seen it, too, only to find the same look of shock in his smile as he turned to her. Together, they shared a laugh.

Peyton reached out and started unlacing his tennis shoes. "So, you like spending time in the water?"

"Love it. Every summer Josh and I visit the..." Her words faded when he pulled one sock off and tucked it in his shoe. "You're not going swimming, are you?"

He frowned, shrugging. "Is it safe?"

"Umm...it is. It's just late and..."

He rolled the hem of his jeans up around his ankles. "Let's go."

Her smile fell. "I'm not going for a swim."

He gave her a sideways look. "You're not?"

It didn't sound like a question—it sounded like a threat.

Surely, he wouldn't.

Peyton pushed himself off the ground, crossed the few yards of damp soil, and stepped into the murky water that lapped gently against the bank. He didn't stop there. He kept walking until the rolled hem of his jeans were submerged. Then his shins. Then his knees. He turned around and scooped a handful of water, tossing it in her direction. Thick drops peppered her as she screeched. "What do you think you're doing?"

He laughed a quick, amused chuckle.

Behind her, Josh cheered. "Mom, can I go swimming, too?"

"Only if you want to walk back to the farm soaking wet," Mom said.

Josh took that as an affirmative and kicked off his shoes. He tugged each sock on the way to the water's edge, leaving a trail of shoes and socks behind him. He sprinted against the tiny waves and kicked as hard as he could, splashing Peyton in the process.

Peyton stood with his arms wide at his side, water dripping from his hands. "Josh, I thought we were a team, buddy! We're supposed to go after your sister."

"Yeah!" Josh spun around and smacked his hands against the water, sending more sprinkles through the air.

The cool drops landed on her hair and trickled down her neck. "The two of y'all can make the walk back all wet, but I won't be joining you."

Grinning, Peyton raised one eyebrow. He wouldn't drag her in, would he?

"You're only young once," Pepaw mumbled.

She didn't want to give Peyton a chance to sweep her off her feet and discover her full weight. So, she took off her shoes and socks, pulled the clip from her hair, and followed them into the water. She dipped both hands and managed to shower each one of them with a handful of lake water.

That action triggered a splashing riot as squeals and yelps filled the air around them. Even her parents' chuckles reached her ears over the sloshing. Josh kicked, sending a spray across her face and eyes. She let out a scream and cupped both hands together, enough to drench him and gain a gasping smile beneath the water that dripped from his nose and chin.

Peyton was next. She pivoted and splashed in his direction. He stepped just out of its reach and returned fire. It was a failed attempt, but with the lake at his back, he had nowhere to go. So, she doubled down with another scoop of water and sent it higher. The wave landed on her target, and he released a rich laugh.

Content that she'd gotten revenge on both of them, Olivia fought a grin.

But the look in his eyes told her Peyton was interested in the challenge. He came closer and she rushed for the bank. But he was too fast, too strong against the weight of the water. He splashed again, causing her to close her eyes, and when she did, he snaked his arms around her middle, his chest to her back.

Josh burst into a series of maniacal giggles at her plight. Peyton lifted her as if every worry she'd ever had about her weight never existed. She pushed, but his arms held tight as he fell backward into the water, taking her with him. Everything went dark and the urge to laugh had to wait until she gained her footing and stood. Peyton laughed, too, as he stood, water dripping from his hair and over his lashes.

"Nobody said anything about dunking." With one burning eye closed, she put her hands against his shoulders and shoved, not surprised when he didn't budge. She didn't think he would.

But she had a secret weapon. Wiping her fingers against her eyes, she regained her vision. "Josh, if you join *my* team, then tomorrow I'll make you some strawberry cream puffs...dipped in chocolate," she added for good measure.

Peyton closed his eyes and groaned. "Do you promise?"

Olivia giggled and Josh didn't hesitate. He waded over to Peyton and wrapped his arms around Peyton's waist, gritting his teeth as he attempted to bring the grown man down. Peyton grunted, struggling against Josh's attack—an act, obviously. Josh repositioned himself, reaching for Peyton's arms instead. Peyton chuckled as he bent low, put his shoulder against Josh's, and pushed.

Hair stuck to her face and eyes blurry with lake grit, Olivia stilled.

Peyton wasn't putting on an act. He was meeting Josh's energy and giving her brother something to wrestle with in his own strength. The fighting paused for a heartbeat or two as Peyton explained to Josh where to leverage Peyton's weight against himself. Josh followed the instructions, forcing Peyton to stumble backwards. Peyton caught his balance before plunging beneath the water and nodded proudly at Josh's effort.

In this moment, Peyton wasn't a stranger who worked for her dad. He was the big brother she and Josh never had.

This day would end, and everything might very well go back to the way it was, but for now Peyton was creating memories that Josh wouldn't soon forget. Both boys chuckled as they went up against each other again. Theirs was a dynamic Olivia couldn't give Josh. Catching bugs and playing pranks were the best she could do for him. And while she knew Josh loved every second of their relationship, having a brother-figure to just be a boy with was something she didn't realize he needed until this moment.

Olivia retreated until she was at the edge of the water, and as night wrapped around them, she watched Peyton teach Josh how to believe in himself.

Laying with his back against the smooth, wide cedar, Peyton breathed a contented sigh as he listened to Olivia sing. Clasped hands resting on his stomach and legs crossed at the ankles, he'd already put his shoes and socks on, now damp from the hem of his jeans. His hair had dried during the time it took him, Josh, and Olivia to catch a dozen fireflies as the last shades of evening leaked out of the western side of the sky. Above him, a blanket of velvet night and winking stars cloaked Hill Country.

"Thirsty, we were thirsty;
The King holds to our lips
The cup of salvation.
Bread of Life, Living Water.

Desperate, we drink deeply;
It spills upon our face,
Drenches us in grace.
Orphans called sons and daughters.

We didn't know we needed this
Until He set us free.
We only knew we craved His love,
And now we sing jubilee."

The family sang along to the song Peyton had never heard before. The campfire crackled in his background and the smell of coffee drifted in the wind. Even though every instinct in his body had told him not to come on this hike, he was grateful he hadn't listened. If emptiness plagued him later tonight, he'd gladly battle it. For now, the world held no troubles.

"Supper's gettin' cold, kids," Gianna said.

With an exhausted grunt, Peyton pulled himself from the cedar and went to the log where Josh sat with a jar of fireflies in one hand and a piece of cornbread in the other—Bear asleep at his feet. He eased down beside the kid and took the metal plate Gianna handed him. A pile of blackened catfish sat before him and his stomach released a growl.

"Ever had fresh fish before?" Vern mumbled, seated on the ground, his arms hugged across his chest and his back resting against a stump.

Peyton nodded. "My grandparents used to cook fish on a rock when I was a kid."

"A rock?" Olivia barked a laugh as she stepped inside the circle and took a seat on the log adjacent to his and Josh's, a damp braid hanging over her left shoulder. The firelight flickered across her features as she took the plate her mom held out, and she didn't rush to hide when he looked her way. "How d'you do that?"

He paused to swallow a bite, noticing the Whitmore family had cooked theirs on a cast iron skillet over a wire rack. "My grandparents always said it was so hot in New Mexico, and you could cook anything on a rock in hundred-twenty-degree weather. But I'm pretty sure they just heated it over the campfire."

A harmony of exhausted laughs filled the night air.

"I was probably five years old when Pops threw a piece of fish on there and my eyes turned into saucers, thinking it was the atmosphere making it sizzle and not the flames licking the side of the rock." Peyton smiled. Nan and Austin had chuckled at his small gasp and reminded him to never walk barefoot on sidewalks in the summer, or his feet would cook as fast as the fish did.

"When was the last time you got to visit your grandparents?" Gianna asked.

"Actually, they made the drive down a few months ago for my niece's birth. But I haven't spent a summer there since I was...sixteen." Wow. He hadn't realized the time had passed so quickly. Sixteen was the year he got his first car, his high school baseball team had gone to state, and his brother had reappeared in his life after eight long years. Peyton swallowed and pushed a bite of fish around on his plate. "Life got busy. I graduated, went to college, and started working straight outta the gate."

Daniel hummed, sitting directly across from Peyton. He leaned forward and picked up a percolator sitting beside the skillet. He poured a long stream of coffee into a tin cup. "Gotta get away every once in a while."

Peyton took another bite. That was part of his problem. He'd burnt himself out on the predictability of city life and had forgotten what it was like to sit on the water's edge, listening to wildlife chirp, croak, and howl, surrounded by people he enjoyed spending time with.

Beside him, Josh slid to the ground, twisted against the log, and laid his head on his arms. His blinking jar of fireflies balanced on his lap.

"It's easy to get caught up in the routine of things," Gianna said from where she sat on a single stump between Vern and Daniel. "But we have to remember there's no good reason to live in a rush."

Daniel took a sip of his steaming cup. "We all grow up thinking time is money and if we've got free time on our hands then we're losing money. But that's not how God created us to live."

"The Bible says by resting in Him we'll be saved, and strength is found in our stillness. We've got to stop trying so hard to get ahead all the time." Gianna shook her head. "He's already got everything figured out. We just need to trust Him with the plans."

"We've got to learn how to appreciate the wild side," Daniel said, lifting his cup in Peyton's direction.

Peyton huffed a tired laugh. "I've lived more life in the last two days than I have in the past ten years," he admitted, setting his plate on the ground. He was sure he could sleep straight through the next month. "I never wanted to get caught up in it, but that's what everybody teaches you as a kid. You grow up so you can go to work, and you go to work so your kids can grow up." He stared into the dancing flames, horrified. "And it never ends. That's not living."

"God loves a hard worker, Peyton, but what did He tell Martha when her sister sat at His feet to hear Him speak?" Daniel asked.

"Mary hath chosen that good part, which shall not be taken away from her," Peyton said.

Vern's head came up, pinning him with a look of surprise.

Did he think Peyton didn't know the Good Book?

Daniel nodded. "What's the point in working the life out of ourselves if we never stop to appreciate the beauty of it?"

That made a lot of sense. It explained so much.

Everything, in fact. "You're right. I've been working day and night thinking God would be proud of my effort, and He'd somehow see my exhaustion as a—I don't know—a badge of honor. Like I could earn His attention with it."

No wonder he was burnt out.

"What are you holding onto that makes you feel like that's the only way to get God's attention?"

Peyton looked up at Daniel, the question cutting him to the quick. He cleared his throat. "I can't really put my finger on it. Both of my parents worked full time after their divorce..."

Four sets of eyes watched him, waited. He wasn't emotionally prepared to share his life story with the whole family sitting before him.

But then again, he knew them well enough now to know they held no judgement toward him. They weren't looking to bury him with his past—they were picking up shovels and helping him look for something he'd lost.

"Vacations and birthdays and weekends were never the same. They just worked. They didn't have time to...to stop and enjoy life around them. I think they were probably, uh...running." Something in his brain shifted. Like a dusty window that suddenly swung open. "They were all running. Even my brother. They were running from themselves. But I didn't. I stayed put. I waited for things to come around."

"But they didn't, did they?" Daniel asked.

"No."

Daniel dipped his head. "Sounds like it's time to forgive your parents, son."

Peyton lifted his chin, sitting straighter. "I already have. Years ago. I adore my parents. I could never hold that against them."

Daniel shook his head, eyes closed as he did. "Not holding their mistakes against them is all noble and good. But when you let their mistakes define you, that's the part you're holding onto when you shouldn't be."

Peyton cringed as if the man had tossed a bucket of ice water over him. He took it like a punch to the gut. And boy, did it hurt.

"What do you feel like you lost when they divorced?" Gianna asked.

Peyton looked into the flames, letting out a chuckle that he was sure the entire family could see straight through. "I just, uh...I've never been able to shake the feeling that, uh...they took something beautiful away from my childhood." He swallowed the stubborn lump that jumped into his throat. "Something that they gave my brother when he was my age but couldn't give me."

Gianna nodded softly, her bottom lip tucked between her teeth like she could feel his discomfort.

"I feel like I'm always trying to figure out who I would have been if they hadn't divorced."

Olivia's head came up, and her eyes landed on him as if she could feel it, too. He offered her a smirk that felt more pathetic than assuring.

As the fire crackled, he thought maybe she could relate. Josh, too, though he was asleep. Maybe they were missing part of their story because they were adopted. Who would they have been if their birth parents had raised them? And Vern, the accountant-turned-cowboy, who had spent a majority of his life yearning for a dream instead of living it. And what of Daniel and Gianna? Did they have scars left from the moments in life that should have been milestones, but only turned into disappointments that they couldn't make sense of? When life felt less like a celebration and more like missing a step and falling face first against the pavement.

Did everyone feel the way he felt?

"You wanna know how to fix it?" Daniel asked, shadows from the flames dancing across his face.

Peyton lifted his chin once.

"Let that part of you go. Grant that boy the permission to be with Jesus. Know that he's in good hands, and he turned out to be everything he was created to be. And when you finally walk away from him, you'll realize you were bearing mountains that were only meant to be moved."

Seven years old and shivering beneath his blanket, Peyton squeezed his eyes shut and pulled his pillow tighter over his ears. The screaming wouldn't stop. It was making

his stomach hurt. Mom and Dad never fought this long before. This time was different, and he couldn't figure out why.

The sound of the window opening made him hold his breath, just to be sure he heard right. When it clicked shut, he knew everything would be all right.

Austin was here.

Peyton sat up in bed and the pillow fell from his face. His heart didn't beat against his chest so hard anymore. "They're still fighting," he said, rubbing one eye. "They won't stop."

Mom and Dad's voices got louder on the other side of the door.

"They will," Austin said, pulling his hoodie over his head and throwing it on top of a pile of laundry on the floor. "Go back to sleep, buddy."

Peyton listened, tucking himself beneath the blankets again. If Austin told him it was gonna be okay, then he believed him.

The sound of his brother getting into his own bed made him smile. He remembered the baseball card they found today, the one sitting on his nightstand right now. He couldn't wait to wake up in the morning and—

Dad yelled again. And then it was Mom's turn. They sounded so angry that it made Peyton worry that he'd done something wrong. But he'd finished all his chores and he'd done everything they asked him to do today. Maybe Mom found out he didn't finish his homework.

"Austin," he whispered, hoping his brother wasn't already asleep. "I'm scared."

Austin didn't answer back. But Mom and Dad also stopped screaming, too. Peyton opened his eyes and waited to see what would happen next, so he could either go to sleep finally or—

"I can't do this anymore," Mom said from the kitchen on the other side of the door.

"What do you want to do, Jenny? Send our son off to military school?" Dad said, and Peyton swallowed a gasp. Maybe they had found out about his homework. "His third fight this semester! Doesn't he realize there's only so many chances before they kick him out? The boy just doesn't have *any common sense."*

No. They were fighting about Austin. Again.

"I'm not talking about Austin," Mom said. "I mean this."

What was "this?" What was she pointing at?

"This?" Dad asked.

"I can't keep fighting with you, Jake. I'm tired. And this is our son, not some kid off the street. We can't just send him off like a criminal. And we can't keep tearing each other down because we're disappointed in him."

Peyton finally gasped. He'd never heard Mom, not even once, say that she was disappointed in them before. If she was disappointed in Austin, then she would definitely be disappointed in him.

There was finally silence. Long enough for him to think about all the ways they might punish him for not doing his homework. Maybe they wouldn't let him go to his friend's house down the street. Or they might tell him to do extra chores. Or they might take away his baseball card!

"You want me to leave?" Dad asked.

"No, I don't. But we can't keep doing this. We're not making any progress. Life isn't getting any easier. Austin isn't acting any better and this is the last thing he needs in his life right now." Mom started crying. "And I can't keep pretending like we're still in love when we don't even kiss anymore."

Peyton wanted to sit up in bed again, to get his bearings, because he'd never heard his parents talk like that before. But he didn't want to disappoint Austin.

"I...I'll come back for my stuff in the morning," Dad said. But his voice was quiet. "If the boys need me, I'll be at my brother's house."

The front door opened and then closed. He couldn't hear his dad's voice anymore, but he could hear Mom crying. Then she made a sound that felt like someone had hit him in the heart.

"Austin?" Peyton called out, unable to follow his brother's instructions.

Austin cleared his throat. "What?"

"Can I sleep in your bed?" He knew he probably shouldn't ask, but he couldn't stop himself from shivering. And being near Austin always made him feel better.

"Come here," Austin said, the sound of his blankets rustling.

Peyton kicked at his own, hustling to get out of his bed and crawl in next to Austin whose body was big enough to feel like a bear. He wanted nothing more than to curl up next to his brother and finally sleep.

Peyton's bare toes were cold, so he tucked them against his brother's warm leg as he grabbed onto Austin's arm and hugged him close. Peyton felt Austin's hand mess up his hair and then he kissed his forehead.

"It'll be all right, kid."

Peyton smiled. His brother knew everything. Nobody knew more than Austin. If he had his brother close, then things couldn't be that bad. Even on the nights that Austin snuck out and their parents fought, he always came back. He always listened when Peyton told him how scared he was. And he was always there to let Peyton huddle close.

"Where did Dad go?" Peyton asked.

"He went to Uncle James' house for a little while."

Dad did that sometimes, but never late at night. "Will he come back when we wake up?"

Austin was quiet for a moment. Peyton didn't mind waiting. He wasn't shaking so much anymore and his heart felt normal, and he could breathe easier when he was with Austin. Austin always made it all feel better.

"Not this time," he answered.

Chapter Ten

One Month Later

The flatbed trailer shook with a loud clap as a damaged railroad tie came to a rest on it. Peyton swiped his sleeve against his forehead as he surveyed the area for more debris that Vern had sent him to clean up. At the edge of the yard between the cabin and the treeline, there was nothing left of the old junk pile except for dead grass and a handful of jittery grasshoppers. On his way to the tractor sitting in front of the flatbed, a field mouse skittered across his path, nearly meeting its Maker under Peyton's shoe.

As he passed the trailer, an orange piece of bailing twine stuck out from between the tires. He bent low to snatch it on his way by, but the cord held fast. He went down on one knee and peered beneath. The rope had made itself one with the hub. He pulled his knife from his pocket, flipped the blade open, and cut the twine loose. It pulled free with a little coaxing, and he tossed it on the trailer with the other trash as he flipped the knife closed.

Grabbing the tractor's steering wheel, Peyton swung himself into the seat, turned over the engine, and set his sights on the burn pile beside the pond—the one Vern had him start a few weeks ago. As he traversed over the terrain, he tugged off his gloves and leaned up far enough to tuck them in his back pocket.

In the thirty plus days he'd spent at the ranch, he'd learned more lessons than he could keep count of. And while tending the garden had become his favorite chore, he couldn't deny how good it felt when he'd learned to tame the old blue beast beneath him. Even Vern had doubted his ability. But Peyton had proven that he had what it took to take the tractor out on his own, and Vern had given him his blessing.

The hills came into view and Peyton couldn't take his eyes off of them. "Lead me to the rock that is higher than I," he whispered.

Near the cabin, the temptation to make a pit stop for a water break was too strong to ignore. He left the tractor parked at the edge of the mowed lawn and hopped off, crossing the yard and cutting through the patio. Sweat tickled down his temple and dripped into a thin beard he'd managed to grow out here in the wild—a privilege his former nine-to-five life had never let him afford.

Cold air splashed over him when he stepped inside the empty kitchen. At the sink he washed the dirt from his hands. He could hear Daniel's voice coming from the living room as he reached into the fridge for a bottle of water, the perspiration collecting on his fingertips as he twisted the cap off and tipped it back for some much-needed hydration.

"So, neither one of you know anything about an airhorn attached to the seat of the lawn mower?" Daniel asked, his voice as serious as Peyton had ever heard it.

Peyton let the fridge door fall shut and made a couple steps toward the doorway as he took another drink.

"I know nothing," Olivia said from the living room.

"Nothing at all," Josh tacked on.

"Let me tell you about it then," Daniel said with a frustrated chuckle in his voice. "Last Sunday at church, Mrs. Carmine approached me about the possibility of using my lawn mower for her yard. And today she came by to pick up said lawn mower."

Olivia gasped and Josh grunted an *uh-oh* sound.

"Imagine her surprise when she tried to load it on her trailer."

Peyton snickered under his breath. He'd heard the sound echo across the fields this morning but hadn't thought anything of it.

"She wasn't supposed to!" Josh yelled, caving under the pressure to tell the truth. "It was meant for Pepaw to find!"

"Yeah," Olivia added, a chiding cord in her tone. "What kind of place is this that the men let a little ole church lady load up a lawn mower on her own?"

"No, no. The two of you aren't explaining your way out of this one."

Peyton was interested to see how this played out. He stepped around the corner and into the living room. Daniel stood with a bent leg perched on the coffee table across from the couch where Olivia and Josh sat on opposite ends. Gianna stood nearby, her arms crossed, looking none too proud. Peyton plopped in between Olivia and Josh, propping one steel-toed sneaker on the coffee table in front of him and tossing his ball cap beside it. He took another drink and shoved his moist hands through his hair that had gone without a trim for far too long.

Daniel looked at him wide-eyed, his mouth hanging open as if he were searching for his next word. A wrinkle appeared between his eyebrows and his attention floated between Olivia and Josh. "I don't care that your prank was meant for...for Vern. You could have hurt an innocent lady."

"We're lucky she didn't pass out right there in our yard," Gianna added.

Peyton nodded. "That could have been bad."

"And uh...the other pranks you two..." Daniel stammered as his eyes landed on Peyton briefly. "Have pulled. Replacing the eggs in the coup with ceramic eggs and letting the milk cow loose. I..."

There was a lull and Daniel looked over his shoulder at his wife. Gianna shrugged, one eyebrow arched. Daniel turned again, resting his forearms on his bent knee. "Where was I?"

"We're getting lectured," Peyton offered.

"Yes—no." Daniel shook his head. "Not the three of you. Just..." He gave a resigned sigh. "Olivia, Josh, get your acts together. Peyton..."

Peyton tipped his chin up, waiting.

"Same goes for you," he said as he dropped his leg from the table and walked toward the kitchen. "The three of you are dismissed."

Gianna followed hot on his trail and left them sitting shoulder to shoulder. Peyton let a deep breath bury him in the comfiness of the couch as he rested his head for a moment. "What else are we planning?"

"Well..." Josh said with a sarcastic tone. "We can't talk about it in here or else we'll get in trouble again."

Olivia laughed, her hair long and unruly today, spilling over her shoulders. The three of them stood, Peyton grabbing his hat as he did, and went for the door. With a wagging tail, Bear followed them across the patio and through the yard to where Peyton had parked the tractor. They made sure they were far enough away to plot without being spied on by the parents standing at the kitchen window right now.

"Josh and I were thinking about tying a fake snake to the inside of the trash can lid," Olivia said with her hands on her hips, sashaying through the long, beige grass.

Josh broke out into a series of giggles. "Yeah, and putting bacon grease on Pepaw's door handle."

Peyton chuckled. "What if you tied a bunch of tin cans under Pepaw's work truck. Make 'im think he's dragging a house around."

Olivia and Josh shared a stunned look, eyebrows arched high. They reached out and gave each other a high five.

"We've *gotta* do that," Josh said.

Olivia squinted toward Peyton, head tilted sideways. "You might just turn out to be a Whitmore after all."

"The adoption papers are ready whenever your parents want to sign them."

She grinned. "All right. I gotta get back to town. I had one last delivery to make when *Josh* called me because he didn't want to get in trouble by himself."

"It was *our* idea!" Josh complained. "I wasn't going down for that by myself. Besides, Dad was yelling before you got here, Olivia. I had to hide behind Pepaw's recliner."

"And Peyton was a huge help," Olivia said.

"How so?" Peyton squinted at her.

"When you showed up, Dad forgot how he was gonna punish us. I think that's the first time I've ever seen him speechless."

Peyton took a bow. "It was my pleasure."

Past his reflection in the glass of the kitchen window,

Daniel watched his children laughing together near the tractor. Olivia and Josh high-fived one another, Peyton gave a pretend bow, and the little dog called Bear laid in the middle of their circle, tongue hanging out. As Josh chatted away, Olivia stepped up on the flatbed and balanced on a railroad tie, arms stretched at her sides.

His children.

"You know when it comes time for Peyton to leave it's gonna feel like losing another one of our foster children?" He glanced over his shoulder.

"I know." Gianna stepped closer, wrapping her hands around his bicep and hugging him close. "But that's not my biggest concern."

What could be bigger than breaking off another piece of their hearts, same as the others had? In the time it took for him to ponder her statement, he watched Peyton reach out and take Olivia's hand to steady her walk across the narrow beam. He kept pace with her, smiling as she talked. Then she gave the boy a sideways look and Daniel's throat tightened.

"He's gonna be the one to take her away from us, isn't he?"

"I think so." Gianna's slender fingers tightened on his arm. "We knew she wasn't gonna be ours forever."

He swallowed, letting this image of his kids burn into his mind so that he'd never have to forget it. "A daddy could hope."

"Our little butterfly has been anxiously waiting to see the world." She sighed. "If Peyton is the one God wants to teach her how to fly, then all we can do is pray. For both of them."

At the end of the flatbed, Olivia stepped down into the grass, the afternoon sun glinting off the red sheen of her hair as Peyton held onto her hand a heartbeat longer than what was necessary.

"I don't think she knows she's in love with him."

Gianna giggled. "I don't think either of them know it just yet."

He looked down at his wife and found the same watery sparkle in her blue eyes that he felt gathering in his own. She gave him a soft smile, the kind that always promised him everything would be okay even if it didn't feel like it.

He looked out across the lawn again, this time to find his

JESSICA ALYSE

kids going in three different directions—Josh to his treehouse with Bear, Peyton on the tractor, and Olivia toward the living room doors.

Daniel stretched the muscles in his back. "I'm gonna have a talk with Peyton."

Gianna tugged him closer to her. "You're not gonna chase him off, are you?"

He fought a grin. "Not yet."

They shared a quick kiss, and she released him. As he stepped into the summer heat, Olivia was opening the living room door. "Where you headed?"

She hesitated, taking a half step back. "To the bakery. I've got one last delivery to make before Caroline closes shop. Hey, do you know where the vendor signs to my bakery are? I'm thinking about setting up a table at the Fourth of July parade."

"They're in the barn. In my workshop. I'll head there now and grab 'em for you."

"That'll be great. Thanks, Dad."

He gave her a nod. "Love you. Be careful."

"Love you, too." She was gone.

Ten minutes later, Daniel hauled Olivia's signs downstairs. Sights set on the house, he was pleasantly surprised to find the tractor parked inside the barn, the trailer empty. He set the signs on the trailer and looked around for the driver.

Peyton was at the other end of the corridor, down on one knee in front of a stall gate, a drill whizzing as he drove a screw into the splintered wood.

"You're gonna have this place looking new in no time," Daniel said as he leaned one elbow against the gate on the next stall over.

Peyton stood, dusting bits of hay from his jeans. "I'm convinced Vern walks around breaking things just so he can tell me to fix 'em."

Daniel couldn't help but chuckle. Peyton carried the drill and broken hinge across the breezeway and set them both on a worktable. The boy had changed what seemed like overnight. He sported a short beard that he hadn't arrived at the *Higher Rock Ranch* with and his hair now curled from under the brim of his hat. He had a deeper shade to his skin and a broader width to his neck. His clothes were work worn in the elbows and threadbare around the knees. At one point he hadn't believed Peyton was twenty-six, but now he looked it.

"How're things going?"

Peyton looked over his shoulder at him, a confused frown on his face. "It's goin' great unless this is a trick question."

Daniel shook his head. "I'm just checking in on you."

"Since you mention it," he said as he turned around and leaned against the worktable, crossing his arms. "I feel like someone's been up at the homestead."

Daniel's back muscles tightened. "What makes you think that?"

He shrugged. "Seems like things get moved around every couple weeks or so. Items on the counters. In the bathroom. There's a plank of wood in front of the fireplace that was dislodged when I got home last night."

Daniel scrubbed one hand against his goatee. He'd had the same feeling the day he'd helped Peyton move in last month. The door was unlocked when it shouldn't have been. But he'd brushed it off.

"You didn't stick me in a haunted homestead, did you?" Peyton asked with an eyebrow raised.

"Is there anything missing?"

Peyton shook his head. "Not that I can tell. The boxes I moved upstairs are still there, and my belongings are accounted for. It's just...a feeling."

"It's probably Josh playing around," Stu said as he walked between the two of them. "We all know how Josh tags along like your shadow, Brooks."

Peyton wore a wrinkle between his brows as his focus followed Stu until he stepped out of the barn. Daniel hadn't seen that look on the kid's face before. He pulled himself away from the stall gate and crossed the breezeway, stopping at Dagger's stall to the left of Peyton.

He leaned his arms against the gate and tipped his chin. "What's that about?"

Peyton shook his head. "He's not my biggest fan and I'm not his."

"Why's that?"

Peyton's jaw ticked as he turned and matched Daniel's

stance, his forearms crossed and resting against Dagger's stall. "Some remark he made last month that..." He shook his head with vigor, looking up at the horse. "I didn't care for."

"Anything that I need to take into account?"

Peyton's shoulders rose where he pulled in a breath and then sunk when he let it out. He scratched his forehead with the back of his thumbnail. "Not particularly unless you're looking for a reason to pummel the guy."

A truck sounded in the distance outside the barn door and Daniel assumed it was Stu heading out. "What'd he say?"

Peyton shook his head again, frowning as he did. "He called Olivia a nickname that he said everyone used in high school and I wasn't too happy about it."

Daniel's breath hitched. "To her face?"

Peyton shook his head.

Daniel breathed again. It wasn't a fireable offense. But it was enough to get Stu on Daniel's bad side quicker if he ever warranted it. "Got it."

"That's all there is to it."

Daniel let a long sigh spill out of him. "Unfortunately, my daughter has had her fair share of bullies and nicknames. It was something we knew she would face, and we thought we'd done enough to prepare her for it. Maybe we did or maybe we didn't, but, uh...I know she's let that birthmark stop her from living life to the fullest."

When Daniel looked at Peyton, he found compassion softened in his eyes—further confirming his and Gianna's suspicions about his feelings for their daughter.

"I uh...I'm pretty sure that's why she's sworn off marriage. She's afraid a man's never gonna want her with that mark."

Peyton shook his head boldly, his eyes skimming over Dagger, but he didn't speak.

"It probably won't win me "Father of the Year" to admit this, but I never much tried to talk her into settling down and getting married. A dad never wants to imagine his little princess growing up and running away with some man. You'll understand what I mean one day when you've got a daughter."

A smirk pulled at the edge of Peyton's mouth.

"It's been twenty-two years and I'm still learning to trust God with Olivia's heart. She's been through a lot with that birthmark, and I've done everything in my power to protect her from the harsh reality of this world."

He swallowed. "Peyton, I would never tell her this, but the reason why her birth records are sealed is because her birth parents don't want to be contacted. The birthmark is why they gave her up. They didn't have the emotional or financial capacity to—"

A noise behind them had Daniel turning to the open doorway. There stood Olivia, hand over her mouth and eyes pinched with pain that cut him to his heart. She turned and walked out of the barn.

Have mercy.

Daniel started after her, his heart shattered in his lungs, making it hard for him to breathe. But he hadn't made it more than three steps when Peyton passed him. As he moved with urgency, Daniel stopped where he was, some invisible force holding him in place as he watched this man go after his daughter, disappearing around the corner where the sunlight turned the fields glaringly white. The world as he knew it flipped upside down and the secret he swore he'd never tell a soul was now hers to be crushed by.

As reality came whirling back to him, Daniel forced himself to move forward.

She was headed for her truck parked near the others, a dust trail flying on the wind where Peyton ran to catch up with her. She reached for her door handle, and he grabbed her arm. With a sob, she pushed him away. Peyton took both of her hands and coaxed her around the front of the truck, to the passenger side where he helped her in.

Daniel watched as Peyton climbed behind the wheel of his daughter's truck and pull out into the driveway without a backward glance. "Lord, what have I done?"

She'd cried until she couldn't cry anymore. Olivia watched the country road ahead through sore, swollen eyes. No clue where she was, she tried in vain to distract herself from the ache that pierced her chest. But her sound reasoning collided with her emotions, and she couldn't get her head above the waters of doubt.

Why hadn't her parents ever told her?

Her birth parents didn't want her because of her birthmark?

They didn't have the emotional capacity?

She was a financial burden?

"What else did he tell you?" she asked breathlessly.

"Nothing else." Peyton sighed. "I'm not sure why he told me that much."

Fire in her lungs dragged her back to the bottom of a pit of despair. How was she supposed to survive this? How could she ever hope for a normal life knowing what her parents knew—and now Peyton.

Who else knew? Caroline? Josh? The ranch? Their church? Did the whole town know? Did people buy from her bakery because they felt bad for her? Was every aspect of her life a carefully orchestrated charade to ensure the pathetic girl with the birthmark on her face would have the charity she needed to get through life?

Breath fled her lungs and refused to return until she found an answer. Every second, a moment of surrender she had no control over.

"I'm pretty sure I'm the only one he's ever told."

She looked at him then, air filling her lungs. Had he been reading her thoughts? While he watched the road ahead of him, one hand propped on the steering wheel, his mouth was downturned, his signature smirk nonexistent. Did he pity her or was he walking through the same emotions she was walking through?

"How can you be sure?"

He glanced at her, his brows lifted in the middle to give him the same sad appearance that she felt inside. "Because..." A quiet grunt interrupted him, as if he were wrestling with what he was about to say. "He said he never wanted you to know. That tells me he's been living with that secret locked inside for a long time."

"Why didn't he just tell me?" The words came out in a cry, even though she knew Peyton had less answers than she did.

"Olivia..." A wrinkle appeared between his brows. "Look

in that mirror right there and tell me at what age you would wish this heartbreak on yourself."

He blurred through new tears, and she looked at the road ahead. He was right. It didn't matter if she was ten, twenty-two, or a hundred, the ache wouldn't have felt any different. The child she'd been wouldn't have survived this truth. She would have isolated herself from the world until she turned to dust. The bakery never would have opened. She never would have lived the life or dreamed the dreams that Olivia had today.

But she couldn't see how the person she was today would survive it either.

The truck slowed, coming to a gentle stop. Peyton pushed the gear in reverse and looked over his shoulder as he backed into a space between the trees. The main road lay a couple dozen yards away where a car whizzed by. A scattering of leaves drifted to the ground in the summer heat. He parked and turned the key in the ignition. When the truck went quiet, he fell against the seat as if the weight of her emotional rollercoaster wore on him.

"I'm so humiliated." Her eyes pinched shut as the words left her mouth, their weight pelting like rocks against her heart as she said them.

"How so?" The innocence in his voice drew a frustrated chuckle from her. Was he serious or was he trying to brush things over?

"How would you feel if you just found out you weren't wanted?"

"Who said you weren't wanted?"

She laughed again. What was happening? "You heard what my dad said. My birth parents gave me up because they couldn't stand to look at my face." Her eyes watered again. "Wouldn't that make you feel humiliated?"

His eyes roamed over her features, tracing the lines of her disfigurement, she was sure. She turned her head away before he could feel the same thing her birth parents had felt the moment she was born.

"You're not unwanted, Olivia," he said, his voice gentle. "What your dad said back there, it doesn't mean you're not wanted. You had birth parents who were scared—scared to face the same reality you live with every single day. It didn't mean they didn't want *you*. It meant they did what they thought was best for you when they realized they weren't the people who could give you everything they wanted to."

Olivia swallowed. Wasn't that what she'd assumed this whole time—that she'd been put up for adoption because her parents couldn't give her the life they wanted to?

"Look at your mom and dad and Josh and Vern. That's the life your birth parents wanted you to have. It's a life they knew they couldn't give you."

She scrubbed away a tear with the inside of her wrist.

"And I have no doubt that if they met you today that they'd fall in love with you. Beauty mark included," he said with a slow grin.

She looked up at him. "It's gonna take some time for me to share that belief with you."

"Take all the time you need."

Peyton stepped out of the truck then, coming around to her side. He opened her door and with one shoulder leaned against the edge, he held his hand out for her. She hesitated, not sure what he had in mind, and he tipped his head to the side in one quick motion, a gesture for her to trust him.

She did. So, she offered her hand and let him help her out of the truck. They were parked on the edge of a field that overlooked a prairie of pale grass and a few green hills in the distance. The sun high overhead painted everything in bright, vibrant colors. She didn't know who owned the property, or if they were even trespassing. "Where are we?"

"Not sure." He dropped the tailgate and looked over the landscape with a slow, sweeping scan. "But this is where I stopped the night I crossed paths with you."

Caught off guard by the reminder, she looked up at him with a smile.

"I needed somewhere to stretch my legs and rest a bit before I drove through the night, and I found this place."

She took a seat on the tailgate, letting her legs dangle against the untrimmed grass below. Peyton sat to the right of her—where he had a personal view of the blemish she wanted nothing more than to hide right now. So, she let her hair fall across her face as she looked out at the white billowing clouds in the distance and the ocean blue sky that swam around them. Fresh air filled her lungs, and she held it hostage for a handful of seconds.

"You know what we haven't talked about in a while?" he asked, his arms braced behind him and his face tilted toward the sunshine. When she waited for the answer, he squinted at her with a grin. "Your dream job."

"Right," she drawled as she nodded. It had been a month since they'd discussed the ridiculous topic. The last few weeks had been filled with family dinners, shenanigans between her, Josh, and Peyton, and crazy outings with Caroline. Though she hadn't forgotten her list, she was almost positive he'd forgotten his.

Almost.

She wasn't really in the mood for silly games, but she welcomed the distraction. "We were on dream number three, weren't we? You first, then I'll tell you mine."

"Fair enough," he said as he straightened and dropped his hands in his lap. "I wouldn't be too torn up if I could run a food truck."

She blinked at him, a smile growing on her lips. "Really? I didn't know you cooked."

"Actually, you might be surprised by how well I can reheat leftovers."

A much-needed giggle fell out of her, loosening something in her soul that had hardened in the last half hour. "So, you're not cooking comfort food or Tex Mex or anything like that?"

He shrugged. "Nothing specific. Just all of my favorite foods."

"And what would that be?"

A guilty smirk tugged at his lips. "So far everything you and your momma's cooked."

Olivia tossed her head back and laughed deeply.

"Your turn. What's your number three?"

She took in a deep breath and looked out to the horizon. "I wouldn't mind being a professional bridesmaid."

"Professional?"

She nodded. "That's someone who stands in as a bridesmaid for a bride who doesn't have a lot of friends. I never want a woman to have to stand up there and get married without a friend, even if it's a temporary one." The idea of it broke her heart when she was a kid and she'd been happy to volunteer her services ever since.

"Wow," he breathed. "You're an incredible woman, Olivia."

A shy smile tugged at her lips. "Thank you."

"But you're determined not to have a wedding of your own?"

Olivia swallowed, glancing out at a flock of ducks that crossed over the prairie. "Oh, yeah. It's way too mushy for me. I'm not the hopeless romantic type. I'm a little bit too spoiled with my independence. As a matter of fact, I dread the idea of ever having to share it with somebody. I mean, I can't point to one aspect of my life that I would be willing to give up in order to have a wedding and settle down with someone."

With his head tilted to the side a bit, he stared at her, a smirk on his face like he was reading all of her innermost thoughts. "Love wouldn't ask you to give it up."

Her smile melted from her face. She'd spent years building these walls, how dare he try to disassemble them in a matter of minutes.

"I don't think you mean that—I don't think you've actually written off marriage."

Her emotions were already fried, and he was getting too close to a broken place. "I have, Peyton. Believe me. I've given it a ton of thought and it's not something that suits me."

"Why not?"

A frustrated laugh tumbled out and her fingers tightened on the edge of the tailgate beneath her. They were friends and there were some conversations that were meant to stay between friends. "Because. People only spend their love on beautiful things. And if a woman isn't beautiful then she's not a candidate for love."

"Every woman is beautiful, Olivia," he said with a chuckle as if it were a fact that she wasn't aware of. "And for every woman out there who doesn't think she's beautiful there are a hundred men looking for her specific type of beauty. They just haven't met those men yet."

"You don't know what it's like to be passed over in a room full of girls who look like they've stepped out of a magazine. To stand next to someone as beautiful as Caroline and the guy doesn't even see you there. Or to try to talk to a man and he can't even look into your eyes because he's disgusted by the mark on your face." She flicked her fingers across her face and threw her hair out of the way. "What you're saying is a theory. It sounds great but it's not reality."

He shook his head gently. "It's not a theory. You may not think you're beautiful, but when you meet the right one then you'll have to trust that he does."

"You're wrong. It doesn't work like that."

"I promise it does."

Her eyes stung with tears. "And I promise it doesn't. I did trust him, Peyton. I trusted him with my whole world, and he made it clear to me that only beautiful things deserve love."

His smirk faded as he lifted his chin. "Who, Olivia?"

She bit down hard. She'd said too much. That story was never supposed to leave her lips. Nobody knew. Not even Caroline. It was too humiliating—the experience nearly shredding what was left of her confidence.

But maybe if she explained it then he'd understand.

"In elementary school there were three of us. Me, Caroline, and a boy named Rhett. We'd known each other since we were babies, and we were inseparable. We did everything together and when I got picked on at school..." She paused to swallow the lump in her throat. "Rhett would stick up for me. He'd put the bullies in their place, and he made me feel loved and appreciated and beautiful, y'know? And then the summer we went to middle school..." A tear trickled down to her chin, her cheeks burning with embarrassment. "I kissed him. Because I thought I loved him. And...he didn't kiss me back. He stepped away and said, 'I'm sorry, Livy. I only like girls who are pretty.'"

With a tense smile, she nodded adamantly. That was her fate and it was sealed. Love was out of the question for a girl like her and everyone who tried to convince her otherwise was just part of a cruel joke that never ended. "We never said two words to each other after that day. His family moved to another state the year we went to high school, and I haven't seen him since."

"I'm sorry, Olivia," he whispered, his voice thick.

"Don't be. I'm glad it happened. I needed to know at a

young age so that I didn't waste my life chasing after something that wasn't there."

"No." He twisted, facing her fully and propping one bent leg on the tailgate between them. "You can't stake your entire future on something a—what, twelve-year-old kid said. Just because he didn't see your beauty doesn't mean it isn't there."

Her jaw tightened and she pinned him with a look. "I need you to understand—"

"My goodness, you're stunning, Olivia. You have the most amazing eyes a person will ever get to look into, and your hair is incredible and your smile is breathtaking. But the greatest man on the face of the earth could tell you all of that but you won't believe him. Do you hear me? You won't believe him. Because some random kid in elementary school told you he's not into your kind of pretty."

She gasped and snapped her lips closed. She'd never thought of it like that before. It had never occurred to her...

And just like that, her entire world righted itself. The wall of heartache she'd hid behind for most of her life no longer existed. Defenseless, she was out of options that gave her something to do besides imagine a future where she might actually be able to experience love. This was new.

This was dangerous.

Maybe her birth parents had given her the best possible life that they could afford. Financially and emotionally. And maybe her parents had lived with that heartbreaking secret for longer than they could stand. And maybe her childhood best friend hadn't been the boy meant for her after all. And if a man ever did call her beautiful, she wouldn't believe him because she'd already decided she wasn't. "Maybe you're right."

"You'll see," he said. "After you get past today, you'll see it all clearly. I promise."

She nodded slowly, her thoughts swimming. "I've spent so long fighting with the idea that I don't belong."

"That's because you're a masterpiece in a world looking for mirrors."

His words dipped deeply into her heart, to a place that hadn't seen light in years. She thought her desire to be loved had faded into embers, but Peyton breathed on it just enough to make those flames return.

"It's easy to feel alone when everyone else is looking out for themselves," he said. "But God has something a little bit different in mind for you, I have no doubt. In fact, the next time you look at Jesus, I want you to see Him as the King you call Father. And when you do, you have to know that makes you royal by blood. Who can stop you then?"

Something was different within her. She could feel it surging through her veins and racing to her soul.

"You see that view out there?" Peyton tipped his head to the wonder that was Hill Country. "You're even more beautiful than that. Because Jesus didn't die for that. He died for you."

CHAPTER ELEVEN

The truck rolled to a stop in front of *Slice of Heaven* and Olivia hopped out. It was one of the few times she'd ridden in the passenger side of her own truck—usually with Dad behind the wheel—but Peyton had convinced her to let him make the drive to the bakery. It had felt nice sharing small talk about their favorite movies, hidden talents, and guilty pleasures—for which she was comically surprised to find out Peyton's was singing in the shower.

She met him on the sidewalk in front of the truck with a grin that turned into a giggle.

"You're not gonna let me live that one down, are you?" he asked, looking up at the awning that stretched over the walkway.

No, she wasn't. "You should share your voice with the world. Sing in public. Maybe audition some place."

"I'm strictly a shampoo bottle singer," he said as he rolled his sleeves to his elbows. "But you, on the other hand, have a gift. Why don't *you* share it with the world? Audition some place?"

Olivia smothered her mirth with a deep breath. "I only sing for my family."

"What about church?"

She scrunched her nose. "It's a whole big thing. First you have to get the pastor's approval, then rehearse with the band. It takes a few weeks—and besides, the worship is already perfect. There's nothing more I can bring to it."

He squinted at her as if she were lying. Then he reached for the door and pulled it wide. "Promise me you'll consider it?"

"I promise." She squinted back at him as she stepped

inside. The smell of chocolate bread splashed over her. "Here it is. You finally get to see the place for yourself."

"Do I get the employee discount?"

She winked. "I'll fix you up."

"What do we have here?" Caroline's voice echoed off the white walls of their little shop as she took the debit card of a waiting customer. "You two are finally dating, is that it?"

Olivia rolled her eyes as she stepped behind the counter. "Very funny. I've got a delivery to make, and Peyton offered to drive me. And give me a hand." She tacked on at the end and was rewarded with a thoughtful frown as Peyton nodded.

She snatched a square of parchment paper from the dispenser and plucked a pastry from behind the glass, handing it over the counter to him. "Today's special. *Pain au Chocolat*. It's a French pastry. In America, we call it chocolate croissant."

He took one big bite, and his eyes rolled closed. "Only you can make bread taste this good."

Olivia looked over at Caroline who had stilled as she handed the bag to the customer who had also frozen. Heat warmed her cheeks, and she stepped from behind the counter, gesturing for Peyton to follow her to the back.

"So, this is where all the magic happens?" he asked before taking another bite.

"Something like that." She stopped in front of the boxes of chocolate chip cookies and sprinkle-covered brownies that were meant for the daycare a few blocks away. She double checked her notebook and the inventory, remembering she'd packed a few extra boxes meant for the ranch. Tomorrow she'd spend the day baking for the Fourth of July dance. She tapped her pen on the paper. Maybe she'd forgo setting up a table at the parade this year.

The door swung wide, and Caroline stepped through, her silky blonde ponytail high on her head. "Let's hear it, Peyton. What's your first impression of the place?" Caroline stopped beside where Olivia double checked her inventory and leaned back against the counter. "Do we win Heavenly's Business of the Year award?"

"There's not even a close second."

Olivia glanced over her shoulder with a snort and turned

to check her inventory again. "Peyton, would you do me a huge favor?"

"You need someone to taste test?" He was suddenly at her side—his shoulder pressed against hers as he peeked at the boxes.

She opened the lid on the top box meant for the ranch, revealing perfect rows of peanut butter cookie sandwiches. "Let me know what you think of these. I might add them to the menu."

He picked one up and took a bite. "What's in the middle?"

"You don't like it?"

"When did I say I didn't like it?"

She smirked. "It's a salted peanut butter cream."

"Add 'em to the menu." He stuffed the rest in his mouth.

She tipped her head once, made a note in her book, and touched the stack of boxes. "Will you take these and put them in the backseat of the truck?"

"Yes, ma'am." After wiping his hands on his jeans, he scooped the boxes up and backed through the kitchen door.

The door swung closed and Caroline stared at her with her smile hanging wide. "That boy is in love with you."

"You've got to stop saying stuff like that." Olivia rolled her eyes as she went to the storage room and grabbed the handle of the wagon sitting in the corner. She pulled it into the kitchen and started loading it with boxes.

"Girl, he can't resist you. Did you see the way he looked at you when you said, 'you don't like it?'"

Olivia glanced at the door. They were still alone. "I don't feel like enough of a woman to evoke any emotion in a man, let alone love." She tucked the last box in the corner of the wagon bed. "Besides, he already said he isn't dating anyone. And he doesn't even act the least bit like he's interested in me. He treats me more like a sister than anything."

Caroline hummed skeptically, twirling a piece of hair around two fingers. "Yeah, sure. When was the last time you heard a brother say, 'yes, ma'am' to his sister?"

"He's polite."

"He's smitten. And just because he's not dating anyone doesn't mean he's not in love with you."

"Shhh." Olivia grabbed Caroline's arm and pulled her closer. "Stop talking like that."

The door swung open, and Peyton reappeared. Olivia dropped her focus to the wagon in the event that her face was as red as it was warm. "These need to go to the daycare down the street. It's only a few blocks away, so I usually walk."

He took the handle from her and started toward the door. "Lead the way."

Olivia hopped to it, holding open the kitchen door until the wagon cleared it. Before she let it swing shut, she caught sight of Caroline wiggling her eyebrows. Fighting the urge to growl—but unwilling to have Peyton ask what the sound effects were for—she opened the shop door for him and then gestured toward the right.

"You make deliveries like this often?" he asked as she fell in line beside him and set the pace.

"The daycare is my only delivery by wagon, typically. But I do make deliveries to someplace every day. I'll get orders from the retirement home across town, or the high school, or a birthday party or two." She shrugged as they passed the cafe where the smell of coffee swam through the open door when a customer walked out.

They passed a few waiting cars at the traffic light on the corner of main street. "This is where we have parades through the year. The fair parade. Christmas parade. Homecoming parade. The Fourth of July parade is tomorrow."

He nodded as he pulled the wagon up the concrete ramp to the next sidewalk. "Tell me more."

A thrill of delight soared through her. She pointed across the street to an art shop. "That used to be the driving school where I got my license. And right back there was the first red light I ever ran. It was an accident, of course," she was quick to add. Then she pointed toward the building coming up before them. "And this is the salon where I got my hair and makeup done for prom."

"You went to prom?"

"I did."

"You danced?" he asked.

"Mm-hmm. I love to dance."

"That's good to know. You, uh, plan to dance tomorrow night?"

"Yeah," she pushed the word out. "I usually dance with a couple of guys from church. And then Dad will probably dance with me." The reminder felt like a stab in her heart. Had he truly carried her secret for so long that he couldn't bear it anymore?

"Where can I add my name to your dance card?"

The question pulled her from her thoughts. She smiled at a couple of older women carrying shopping bags as they passed. "Well, the line to dance with me isn't exactly wall to wall, so I think you'll get a spot pretty early."

They passed by the antique store. "Over there is my favorite place to shop. Most of the decorations in my house are from there. It's the cutest stuff and for good prices, too."

They navigated the last crosswalk.

"And that ice cream parlor right there is some of the best ice cream you'll ever taste in your life. Our class used to take field trips there all the time when I was in school. And you already know about the hardware store, I assume."

He sighed. "It was one of the first places Vern took me to. Felt like a five-year-old kid again, listening to my grandpa talk about boring things that I had no clue about."

She laughed softly. "Pepaw said you had an idea about opening up a men's ministry."

Peyton's eyes were wide for a second, then he grinned. "I didn't think your dad would tell the whole family. It was just a dumb idea."

"I don't think it's dumb. And I would be willing to bet my dad doesn't either. What led you to it?"

He took on a faraway gaze at the sidewalk ahead of them. "I know how much the ranch changed me on the first day." He shrugged. "I was thinking a lot of men could profit from something like that. Get in touch with the wild side of the heart for a change."

Olivia dipped her chin. "That would be amazing. I'll pray that God will bring it to pass if it's in His will."

He gave her a smirk that told her he appreciated that.

She slowed to a stop in front of the daycare building that sat on the outskirts of downtown, where a fence in the back protected the playground from city life. She opened the door, and he wheeled the wagon inside.

"Well, this is new," Sabrina, the administrator, said as

she rose from her desk. "Did ya have some help today?"

"Sabrina, this is Peyton, he works for my dad. Peyton, this is Sabrina. She owns *Little Meadow Academy*. Which is the best daycare you'll find in Hill Country."

"Nice to meet you, ma'am." He dipped his chin.

"Y'all can go on in. The kids will be over the moon to see those pink boxes," Sabrina said, gesturing toward the door. She leaned over the edge of her desk and waved for Olivia to come close. "And uh, keep an eye on your...friend. He's new in town and some of the girls working here are...unmarried. If you know what I mean."

Olivia nodded, biting back a smile. As she reached for the doorknob, Peyton caught her wrist, a wrinkle between his brows. "Maybe you should go. I've been working all day. I don't exactly blend in."

She dropped her focus to his work-worn sneakers, the grass stains around his knees, and the dirt smudged on the front of his white T-shirt, hidden behind the edge of his plaid button down. "Nonsense," she said. "Kids are always dirty. You'll blend right in."

He ran his tongue across his teeth behind a closed grin. She opened the door and a room full of little kids sitting in front of a projector screen looked over their shoulders. When they realized who had come to see them, they let out a triumphant roar.

"Macaroni and cheese!" one of the teachers called out.

"Everybody freeze!" The kids yelled in unison, falling quiet enough for the teacher to gain their attention.

"Give Miss Livy a few minutes to set up her treats and then we'll form an orderly line so everyone can get one. Sound good?"

"Yeah!" they shouted.

Olivia laughed softly, taking the boxes Peyton held out and setting them along the table on the back wall.

"Miss Livy?" he asked, holding tight to the next box he handed her with a glimmer of amusement in his eyes.

"It was my nickname in high school."

"I like it," he said, releasing the box. "Suits you."

Something in her stomach warmed as she opened the lid. "I, uh, outgrew it sometime around my senior year," she whispered. "The name Livy was associated with a lot of...unfortunate nicknames that some people used. So, I started going by Olivia."

Something darkened behind his eyes, and he nodded. Maybe that was too much information.

One of the younger teachers—a girl named Nova—brought her a stack of kiddie plates and boxes of room-temperature juice. She leaned back against the table, her green eyes twinkling with interest.

"What's your friend's name?" she whispered.

Olivia gently cleared her throat as she dispersed the plates. "Uh, Peyton."

"Are you dating?"

"No," Olivia rushed to assure her. "Not at all."

When Peyton set the last box on the table, he came to stand beside her, and she handed him a plastic spatula. "Can you scoop one treat onto each plate?"

"Yes, ma'am," he said quietly.

Nova snorted. "Not yet." She raised one eyebrow and stepped away from the table.

What was that supposed to mean? Did she plan to make a pass at Peyton? He was fair game. Olivia wouldn't stand in her way.

She checked over her shoulder. The young woman whispering in the ear of another teacher, both of them looking in their direction. Olivia shook off the feeling that these girls were about to descend on Peyton from every angle. Sabrina had warned her—and she had known as much. Heavenly was a small town. Eligible bachelors were rarer than shooting stars.

Once they had the plates ready, with an exhausted huff Olivia blew a strand of hair out of her face. "How are you with kids?"

"What?"

"Brace yourself."

He looked confused. But not for long when the kids lined up, took a plate and a juice, and then gave Olivia either a high-five or a hug as they passed by. Because Peyton was there, too, he got in on the action. Taking a knee on the cityscape carpet, he matched the energy of each kid—enthusiastic when the boys roared a thank you, and gentle when the girls leaned in for a hug.

After the last kid took their snack, each one was seated in front of the screen, munching and slurping. Olivia started packing the mostly empty boxes back in the wagon when a little boy named Hudson approached. No older than four, he reached both arms out for her. She'd known Hudson since he was born, his dad a couple grades older than Olivia. She scooped him up and set him against her hip.

"What are you doing? You're supposed to be watching the movie, little man." She tapped his nose and watched his brown eyes widen.

His full cheeks puffed up when he smiled. "Can I have another cookie?" he whispered.

She faked a look of shock. "But one cookie is all you're supposed to have."

A soft, guilty giggle poured out of him. "Can I have two?"

"Hmm," Olivia hummed as she looked across the room at his teacher. The older woman offered a warm smile and nodded gently. "I don't see why not.

When she turned to Peyton to ask for a second treat, she was caught off guard by the look in his face. Brows low, mouth slightly agape, he had the look of a man who had just seen tomorrow's winning lottery numbers and didn't know what to do about it.

"Can we get a second cookie, Mr. Peyton?" she asked.

He blinked himself out of whatever trance he was in and held the box open as Hudson plucked one out.

The evening sun set low behind the hills as Peyton turned into the ranch driveway. They had driven around for a couple hours while Olivia had talked about her life in Heavenly and laughed about memories that made her eyes light up. But as they drew closer to the house, she'd grown quiet. Knowing the unfortunate conversation that lay ahead of her, Peyton had done nothing but pray since silence had filled the truck. He wasn't sure what the outcome of it would look like, but he was certain of one thing.

"No matter what happens, you need to know that your parents love you more than life itself."

Her lips parted in surprise. She looked at him. "How do

you know what I'm thinking?"

He smiled, rolling his tired eyes back to the driveway. "You're an open book, Olivia."

"I've lived with my parents for twenty-two years and even *they* don't always know what I'm thinking."

He shrugged, grinning. "Some of us like to read."

She grew quiet again, turning to look out her window.

Past the woods and wildlife and dried creekbed, the cabin came into view and Birdie and Boone stood at attention on the porch. Their patrol didn't last long, though, once they realized the truck belonged to Olivia. Trotting in a half circle, both dogs returned to their places and collapsed in panting piles of fur as Peyton shifted the truck into park.

They got out and he met her in front of the porch steps. "I think I'm just gonna head to the homestead."

"No, you have to come have supper with us." The disappointment in her voice was almost more than he could take. But she needed this night alone with her parents. He didn't want to intrude on that.

"Tomorrow night, I promise." He thought to reach out and tussle her hair like he might do Josh's but stopped himself. She was a woman in every sense of the word and his deepest instincts demanded that he treat her like it. He cleared his throat and took a few steps backwards. "I'll go grab the boxes out of your truck."

"Leave 'em. I'll have Josh or Dad do it."

He nodded, turning to go.

"Wait." She held one hand up as if her palm had the ability to make him stay planted in one place.

It did.

She closed the distance between them and pulled him into a hug, wrapping her arms around his neck as she went up on tiptoe. Peyton tightened his grip on her, his heart beating victoriously at the realization that she fit into his arms perfectly.

But what did it matter to him if she did?

"Thank you," she whispered.

Every natural response that came to his mind seemed insufficient and shallow. She was neck deep in a situation that would shake anyone to their core and challenge their beliefs, and she was gonna have to cope with that for the next few days. So, as she pulled her arms away—a chill meeting him where her warmth had been—and took a step, he held tight to her arm and offered her the only thing that would mean anything.

"Can I pray for you, Olivia?"

Her happy brown eyes widened for a heartbeat. Her smiling lips opened as if she were about to say, 'yes,' but she nodded instead.

Permission granted, Peyton lifted his other hand to the back of her head as she closed her eyes. He dipped his chin, his embrace like a covering over her. Her hands rested on his lungs, making it hard for him to breathe.

"Father, I ask You to watch over Olivia. Give her the strength she needs to overcome every obstacle the enemy throws at her. Walk with her through this night and let her eyes always see Your light, no matter how dark the world may seem. Show her how loved and beautiful You made her. May Your name be glorified in all that she does and all that she's called to be. In Jesus' name."

She lifted her chin and though she was still smiling, her eyes were glossy, reflecting the sky behind him.

"Thank you," she whispered again, backing away until her hands fell.

Something about that felt wrong and suddenly he was looking for more reasons to pray with her.

"Goodnight, Olivia."

"Goodnight, Peyton." She turned and walked up the stairs, crossed the porch, and disappeared behind her parent's front door.

That's when he realized he'd been watching her for no legitimate reason that he could think of. Shaking off whatever dazed state his head was swimming in, Peyton stepped onto the lawn and made his way around the corner of the house, heading toward the barn that was hiding behind the purple evening shadows. A navy sky outlined the orange glow of the setting sun behind the faraway trees. He pulled in a deep breath that felt like it caressed something in his soul.

He could get used to this.

A minute later, he was at his truck, reaching for the handle when he realized Daniel's was still parked beside him. Even though the man was known to work long past daylight, a twinge of compassion tugged at Peyton's heart. He looked to the barn where the door was still open wide, golden light spilling out onto the concrete. Inside, he found Daniel standing in Dagger's stall, stroking the shimmering black horse with a brush.

He looked over his shoulder, his eyes widening when he registered Peyton's presence. "Olivia?"

"She's up at the cabin with her momma."

Daniel's shoulders caved as if he'd been holding up a mountain on his own for half the day.

"It wasn't...as bad as you might think it was, Daniel."

He scrubbed one hand against his temples. "I've fought more battles in my heart today than my whole life combined."

Peyton stepped into the stall. "We all make mistakes. But for what it's worth, I think this is something she needed to go through."

Daniel froze, staring at the ground between them before he slowly lifted his eyes. "You think so?"

Peyton nodded, looking down at the invisible string that he fidgeted with in his fingers. "I do. I think..." He paused, rubbing the back of his neck, unsure if he had a right to say what he was about to say. "I think she's been a girl for so long and she's been waiting for someone to give her a reason to be a woman. I think what happened today gave her something to fight for. Something to build from." He growled under his breath and dropped his hand. "If any of that made sense."

"It did. Thank you, Peyton. And thank you for seeing her home. She might not have come back to us if it weren't for you."

He shook his head. "She would've. She's too smart. I didn't tell her anything that she wouldn't have come up with on her own."

"Yeah, but because of you she didn't have to go through it on her own." He lifted the brush in his hand with halfhearted effort. "I promised myself I'd take that secret to the grave, but I just had a moment of weakness, I guess. I thought...I was wondering—"

"Don't worry about it. It's behind us." Peyton waved off

any need for an explanation. Olivia would be waiting up the hill for her daddy to come home. "Goodnight, sir." He dipped his chin as he turned to leave.

"Peyton."

"Yes, sir?" He spun around.

"Do you love my daughter?"

Peyton's heart dropped into his stomach. Any knowledge he had of breathing now lost to him. What was Daniel thinking? How could he jump to conclusions like that and spring them without warning? How could he make such a massive assumption when Peyton had only known the girl for a month?

And how was he supposed to tell the man that he'd taken one look at his daughter holding a kid today and had seen her future—a ring on her finger, a baby on her hip, and a house they'd built together?

"I do," Peyton breathed.

Daniel's hardened jaw ticked and after a long second, he tipped his head. As if the thought weren't a surprise to him. "I thought you might."

"I think the moment I met her on the side of the road that night and she told me about her dreams...that's when I fell for her." But he hadn't considered it until this moment—hadn't given himself a chance to realize it. "She's everything good in the world, Daniel. I wouldn't mind spending the rest of my life making sure she knows that."

Daniel's brows lifted a fraction, a faraway look in his eyes. He set Dagger's brush on a small ledge on the wall and closed the distance between them. He reached out to shake his hand. "Welcome to the family, son."

Peyton shook his head, freezing their handshake in place. "She doesn't know how I feel about her, and I want to keep it that way. What I said when I got here still stands. I want to get my heart right with God." Peyton let his hand fall away. "I spent too many years dating and thinking a woman's presence would change my heart." And while Olivia had certainly impacted him, she wasn't the answer he sought. "I want Jesus to fill that place, first."

Daniel nodded, as if he could respect Peyton's decision. "I believe that He will, son. And I can rest knowing my daughter is in good hands."

Peyton shoveled one last pile of weeds into the wheelbarrow and paused, propping his calloused hands on the top of the handle as he watched the same orange sky he saw every evening. Hundreds of dragonflies flew figure-eights through the air, shimmering in the sunlight. In the distance, mourning doves cooed a low hum and cicadas had started their nightly chants.

This land never gave him a chance to tire of it, each sunset, sound, and shade different from the next. For a few minutes every day, he was at its mercy, arrested by the idea that God would create something so rich just for his eyes to behold.

Peyton gripped the shovel again and observed his work. It was a good day when Daniel had him pulling up the harvest, breaking ground with the tiller, or dropping new life into the soil for the fall season. Out here he could think clearly. Nature gave endlessly without expecting anything in return and he couldn't get enough of it.

The ground beneath his shoes called his name. As the other workers retreated to their own homes to get ready for the dance, he stood at the edge of the garden watching thick gray clouds flock the late sun. What were the chances that those clouds would turn to rain and give this place a much-needed shower?

He closed his eyes and breathed deep, willing the peace to reach his soul. Like always, the feeling ricocheted off his heart as if there was no good place inside of him to plant the seeds of assurance. Disappointment soared through him as he turned his focus back to the task at hand—planting summer squash. He set the shovel against the wheelbarrow and went down on one knee. From a crate, he lifted a small pot with the green stalk of squash already sprouting through the top—a head start Gianna had been growing in the greenhouse over the last few weeks.

Peyton shimmied the block of dirt from the pot and handled it gently, so the new growth didn't snap off during the transition. He burrowed out a shallow hole in the empty row and loosened the roots in his hand before planting them. Then he moved onto the next. He was nearly halfway down the row when he felt something stir in his spirit.

Watch your left.

The thought was so random, he nearly ignored it. But curiosity was strong. He glanced to his left at the cabin sitting proud at the top of the hill. Everything seemed normal. Peyton picked up another pot of dirt and shook the young squash out into his hand.

Watch your left.

The words didn't seem to belong to him. They were the same tone of his thoughts, but they weren't pulled to the front of his conscious by his own command. He looked toward the left end of the empty row waiting for squash. Maybe he needed to pick up the pace, so he had time to shower and get dressed. He took two more shifts to his left from his knees.

Watch your left.

Struck by the persistence of the thought, Peyton turned his full attention, scanning the row of soil, the cabin, and whatever was over his left shoulder.

A few feet away lay a cottonmouth snake circled around itself with its head in striking position. Peyton shoved himself until he was crawling backward and then pushed off the ground to stand. He dusted off his clothes and wiped his shirt as if the scaley thing had been draped over his shoulders. He hadn't been this close to a venomous one yet. And by the looks of it, the snake was just as disturbed as Peyton was.

"Not today, pal." Peyton walked to the far side of the row where he'd left the shovel. He plucked it from where it sat and made his way to where the crate of squash and the snake waited.

But the snake had moved on.

Peyton scanned the rows to his left and then right. But there was no snake in sight. It hadn't been a little thing, either, so it wasn't like it could hide under a plant. With the sharp end of the shovel resting against the ground, Peyton waited.

What had told him to watch his left? There was no way for him to know he was moving right into the path of a snake. He wasn't the kind of man who believed the universe sent out signals—there was only One Peyton gave credit to.

"Was that You, Lord?" The moment the words left his lips affirmation settled on him like a weight.

It was God. It had earmarks of His power all over it. An answer Peyton hadn't asked for. A miracle he hadn't been expecting.

And something about that reached deep inside Peyton and stirred a feeling he hadn't felt in years.

Belonging.

He was God's. Peyton's heart belonged to the Lord. Always had. And he'd always taken that for granted. Even in church when the hymns demanded he know God's love for him and when he'd been surrounded by family that echoed it. Being told Jesus loved mankind was one thing.

Knowing it was another.

"Lead me to the rock that is higher than I," he whispered.

Heaviness settled in the center of his chest, a drive to worship. He released the shovel and heard it crash against the dirt. With his eyes lifted to the gray sky above he let the golden warmth of the sun bathe his face. He lifted his hands at his sides, surrendering whatever the Lord asked of him.

"God, I love You." His voice was husky even to his own ears. "I want You so bad. Lord, I can't settle for less." When his voice failed, he let his heart do the talking.

God had always been there for him, through sin and success. On his dark, lonely days, and the ones that held memories and milestones. When he thought he'd failed, run too far, or done too much to belong to Him—God was there. And as if every prayer was answered in the same breath, he could envision Jesus as a mighty lion settled in front of a blinding light, at ease. Confident, wild love radiating from Him. Unconcerned, there was a gentleness in His eyes as if He were weighing Peyton and conveying, 'Why didn't you just trust Me? I knew your story all this time.'

A fierce growl ripped through the sky overhead and shook the earth beneath his feet, freeing the bands that had held Peyton's soul firmly to the pit of his stomach.

"Is this it, Lord?" He asked as a tear trickled down to his jaw. "Is this what You've been waiting to show me?"

The answer came in the form of a rushing wind that moved through the trees and a crashing rain that drummed against the earth and then a still small voice as Peyton fell to his knees, overcome by a taste of grace that he hadn't known existed.

It is.

CHAPTER TWELVE

Since Peyton had started working at the ranch, he'd been to the Whitmore's event hall twice, but never when it was this lively. The sound of music reached his ears before he stepped out of the twilight and into the chandelier light that spilled over some two hundred happy people.

Most were in the middle of the barn-shaped building, dancing to the band that played on a stage at the far side of the room. Many were gathered near tables lined with food that stood against the walls. Some were filtering in and out as the doors opened and closed, tracking the floors with the rain that had ended a few minutes again. Faraway thunder promised more to come.

As he scanned faces for someone he knew, Peyton picked a loaded potato skin from a tray on one of the tables and popped it into his mouth, the savory flavors settling on his tongue.

"Well, how—*dee*, cowboy," a woman said, the voice so painfully familiar that he rolled his eyes as he looked at her.

"Caroline," he said with a nod.

The woman was dressed in a bright pink skirt, a cowgirl hat to match, and a baggy white blouse. Most everyone else wore jeans or jean shorts. She stuck out like a diamond in a coal mine. But if she had come to blend in then she wouldn't be Caroline.

"I like the lumberjack look you've got goin'." She tipped her head to his beard, her eyes scanning the plaid button down he wore, and winked. "Did anyone ever tell you I've got a thing for lumberjacks?"

Fighting the urge to let his smile turn into a cringe, he picked up a fried ball of something and paused before he tossed it in his mouth. "Was that before or after you had a thing for baseball players?"

She grinned. "After." She tipped her head to the side, a silky ponytail catching on her shoulder as she did. "Dance with me, cowboy."

"Actually, I'm looking for—"

She had her slender fingers wrapped around his forearm, pulling him onto the dance floor before he could protest. There was no harm in sparing her one dance. Though he wished he was sharing the first with someone else. Her fingers slid down to his as she led him deeper into the swarm of dancing couples. She spun around in her sequin cowgirl boots and rested her free hand on his shoulder.

With enough space between them so that he didn't send any misguided signals, he set one hand on her waist and held the other firmly in his. The song was slow enough to not have to spin her around, but fast enough that he wouldn't have to feel like he was at prom.

"Ranch livin' has been kind to you," she said, a prissy smirk in the purse of her lips. "You really ought to consider moving to Heavenly for good. Might change your life."

He sighed, unconcerned if she heard it or not. "I've got too many plans in the works."

Her eyebrows raised as if she were hanging on his every word. "Plans to see the world?"

Peyton cleared his throat as he shook his head. "Just to see my grandma."

Over her head, he scanned faces again. Would he find Olivia dancing with another man? Something about that mental image forced him to swallow a bad mood. He'd never felt better in his life—why would he let something like that ruin his night? So what if she was. She already told him that she liked to dance. It was his own stupid fault for not getting here sooner.

"You can stop playing hard to get, cowboy." There was something different in her voice, something serious that drew his focus to her blue eyes. Caroline rolled them as she shook her head. "I know I'm not the one you want to be dancing with right now. But this town is full of bachelorettes and if I didn't snag you up then one of them would have." She tipped her head.

Peyton looked over the crowd again, most were talking and minding their own business. But then he saw it. A few women were looking his way. One, while she was already dancing. He wanted to slink back to the food table and maybe hide under a tray of pigs in blankets for a bit.

Instead, he looked down at Caroline, resigned to accept that she was simply a harmless flirt who couldn't help herself. But she wasn't a bad person. "Thank you."

The edge of her mouth perked a bit at his praise. "Don't mention it. We'll just kill a little bit of time until Olivia notices you're here."

Her name felt like a firecracker in his lungs. "How'd you know I was looking for Olivia?"

"Oh, please. Half the husbands here don't even look at their wives the way you look at her."

That little detail brought a smirk to his face and sent him scanning for her again.

"And she once locked herself in her room for an entire week when she was a kid because her parents canceled their vacation. She's that stubborn. She'll never tell you how she really feels about you."

The earth stopped turning for a moment. "What'd you say?"

Caroline snorted and leaned closer. "I'm not supposed to tell you this." She paused, a sigh bringing her shoulders down. "But I've never seen this side of her before. She spent her entire life like she was searching for something that makes sense." If he was seeing things right, Caroline's eyes shimmered with emotion. "Since you showed up, she acts like she found it."

Peyton forced himself to breathe.

"She's my best friend and I want to see her happy. She deserves it more than she'll ever know. So, I'm giving you a heads up." Her serious eyes found him again. "If you have even an ounce of feelings for her, then I think you should both see where they might lead."

Say no more. Peyton loosened his grip on Caroline and turned to walk away.

"Not so fast, cowboy." She grabbed his sleeve and pulled him back toward her. "We've got to make her jealous first."

"I thought you said she was stubborn," he said, shaking

his head.

"Don't worry. We'll give her enough time to get her hackles raised, then you can sweep her off her feet, and she'll be like putty in your hands. Trust me. She's the only sister I've ever had. I know how she thinks."

Peyton swallowed, hesitant to carry out Caroline's scheme, but willing to let the girl have her fun. If she was right, then he'd risk it all to have that woman in his arms.

Lifting his attention to the crowd once again, his heart stopped in his throat and nearly made him lose his mind when he found her already looking at him. Her hair pulled away from her face but spilling down her shoulders, a pretty little smile on her lips, and a jean jacket over a white sundress that flowed around her knees as she danced in another man's arms. The only man he didn't want to pick up by the collar and toss out into the parking lot.

Her dad.

"Have I ever told you how proud I am of you?" Dad asked.

She smiled up at him as they danced. "About a thousand times."

He chuckled. "Then make this a thousand and one. Every day you make me the proudest dad in the world."

"Thank you." She tipped her chin. "I couldn't have done it without you and Mom."

He beamed and for a moment they simply danced.

"You know what I noticed?" he asked.

Olivia looked up at him. "What's that?"

The smirk on his face braced her for a teasing comment. "You seem to be coming around to the house a lot more lately."

She tilted her head slightly. "Have I?"

"I was wondering if it was because you were missing your family." He raised one eyebrow. "Or maybe it was because of a young farmhand."

She nearly gasped, catching herself before the sound came out. "Dad, that's ridiculous. You know I have no interest in seeing anyone. I think you're imagining things."

Dad looked at her, his dark eyes seeing more than she

wanted him to see right now. So, she dropped her focus to his throat where she could see him swallow. "Olivia."

The depth of his voice pulled her attention to his eyes. There was a earnestness there. "It's okay if a man comes along and makes you change your mind."

Feeling like the walls were suddenly falling around them, she looked past Dad's shoulder, her eyes connecting with Peyton's again.

The song ended and applause tore through her thoughts. She didn't know what to say. Whatever her dad was thinking, it wasn't the truth.

Another song started up and Olivia followed her dad to the table where Momma was organizing platters of food. Pepaw sat in a rocking chair on the stage with a few of his friends as they watched over the event, gossiping no doubt. Josh kept disappearing with his friends, only returning when he needed another bite of food. And Peyton was still dancing with Caroline in the middle of the dance floor. The sight of them together dropped a brick of dread into the pit of her stomach.

Olivia picked up a fried cheese stick and took a bite, refusing to look over her shoulder at them even one more time. It was bad enough that he'd caught her staring twice. Once more and she was determined to crawl under the stage and sleep there until morning.

"They're trying to make you jealous." Mom moved closer as she rearranged empty trays, loose napkins, and scattered plates, her lashes fluttering briefly as she looked up at her.

Even if she was right, Olivia didn't care. "What makes you think that?"

"Because they're over there giggling like a couple of kids up to no good."

She took another bite and raised an eyebrow. "Maybe they're in love."

"Mm-hmm." Mom's dimples appeared. "He doesn't look at her the way he looks at you."

She scoffed. "He doesn't look at me like he looks at desserts, Mom."

"I beg to differ. I've been married to your daddy for more than thirty years. I've seen that look a time or two and he wasn't looking at pastries."

Olivia picked up a napkin and wiped her fingers, shaking her head.

"It's okay if you don't see him the same way. There's no heartbreak in it if he's not the one for you."

Against better judgement, she looked at the dance floor one more time. He wasn't hard to find. There was a light about him that spoke of a heart that knew the Lord intimately. It had been easy to ignore over the last month, but tonight she couldn't deny it. The way his dark blue eyes held her up, she knew in that moment that there wasn't a single mountain she couldn't climb, a river she couldn't cross, or a dream she'd have to give up.

"Not this one, Momma. He's gonna break my heart whether he stays or leaves. He's changed me. Love has always been a longshot for a girl like me, but he's changed the way I see every other man now."

Her mom hummed a melodic acknowledgement.

"And I don't think any other will ever suit me." Even if Peyton never wasted a thought on spending another day with her—even if he never entertained the idea that she was worth spending a lifetime with—he was the only man she'd be willing to trust with her heart. "I've got a feeling he's gonna say, 'I promise' and I'm gonna be able to believe him."

Olivia tore her gaze away from him, turning to face the tables of food. Which was probably a much better use of her time. The day they'd spent together yesterday had been so good, so sweet that she wasn't quick to surrender this friendship to any ideas about love. She loved him, there wasn't a doubt in her mind, but she would build a dam from toothpicks before she let that love spill over into notions about romance. She'd ruined her friendship with Rhett because of silly fairy tales.

She wouldn't lose Peyton to those same dragons.

The song changed, something a little quicker this time. Josh jetted between Olivia and the table, grabbing a handful of chocolate chip cookies and racing away with a giggle fueled by an overdose of sugar. He was gone as quickly as he'd come, and Olivia grinned as she tucked a cube of watermelon in her mouth.

"You gonna sing tonight?" Peyton asked, suddenly behind her.

Fighting a smirk, she turned to face him. There was something different in the depths of his eyes. Something sure. Something that she felt in the pit of her stomach. "I don't sing at these kinds of things."

He lifted his hand and held it out to her. "Do you dance at these kinds of things?"

"I do." And even though she'd told him as much yesterday, right now she wasn't emotionally prepared to be held in his arms.

But turning him down would feel like missing out on a once in a lifetime opportunity.

So, she swallowed her fears and placed her hand in his. His touch was warm, his grasp firm as he led her through the spinning and twisting couples energized by the fast-paced song. They were somewhere in the middle of the dance floor when he turned toward her, set his hand on her waist, and moved to the rhythm with more finesse than he had a right to.

Wholly convinced that she'd made the right move, at least for one night, Olivia matched his flair, swaying twice to the right, then as quickly to the left. He held her hand above her head and spun her around. A thrill of delight drew a giggle out of her as she returned to his arms, shocked by how well they moved together.

Olivia tossed her head back and let out a laugh. "You didn't tell me you knew how to dance."

His smirk lifted a little more on one side, tufts of untrimmed hair falling across his brow. "Mom taught me and my brother when we were young. Dad taught us how to fight, and Mom taught us how to dance."

"Mm-hmm. And who did you get your charm from?"

He winked. "My grandma."

When she laughed again, he pulled her a little closer. She'd never shared space like this with a man before. Not even when she'd danced with Sophie's cousin and someone's brother at the wedding last month. Those dances had been professional and demure. This was different. This was...electrifying.

Their dance slowed into a modest sway and Olivia looked up into his smiling eyes, bright with something she hadn't seen in him before. "What happened?"

"What happened when?"

"To you. You look like you just discovered some kind of buried treasure."

His smirk turned into a grin. "Something like that."

She squinted at him, tilting her head. This man. He'd whirled into her life on one of the scariest nights she'd ever experienced, had talked her into wearing her hair out of her face, and had made her forget all about how she didn't like the way she looked when she stood next to other girls.

"What?" Peyton asked, his eyes never leaving hers.

"I'm just thinking about..." She couldn't really repeat aloud what she'd been thinking. "How different everything is since you walked into our lives."

His smile sobered a bit. "Meeting you has changed me in ways I didn't know I needed to change."

Olivia nodded. His "you" included her family. She refused to read into it any more than that. "We've changed, too. My parents act like they got a new son. Josh treats you like the brother he never had. Even Pepaw is talking more than I've ever heard from him before."

"And what about you, Olivia?"

She swallowed again. Her? She'd changed the most out of them all. "For the first time in my life I can simply be me." The reminder was like a breath of fresh air. "I don't have to wait for permission from everyone else in the room before I come out of my shell. I can just be." Tears burned in her eyes, but she refused to let them fall. Not here under the golden glow of the chandelier light where everyone else was having the time of their lives. "To me, that's worth a thousand flat tires."

Understanding passed over his face slowly, drawing a chuckle from him. The song ended again, separating them long enough to applaud. When a gentler, more romantic song started playing, she half-expected him to lead her off the floor. But he pulled her back into a dance instead. She let him, resting her hand a little easier on his shoulder this time.

His focus lifted to something behind her and the joy in his eyes dissipated. Like the flip of a switch, his excitement turned intense.

She tightened her grip on his hand. "What's wrong?"

He snapped out of whatever trance he was in and looked down at her. "Nothing. It's stupid."

His tension left, but she wasn't letting him get away with it so easily. "How stupid?"

The tick in his jaw beneath his beard didn't go unnoticed. "What do you think of Stu?"

All the little fairies that whispered romantic notions over her in the last few minutes flew away at the mention of Stu. Where had that question come from? "I think he's a bit of a creep, but not a bad person to my knowledge. He used to pick on me in high school, but when he asked my dad for a job then I knew I had to put that behind me."

A wrinkle formed between his brows. "You want me to turn him to dust?"

She huffed a laugh. "No, but I appreciate the sentiment." After a moment passed, she shook her head. "Why do you ask?"

"He's been acting strange lately. Stranger than when I first met him."

Olivia let her eyes stray from his face and scan the crowd in the off chance that Stu was somewhere in the room. Against the front wall, near the doors, she found him. He was already looking their way. A couple danced passed between them, and Stu was gone.

A chill snaked down her spine and Peyton pulled her closer.

She cleared her throat. "I've kept my distance from him because I know he doesn't care for me, but I don't think he's too much to worry about."

Peyton nodded, raising her hand so that she was circling in a slow spin. Once she returned to him, he tucked one hand against her back and lowered her into a slow dip she hadn't been expecting, but welcomed, nevertheless. When she stood again, her hand was on the nape of his neck and his was tucked against his chest with her fingers clasped firmly within. She let herself revel in his nearness.

If only for one night.

Olivia looked up at him, the curl at the ends of his hair brushing across her knuckles. "Did you ever come up with a dream job for the top of your list?"

A gradual smirk crawled across his lips. "I did. But you

have to promise you won't laugh."

A soft squeak escaped her throat. She couldn't imagine what he'd drummed up that she would find amusing. "Okay. I've got my sense of humor in check."

He sucked in a deep breath and let it out slowly. "Farmer."

That one little word made her heart feel like a fish that had been hooked. An unnerving reaction for a silly inside joke they'd kept running for the last month. Promise broken, she tossed her head back as a series of giggles bubbled out of her.

"You weren't supposed to laugh."

"I'm sorry. I'm not laughing at you. It's just..." She sighed deeply. "Perfect. It suits you. More than you realize, I think. You're a natural on the farm. You've loved every moment of working with my dad." She looked down at his beard. "Farm life looks good on you."

He grinned and she suddenly wished she could stuff the words back in her mouth.

The song ended—a needed moment of cool air as they separated. She fought the urge to swipe the sleeve of her jacket against her lips. As if he could read her thoughts, Peyton took her hand and led her through the people who were waiting for the next song. He didn't let go until he found her parents standing in the corner near where Pepaw sat alone in a half circle of empty chairs. Josh and his friends were picking through another table of goodies.

"Hot in here, innit?" Pepaw tipped his chin as Olivia reached for a cup of punch.

"Dad," Mom chided under her breath.

Olivia's eyes widened over the brim as Peyton circled around in front of her, blocking her view of the family who was bent on watching her squirm. He picked up a brownie and broke it in half. "A deal's a deal." He smiled as he tucked one half in his mouth. She watched him through a suspicious squint as he smirked. "What's your number one dream job?"

Pursing her lips, she shook her head. "To tell you the truth, I'm not sure I remember what my number one dream job is."

"I'm not buying it."

She swirled the red liquid around in her cup and shrugged. "I don't know what to tell you. I'll have to go through my old diaries and try to refresh my memory."

"How long might that take you?" Peyton asked, grinning.

"I know what her dream job is!" Josh called out.

Peyton turned, along with her family to look at her brother. Olivia laughed. There was no way he knew what her *real* dream job was.

"What is it?" Peyton asked.

"She wants to be a wife and a mom," Josh said, as serious as she'd ever seen him before.

Her heart dropped into her stomach as she set the cup on the table. Everyone turned to look at her, as if waiting for confirmation. But her breath stuck in her lungs, and she couldn't think up a quick enough lie to pacify them.

"How do you know that?" she asked breathlessly.

He shrugged, cookie crumbs on the edges of his mouth. "I saw it on the paper behind your computer when I played *Mutant Firestorm Conquest*."

Olivia tried to fill her chest with air. She could feel Peyton's waiting eyes on her. She refused to look at him. Refused to cement this moment to her memory if she found a look of pity resting there. As everyone waited for her to respond, the earth crumbled around her.

How could she ever expect to become a wife with this *thing* on her face? What made her think she'd be able to have babies who wouldn't cry when they looked at her? That life wasn't possible for her, and she was painfully naive to have ever written those words down to begin with.

Her family blurred before her, and she couldn't take the heat of their curious stares a moment longer. Olivia turned and rushed through the people gathered at the edge of the dance floor, elbowing and excusing herself through them. Her head low, the agonizing urge to release her hair from its clip and let it fall over her face was strong.

When she reached the doors, she pushed them open and all but fell into the night air that was damp with coming rain. She sucked in as much as she could swallow and swore she wouldn't cry. Not here. Her high-heeled boots thudded against the concrete walkway as she rushed toward the parking lot. Checking both directions for traffic, she felt for her keys in her jacket pocket once she reached the tailgate of her truck. Before she could slip her hand inside, someone grabbed her elbow and spun her around.

Peyton.

With his hands on the backs of her arms, he held her close. "Where do you think you're going?"

She pressed her hands against his chest, pushing with a halfhearted effort. Her heart ached from the burn of shame and tears finally escaped against her will. She sobbed as she sucked in a sudden breath. "Nobody was supposed to ever know that."

"And why not?" he said, his breath brushing along her jaw.

She tried to push again, but the need to fight was lost on her. She blinked long and slow until her eyes were free of tears. "Because it's humiliating."

"It shouldn't be."

She finally let herself look up at him, bracing every emotion for what she was about to find in his eyes.

There was no pity there. No disgust. No horror at the idea that she would want the kind of a life that seemed to come so naturally to everyone else.

He shook his head softly. "You have every right to stand on the tallest hill in Texas and let the whole world know what you want."

"How can I ever expect to have that when I look like this?" She tipped her chin a little higher in case he hadn't been paying attention to the mark on her face over the last month. "The only boy who was ever there for me couldn't even stand the way I look."

His hand was suddenly on the curve of her jaw, his fingers pushing through her hair, and his thumb caressing the mark that had never known the touch of another human being aside from her parents. He was intentional about it, his skin discovering the inky edges of the blemish, the tiny hairs that covered it, and the dark ridge that crawled up the side of her nose and into her eyebrow. She closed her eyes and leaned into him as he caressed the part that ran just beneath her eye.

For a wink in all of eternity, she was a priceless diamond found by a man who'd searched his whole life for something beautiful and wasn't afraid he'd find a single flaw. Like a woman thirsty for belonging, she knew she could live a thousand lives and never forget the way Peyton held her in this moment.

She opened her eyes to find him looking at her lips. She swallowed hard. Surely, he wasn't thinking about—

Fireworks went off in the distance behind the barn, the sudden pops causing her to lose her train of thought.

But not for him...

Her head swam, and her heart pounded against her throat. As much as she craved the taste of a kiss that wanted her for who she was, her spirit rebelled. Peyton wanted the Lord—he'd made that clear from the beginning. He needed to get his heart right with God before he settled down with anyone. He'd said that. And she wanted that for him with every ounce of her being.

Even more than she wanted to know his love.

A tear fell from her lashes, and he erased it with his thumb. "Olivia," he said, his voice quiet and warm. "I would have kissed you back."

Her eyes widened, her mouth fell open as his words swept her into the past and rewrote the story of a twelve-year-old girl who took a gamble on the boy she loved. But instead of another, she imagined a young Peyton in his place, promising her a future where she didn't have to hide behind her hair or stand at the back of the room or keep her head downcast. She saw his dark blue eyes and the quiet assurance that rested there when he looked at her.

And just like that, she forgot why she was ever afraid to begin with.

A smirk he didn't have the heart to hold back pulled at Peyton's lips. The woman in his arms would run away with him and change her last name right this minute if he asked her—he could see it in her eyes. The temptation was gravitational. It was hard to look at Olivia and picture another woman walking down the aisle toward him. Hard to imagine going on another date where she wasn't sitting across the table from him. Hard to visualize a scenario where he wasn't able to hear her laugh every day for the rest of his life. He couldn't explain how he knew it—this woman was gonna be his one day.

But not today.

A shadow passed over his soul, reminding him that despite the racing beat of a heart falling in love, and the thrill of hope he'd felt in the garden hours ago, there was still something dark following him. Something he'd learned to question less, trained himself to ignore more. But as he looked into the eyes of his future, he couldn't deny something in his past still hunted him.

"What's wrong?" she whispered, shattering his thoughts like a glass wall between them.

He shook his head and pasted on a smile. "Nothing."

It was something Olivia would never know about. Not if he could spare her from it. Even if God never gave Peyton the green light to pursue her heart, he could gift her the freedom to walk away from his brokenness.

"I need you to promise me something," he whispered, dropping his hand from the soft curve of her cheek and taking both of her hands in his as she nodded gently. "I need you to walk in that building and dance with me and if anyone gives you grief about being a wife and a mom one day, promise me you'll roll your eyes at them in that way you do."

With a huff, she incidentally rolled her eyes at him. A grin finally tugged at her mouth. "I guess I could do that."

He laced his fingers through hers and led her across the parking lot, through the double doors, and onto the dance floor. As the space grew more crowded, Peyton set one hand against the small of her back, guiding her to the center again. He glanced to his left and noticed the attention of the daycare worker that Olivia had called Sabrina, a telling smirk on her face as she sent him a single nod. Hopefully the other women Caroline had warned him about were looking, too. He hadn't staked his claim on this girl yet, but the sand was swiftly falling.

He spun Olivia in a circle, and she answered his invitation with a double turn that had her long, auburn locks dancing around her. She returned to his arms in no time, one hand in his, the other curving around the back of his neck as he pulled her close and swayed with a rhythm that she matched energetically. There was no doubt in his mind that he was holding the belle of the ball. Her smile glowing, she wore her heart on her sleeve with the way she watched him. He'd have to dance with her for the rest of the night to avoid the line of men who no doubt wanted their shot with her.

It was only a few minutes later when he got tapped on the shoulder—happy to see that it was Daniel who wanted the next dance. Peyton bowed out and let him cut in. As the night unfolded and the fireworks grew more frequent, the building emptied slowly until there were a handful of people left behind to clean up. Olivia had gotten tugged by Caroline through the double doors with Josh quick on their heels, but not before they shared a glance across the nearly empty building. His heart so full that he could explode, Peyton downed what was left in his cup and tossed it into a nearby trash can.

"Make yerself useful and take these to the truck, will ya?" Vern pointed to the short stack of boxes leftover from Olivia's baked goods.

"Trying to put me to work during my off hours, huh, Vern?"

"And you'll be happy with it, or I've got a scrap pile that needs to be relocated tomorrow," Vern said as he lifted a cooler and hefted it past Peyton.

Sneaking a kolache from under the top lid, Peyton stuck it in his mouth and picked up the boxes. Outside, the wind was a little colder and humid. He set the boxes in the backseat of Daniel's truck where Vern had left the door wide open. To the west, faraway lightning turned the sky stark shades of purple. Billowing clouds outlined in blue-gray wisps of light guaranteed a storm that nobody wanted to get caught in.

"Sometimes you pray for rain..." Vern said, stopping beside him, hands empty. "And sometimes you pray the rain doesn't wipe out your crops and drown your livestock. I've got a feeling we're about to be asking the good Lord for the latter."

Peyton turned to the old man who watched warily, a wrinkle between his brows. To their right, cannons echoed as the sky lit with a different kind of light, the sizzle and thud of fireworks exploding.

"Fireworks are a lot like women. Easy on the eyes but a danger to men."

"Yeah, but fireworks might take your fingers," Peyton said as Vern turned to look at him. "A woman'll take your heart."

Vern barked a laugh that mixed with a cough. He shook his head and turned back to the show. Red, white, and blue filled the night sky behind the venue, the loud *pop-pop* of the display followed by cheers and oohs.

"You're not wrong about that, my boy." Vern said, his shoulders lifting where he took in a big breath. "Problem with that is deciding which one might hurt less." He shuffled toward the building.

Peyton watched the man disappear inside, his gut telling him to follow and grab another load, but his feet stayed planted. That last statement felt like Vern was relaying a message.

He hadn't bothered to hide his feelings when he followed Olivia out of the barn a half hour ago. And it didn't matter to him if everyone assumed he felt something for her. But what was Vern trying to say? That she was gonna hurt him? That she was worth the risk?

The whistle and bang of a firework going up behind the barn caught Peyton's attention as it filled the night sky. Then the rumble of thunder to his left stole it next, where purple lightning shone through massive clouds. Vern was right about one thing.

Something chilling clung to the air.

CHAPTER THIRTEEN

Peyton dropped the last box of leftovers on the kitchen counter with a thud. The space was dim, everyone too sleepy to bother flipping the switch—Peyton included. He rubbed the backs of his knuckles against his tired eyes. "Tonight was fun. See you guys in the morning."

Gianna stopped him with a hand on his arm. He paused long enough for her to rise on tiptoe and press a kiss to his cheek. "Thank you for everything, Peyton."

Stunned by the maternal warmth reflecting in her blue eyes, he nodded, understanding that she was referring to more than just bringing in leftovers. Wearing a smile, Daniel stood in the kitchen doorway, only illuminated by the lamplight from the foyer.

"The thanks should be going to y'all. You've done more for me than I'll ever be able to repay."

Gianna laughed softly, sleepily as she stepped past him. "Having you here has been a joy for us, Peyton." She opened the fridge and started placing dishes inside. "You're like part of our family. We wouldn't have it any other way."

His chest tightened. When was the last time he'd felt so...accepted?

With one last nod, he passed Daniel, and the man patted him on the shoulder as he walked past. "Goodnight, sir."

On the porch, where Birdie, Boone, and Bear were fast asleep—Bear on his back with all four legs pointing upward—Peyton pulled the door shut behind him. He chuckled at the little dog's slumber, stopping short when he noticed Olivia coming up the stairs. Sudden thunder overhead shook the ground below.

"I thought you were headed home?"

She slowed to a stop on the top landing. "I had a couple of leftovers I needed to drop off first." She shrugged, gesturing to the huge bag hanging from her shoulder.

"Let me help with that," he said as he stepped forward.

"I've got it," she said with a laugh hanging in her voice. "It's not much. Only a few things."

Peyton nodded, stopping a few feet in front of her. "You have work in the morning?"

She shook her head. "Tomorrow's our day off."

Good. That was good. Why? Peyton cleared his throat. "Maybe after I get off work we can go do something?"

Her mouth fell open, her eyes widened, but just as quickly she shook her head and looked down at something in front of her shoes. "What did you have in mind?"

"Well, I've been here for a whole month and Vern never gave me a tour of the town."

She laughed and he smiled.

"Maybe we can do that. Ride around Heavenly. You can show me the lay of the land. Maybe we can stop at your favorite place to eat. Take a walk through your favorite antique store. Stay a while."

A grin as fast as wildfire appeared on her lips. "Sounds good to me."

"Good," he echoed as they both moved around the other, trading places. "Goodnight, Olivia."

"Goodnight, Peyton," she said as she walked backwards to the front door, a smirk on her face that teased him to follow her inside and spend the rest of the night talking.

He shook his head and let out a quick whistle. "Wanna go home, Bear?"

The little dog wiggled like a worm until he turned over on all fours again. Ears perked high, he stretched his front legs for a long second.

"Home?" Olivia stood in front of the door.

He shrugged. "It feels like home."

"I was hoping you didn't mean the city."

He rubbed one hand over his chest where something stirred. "I've got no plans for that anytime soon."

"Good," she said as she let herself inside. "I didn't want to miss out on tomorrow."

The door clicked shut but Peyton was held hostage. His

head swam. Every one of his thoughts flipped upside down and everything he believed about life was suddenly unimportant. There were only three things he was sure of. Jesus was his Savior. He had no intentions of heading west. And...

"I'm gonna marry that woman."

Bear yipped, pulling Peyton back to the present. He did an about-face and trotted down the stairs as the skies opened up and let the Heavens spill out. Rain drops pelted his shirt and hair, but he couldn't care less. He opened the passenger door and let Bear inside first, then rounded the truck and hopped behind the wheel. Headlights cut through the blanket of rain, but he could see just enough of the path ahead to make it to the homestead.

Bear stood on the seat with his front legs on the dash, tongue hanging out as if Peyton were about to put the truck in turbo speed and he didn't want to miss it. He reached out and patted the little dog's head. As the homestead came into view, it wasn't as dark as Peyton was expecting it to be. He eased down on the brakes, stopping at the edge of the treeline, still obscured.

The lights inside were on. Every one of them. And he very specifically remembered turning them all off. Especially the ones upstairs since he never went up there. He had no use for them.

He flipped the truck off. The headlights splaying across the rainy yard fell dark. Nothing but pitch black covered the short distance between him and the house. He waited, watched for movement.

There was none.

Shoulders tight, he stepped out and let Bear follow him through the driver's side. The dog hit the ground and ran to the closest tree, lifting his leg. Peyton moved toward the house. If he needed backup for some reason, he hoped Bear was fierce enough to attack an intruder. The rain drummed out any squeaking porch steps as Peyton slowly made his way across, peering through the windows. He reached for the doorknob, stopping short when Bear suddenly let out a low growl behind him.

Peyton looked over his shoulder to find the dog at full attention, the fur on his back standing on end to make him look more like a wolverine than a dog. Head down, he stepped slow and gradual as if there were a bear trap hidden in his path. Dread snaked up Peyton's spine.

On second thought, if there was someone inside waiting for him, then Bear might not be the best help. "Stay, boy," he whispered loud enough that the rain didn't take his words.

Bear licked his snarling lips and eased down on his belly.

"Lord, cover me." He twisted the knob and stepped inside.

His heart ricocheted off his ribcage. Everything was ransacked. Couches were moved, slats of wood pried away from the flooring, drawers emptied and scattered. Even the fireplace had been stirred through. From what he could see, the kitchen was in the same shape. Cabinets hung open, dishes on the countertops and some broken on the floor. The oven and fridge were both open.

If he wasn't alone here, then getting to his gun was the first thing he needed to do.

His bedroom door stood open, the lamplight filling the small space. He dropped down on one knee beside the bed that had been stripped of the quilts and slid his hand beneath the mattress.

It was gone.

An icy chill ran through his veins. The door at his back squeaked. He wasn't alone. And the person behind him had his gun, he could be sure of it. Peyton rose slowly, his muscles aching with adrenaline. He sucked in a deep breath, making peace with death if that's what God wanted for him tonight. Then he turned, awareness mixed with shock coiling through his body.

"Stu?"

The man stood in the corner between the half-closed door and the closet that he'd clearly emptied. Boxes thrown against the opposite corner to his left. Peyton's clothes were in a pile on the floor. Stu stood with one arm extended, Peyton's gun clasped tightly in his grip.

"I'm not a killer, Brooks. I'm not here for that, but I'm desperate enough to do whatever it takes to get out of this place."

"I don't have anything you want so you're free to leave."

A wicked smile split Stu's face. He lifted something in his other hand. It was a red tin—the same red tin that Peyton had tucked away in the storage at the top of his closet after Daniel had told him to store the box last month. "Oh, yes you do."

Peyton shook his head. "That's not mine."

"It doesn't matter." Stu shook the gun, punctuating his sentence. "It's mine now."

Peyton didn't care what the man wanted or thought he had. He just wanted his gun and a little solitude. On the nightstand, to his right, a vase without flowers still sat next to his Bible and a handful of change. With careful movements, he reached out, taking a half step toward the nightstand.

"Don't try anything, Brooks!" Stu followed with the barrel of the gun.

But Peyton had to know. He had to be sure. He reached the vase, lifted it enough to give it a shake, and heard the bullets jumble together at the bottom. Bullets he'd placed their last month when he'd relocated his gun from his truck to the mattress. He set the vase down, relieved that the gun pointing at him wasn't loaded. Even as breath filled his lungs, he still wasn't out of the woods.

"I told you, I'm desperate." He clutched the tin to his chest as if a sweaty grip might cause him to lose it.

"Then go." Peyton tipped his head toward the open door.

Stu smiled again, but this time it was a little less confident. "The moment I reach the treeline, you'll be in Daniel's back pocket telling him I'm the one he's looking for. Cops will be all over this place in less time it'll take me to get to the main road."

The one he's looking for? His wording sounded too specific for this to be a random burglary. Peyton looked down at the tin again. "What's in there?"

A deep, empty laugh echoed off the walls. "Look at you, Brooks. You rode in here like a long-lost son that the Whitmores didn't even know they had—they give you a job, a paycheck, a house, they feed you while the rest of us work like dogs just to make ends meet!" He shook the gun again.

"Those were the deals we cut with Daniel when we agreed to work for him. If you don't like working here, then go find something else to do."

"I didn't have to." He shook the tin. "Until you came along and took over this place. The homestead was my own private bank where I could get an extra few hundred dollars whenever I needed it. And then here you come along to ruin that for me. You've got the worst timing, Brooks."

Realization washed over him. "The money. The ten thousand dollars. You took it."

"I've done enough for that man on this farm that it should have been mine to begin with." Spit flew from Stu's mouth.

"Stu, this isn't a big deal. Just tell Daniel why you took it. I doubt he'll press charges against you."

"You don't understand. I'm taking it with me."

Peyton bit down until he felt his jaw tick. "Then what are you still doing here?"

Stu took two steps until the barrel was directly in Peyton's face. "I'm not convinced you won't have Daniel on my trail three seconds after I clear that door."

"You want a head start? Fine. Go. I won't mention it to him 'till morning."

Stu shook his head, a bead of sweat dripping down the side of his jaw. "No, Brooks. I'm telling you not to say two words to Daniel about the money *ever*." The man's eyes lightened for a brief second. "And if you do...then I know exactly where to find Olivia at any given moment of the day."

Peyton lifted his chin. Whatever chances the man had of leaving this house tonight plummeted to zero. There was only one way out now. And that was through him.

Peyton reached for the gun, grabbing Stu's wrist as the empty chamber clicked. With the other hand, he gripped Stu's collar and pushed the man until he was up against the wall. The gun clattered to the floor and Stu pulled his hand free, taking a swing at Peyton. Knuckles met Peyton's chin, blowing his head back with a snap of pain to his neck.

He swung, connecting with Stu's nose and splintering the panel behind him. With a roar, Stu lunged at him, lifting Peyton off the ground and sending him against the foot of the bed. The screech of wood against wood sounded as the bed moved, the tin clattered against the floor. Peyton gained his footing before he hit the ground and gave Stu a shove, sending him backward far enough to clock another punch.

The man spun and stumbled out of the room. Peyton followed, grabbing Stu by the shirt and swinging again.

Stu flipped over the couch and thudded against the floor. Before Peyton could reach him, he had turned over, scrambling to his feet. Stu came at him, catching Peyton around the middle and sending him against the wall beside the fireplace. He felt sheetrock collapse against his back, pain searing his bones at the impact.

Peyton shoved Stu, stumbling to one knee as he did. Stu made a glancing blow at his temple, pain searing where his knuckles landed. Peyton landed one to Stu's stomach, doubling him over as he groaned. Warmth spread across Peyton's brow, blood dripping into his line of sight on his right side. He wiped it away with the edge of his hand and pushed the sole of his shoe against Stu's ribcage, shoving him on his back. Before he could regain his stance, Peyton picked him up, the sting of pain rushing down both forearms as he lifted the man off the ground. The smell of fire filled his senses.

"If you ever threaten her again, there aren't enough men in this world to stop me from finding you."

From the time his daughter had walked through the front door, she'd worn a smile that told a story to everyone in the room who was paying attention. She was in love. And the boy living just down the hill had put that smile there, Daniel was sure. Tossing another pinch of monkey bread in his mouth, leftovers from the celebration still sitting on the kitchen counter, he watched her organize containers in the fridge.

"Have fun tonight, did you?"

Gianna stopped beside him with a giggle and pinched off a bit of bread for herself.

Olivia hummed a laugh. "This year was a good one."

Daniel shared a knowing look with Gianna. In her raised eyebrow, his wife was sharing the same thoughts he was.

"Maybe we should start having a Fourth of July every year," Gianna said.

"Mm-hmm."

They chuckled together. The girl was on cloud nine.

"Maybe Peyton will be around for that one, too."

With one hand on the fridge door, she paused. Long enough to go through some kind of thought process only known to her. "Maybe so."

Daniel nodded, pausing before he tucked another bite in his mouth. "And maybe he'll be ready to settle down by then."

She shut the fridge and turned to face them. "On that note, I'm going home. Love you both. Goodnight."

"Are you sure you don't want to stay here for the night?" Gianna asked, coming around to Daniel's other side so that she was closer to Olivia. "That storm sounds like it's gonna be a big one. Your old bedroom is still here...only it's a guest room now."

"That's okay. I'm too comfy at the cottage."

"If you're sure." Gianna went to give her a hug, kiss on the cheek. "Love you, sweetie. Goodnight."

Daniel followed suit, pressing a quick kiss to his little girl's forehead and realizing that she was very much a young woman now. He cleared his throat. "Goodnight, darlin'."

"Love y'all," she said and headed for the front door.

The foyer lamp flickered once. Twice. On the third time, the house powered down altogether.

"Perfect timing," Olivia laughed as she opened the door to a darkened porch and a torrent of rain beyond it.

Daniel's gut stirred. Something was wrong. He didn't know what, but it tightened his lungs. "Maybe your momma's right, Olivia. Why don't you stay the night here?"

"I'll be fine. I just need to make it through this hurricane and my truck is right there." She looked over her shoulder, and though it was dark, he thought she was smiling.

He grabbed a cowboy hat from the hook on the wall. "Be safe."

She nodded and pulled the door closed behind her.

"Who fergot to pay the light bill?" Vern bellowed from down the hallway. "I'm in there digging through the drawer and I can't tell my skivvies from my socks."

Daniel chuckled. "I'll go fire up the generator. Give it a minute and you'll have your skivvies in no time."

Vern plopped down on the couch beside where Josh was

curled up, asleep. He stirred. "Mom? Dad?"

"We're here," they said simultaneously.

"Why's it so dark?" He pushed himself into sitting position.

"Power went out. I'm 'bout to turn it back on now." With that, Daniel grabbed a flashlight from the drawer and his jacket from the coat rack, pulling it on as he stepped out onto the porch. Down the stairs and across the lawn, rain pelted like rocks. Had he walked out into a hailstorm? Around the corner of the house, he reached out only to collect water in his hand. No hail.

He pulled the old, splintered door to the shed open. Behind him, a faint bark. Daniel froze, unsure if he was able to hear anything over the rain at all. He turned and looked down the dark lane that led to the homestead. Was that Bear that barked? Rain dripped like a faucet from the front of his hat as he angled his head and listened harder.

Another bark. Closer.

The little dog appeared through the haze, running like his life depended on it. Daniel let the shed door fall shut, his instincts pulling him in the dog's direction. Bear stopped a dozen feet away and launched into a series of panicked howls. From the porch, Birdie and Boone stood and joined the chorus of howls with deep, earth-shaking voices of their own.

That couldn't be a good sign.

He jogged back to the porch and soared through the door, leaving it open behind him.

"What's wrong?" Gianna stood from where she was sitting on the armchair.

"I'm not sure—I'm not sure if anything's wrong," Daniel said as he swung open the picture on the wall beside the door and pulled a handgun from the case hidden inside. He shook his head as he loaded the gun, unsure if he was just being an overprotective dad or not. "Bear came from the homestead on his own and he doesn't look too happy."

Vern hustled from the couch. "Go find the boy. The cavalry can hold down the fort here." He left the room—to retrieve his own firearm, no doubt. Daniel wasn't even sure they needed to be armed. But with each second that ticked by, his heart told him something wasn't right.

He shared a quick look with Gianna, and she nodded once. He was gone as quickly as he came in, racing to his truck. He opened the door, and Bear beat him to the seat. Hoping over the console, he settled on the passenger side, bracing his front legs on the dashboard. Daniel flipped the truck on and hit the gas, glancing in the rearview mirror and half wishing he'd forced Olivia to stay at the cabin tonight. His kids were in three different places and if there was trouble in this storm, then he was only one man and couldn't reach them all.

"Lord, protect them," he whispered as he turned the minute-long drive into a thirty-second one.

Peyton's truck blocked the driveway into the yard. Through the rain, the house looked dark except for a flickering orange glow inside. His heart leapt into his throat as he stepped out into the rain, Bear on his heels.

By the time he reached the house, he could see the glow of a fire through the living room window. "God, have mercy."

With one foot on the bottom step, the front door flew open, and a man came stumbling out. He landed in the mud with a grunt. Daniel stepped away from the porch when Peyton followed, blood streaking down his face as he trotted down the stairs and helped the man to his feet.

Stu?

"What happened?"

Peyton swiped his hand against his face, panting for air. "He took the money, Daniel. The ten thousand. He's the one who took it." His shoulders bowed forward like he was a man out of fight. "And he threatened Olivia."

Daniel withdrew his firearm, holding Stu right where he was. "You what?"

As Peyton went back into the house, Daniel pulled his phone from his pocket and dialed nine-one-one.

Once they had all the information they needed to send a few officers out, Daniel waited until Peyton returned. He sat on the second stair as if his body didn't have one more ounce of energy left. Arm outstretched, he held a red tin box in one hand. Daniel took it, assuming it was the money stolen from them.

"The fire?"

Peyton nodded, his eyes pinched closed. "It's out."

"Take a minute to rest, son, but we need to move those trucks when the police get here."

Peyton pulled himself away from the step and dropped his hand on Daniel's shoulder as he past. "Don't let him get the drop on you. He's a heck of a fighter."

Stu stood huffing and whimpering in the rain, drenched and most of the blood washed from his face. "Why'd you do it?"

He shook his head as if he didn't know.

"*How'd* you do it?"

"The contractors..." Stu said between heavy breaths. "They asked a few of us to help them carry the tub. For the remodel. Upstairs. And...I was the last one out. I saw the safe in your closet. It was easy...to pick."

Daniel wanted to spit the taste of disgust out of his mouth. He'd trusted this man. Had seen him through many tough times. If he needed the money that bad, Daniel would have loaned it to him. Or given him a raise within reason. But the fact that he went through his wife's closet to get to their savings was more than he could cope with. And threatening Olivia...

He needed time to process this.

Daniel took out his phone again, this time to let Gianna know why the cops would be passing through their driveway in a few minutes.

Thunder rattled the ground beneath the cottage. A lantern on the corner of her desk, her only light. Olivia fell back against the quilts on her bed. Half-tempted to crawl beneath them in the same clothes that she went to the dance in, she let a deep breath flood her lungs and release slowly. Today was a good day.

A very good day.

Tomorrow couldn't come soon enough. Her heart raced at the thought of what it held. And who she would see. And what he would say.

Pulling her exhausted body from the bed, she made her way over to the computer where she'd hung her list of dreams on the wall behind it. No wonder Josh had been so quick to offer up the information. He'd seen this list at least once a week for the last month. She hadn't even thought twice about it. Hadn't thought her little brother would ever notice.

She plucked the paper from the wall, letting her eyes rove over the script from every version of her younger self, seeing it through fresh, new eyes. Eyes of a woman who was no longer afraid to admit that yes, she wanted to be a wife and a mom more than anything else. More than being an ice cream taste tester, a professional bridesmaid, a water slide volunteer, or even a baker.

The idea that she potentially had a husband out there in the world made her giggle. But the idea that she had kids who were waiting to be born or waiting to be adopted stung her eyes. She pressed her knuckles against her lips. She would lay down every dream she ever had to hear her family's banter, her husband's laughter, and the pitter-patter of little feet running through their home. She would sacrifice it all to feel the warmth of their hugs, to hear their little giggles as they played hide-and-seek, and to pray in the hallways where they slept. To celebrate holidays with sweet treats, and summers with ice cream cones, and to wrap birthday presents for them with Peyton.

Olivia gasped.

It felt awkward but slipping him into that role was too easy. After all, he *was* the man who took a jackhammer to the walls around her heart and brought every one of them tumbling down around her. She felt different. Felt like for the first time in a long time, she wasn't done chasing her dreams. Pressing the paper to her collarbone, she closed her eyes.

"Lord, if it's him...if Peyton's for me, please heal his heart. Let him line up with You. Whatever journey he's on, let him find what he's looking for."

With peace settling around her, she folded the paper and tucked it in the top drawer of her desk. She'd let it rest with God.

Olivia went to her dresser and pulled a pair of pajamas out. In the bathroom she changed and then pulled her hair back in a clip. She grabbed a wipe of makeup remover and smoothed it over her eyes, and then her beauty mark, and then the rest of her face.

In the middle of washing her face, her phone rang from her bedroom. Rain pelted the roof as she hurried through the task and grabbed a towel on her way out. She dabbed her face as she went to her phone.

One missed call from mom.

She tapped to return the call and waited.

"Olivia Rose Whitmore, you answer this phone when I call you."

Olivia was taken aback. "I was in the middle of washing my face. I couldn't get to it."

Mom sighed a long, heavy sigh over the phone. "I was worried."

"What's wrong?"

"There's been an incident at the homestead."

Her breath froze in her lungs, heart in her throat. "Where's Peyton?"

"He's with your dad. I don't know the details, but it sounds like Stu is the one who took the money from us, and he was keeping it at the homestead. Tonight, he went to find it and Peyton caught him. The police are on their way."

Olivia swallowed the panic rising in her throat as she went for her tennis shoes in the closet. "Is he hurt? Have you heard from him?"

"I haven't. I'm not sure how bad it is. But I wanted to let you know."

"I'm coming," she said as she slipped her feet inside, grabbed a jacket, and picked up the lantern.

"Come straight to the cabin. Your dad is with Peyton."

"I have to know he's okay, Mom."

"Olivia, we don't know exactly what's happening. If you put yourself in harm's way there's nothing those two wouldn't give up to keep you safe. Don't force them to make that decision."

She slid the jacket on as she pulled the door shut behind her. Mom was right. "I'm leaving now. Please let me know if you hear anything."

"I will. Drive safe," Mom said before she hung up.

Olivia never stopped praying for the five-minute drive. By the time she reached the driveway, two cop cars were headed down the lane toward the homestead. Her heartbeat lodged in her throat. She jammed the truck in park, yanked the keys out, and ran through the rain. Up the stairs and across the porch where lights had been restored by the generator, she burst through the door. "What happened?"

Mom stepped out of the kitchen, her curls wild and her eyes tired. "Don't worry. I talked to your dad. Peyton's fine. You should see the other guy. Those were your dad's words."

Olivia breathed freely, though her nerves were on the verge of exhaustion.

"Go sit with your brother and keep him company. Pepaw retired to the sitting room and I'm pretty sure he fell asleep in the recliner."

Olivia nodded, even though sitting was the last thing she wanted to do. She made her way over to where Josh was building a miniature log cabin on the coffee table and plopped down on the couch beside him.

Josh gave her an innocent smirk and held out a log. "Wanna help me build a fortress?"

With a sigh, she scooted to the edge of the seat and accepted it. They'd built two fortresses by the time Birdie and Boone started howling an alert. Olivia sprinted from the couch with her brother, throwing open the front door to the sight of three police cars and an ambulance leaving the circle drive.

The rain had lessened and now peppered the house with gentle drops. It wasn't long after when headlights appeared through the trees and Dad's truck pulled into the driveway. Peyton's was right behind him. The moment both trucks parked, Olivia trotted down the stairs and crossed the driveway.

Peyton's door opened and he slowly stepped out. Bear followed him, his feet hitting the pavement and darting up to the porch. Olivia stood still for a moment, too frozen with worry to know what to do. Then she did what she wanted to do more than anything else. She hugged him. He hugged her back, favoring his left arm. She wrapped one arm around him, headed toward the stairs, but he walked with a limp.

"You're hurt," she said.

"I'm sore," he said with a chuckle.

Once they were in the house, Mom brought them both

towels. As he dabbed his face dry, Olivia caught sight of a gash above his right eye, and a bruise forming on his left cheek. She took Peyton's hand and led him to the kitchen where she pulled out the chair at the end of the dining table and pushed him into it.

"I'm soaking wet," he complained.

"Chairs can be dried. You need to rest." She went to the kitchen sink and sank down on her knees, shuffling through the cabinet for a first aid kit. "You didn't let the EMTs take a look at your face, did you?"

"What makes you think that?"

"Besides the fact that I know you don't like to ask for help? You look terrible." She found the kit and carried it to the table where she pulled a second chair up alongside his, opened the box, and looked for butterfly bandages, alcohol wipes, and ointment.

"You really know me that well?"

Considering that they'd spent nearly every day together over the last month and he'd consumed her thoughts even when they weren't together? "Yep."

He chuckled until she swiped the alcohol wipe over his brow, then he let out a cringing hiss. Pushing back the wet hair plastered to his forehead, she eased her technique, dabbing instead of rubbing.

"You'll probably have a scar."

"What's one more?" His voice was gravely and exhausted.

He kept leaning away, in pain no doubt, so she cupped her right hand against his jaw and stilled him so she could finish the task.

He looked at her then, a long, sleepy blink doing nothing to deter the gaze he gave her. "You're gonna be an incredible mom, Olivia."

Olivia glanced at the entry to her left to see if anyone had heard him. But the living room was empty, quiet. She set the wipe on the table and grabbed the ointment. Dabbing a small dollop on her finger she placed it on his cut gently. "I think you might have a concussion."

"Trust me, this is no concussion," Peyton said.

She pressed the butterfly bandage firmly to his cut, smoothing out the edges with her fingertips when he reached out and captured her wrist. His chair creaked in the quiet room as he leaned forward. Her first instinct was to bolt. To call it a night and return to her cottage. She needed to sleep. They both needed sleep.

But she stayed.

And in the seconds that he hesitated she could see her future in his eyes. She could see homegrown Christmas trees in a house they built together. Two rocking chairs on a wide porch that overlooked a thousand sunsets. A green lawn where their kids would play in sprinklers. Peyton blurred through watery eyes as he leaned in to kiss her.

She was ready for him.

But the drum of running feet through the house had them both sitting straighter, leaning away from each other. Josh burst into the kitchen, breathless as Olivia collected the first aid kit and trash beside it.

"Dad said you fought Stu!" Josh declared, his voice squeaking with exhaustion as he reached Peyton's side.

"Unfortunately," Peyton said, clearing his throat. "He was up to no good."

"Did he hit hard?" Josh gave the air a left hook then a right hook.

"He did. But lucky for me I hit a little harder."

Josh laughed. "Can you teach me how to fight like that?"

Peyton nodded gently. "One of these days."

"Did he have a weapon?" Josh asked like he was recounting an action movie.

"He put my own gun on me."

Olivia gasped, raising her fingers to her lips.

"Didn't have any bullets in it at the time. I knew that so I didn't have much to lose."

"You weren't afraid?" she asked.

He shook his head, blinking slowly. "He was threatening you."

Her heart dropped into her stomach. "Why me?"

"He was trying to scare me into a corner so I'd let him go."

Josh made a noise that was mixture of awe and amusement. "But you don't scare easily, do ya, Peyton?"

"Not when it comes to her."

CHAPTER FOURTEEN

Homeless again.

It hadn't been so bad the first time. Peyton had signed up for it. But this time was different. The fire—an electrical fire caused by faulty wiring behind the wall that Peyton had crashed into—had caused too much damage. And while he and Daniel had packed his only belongings into his truck, Daniel had assured him that he was welcome to stay at the cabin for as long as it took to get the homestead back up on its feet again.

But none of this felt right.

In the bathroom mirror of the guest room, Peyton pulled his hand down his beard. His hair styled for a date that he wasn't sure was actually a date, he hardly recognized himself. Besides the bandage near his brow and the bruise on his cheek, he was quicker, stronger, and braver than he'd ever been in his life. For that, he was thankful. But there was still a sadness behind his blue eyes that he couldn't explain.

Though his heart leapt at the idea of spending a night on the town with Olivia, he was tired. Probably from last night's ordeal combined with a full day's work against everyone's better advice. But laying up in the guest room all day wasn't an option. He had too much to get done. He had work on himself to do.

Because he was out of his mind for thinking last night was a good time to kiss Olivia. Wanting her to know how well-loved she is was killing him, but eighteen hours and a clear head later, he was crazy to think *that* was a good move to make. A woman like her deserved the world. A world he couldn't give her in his present state.

Where had his peace gone? Where was the joy he'd felt

yesterday in the garden? Arms braced against the sink's edge, he dropped his head, a twinge of pain between his shoulder blades. Why had it been so easy to talk to God yesterday and now he felt like he was back at square one? Shaking his head, he felt something in him grow eerily desperate. Like a dying man thirsty for water.

Something had to give.

And if it ended up being him who had to give up something, then...

"Lead me to the rock that is higher than I." The strain in his own voice scared him.

For most of his life, he'd tried and tried again. Failed and then failed harder. And just when he thought he was catching his breath, something knocked the wind out of him. What was he getting wrong?

Swallowing the questions and doubts and confusion, he pushed himself away from the sink. In the bedroom, he grabbed his phone and and wallet, tucking them in his pockets. He flipped off the light, pulled the door shut, and made his way downstairs. Vern stood at the kitchen counter drinking a glass of tea.

"You know where Olivia is?"

He gestured with his cup toward the glass doors. "Last I saw, she was hauling food to the patio for the ants."

Peyton paused. They were supposed to be going for a drive. Then he realized...

"Thanks, Vern." He stepped outside into the warm sunset, every trace of last night's storm gone. The electricity had turned on sometime in the early morning hours. And the pond at the bottom of the hill was the fullest he'd ever seen it.

To his right, Olivia stepped out from under the patio roof. She was dressed in jeans that stopped below her knees, a pair of converse tennis shoes, and a pale pink shirt with a collar close to her neck and wide sleeves that covered the tops of her shoulders. She was a dream in every sense of the word. He couldn't help but smile as he followed the pavement to meet her.

"I thought we were going for a drive?"

She lifted her chin, her smirk growing a little more mischievous. "And I thought you were supposed to be resting today."

Tossing his head back, he looked at the dim blue sky with a chuckle. "I rested through the night. I'm good."

He stopped when he was close enough to smell her perfume or shampoo or whatever made him envision flowers and fruit baskets.

"There's plenty of time left in the summer for us to take a drive some other time. I thought we could have a picnic today."

Peyton nodded, taking in a deep breath as he looked over her again. "You look stunning. I'm afraid I'm underdressed for a picnic."

"I don't think you'll make a spectacle of yourself in that outfit." She wrinkled her nose in that way of hers and reached out for his hand.

He offered it freely, letting satisfaction fill him. Her touch was warm, her guidance gentle. He'd never been drawn to any other woman's femininity the way he was drawn to hers. Every soft and sweet thing about Olivia awoke in him an innate desire to lay himself on any landmine that she may find on her path for the rest of her life. Where these feelings had emerged from, he had no clue. But neither did he want to question any of it.

Every moment spent with Olivia was a good one.

At the porch swing that hung from the front of the patio, she had set up a makeshift table that held a tray with meats, cheeses, crackers, and pastries. Two sodas and a stack of napkins sat in the center. Peyton chuckled as he snatched a square pastry from the corner of the table and took a seat beside her. He tasted chocolate, coconut, and pecan. It was both chewy and crunchy.

"Mmm," he hummed as he melted back against the seat. "Is there anything you can't bake?"

Her crossed arms hugged her middle. "Puff pastries are my sworn enemy."

Across the distance, the sun was setting behind the tallest trees. Peyton breathed in deeply and let it out slowly.

"You said that we would go eat at my favorite restaurant in town," Olivia said, leaning toward him just a bit. He opened his mouth to promise to make it up to her, but she continued. "This...is my favorite spot in town. Right here."

"You've got good taste."

She laughed and he soaked up the sound. There wasn't a single thing about this woman that he could imagine living the rest of his life without. Even her imperfections were perfect on her. Whatever ministry or mission the Lord sent her into, there was no doubt in his mind that Olivia would carry it out with grace and victory.

"What?" she asked.

He must've forgotten to look at the sunset. "Can I ask you something?"

She dipped her head.

How to go about this? Peyton cleared his throat. "I wanted you to know that...I really liked spending time with you in the backyard yesterday."

An amused giggle rushed out of her.

"So, I, uh, was wondering if you'd like to be my best friend." He didn't mind that she found it funny. If it worked for Josh, then it would work for him. "Being best friends with a girl like you is right where I want to be." Because he was getting to see sides of her that the other guys didn't get to see. She was able to trust him enough to be herself when he was around.

And he wouldn't have it any other way.

Her brown eyes sparked with joy as she nodded. "I would like that."

Even though his question was silly, his chest still filled with relief that she hadn't turned him down.

"Can I ask *you* something?" she asked. "And I don't mean to step over any boundaries."

He looked over her, letting his eyes memorize the outline of her face, her jaw and eyes, the beauty mark that was so intrinsically her that he rarely noticed it anymore. "There's nothing you can't ask me."

"What were you running from?"

Peyton's heartbeat sped up a bit. That wasn't the question he was expecting.

"When you left the city. And came out here. What made you leave?"

He shifted a little straighter, determined to hold true to what he'd just said about asking him anything. "Uh...um. Basically myself." How could he make a twenty-six-year story short? "I...haven't heard from God the way other people seem to. Ever."

"I remember you saying something about that when you first got here."

He couldn't exactly remember what all he'd told the Whitmores about his journey, but they knew enough. They knew what they needed to. The dark parts, Peyton wanted to keep as far away from Olivia's light as he could.

"So it wasn't, like, a bad event?" she asked.

He shook his head. "No. Life was good. More on the boring side than anything. But it wasn't like a traumatic thing happened."

With a sideways look, she nodded.

"You don't believe me."

"I do. It's just..." She hesitated as she looked off into the yard. "You always seem like you're trying to stop people from getting too close. Like you don't want anyone to see the real you."

He pulled in a deep breath and leaned forward, propping his elbows on his knees. "Yeah, but I think that's pretty common. Right? Most people don't want the world to know their deepest, darkest secrets?"

She leaned forward to tuck both hands under her legs at her sides. "I guess you're right." She laughed gently. "Except I think you're the only one to witness my darkest, deepest secret."

He gave her a curious look.

"The reason why my birth parents gave me up." She pointed to her face.

He let his gaze linger over the beauty mark. "But you didn't let that take you down."

"It would have...if it weren't for you." She shrugged.

Peyton couldn't help but smile. "Thank God for that, then."

She gave him a sweet giggle, and he looked at the bench behind her. While she was leaned forward, now was a good time to make an inconspicuous move. He stretched his arms out in front of him, pretending to work out a kink in his shoulders—which turned out to not be an act—and set both arms along the bench on each side.

She pursed her lips to the side and raised an eyebrow.

Uh-oh. Did she catch it? She leaned back until her shoulders were pressed against his arm. A deep stream of gratification settled over him. Yep. This was the life he wanted to live.

"Okay. So, what horrible incident happened in your life that would have been different if *I* had been there?"

Peyton grinned. This was gonna be fun. There were lots to choose from. "Let's see...there's my parent's divorce—but I had Austin there for that. Or there's the first fight I ever got into when I went to high school—Austin wasn't there for that one, though."

Flashes of a different event shot like lightning through his memories. An event so dark that he didn't wish it on his greatest enemy. One that had so clearly defined his life that he hadn't really thought about it that much. It just...*was*. Nobody ever asked him about it. It was his to live with—a normal, ordinary day for the rest of the world. But for Peyton it had been the first time he felt this proverbial sadness he lived with today.

"Peyton?" The concern in Olivia's voice sliced through the disturbing cloud that closed in around him.

"Yeah?"

"What's wrong?"

He shook his head. "I was thinking..."

"About?" She was suddenly a little closer, a little more tucked against his shoulder.

The easy way she fit against him was enough to wage war between light and darkness in his thoughts. The memories, a long-abandoned prison cell he didn't care to revisit. And Olivia, a sunrise he never wanted to miss.

"Uh..." There was another event—a milder one that he didn't mind sharing with her. "Before I got my license and still rode the bus to school, one of my bus drivers ended up drinking on the job and a few of the upper classmen on our bus caught him."

She gasped softly. "That's terrible. Was there an accident?"

"Almost. But they were able to contact the school and get a cop out there to handle things. He wasn't too happy about that one," Peyton chuckled.

"Wow," she hummed as she looked off into the distance. "The worst thing my bus driver ever did was split me and

Caroline up because we talked too much."

Peyton huffed a laugh. But the amusement was lost on him.

Something wasn't right.

With the sun long gone, the family sat around the patio where Peyton and Olivia had just been a few hours ago. Nobody needed to know about their date which turned out to be a real date after all. At least, it felt like one to Peyton.

And it didn't set well with him.

"Lead me to the rock that is higher than I," Peyton whispered.

The firepit flickered and everyone gathered around, chatting and laughing like the happy people they were. Even Caroline had made it for supper and now sat next to Olivia at the booth, both girls giggling together. Peyton could only imagine what their bus driver had to deal with.

Olivia looked at him then, caught him staring, and then double glanced with a raise of her eyebrows. He didn't mind that she'd caught him. As of late, he hadn't bothered hiding the way he felt about her from anyone.

But he'd sworn he wasn't dating—not until the Lord moved in his life. And while he was sure God had done that very thing yesterday evening, today hope and joy were gone.

Peyton looked out across the dark hills, hidden by the night. This wasn't good. His soul felt like it was filling with poison. While he'd given his all to ignore the memories that his conversation with Olivia had brought back, he was starting to remember now.

And it was taking him under.

He was homeless, tired, and darker than he'd ever felt before. And while the woman sitting on the other side of the patio promised a life with never-ending sunshine, Peyton would do whatever it took to keep his darkness from reaching it.

Daniel strummed his guitar, drawing a curtain of quiet over the patio. A few chords in, Olivia started singing.

"I was guilty,
And I was broken—
Hollow heart,
And heavy eyes.

I'd been filled
with all the world could give,
Yet I couldn't
Find the Light."

Her voice strengthened, passion tangible in the way it rasped and rose.

"But You reached out
And pulled me close.
Death called my name,
And You said "No."

You chanted the anthem
With a thousand angels:
"No more chains, no more shadows"
Now Your love is all I know."

Peyton's heart ricocheted off his lungs until the air there grew hot and thick. He couldn't do this right now. He couldn't be here.

As the family joined her in the song, he slipped off the barstool and backed up until he bumped into the column. Arms crossed, he leaned his shoulder against it and waited. When everyone seemed to be focused wholly on Olivia, Peyton stepped backwards into the shadowy edge of the yard and turned to face the darkness.

He needed to leave.

Peyton may have meant to slip away without anyone noticing, but Daniel didn't miss the way he stalked across the shadowed yard with the walk of a man on a mission. The part that puzzled him was that he'd done it while Olivia was singing. Since the day he'd decided to stay, he hadn't missed a single one of her songs. And more often than not, he'd stared at her with the look of a fan meeting their favorite celebrity. But not this time.

Daniel glanced down at his guitar as he strummed the last chords of the song. If the boy needed a moment to himself, then he had a right to it and Daniel would pray that the Lord would intervene in whatever battle he faced.

But the moment Olivia finished singing, Daniel's fatherly intuition signaled hard.

He stood and set the guitar in his chair, pleasantly surprised when everyone continued chatting with each other. He stepped off the patio into the darkness and headed in the direction that Peyton took a few minutes ago.

Soft grass crunched quietly under his boots, supple from yesterday's downpour. At the bottom of the hill, he passed the garden, the greenhouse, and the pond without seeing Peyton. The barn was on his left. On his right, Josh's treehouse. Daniel looked in each direction. Why would he go to either of those places? If he needed time to get away on his own—

Daniel lifted his chin, looking straight ahead at the hill full of Christmas trees.

The wild. That's where men went when they wanted to find themselves.

A handful of minutes later, Daniel was walking down the furthest lane of trees, straining his eyes to see the familiar form of the man who'd become like a son to him over the last month. The sharp scent of cypress filled his senses. He reached out and brushed the needles with the palm of his hand as he passed. Close to midway, he thought he saw a figure. Squinting in the twilight, Daniel decided it was Peyton standing in the middle of a clearing where disease had killed a handful of young trees and left a bare spot in the perfect rows and columns.

He walked in a slow circle, one hand in his pocket, the other holding something white that flipped through his fingers like a magic trick. Daniel stepped on a branch and Peyton looked up. When Daniel approached, Peyton turned around, facing the sunset that was no longer there.

"I wanted to come check on you, son. Make sure you weren't putting in overtime."

Peyton looked at his hands, shaking his head.

Something was wrong. Daniel could feel it. He tipped his chin. "What's that?"

"Samuel Ace Wooledge." Peyton flashed a baseball card—the same card Gianna had found on his nightstand last month. He slid it through his fingers like a cardist. "Pitcher for the Chicago Comets. '81 to '92. Rookie sensation with a fastball. Lost the '87 World Series in crushing defeat. Career ended with Tommy John surgery," he said without ever looking at the card.

"Worth anything?"

"Not a penny." He huffed a sad laugh. "My brother told me it would be cool to find one and when I finally did, everything changed."

Daniel waited.

"Happened to fall on the very day my dad moved out."

Daniel nodded slowly, though Peyton couldn't see him. "Is that why you kept it all this time?"

"I didn't realize it. Not until I came here. I thought it was just a good memory. Turned out to be one more way I defined myself because of someone else's actions."

The boy had a habit of doing that. Cicadas and locusts filled in the conversation while Daniel waited in silence.

"Why does life have to be so hard?"

Lord, give him the right words to say. "I suppose it's to remind us how desperately we need God."

Peyton nodded adamantly. The man was fighting demons.

"Have you ever been treated unfairly before?" Peyton asked and then sucked back something that sounded like sadness.

"Plenty of times."

"I mean...I mean so needlessly unfair that you didn't want to live anymore. Not that you want to die...but that you just don't want to be here?"

Daniel swallowed. He wasn't sure he had the right words for that one. "Can't say that I have."

Peyton chuckled quietly. "It's not too much fun. I wouldn't recommend it."

"You want to tell me about it?"

Peyton finally turned—painfully slow. It was too dark to

see, but in the way he kept his head down, Daniel could only assume he'd find tears on his face if there was any more moonlight to reveal them.

"I'd completely forgotten about it. It had always simply been a fact—a thing that happened and there was nothing I could do to change it." His voice was thick with something haunting. "My...uh...brother was always there for me. For as long as I could remember."

He shook his head staunchly, as if the words were coming from some place deep in his soul. "He was my hero. Whenever our parents fought, Austin was there. When life got rough, Austin was there. When I didn't know what to do, Austin was there. I was either waiting for him to come home through the window, or I was sleeping in his bed next to him, but he was always there. No matter what."

Daniel waited, his heart thudding against his chest as the boy drew something to the surface of his well of memories.

"When there was a thunderstorm. Something tragic on the news. A bad day at school. Austin was there for me. He was ten years older, so he already had life figured out in my eyes. Maybe I was the idiot for thinking that."

Daniel shook his head. "You were a kid. Every kid looks up to their older sibling."

He nodded and peered out toward the cabin, the bandage on his head stark in contrast to the darkness swallowing him. "And mine was the best there ever was. If you could have seen him through my eyes, you would have thought he was the world's strongest man. Nothing could shake him. He always knew what to say and where to be when I needed him the most. I didn't have to worry about a thing when Austin was there."

"What happened, Peyton?"

"He left."

Daniel waited. There was more to it than that. Had to be. This emotion wasn't coming from an older brother moving out.

"He...uh...left. When I was eight. No older than Josh. The year after my parent's divorce and I was living with my mom, and uh—" His voice cut out for a brief second. "All I remember is being in the backseat and she was crying and wouldn't tell me why. And then my dad came to the house, and he cried, too. But, uh, he wouldn't tell me either. I had to go play in my room.

"And I did. For the rest of the day, I stayed in my room...waiting for Austin to show up. He would tell me what everybody was crying about. And then the day past and I...uh...slept in that room all alone, waiting. And the sun rose in the morning, and Austin was still gone. And Mom never came to get me. And Dad didn't stay to see me. I was alone. I was hungry. Everything was quiet. And I waited. I just...waited."

Daniel glanced up at the cabin, imagining that scenario with Josh—his eight-year-old in a room by himself, waiting for Olivia to come back and reassure him that everything is fine. But she never comes. "I imagine that was hard to endure."

Peyton shook his head again. "He was gone—he decided to move away without telling anyone—but it felt like he had died. My parents had thought that too, but he called a week later to say he'd gone out on his own." He scrubbed both hands down his face, the card fell to the ground. "And nobody told me. I was more alone than I'd ever been in my life, and nobody explained it to me. Austin—it was Austin who had always been there for me, to teach me about life, to tell me how to cope with something I'd never faced before.

"And he left me, Daniel. He just left me there." His hands fell away, and Peyton went down to one knee, a sob hanging in his voice. "How could he do that to me? I needed him! I was eight. I was just a kid. My parents weren't there for me. It was Austin who raised me—it was Austin who made sure I had everything I needed, and he just left me there."

Daniel's throat grew tight. The man he'd come to know had turned into a boy before his eyes. A kid screaming to be released from the prison of his room, a prison he never asked to be locked away in.

"Everything about life changed that day! The brother I played with was gone. Every birthday, every holiday, every good day I ever had went away with him. Both of my parents worked full time jobs, they didn't have time for me. Austin was all I had, and he left me! I don't understand how someone could do that to a kid!"

Daniel moved until he was directly in front of Peyton and

lowered himself down on one knee.

"I don't understand what I did to deserve that. Maybe if I had been a better brother then he would have stayed. I was too immature or dumb or annoying."

"No—no, son."

"My parents didn't even tell me what happened to him. I didn't know if he was okay or not. They just told me to go to my room."

Daniel pinched his eyes closed. "And you stayed, didn't you?"

Peyton cried. "He didn't even care that I was there all by myself. He didn't care that I needed a friend and had nobody! He was my whole world, Daniel, and he died the day he left, and nobody let me bury him and I still have to live with that to this day."

Daniel's eyes stung, compassion for the boy flooding his lungs until they burned. He reached out and cupped the back of Peyton's head, pulling him to his chest. Peyton fell on both knees and wrapped his arms around Daniel like he was the only lifeline he'd ever been offered.

"Oh, God, why did he do that to me?" he cried, his wails nearly more than Daniel could take. "I needed him. I needed him so bad it hurt."

"I know," Daniel said past an aching throat. "I know it hurt."

"He treated me so good. He loved me better than our parents did. I was able to be a kid when Austin was there. And then he left."

"It's safe, Peyton. It's safe to come out of that room and leave it all behind."

He wailed harder, his chest exploding against Daniel's when he did. "Nobody ever felt like home the way Austin did. I lost everything that day."

The pain was tangible in the air around them. Lord, have mercy, the boy was at war with himself. Daniel held him tight, holding him upright when it felt like he was about to collapse.

"I hate him, Daniel. I hate him more than anything else I've ever hated in my life."

Daniel opened his eyes and stared out through the night. Hate wasn't progress—but often it was one of the first steps toward it. "That's okay. Get it out of your system."

A moan tore free from Peyton. "I hate him more than I've ever hated myself. I want him to feel the hurt he made me feel."

Daniel sighed, closing his eyes. This journey might take him a little longer than he wanted it to. "There's no room for revenge in this situation, Peyton."

"I want him to know. He has to know how bad it hurt." Peyton finally loosened his grip and fell back on his heels. He let out a rushed breath as if he'd ran a sprint. "He took my world away from me. It's been eighteen years, Daniel. I've wrestled with sadness ever since that day."

Daniel reached out and gripped his shoulder, gently gaining his attention. "That feeling will pass. You're processing something that you've kept inside of you since you were a child and it's time to let that anger out. But you're not gonna hurt him."

He swiped his wrist against his nose. "I won't hurt him. But I don't want to see him again for the rest of my life."

Daniel released his hold on Peyton and leaned back on his heels. "Let it heal before you make a decision like that, son."

Peyton shook his head, a faraway look in his eyes. "I don't want anything to do with him. He wrecked me. He took everything away from me. I could never look at him the same after this."

If anger was what the boy needed to express in order to mend, then Daniel was okay with that for as long as he was on the ranch. He would need accountability now more than ever before. Daniel was willing to walk through that fire with him if that's what God had brought him here to do. Somewhere deep in his heart, the words God had given him came rushing back.

Don't worry. He'll stay.

CHAPTER FIFTEEN

The storm wasn't over.

Thunder rumbled in the distance as Peyton took Daniel's outstretched hand. He pulled himself from the ground and dusted his jeans off. Before Daniel released him, he leaned in and hugged him, patting him firmly on the back. When they separated, Daniel turned and walked down the dark aisle flanked by Christmas trees. Peyton took a step and stopped short.

The baseball card he'd held onto for most of his life laid in the dirt. He picked it up and wiped it off. For the first time in almost twenty years, he looked at the card and didn't question his existence.

He was tired.

He tucked the card into his wallet and continued down the path. Daniel waited for him at the end, where the dirt road would take them back to the cabin. Together, they traversed the darkness.

"You're anointed, Peyton," Daniel said. "You're meant to be doing a lot more with your life than what you were doing with it before."

Peyton looked up at him. "How do you know that?"

Daniel shrugged. "Gut feeling."

Gut feeling. Peyton was hoping for a little more than that. If it was true, he wanted to know it for a fact.

Through the woods at the bottom of the hill, an orange glow peaked through the trees. A fire raged between the fence and the pond.

"Vern's been itchin' to burn that pile since he had you start it."

Peyton drew a quick sniff to clear up what emotion was

left from a few minutes ago. "Tell me about it. My arms are still sore from everything he had me throw up there."

Daniel chuckled with him as they cleared the trees.

"Looks like Caroline went home," Daniel said, gesturing to where Olivia and Josh were laughing and running circles around the pile.

As they neared, Daniel continued on to the cabin, but Peyton veered off. Olivia and Josh's company was preferred over the guest room right now.

"Hey, Peyton!" Josh called out over the crackle of the fire. "Wanna catch crickets with us?"

"Why not?" he said, hating how hoarse his voice sounded.

Olivia watched him with a concerned gaze, following his gait as he came closer and stepped up on a railroad tie that was too far away from the pile to burn. He kept his head down, focusing on his next step just in case she caught sight of his eyes.

"Is everything gonna be okay?" she asked, coming closer.

He should have known she could see right through him.

He tipped his head. "Yep."

While Josh ran figure-eights around the burn pile after a fluttering cricket, Olivia stepped up on the opposite end of the railroad tie and balanced her arms at her sides. "Y'know, sometimes when I'm feeling down, s'mores cheer me up."

A chuckle spilled out of Peyton. She knew him too well. Not that she knew that sweets would cheer him up—but that she knew he was facing a battle. And she was getting too close to that battle.

He would do everything in his power to prevent that from happening.

She stopped directly in front of him and tilted her head to the side, looking deeply into his eyes. He let her. Laid out everything before her. Sadness, ruin, and scars. Maybe it would scare her enough to take a step back and go join Josh in his hunt.

Instead, she winked. His breath stuck in his chest with the tiny gesture. "Wanna go get some?"

He shared a smile with her and nodded.

She stepped off the tie and walked out across the lawn. "Josh, you wanna go get stuff to make s'mores?"

"Yeah!" He leapt through the air with a fist and jetted

toward the cabin.

Peyton followed, too, stopping only when he came closer to the heat of the fire. He looked down into the warm flames licking at the humid air. He pulled his wallet from his pocket and slid the baseball card from it. With the same dexterity his dad had taught him to use for magic tricks he flicked the card into the blaze. It disappeared so quickly it was as if it never even existed.

Eight-year-old Peyton sat in the backseat of his mom's car, working to perfect the magic trick his dad had shown him how to do with his baseball card. It made a halfhearted summersault between two knuckles and then fluttered to the floor. He reached down to pick it up the same time Mom's phone rang.

"Hello?"

Peyton tried again, eyeballing the thing so mightily that it might move on its own if he had enough willpower.

"What do you mean? He's not with me. Haven't you talked to him?" Mom said and her voice sounded mad.

He lowered the card and looked at the side of her face.

"Maybe he's at a friend's house." Her smile from a few minutes ago was gone. "Knock it off, Jake. Austin has friends."

But Peyton knew he didn't. Austin once told Peyton friends would stop him from being able to hang out with his little brother. A memory that made Peyton smile.

"I don't—I don't know. Just keep calling him. If we don't hear from him soon then we'll call the police."

Peyton's smile fell and he swallowed.

Mom hung up the phone and threw it in the passenger seat. She was quiet for a long time, and she started to drive home a little faster.

"Mom, where's Austin?"

She glanced at the rearview mirror, but never really at him. She didn't answer and his stomach started to hurt.

"Mom?"

"Yes, sweetie?" she said quickly.

"Is Austin all right?"

She flipped on her blinker. "Uh...yeah. You know your brother. He does this sometimes."

Peyton nodded. She was right. Austin always did this. Sometimes he'd stay out 'till midnight and sneak back in without anybody but Peyton knowing about it. Peyton loved the sound of the window clicking shut as he slept. It meant Austin had come home and everything was gonna be okay.

When they were home, he followed her inside, clutching his baseball card in one hand. She picked up the phone on the kitchen counter and pressed one hand against her forehead as if she were checking for a fever.

"Jesus, Jesus, Jesus," she whispered.

"Mom?"

She tapped the numbers on the phone and held it up to her ear, waiting. "Mrs. Buford, have you seen Austin's truck in the neighborhood recently?"

Peyton walked up to the counter and rested his chin against it.

"Okay. Thank you. If you see him, will you please call and let me know." She hung up the phone and turned toward the kitchen window.

"Mom?"

She didn't listen. She kept shaking her head and tapping numbers on the phone.

"Mom?" he said a little louder.

"Peyton. I'm sorry. I can't talk right now. Will you please go play in your room for a little bit? I'll come get you when supper's ready."

He nodded, glancing at the clock. Supper wouldn't be ready for all day. But he did what she said, taking his card to his room. Hours passed before he heard the front door open and a familiar voice come inside.

"Austin!" he gasped, jumping to his feet.

He raced across the room and reached for the doorknob.

"Why are you asking me, Jake? I don't know what to do. He's never been gone this long before."

Oh. It was just his dad. Peyton let his hand fall away and went back to the corner of his room where he played with a pile of blocks. In a few minutes Dad would come play with him like he always did.

But this time was different. The sun was starting to set, and his parents were still arguing even though they weren't married anymore. The front door opened again, and Mom told somebody to come in.

Peyton went to his door and pressed his ear against it. The voices were muffled, but there was a man in there with his parents. One who had a deep, serious voice like a principal. Peyton growled. This door was too thick! He reached for the knob in front of his face and twisted slowly so nobody would hear it. He pulled until there was a tiny little crack that he could see through.

Peyton gasped. It was a cop! He wrote something on a notepad as Mom talked, and Dad sat on the arm of the couch.

"Eighteen you say?" The cop asked.

"Yes, sir. He had a birthday a few months ago."

He shook his head as he wrote something down. "We'll see what we can find, but I'll be honest with the both of you and you're not gonna want to hear it, but if he's eighteen then there's not much we can do about it. He has the right to disappear if he wants to."

Mom uncrossed her arms and held them out in front of her. "But how do we know he's not lying dead in a ditch somewhere?"

Peyton slapped his hand against his mouth to hide the whimper that threatened to expose his location.

"Like I said, we'll see what we can find," the cop said. "We'll run the plate for sure, but I can't make you any guarantees."

Mom turned around and covered her face with both hands. Dad stood and stretched out his arm to shake the cop's hand. "Thank you, officer. We appreciate it."

"It's no problem. Goodnight, folks. If you hear anything from Austin, call and let us know."

When the cop left, Peyton eased his door shut. He backed up slowly until he was sitting on Austin's bed closest to the door. Was his brother...dead?

Mom and Dad talked a little bit more. Then the door creaked open and shut again. Did Dad leave? Without seeing him? The sound of a truck outside told him it was true. Peyton shivered when he realized he was all alone.

And everything was quiet. And Austin was gone.

No! He couldn't be gone. He was Austin!

Peyton sprung from the bed and ran to the window. His brother would be home anytime now. Maybe even in a few hours. But he didn't mind waiting—Austin would be back. He always came home. And just so he didn't miss him...

Peyton marched over to his bed and pulled the quilt and pillow from it. He dropped it in a pile on the floor beneath the window and laid down. When his brother returned, Peyton would be the first one to know about it. Then everything would be okay again. They would play in the treehouse and throw rocks in Lady Bird Lake and eat ice cream cones from the truck down the street. Everything would be okay.

But Peyton woke the next morning to sunshine in his eyes. His belly hurt with hunger. He looked up at the window above him, still firmly in place. He shoved himself away from the quilt and looked at Austin's bed.

Empty.

His heart raced in his chest. Where was his brother? He pushed himself off the floor and wavered on his feet. What if Mom was right and Austin was dead? Tears stung his eyes until he couldn't see anymore. A sob shook his shoulders as he shuffled to the door. It creaked open to an empty kitchen and living room. Nobody was home. Not even Mom.

He cried a little harder, using the collar of his shirt to clear his eyes. Through the dim living room, he wandered down the hall to his mom's door. He knocked quietly, so he didn't scare her. Then he knocked again.

She didn't answer.

He went back to the living room and waited, crying until his stomach let out another growl that hurt. He looked at the pantry cabinet where Mom kept cereal and snacks. Peyton swiped his sleeve across his nose again and swallowed his tears.

He opened the door and shuffled through the basket until he found a cinnamon roll. At the ice box, he stood on a chair to reach the milk on the top shelf. He poured himself a big glass and set things right again. He took his food to his bedroom and closed the door behind him. Milk trickled over the edge of the cup and down his fingers. He didn't care. He was hungry.

Beneath the window, he sat cross legged and set the milk on the ground. His baseball card lay near his blanket. He opened the cinnamon roll and took a bite, reaching for the card. If he waited long enough, maybe he would wake up and find out this was all a dream. Or Austin would show up in the window above him. Or somebody would come along and tell him what was happening. And that he wasn't alone.

But he was alone.

Through the rest of the day, even when his mom brought him a sandwich for lunch. And even when his dad came to take him to the park. And even when his grandparents came to celebrate his birthday—he was still alone.

He was alone when he played outside that summer, watching the ice cream truck pass by their driveway. He was alone when the treehouse grew vines and became too worn to stand on. He was alone when he started high school and tried out for the baseball team. He was alone when he grew tall enough for a girl to want to go to the homecoming dance with him. He was alone when he got into his first fight, discovered his first kiss, and landed his first job. He was alone when he learned to drive, got his learner's permit, and earned his license.

And Austin wasn't there for any of it.

Rain pelted the window, stirring Peyton from a shallow sleep. The quilts tangled around his legs, and he wrestled with them for the hundredth time. Sleep may be lost on him, but it didn't mean he couldn't still lay here and get some rest.

Why would Jesus bring him this far just to throw him into the darkness again? The Lord was real—He was there. Peyton knew that. But why couldn't he keep his joy? What would it take to bring his life full circle so that he could be the happy kid he used to be? Like Josh. Like Olivia.

He looked up at the dark ceiling. "What am I missing?"

He was tired of the questions. Sick of the confusion. His head swam with doubts that he'd ever be able to fix himself.

Even with the new desire to worship the Lord again—the way he'd done in the garden a few days ago—he felt like he was drowning and couldn't keep his head above water.

He wanted to go back. He wanted that peace again. Whatever the cost.

"What do You want me to give up?"

His phone buzzed on the nightstand. With slow, aching movements, Peyton rolled over and picked it up. He tapped the screen, squinting at its brightness. Once his eyes adjusted, he read the message waiting for him.

Hey, bud. Good news. The job in Albuquerque is open. It's yours if you want it.

He dropped the phone over his heart and stared into the abyss hovering over him. Shock lasted only a second before reality rolled in. He'd spent enough time here. He didn't even have a place to stay anymore. Living in a kind family's guest bedroom wasn't exactly the dream life. And it thrilled him to get as far away from Austin, Texas, as possible.

But what about Olivia?

He sat up in bed. She was the love of his life. There would never be another like her. He could search for the rest of his days and still have to settle if he wanted to start a family— he was sure of it. But he was further away from hope today than he had been a month ago. Or so it felt.

"What are You doing with me?"

Olivia deserved things that Peyton couldn't give her. And he wasn't sure he'd ever be able to. She was an incredible woman, self-assured with a list of dreams, and he was lost, miserable, and angry. He knew the moment he'd met her that she was out of his league. But sometime over the last month he'd let hope slip in. It was a nice feeling, so he'd welcomed it.

But now he had only two options—move forward and see what Albuquerque held for him, or overstay his welcome here like he'd done everywhere else.

Peyton threw off the quilts and stepped onto the cold floor. Ten minutes later, his bags were packed, bed was made, and his heart was reliving his first night in this room. Back when his darkness seemed harmless. Now his heart felt like a weapon and everyone he loved was in danger. Tucking his phone and wallet away, he shouldered his bag and walked out.

The homestead fire had forced him to pack his belongings in his truck again, so he didn't have much to gather. The timing of it all was as good as confirmation in his eyes. Setting his bag in the chair at the end of the dining table—the one where Daniel sat surrounded by his happy family while they joked and shared stories—Peyton walked through the empty kitchen and out the patio door.

Daniel and Gianna laughed with one another, sitting on barstools and sipping from coffee cups. As he came close, their eyes found him and lit with joy. He had parents of his own, but he'd never forget the way they stepped in and treated him like a son.

"Good morning," they chimed together.

"What brings you out so early?" Daniel asked, lifting his cup to his mouth.

Peyton looked out at the cloudy, gray hills and fog-covered rows of Christmas trees for what could be the last time. He shoved his hands in his pockets. He hadn't exactly prepared a speech for this moment. "I...um..." He swallowed hard. "I'm leaving."

Their faces fell. They set their cups on the bar top.

"I know it's probably a surprise to you both. And I don't mean to just spring it on you. But I got a text a few minutes ago about the job up in Albuquerque." He finally looked up at them, pained by the sadness he saw in their eyes. "I'm gonna take it."

Gianna's brows wrinkled. "Are you sure, Peyton? Don't you want to take some time to pray about it?"

"I did. Kinda. In a way." He shook his head. "I feel like I might've stayed longer than I should have and it's time for me to move on."

"How could you have stayed too long when you only got the message this morning? Do you feel like it's what God wants you to do?" Daniel asked.

Peyton wasn't sure how to answer that. He hadn't heard from God about it. But the coincidence was too much to deny. And it was starting to concern him that he felt worse off today than he had ever before. "I can't stay here at the cabin forever. And I can't spend the rest of my life trying to figure out what I'm missing. And I...can't...give your daughter the life she deserves." He looked up at Daniel. "I'm sorry."

"Well," Gianna said, sliding from her barstool. "I can't believe you're actually leaving." She reached up on tiptoe and pulled him into a hug. He returned the gesture with all the fervor of a son with his mother. "We're gonna miss you more than you'll ever know."

He huffed a laugh as he released her. "Trust me. I'm gonna miss you guys a lot more than that."

She moved past him, headed for the kitchen as Daniel stepped from the barstool. He shook his hand and pulled him into a hug. "I've got to tell you, son. I really thought we'd have the rest of the summer before this day came."

Peyton nodded as he stepped back. "It wasn't what I had in mind. But...uh, given the way things have been lately, I think it's best."

Daniel patted his shoulder. "Do you mind if I pray for you, Peyton?"

A twinge of disappointment ached in his chest. Daniel was a better man than Peyton could ever try to be. "I'd appreciate it."

Daniel kept his hand planted firmly on Peyton's shoulder as if he were afraid Peyton would run mid-prayer. "Father, we come to You today to ask for guidance and insight for Peyton's future—where You're leading him and what You plan to do with his life. We thank You for his time here, fellowshipping with our family. We ask You for mighty blessings and favor on His heart and thoughts, that You would always remind him that You're with him until the end of the world. Amen."

Peyton hugged him again. "Thank you for everything, Daniel. You have no idea how much you've impacted my life. Tell Vern the same, will you?"

"Of course." When they parted, Daniel kept his hand on Peyton's shoulder. "I do want you to know something, Peyton. The men's ministry—the one you mentioned to me last month—it's something I want to do. I'm teaming up with the Lord in prayer right now, but I feel on my heart that there's something there. Thanks to you."

"I'm glad to hear it." Even though Peyton was leaving with more baggage than he'd come with, he could still testify of the way God's Spirit worked on this ranch. More men needed to experience that. No matter what corner of the earth his next chapter called him to, his prayers for this ranch would remain with him.

They both turned and made their way to the kitchen. Peyton collected his backpack from the dining chair and turned to find a sleepy Josh shuffling through the living room in a pair of wrinkled pajamas and a head full of messy hair.

Peyton stopped in his tracks, suddenly taken back eighteen years to the boy he used to be before his brother left. Naive and innocent and joyful. A lump burned in his throat as he went down on one knee before Josh and let his bag slide to the floor.

Josh rubbed his knuckles against one sleepy eye. "Mom said you have to leave."

Peyton nodded, tears surfacing. "I do. I've got a new job waiting for me."

Josh turned his head sideways like he didn't quite understand why Peyton would want to leave for that. "Are you coming back?"

He cleared his throat and looked up at Gianna and Daniel standing in front of the patio doors. "I'll try my best, but I can't make any promises."

His eyebrows bunched like the answer ripped part of his heart out.

It was ripping Peyton's out, too.

Josh leaned forward and wrapped his arms around Peyton's neck. "But who am I gonna play with?"

Peyton cleared his throat again. He hated himself for leaving as much as he hated his brother for doing the same. Maybe he was more like Austin than he realized.

That thought turned his stomach.

He wanted nothing to do with his brother. He didn't want to be like him in any way. He wanted to get into his truck, drive to New Mexico, and forget Austin ever existed.

"You've—uh, you've got Olivia, buddy. She'll help you catch every bug there is out there, and she'll climb up in your treehouse with you, and you'll go fishing and frog hunting together."

Josh leaned away, tears shimmering in his round, boyish

eyes. "But she's not as fun as you are."

Peyton forced the chuckle through his throat. "Sure, she is. You just gotta give her a chance."

He nodded, rubbing his hand against his eyes again.

"Listen, I want you to know something, Josh. I never had a little brother. Not until I got here. And you turned out to be the best little brother a man could ask for."

Josh's lips twitched downward.

Peyton cleared his throat as he tussled Josh's hair. "I want you to know that I love you, kid."

"I love you, too, Peyton," Josh said as he leaned in for another hug. Peyton wrapped him up, closing his eyes, and savoring the goodbye of a boy who reminded him so much of his younger self. A boy he had to let go.

Before Peyton caved, threw in the towel, and rejected the job offer, he released Josh. As he went to stand with his parents, Peyton gathered his backpack and stood. "I really do love you guys. All of you. You have no idea how much your kindness has changed me."

They nodded in unison.

"I'll...uh, stop by the bakery to see Olivia before I leave."

Gianna lifted her fingers to cover her mouth. Daniel reached out and pulled her close. Josh's shoulders slumped as if someone had just stolen his dog. Peyton dipped his head and went for the front door.

He slowed to a stop when he saw Vern standing at the end of the hallway, listening. Peyton opened his mouth to say goodbye, but Vern held up one hand. Then he gave a two-finger salute and disappeared into a room.

Swallowing the lump in his throat, Peyton stepped out onto the porch. Birdie, Boone, and Bear waited for him, all rising to get their respective head scratches. He obliged each one with a scrub behind the ears until Bear sat on his back feet with his paws on Peyton's chest, tongue hanging out as if he were smiling. The look in his eyes asked what adventure they were going on today.

"Take care of Josh, buddy. He's gonna need you when I leave."

Bear dropped his paws, did a full circle, and then sat. Peyton took that as an affirmation and carried on. Inside his truck, he cranked the engine and looked out at the cabin—a place he had no right to ever walk into, let alone feel like he belonged to the family inside. He strapped on his seatbelt as he caught sight of the barn in the fields to the left. With that, Peyton turned the wheel and left the same way he'd arrived.

If this was truly God's answer to his prayers, then why did it feel so wrong? Had he lost every last bit of his faith? Was God mad at him after all? Had he really messed up his life that much?

"I love You, Father, and I'm determined to do Your will," Peyton whispered as he drove past trees that had become familiar to him, wildlife that he could identify off the top of his head, and a swollen stream that flowed freely after the recent storms. Bushels of fire-orange flowers dotted the barbed wire fences on each side of him. A black calf ran and leapt around its mother. A jackrabbit jetted across the road in front of the truck.

"Bless my efforts and heal my heart, Lord. I'm chasing You even if nothing ever changes." It was hard to say. But this heaviness felt like a wet blanket of every moment he ever felt lost and alone. He wanted to throw it off but didn't know how.

At the end of the driveway, he looked right, then left. Then he settled back against his seat and breathed deeply. The *Higher Rock Ranch* sign stood resolute, like a period at the end of a sentence.

He was leaving in a worse state than the one he'd come in. What was it all for?

CHAPTER SIXTEEN

As rain streamed down the small windows on her bakery's back door, Olivia measured out the flour it would take to make a couple hundred chocolate chip cookies. As little specks floated through the air, contentment settled into her lungs. Life couldn't be any more perfect than what it was right now. She reached for the baking soda and stopped short when there was a knock on her kitchen door.

She jumped and turned to find it cracked open, Peyton halfway inside. Her heart skipped a beat. "Hey. What are you doing here?"

"I...uh...came to see you." Why didn't he sound like his usual happy self? "Do you have a minute?"

Olivia nodded as she untied her apron and pulled the loop over her head. She left it on the corner of her worktable and followed him to the front. "Is everyone okay?" Mom would have called her if there was an emergency. "Did something happen at the ranch?"

"No—no, nothing like that," he said as he walked toward the front windows, rubbing the back of his neck. With a hand in one pocket, he leaned up on tiptoe and sank down on his heels. She'd never seen him so unsettled. So uncertain.

"But something's wrong," she dipped her head, not letting herself look away from him.

He turned slowly, staring at the floor between them as he made the walk back to her. Her heartbeat drummed against the base of her throat, so she placed her fingers there and let them fidget with the sunflower on her necklace.

"I don't know how to tell you this."

Oh, no.

"I'm leaving, Olivia."

She sucked in a breath, tears instantly burning her eyes. He was supposed to stay for the whole summer. Maybe longer, her heart had dared to hope. "What?"

"I got a text this morning. About the job in New Mexico. It's waiting for me."

The job. "Right." She nodded. His presence on her family's farm was just a stopover on his way to a new career. Nothing more and nothing less. Their friendship was purely happenstance. "So, today then?"

"Right now."

Those two little words felt like daggers in her heart. What would life look like without him? Without his witty banter at the supper table? Without hearing his laugh while everyone sat around the fire? Without watching him tease Josh on their family hikes? Without seeing him get under Pepaw's skin with his babble? What would happen when she got home, and she stopped looking out across the pastures to catch a glimpse of him working with her dad and grandpa?

"I see," she whispered, the grief ripping at her throat.

He finally looked at her. He took a half step and stopped short. "I need you to know something before I go."

She lifted her chin, determined to be strong. Determined to treat this like a business transaction.

"I love you—"

"—stop, Peyton." Every bit of her determination crumbled before her. She shook her head and waved one hand for him to quit. "Why did you have to say—"

"—I need you to know this." He closed the space between them and cupped both of her arms above her elbows.

She leaned away, tucking her hands against her raging heartbeat. Tears spilled down her cheeks and rested on her jaw as she tried to look at anything but him.

"You're everything good in the world, Olivia. I've never known anyone like you. You're not just kind, you're stubborn about it. Men go to battle with a fraction of the bravery you've got. You're the only woman I know who can look evil in the eyes and find a reason to smile."

A sob wracked her chest.

"And you deserve so many things—" His voice cracked.

She finally let herself look up at him. His dark blue eyes were stormy and turbulent with the same tears she felt welling up in hers. "Starting with a man who can give you the happiness that you're worthy of."

She thought that might have been the man standing in front of her.

"It can't be me." He dipped his head and inhaled fiercely as if he found strength somewhere buried inside of himself. "I want to give you every dream you've ever written down and then some." His attention flittered around her face. "But I'm too lost."

She buried her face in her hands, and he pulled her to his chest so gently that she didn't even realize it was happening. She sobbed as his arms tightened around her. She didn't dare return his embrace—she couldn't for fear of losing all the dignity she had and begging him to stay. She was better than that.

She loved him too much to do that to him.

"I messed up," he said, his voice eerily calm. Disturbingly confident. "I told God that I wouldn't pursue a girl until I got my heart right with Him and I didn't stay true to my word. You're an easy woman to fall in love with and I couldn't help myself. But I haven't healed. And now I'm further away than I've ever been before."

When she'd cried the immediate pain away, she pressed against his chest, breaking his grasp on her. His arms fell away, but the hurt in his eyes was deep and damaging.

"I'll pray for you, Peyton. I'll pray that God keeps chasing you and that one day He shows you how to heal." Even if it was with another woman and a different family. The thought ripped her heart a little more. "And I hope—" She shook her head, swallowing her own selfishness as she reached out and set her hand against his arm. "I *believe* that you will walk in that healing and that everything's gonna turn out like it's supposed to."

He looked at her with the grief of someone walking to their demise. "I'm sorry."

She shook her head and forced a smile, though she was sure she appeared as anything but happy. "Don't say that. God had a plan. He always does." She looked over his face, from his wavy hair to his beautiful blue eyes to his lips and down to the beard that fit him so well. "This meeting wasn't for nothing. You've changed me in ways that I'll never forget. I'm beyond grateful for that even if we never meet again."

He looked down at his fidgeting hands and nodded. Confident that her dignity was no longer at risk, Olivia raised up on tiptoe and wrapped her arms around him. He accepted her without hesitation, embracing her like she was the last person he would ever hug again. He sighed, his breath on her neck, and his chest softened so she fit against him a little better.

When she leaned away, he released her and turned for the door. Without a backward glance, he stepped out of the bakery and Oliva covered her mouth as she released a throat-shredding wail. This hurt. Bad. So much so that it made her humiliation with Rhett feel like a paper cut.

At the edge of the sidewalk, before he stepped onto the pavement, Caroline appeared. Olivia pressed the back of her hand against her lips as she watched what she knew would be another heartbreak. Caroline adored him as much as she did. As everyone in her family did. She only hoped that Josh had gotten to say his goodbyes as well.

Caroline's smile fell and her eyes widened as he obviously told her the news. She pointed toward the door of the bakery, and he dropped his head, shaking it. She reached out and touched his sleeve, her words working to convince him to stay, no doubt. He said something to her and her hand fell away. Caroline nodded meekly as if she understood but didn't like it. Then they shared a hug.

Peyton was the best thing to ever happen to Olivia. A miracle she hadn't asked God for and didn't know she needed. His memory would stay with her for a very long time, if not the rest of her life. Which didn't pose well for a woman who dreamed of getting married and starting a family.

Because the only man she wanted that dream with had just walked out of her life.

Peyton stepped inside his truck, closed the door, and cranked the engine. He looked up in time to see Caroline hugging Olivia behind the windows of their shop.

He fell back against the seat. "God, why is this so hard?"

He was doing what he thought He wanted him to do. Moving forward, seeking answers. The *Higher Rock Ranch* had served its purpose. He was a changed man.

Changed for the better? As he watched Caroline whisk Olivia into the kitchen, he didn't feel like it.

This felt wrong. Leaving this family who had been like a second home to him felt wrong. And walking away from the woman he was certain God wanted him to marry felt wrong.

If he could make it to Albuquerque and start fresh, dive deep and really focus on fixing himself, then maybe he'd find his way back to Heavenly in a few years. Maybe he'd sweep Olivia off her feet and present to her everything her heart desired. He'd wait a lifetime for that woman.

But he couldn't ask her to do the same for him.

She was too young, too beautiful. She had too much life left to live while he was off at war.

Peyton strapped on his seatbelt and shifted the truck in reverse. He backed out onto the downtown road and set his sights west.

Another man would come into Olivia's life one day and give her everything Peyton couldn't. He was sure of it. She would forget all about him, fall in love, and fill her home with kids that had the same happy eyes and stunning smile that she had.

Peyton had a storm to drive into. He had a future to figure out, a past to untangle, and a brother to find forgiveness for before he could even consider love.

Sixteen-year-old Peyton tugged a T-shirt over his head and checked his hair in the square mirror hanging inside his locker door. Not too messy, not too perfect. Just how he liked it. He snatched his wallet from the shelf—a birthday gift from his dad after he'd finally gotten his license a few weeks ago. A birthday where his parents finally seemed like they liked each other again.

They hadn't fought or argued. And they'd both looked at him like they were proud of the man he'd become. Nodding,

Peyton stared at himself. "It was a good day."

He shut the locker, set the lock, and grabbed his backpack. The baseball game went off without a hitch. He'd thrown a no-hitter for three innings before he gave up a homerun. But after he backed up the catcher at home and put the last runner in a hotbox, he was able to redeem himself and tag the out for the win. The celebration from the players and bleachers still rang in his ears and filled his chest.

As he made his way through the gym to the parking lot, he relished in the fact that he would walk through those doors and no longer see one of his parents waiting there to pick him up. No, sir. He was a grown man. He'd be driving himself everywhere he went. It was all London, Paris, and New York from here. He would finish high school in a couple of years, go to college on a baseball scholarship if he had it his way, and find a girl to plant roots with.

Yes, sirree, life couldn't get any better than this.

Peyton shoved through the exit doors outside of the lobby and made a sharp left to the parking lot. Right where Mom and Dad used to park. Except today there was a man there. Leaning back against the tailgate of a truck, legs crossed at the ankles. A familiar man. One he'd never seen before but somehow knew.

Peyton slowed to a stop. His heart skipped in his chest. His bag slid off his shoulder. The whole world stopped turning while he tried to figure out if this was real life or if he was imagining things. Please don't let this be a dream.

"Austin?" His voice was hoarse. He was scared that if he were too loud then the mirage would disappear, and the memory would be gone forever.

But it didn't.

Austin jerked his head up, found Peyton, and started in his direction. Peyton ran for him. Nothing else in the world mattered. Not the backpack on the sidewalk, or the game he'd just won, or the license in his pocket.

His brother came home.

He wrapped his arms around Austin with a cry that had been waiting eight years to come out. Austin hugged him, lifting him off the ground like he was eight years old again and free to be a kid. Feet back on the ground, Peyton's movements were harsh and jerky, but he didn't care. Austin didn't seem to care either. Peyton stayed upright only because Austin held him. Each time his knees buckled, Austin's grip tightened.

His brother was home.

Peyton leaned away far enough to look over Austin's face. Even though Peyton had grown, Austin was somehow taller than he remembered. His hair was lighter, too, but styled like it used to be. His eyes were brighter than he'd ever seen them. Everything else about him looked exactly like the boy Peyton saw in the mirror every day.

But it was his long-lost brother who was looking at him with tears in his eyes.

"I'm sorry, Peyton."

Peyton shook his head. He didn't care what Austin had done. He didn't want an apology. He wanted his brother home again. "I missed you, Austin."

"I missed you too, kid." He reached out and ruffled Peyton's hair like he did when they were young. "I should've come back for you years ago."

Peyton wasn't interested in counting the days they'd missed together. He just wanted this. Today. He wanted Austin. He wanted to laugh again and play pranks on their mom and get on their dad's last nerve and visit Nan and Pop's creek so they could go fishing. He wanted to do it all, every day for the rest of his life.

"You promise you won't leave again?" Peyton begged through clenched teeth, half-scared of his answer.

"I promise."

Good enough for Peyton. He pulled Austin into another hug, burying his face in Austin's shoulder as they held each other. There was an assurance around Austin—a peace that Peyton had never felt before.

"Let's go get your bag, kid." With their arms still locked around the other's shoulder, Austin turned him in a circle. "I caught your game."

"You did?" Peyton couldn't believe it. "The whole game?"

Austin tipped his head once, his smile wide and proud. "I always knew you were gonna be a champ. I never wanted you to know, but you always gave me a run for my money when we competed with each other." There was an *almost jovial air about Austin that was unlike anything Peyton had ever seen before. "I've got ten years on you and most of the time I was still working my tail off to beat you."*

Peyton laughed as Austin reached down and snatched the bag by its strap. "You're different. What happened to you?"

Austin let out a long sigh as they made their way to his truck again. "I'll tell you everything one of these days."

Peyton nodded. They had all the time in the world.

"It's a very, very long story. I could write a book." Austin squinted into the sunset. "Actually, I could write several books."

Peyton tightened his grip on Austin's back. He'd read every one of them.

CHAPTER SEVENTEEN

A fresh start. A clean slate. A new beginning. That's what Peyton needed.

He looked up at the house that belonged to two of the people he loved most in the entire universe. His heart skipped a beat knowing how surprised they'd be by his presence here. They weren't expecting him for a while.

But things change.

Peyton stepped out of his truck and left his bags behind. There'd be plenty of time to grab them later. For now, he was itching to see their faces. Hear their voices. Know that everything was right in the world.

Across the perfectly trimmed lawn and bed of flowers that followed the walkway to the porch steps, he stopped short of the door, remembering the last time he was here and how utterly empty he'd felt. He lifted his hand and knocked three firm times. Pulling in a deep breath, Peyton closed his eyes and prayed for the strength to walk in this new season of his life.

Everything would be different.

The door opened and Austin appeared, shock in his eyes followed quickly by the signature smile of the brother who'd always loved to see him. But Peyton's desperation must have shown on his face, because Austin's joy turned to concern and he stepped over the threshold. Peyton wrapped his arms around his brother and cried.

Just like when he was sixteen.

And just like when he was sixteen, Austin held him up.

"I forgive you," Peyton cried against his brother's neck. "I'm sorry I never said it before."

It had been eighteen years since his brother left. Ten

since he'd returned. And while Peyton had walked through the fire of that grief on his own ever since, he'd never consciously forgiven his brother. He'd simply let it define him. Another event in his life that happened, and he carried it with him. Like his parents' divorce. Like his mistakes in college. Like the sadness that had followed him for most of his life. It had always been part of who he was.

No more.

God was ready to give him a new definition. A higher calling. A solid place to walk in his healing and carry out his anointing. Anointing that felt like warm oil falling down his face and resting on his brother's shirt. Everything broken about him was collapsing, like walls that no longer served a purpose. He was being called into the wild, where love couldn't be measured and hope couldn't be tamed.

And he craved it.

There would be no more conformity after today. Like Daniel, like the love he'd always seen in his brother's eyes, Peyton wanted to be wild and free. He wanted the same wild love that poured from the cross on the day of Calvary. Nothing was gonna stop him from reaching it. Not even unforgiveness.

"I never told you that, Austin," he said when he caught his breath. "I never told you that I forgive you for leaving me."

"It's all right, kid," Austin said, his voice husky as he rubbed Peyton's back. "Everything's gonna be all right."

Peyton stepped into the cool air of his brother's house. AJ, Austin's Great Dane, laid on the patio just outside the double doors at the back of the living room. His sister-in-law, Natalie, stood by the loveseat with their baby girl bundled in her arms. She smiled with tears twinkling in her eyes like she'd heard their conversation. He didn't mind. He hid nothing from these people who loved him and he loved more than anything.

"Hey, sis," he whispered as he wrapped her in a hug, careful not to squish Reese.

She patted him on the back with her free arm and giggled

softly. "Welcome home, Peyton."

He took a second to study the sweet baby sleeping against her momma. She was older and fuller than the last time he'd seen her. She had more hair and longer lashes. Blonde like her momma's with olive skin like her daddy. Peyton ran his knuckles across her tiny cheek and she let out a small sigh.

"The kids are at Gram and Poppa's house," Austin said as he sat on the loveseat beside Natalie. "In case you were wondering where all the noise was."

Peyton chuckled as he sat on the edge of the couch and braced his elbows on his knees. "I've got quite a story to tell," he began. "I never actually made it to Nan and Pop's. I, uh, found a place to work over the summer. Or I should say, that place found me."

They both nodded, taking in his words like they weren't surprised that God could work in mysterious ways.

"It was a ranch. And it was long, hard work. But I loved every moment of it."

"Looks like it," Natalie said gesturing to his beard.

He dropped his head and stroked the beard to hide a grin. "A lot has changed." He melted into the couch, stretching his arm along the back of it. "I found a friend who mentored me, kept me under his wing. And an older man who worked me to the bone, but that's a story for a different time. And there was a woman there who treated me like a son. And a boy there who...reminded me of myself when I was a kid."

He paused to gather his words as he leaned up in his seat again. "That's what led me here. While I was at the ranch, I had to relive those days...when you left, Austin."

Austin dipped his chin, his chest rising and falling as he took in a breath.

"I had to go back to when Mom and Dad divorced. When things were good and even when things were bad. I had to relive high school and college. And I had to look at everything and decide if it was worth taking with me into the next chapter. It wasn't."

Peyton looked down at his fidgeting hands. "Austin, I've always loved you like you were part of me. Like a twin, just ten years older. But last night I had to face some demons and it hurt so bad that I thought...for a second...that I hated you." He couldn't bring himself to look at his brother until he finished his thought. "But this morning when I left the ranch to finally go on to Nan and Pop's, I couldn't. I had to forgive you. The weight was unbearable. I love you too much to carry it."

Austin was looking down at his daughter, hiding the emotion behind his eyes, Peyton was sure.

"So, I turned around and came back to the city." He tipped his head. "I feel the Lord calling me to a new chapter and I have to let go of a lot of old hurt before He sees me step into it."

Austin slowly leaned forward, mirroring Peyton's posture. "I, uh, never told you the real reason why I left, and I think you should know what it is."

"Austin, you're not obligated to tell me anything. I only wanted you to know that I forgive you regardless."

"I know," he said as he nodded. "But I want you to know. I need you to know how big our God is."

Peyton agreed, waited.

"I left that night because I wanted to find a place to kill myself."

Peyton's heart dropped. He slowly rose to his feet, looking at Natalie.

"She knows. It was one of the first things I told her when we met. Again." Austin looked over at Natalie and winked.

But Peyton didn't feel the same calm assurance they shared. "All this time I thought you left because you were rebellious and mad at everyone."

Austin huffed a laugh. "Rebellious? Absolutely. But the only Person I was mad at was God. Because He was the One who made me, and I felt like I kept wrecking everyone's life." He stood and paced toward the fireplace. "I went to Houston, and I jumped off a bridge."

But his brother was still here. Peyton had spent almost every weekend with him for the last ten years. He swallowed hard, his heartbeat thundering in his chest.

"God had other plans. There was a man in the water who couldn't swim and needed to be saved. So, I jumped in to save him. Because I was in the right place at the right time. That man is Gavin Aguilar. The one who comes down from Dallas with his family every few months to spend time with our family."

Peyton knew he had saved Gavin's life somehow, but he'd had no idea...

"From there I was taken to the police department. That's where I met Liam, who turned out to be the best partner an officer could ask for and the best friend a man could find. And he eventually met his wife, Avery. And Avery's dedication to Christ made me realize that I wanted to give my heart back to Jesus. And I did. Then I came home to Austin, mended my relationships with Mom and Dad. You." He turned and looked at Natalie. "Met my wife."

Natalie dipped her chin, a rosy grin on her face as she closed her eyes sweetly.

Peyton could see it coming together, the way God had woven a golden thread through all their lives. How each person was touched and changed for such a time.

Austin moved gradually around the coffee table and dropped a hand on Peyton's shoulder. "That's why it scared me to death when you said you had to go. Get out of town for a bit like I did when I was younger. Because I knew what intentions I had when I left town. And I prayed with every ounce of my being that you weren't experiencing the same hopelessness that I had back then."

Peyton nodded. Though taking his own life hadn't crossed his mind, there had been more hopelessness than he'd cared to acknowledge. But now he knew why. He'd been a boy mourning a tragedy that had never truly happened. Somewhere in his heart a dark seed had gotten planted and it filled him with so much fear that he'd lost sight of joy.

"I never wanted to hurt myself, but I was hopeless," he said in a little more than a whisper. "All I knew is that I would have gone to the ends of the earth to find the same peace and love I see in you, Austin."

Austin tipped his head. "That's Jesus, Peyton. That's Who you see when you look at me. It's Who you've always seen. I'm just a man. But every day of my life I let Him use me for whatever purpose pleases Him. Even when it was hard and even when it didn't make sense. I couldn't love anyone until I learned to love myself. And there's only one way to do that—by realizing that God died to love you first."

Austin dropped his hand from Peyton's shoulder. "That same peace and love can live in you, too. All you have to do is lay your life down at the feet of Jesus. Everything. Every day. No exceptions. No stipulations. No negotiations. It's either yours to carry or His to redeem. But the choice belongs to you."

Peyton nodded, filling his lungs with an electrifying air. He wanted it. Wanted it more than he could put into words. Nothing could compare to the glory of God and Peyton wanted to live in that glory for eternity. No holds barred. Taking with him anyone and everyone who would listen.

"Thank you, Austin." He dipped his chin, and Austin pulled him in for a hug.

When they went back to their seats, Austin gestured to Peyton's face. "What's the story there?"

Peyton lifted his hand and touched the cut near his brow. He chuckled. "Just a co-worker who was desperate for money."

Natalie shared a look with Austin. It was another story for a different time.

Peyton cleared his throat. "There is something else, though."

They both lifted their chins, eyes curious as they waited.

"I met a girl."

Olivia stood in the hallway of her parent's cabin, staring at her reflection in the glass of the picture of Jesus walking on water. She studied her ponytail high on her head, pulled tightly away from the beauty mark that used to hide behind the wavy locks. Not this time. Not today.

Today, she was singing at church.

Olivia giggled, the sound echoing off the quiet walls around her. She still couldn't believe she was doing it. It had been three days since she'd called their pastor and asked if she could lead worship for just one song this week. He'd readily agreed, having heard tales of her voice from her family over the years.

It had also been three days since Peyton had left and she wanted nothing more than to make something of their encounter together. Singing in front of her church seemed the best way to do that. It had been his idea and because he saw more in her than what she could, she was eager to put it to practice.

Now was the time.

She straightened her shoulders and looked more blatantly at her reflection, trying with every bit of willpower that she possessed to see herself as God saw her. Maybe she wouldn't see it today. But one day she would. One day she would look into the dark, stormy waves where Jesus' feet walked...

Olivia looked up at the picture.

Jesus and all of His glory reached out over the waves with one hand and in the distance there was a calm. The God who made the sun and moon to be still. The God who split the sea for His children. The God who pulled men out of fires unscathed. The God who had crafted her with His own hands.

How many times over the years had she looked into this picture to check her own reflection, to hide behind her hair, to worry with her insecurities—when Jesus had been there the whole time? How many times had she looked passed him? How many times had she prayed for strength to be herself when He'd been there all along, promising freedom to be the woman He'd called her to be?

Peyton's words came crashing over her.

She reached out and touched the cold glass with her fingertips. "He's the King I call Father. Which makes me royal by blood. Who can stop me?" she whispered.

The compassion on Jesus' face was so sweet that it caressed her spirit. It was as if He was telling the world, "I love you to Heaven and back."

Tears welled in her eyes. The commotion of her family coming downstairs interrupted her thoughts. She let her hand fall away as they came close, heading for the front door.

"Ready?" Dad stopped and placed his hand on her shoulder.

She nodded with all the calmness and confidence of a beautiful daughter of God.

A half hour later she stood backstage of their little church, a microphone in her hand and tension shaking her shoulders. She'd sang a million times for her family. She had no problem singing in front of God. Why was she so nervous? She wasn't auditioning for anything. Her livelihood didn't depend upon how well she could perform.

Or did it?

"Two minutes, Olivia," the sound tech said as he passed by.

She gripped the mic with both hands and pushed a big breath out of her lungs. Eyes closed, her heart chanted Peyton's words. "Jesus is King and I'm His daughter. I'm royal by blood. Who can stop me?"

When it was time, she stepped out onto the stage, eyes roving over the faces she'd grown up with. Over her mom and dad whose smiles beamed like they were the proudest parents in the world. And Josh who sat at full attention on the edge of the pew. And Pepaw whose wrinkles looked a little less deep, even though he'd gone quiet since the day Peyton had left. And then there was Caroline, nestled against the arm of a man they'd grown up with here in Heavenly. Her blue eyes sparkling and her grin triumphant as she watched Olivia.

"King, give me strength. Be glorified through me," she whispered.

The music started softly. As always. A lovely intro that segued into the lyrics that were so near and dear to her heart.

"I can't explain it—
The way that You came for me.
My mind was a prison,
But You rushed in and rescued me.

Days that would never end,
Nights were filled with tears.
Doubt and pain that wouldn't bend—
But it was You who pulled me near."

As she sang, she looked out over the people that Jesus loved and died for. He heart so full of adoration for them that she let it pour through her voice as the choir filled the background.

"You said You'd move mountains—
You moved mountains for me.
You said You'd heal broken hearts,
And You heard my plea.

You said You would go to the grave,
The cross was the proof.
You said You'd return in three days,
And now we walk with You."

As the church stood and sang along, some with their hands raised in the air, Olivia closed her eyes and worshipped. After another minute, she looped to the chorus again before she brought the song to an end, the words running over her heart like a river.

As she pulled the microphone from her lips, she opened her eyes to the applause of a church praising God. Satisfaction that she'd faced her fears and shared her gift with the world filled her. She was new. Everything was gonna be okay.

She turned to leave, but stopped short, doing a double take. Standing at the back of the church was a man, hands tucked in his pockets in that too familiar way.

Peyton.

He was smiling, nodding. Suddenly he was blurry through her tears. She blinked them away and handed off the mic to the tech. But when she turned around, Peyton was gone.

Her heart fell.

She stepped off the stage and walked down the aisle. She squeezed her dad's shoulder as she passed him but didn't return to her seat like she'd planned to. He didn't seem to question it when she kept walking. She pushed through the wide oak entryway, praying it wasn't her imagination.

Sunshine fell through the open foyer doors onto the emerald green carpet. And Peyton stood just inside, his shoulder leaned against the frame. When he heard the door behind her fall closed, he turned, his smile faltering when he saw her. She stayed where she was, clasping her hands at the waist of her skirt.

If she rushed forward too quickly, she might wake up and

realize this was simply a dream. "Is it really you?"

He tipped his head. "It's me."

"I didn't think you'd come back."

He shrugged. "Vern had a stack of old pallets he needed moved and apparently I'm the only one he trusts with the job."

She couldn't help the laugh that spilled out of her.

"Your dad told me you'd be singing today. I couldn't miss it."

"You came all the way from New Mexico just to hear me sing?"

"Actually..." He took a step toward her. "I didn't go to New Mexico. I went to the city. I had some loose ends to tie up. I had to do some things God was asking me to do years ago. I just couldn't hear Him."

Her heart skipped a beat. "You've heard from God?"

"Loud and clear. And He's made it very straightforward what He wants me to do with my life."

"And what's that?" She dared to ask. Would she like his answer? Would it line up with the desires her own heart was demanding of her?

He looked down at his shoes for a brief second. "Your dad is planning to move forward with a men's ministry on the ranch. And I want to be there for that." He cleared his throat. "It's been heavy on my heart for the last three days and it's getting heavier."

Olivia pulled in a deep breath. She closed the distance and walked straight into his waiting arms. He lifted her off the ground and sighed softly, as if he'd been waiting three days for this moment.

"I missed you so much," she breathed as the tears finally fell.

"I missed you," he groaned. "You have no clue how much I missed you."

Buried against his chest, she waited. She didn't know how much time had passed or if anyone had seen them standing there, holding each other. But she wanted him, needed him in her life in ways she knew was right but couldn't explain.

He finally leaned away. "I never quite understood when people would call their significant other their best friend," he said with a chuckle. "That always sounded boring to me.

But then I met you. Calling you my best friend was something I couldn't turn down. And then I fell in love with you."

"I fell in love with you, too," she laughed, her heart so full it was about to burst.

He released his hold on her and took her face in his hands. "Olivia, if you'll have me, I want to spend the rest of my life winning your heart."

Tears fell as she nodded, the warmth of his fingertips pressing against her neck. His blue eyes sparked with something lively, free of the storm she'd always seen in them, and he leaned in.

She closed her eyes, ready for his kiss, but unprepared for the sudden heat of his mouth against hers. He was kind and gentle and unassuming—as if he knew they had a hundred years to get to know each other, and he wasn't willing to rush through any of them. Joy surged through her like a bolt of lightning when he dipped his head and captured her lips again.

So that's what it's supposed to feel like.

He broke their kiss with a sigh, and she was putty in his hands.

Behind her, a door squeaked. She turned to find Josh slowing to a stop halfway to them, the same hope shining in his wide eyes that Olivia had felt a moment ago.

"Peyton?"

Olivia felt a chill where Peyton had held her as he stepped away. Josh ran the last few steps and jumped into Peyton's waiting arms. They shared the hug of two brothers who'd been separated for longer than either one of them liked. Tears filled her eyes, and she couldn't help the soft laugh that tumbled out of her.

Peyton dropped to one knee until they were eye to eye. "There's a lot more I want to share with you, Josh. So, I thought I'd come back. Stay a while. Maybe forever. Whaddya think about that?"

"Are Mom and Dad adopting you, too?"

Olivia and Peyton laughed together.

"There...might be another way I can join the family."

Smile bright as she'd ever seen it, Josh nodded adamantly. "I've always wanted a brother!"

Peyton ruffled Josh's hair as he stood. He reached out and took both of Olivia's hands—only inches between them. He tipped his head toward her. "And you. Whether you want me as a friend until we're old and gray or you'll let me call you my wife, I promise I won't ever let you forget how loved you are."

She tilted her head and gave him a sideways look, wrinkling her nose. "I wouldn't mind if you wanted both."

A grin spread across his face, and he gave her a look that told her he wanted to kiss her again. "I do."

EPILOGUE

Three Months Later

There was something about a Texas sunset that made Peyton feel like he was alive. Sitting in the bed of his truck beside the prettiest woman on earth, he watched what small part of the horizon they had a view of from the driveway of his brother's house. With Olivia's head resting in the crook of his outstretched arm, warm fall air filled his lungs.

God had truly led him to the Rock that was higher than he was.

Their plan had been to surprise Austin and Natalie with Olivia's arrival. But that surprise got nixed when they'd arrived a few minutes ago and the Brooks' family minivan was nowhere to be seen. Then Peyton worried the family might have made their way down to Houston to visit Liam and Avery.

A quick phone call remedied that worry when he found out that Liam and Avery had come to see them instead and both families were at Zilker Park. They'd have to wait a while longer to meet, but Peyton didn't mind. He was content right where he was.

Olivia groaned and covered her face with both hands. "I'm so nervous."

Peyton squeezed her shoulder, letting his eyes follow the long, silky strands of hair that bunched around his arm where she sat. "What part makes you nervous?"

Her fingers spread and she peeked at him with wide, brown eyes. "The fact that I'm about to meet fifteen people is a little nerve-racking."

"*Well*," he drawled. "If you wanna be technical about it,

you're only meeting four people and eleven kids."

She pinched her eyes shut. "Doesn't help. That's still thirty eyes that are gonna be on me. Thirty eyes that are gonna be questioning whether I'm good enough for you or not. Thirty eyes that are gonna see my beauty mark and wonder why you would pick me."

She shoved herself up using his leg to brace herself. "I can't do it. Take me back to Heavenly. We'll just have to write them a letter."

Peyton grinned. He loved everything about this woman. He pushed himself up and brushed his jeans off. "Not an option. My brother doesn't have a mailbox."

She turned slowly until she found the thing sitting at the corner of the driveway. Then she turned to him with a wrinkle between her brows.

He couldn't help but chuckle. "They're gonna love you, Olivia. I promise."

She wrinkled her nose and fell against his chest, burying her face in his shirt. "But what if you're wrong?"

"I'm not. You'll see in a few minutes. I imagine they took a private jet the moment they realized we were here. They should be landing any second."

Something that sounded like a moan mixed with a laugh spilled out of her. She slowly straightened, her wild, auburn hair sticking out in different directions. "Did you at least warn them about the way I look? Did you tell the kids? They might be scared when they see me."

"I did warn them," he nodded adamantly. "I told them to not act shocked or surprised when they meet you for the first time and find out I'm engaged to the most beautiful woman to ever walk the planet."

She tried to frown but it was a miserable attempt. Her nose wrinkled and her smile won out instead.

This woman really was going to be his soon. "I love you."

Her arms snaked around his middle and pulled him tight. "And I love you."

Her tender gaze swept over his face and he knew in that moment he'd be the kind of husband who stayed in trouble most of his marriage for making her blush.

The sound of traffic coming down the road stole their attention. A minivan and an SUV blazed toward them on the empty neighborhood street.

"There they are," Peyton said as he threaded his fingers through hers and led her to the end of the tailgate. He stepped off the edge and reached back to lift her down.

"Lord, give me strength," she muttered, her hands on his shoulders until her feet were on the ground.

The vehicles parked parallel on the road and every door opened at once. Kids of all ages spilled out onto the lawn and came rushing at them—a couple falling against the grass before they gained their footing.

"Uncle Peyt!" Riley squealed, launching herself into his arms. He snatched her up and nearly tossed her in the air but stopped short. If he threw one kid in the air then the other ten would want to be thrown, too, and that didn't bode well for the arms of a man who'd rather spend the evening holding his future bride.

"Where were you guys?" Peyton asked her.

She shrugged, not caring much about an answer when her eyes landed on Olivia hiding behind Peyton's shoulder. Peyton stepped aside, turning to face her so Riley could have a better view. "Kids, I want you to meet Olivia." Peyton winked when she looked directly at him with uncertainty pinched in her eyebrows. "She's gonna be your Aunt Livy in a few months."

The wrinkle between her brows relaxed and her eyes turned gentle and warm.

Riley reached out one hand toward Olivia. Peyton moved closer, expecting Olivia to take the four-year-old in her arms as the others gathered around. Except Riley didn't want to be held, she wanted to touch Olivia's face. Olivia stepped forward and let the little girl trace her beauty mark with her tiny fingertips.

"Oooh," Riley cooed. "It's so soft."

Leave it to Riley, with her dad's unconditional love and her mom's brave tongue, to cut straight to the point.

"Where did you get that?" Riley asked.

Olivia giggled, her shoulders lifting. "God gave it to me."

"Look!" Riley kicked her legs, a signal that she wanted down, and Peyton obliged. "God gave my cousin, Hannah, two different color eyes! See?"

Ten-year-old Hannah, cousin by friendship, swayed back

and forth as Olivia studied her eyes. Then Olivia looked to him with a gaping mouth as if she were shocked that he hadn't told her before now.

In his defense, he wasn't expecting her to meet the Reed family today.

"Your eyes are absolutely beautiful, Hannah," Olivia said, reaching out and touching the heads of whichever kids were closest to her. They all gathered around, not a single one shied away or acted scared.

Peyton could thank Riley for that. Her headstrong spirit paved a way that the other kids wouldn't be afraid to follow.

"All right. Everyone to the back yard and I'll distribute ice cream cones," Natalie called out from the edge of the group, baby Reese on her hip. "Last one there gets a boiled egg."

All at once the kids took off in the direction of the house. Within seconds the yard fell quiet.

"Now it's our turn to meet the future Mrs. Brooks," Natalie said as she moved in to hug Olivia.

Avery was next. "Oh, Peyton," she laughed. "She's way out of your league, sweetie."

That was rich coming from Avery considering that she was willing to set him up with every available girl from here to Houston.

Austin brushed by him to hug her after that. "Brooks men have a way of doing that, don't we?" He sent Natalie a wink.

Liam was last to welcome Olivia with a hug. "No way. You two men don't get to take the credit, we're all overachievers in the marriage department."

Olivia hugged each one while covering her laugh behind her hand. Peyton cherished every moment he spent falling in love with her in new ways. And seeing her stand among his brothers and sisters, by blood and in Christ, he knew his future was set.

"Olivia, don't be shy. What's the secret? How'd Peyton win you over?" Natalie asked, leaning close enough to Olivia that Reese reached out her arms.

Without hesitation, Olivia took the baby girl and Peyton's chest swelled with respect. "For one, he was the biggest fan of my baking."

The group chimed together like it was no surprise to them that Peyton liked sweets.

"Two, he taught me how to be myself and how to love who I was," she said, her brown eyes trained on him as she swayed with the baby against her shoulder. "And I've never met a man who loved the way Jesus loves until I met Peyton. When I thought I lost him I knew I'd never love anyone else the way I loved him. So, when he came back, there was no question that he was the man I wanted to spend my life with."

Peyton dipped his head, the weight of her words humbling him.

"Aww," Avery and Natalie cooed, sweeping their arms around Olivia from each side.

They moved her toward the house and together the three of them, Natalie, Olivia, and Avery walked arm-in-arm up the stairs and into the house. Three very different women from three very different regions of Texas brought here where they would spend their time as family.

All because of these three men.

All because of Austin and the journey God had laid out for him.

"You did good, Peyton." Liam dropped his hand on Peyton's shoulder, his fatherly eyes shining proudly. "She's a ruby for sure."

"I gotta admit," Austin said, coming around in front of him. "I didn't believe it until you showed up with her. When you told us you met a beautiful girl and she happened to be a woman of God and she was actually into you..." He shook his head. "I don't know how you lucked out three for three, kid."

"I hear it's a Brooks thing," Peyton said.

Austin and Liam laughed deeply.

Peyton sighed. "But I think we all know it's a Jesus thing."

Liam started toward the house. "That it is, Peyton. That it is."

With Austin's arm resting against Peyton's shoulders, they walked to the foot of the stairs where Liam waited. Austin hooked his other arm around Liam and the three of them followed their brides into the house, turning the page on a story that testifies of the trustworthiness, hope, grace, and love of the Living God who still writes stories today.

BOOKS IN *THE FINDING FAITH SERIES*:

THE TRUST CHARM – BOOK ONE

THE ROAD TO AUSTIN – BOOK TWO

UNTIL THE DAY BREAK – BOOK THREE

WILD SIDE OF THE HEART – BOOK FOUR

Note from the author

Just wow. This journey has been the most incredible endeavor of my life. Writing *The Finding Faith Series* has changed me in more ways than I've ever dreamed possible. These four books are truly a testament to what God does in our lives when we surrender our dreams and plans to Him.

I thought my previous novel, *Until the Day Break*, was going to be the last book in this series, but it felt so unfinished. These characters still had a story to tell. And as I mentioned in my acknowledgments, a kind friend suggested I write a story for "sweet Peyton." (*Sweet* is exactly what he turned out to be.) I can't put into words the joy I felt when God finally told me to write it. Everything came together so effortlessly that I have no doubt He has big plans for this book. It means something to Him, and for, that I'm forever grateful.

This story was so full of life and adventure that it felt like I was walking step by step with the characters. Like most of the people in Austin's life, Peyton had been affected by his brother's choices, but in ways he had never fully recognized. The weight of that burden held him back from thriving and truly experiencing the presence of God—much like it does for many of us. Even Olivia carried burdens from the choices of others and had let them hold her back from truly believing in herself. If you find yourself relating to their story, I'm here to tell you that there is abundance in salvation. Christ spared no expense to ensure hope reached you today. Ask Him into your heart and you'll see that the love you've always craved was waiting for you. Trade your burdens for His joy. He would love nothing more than to meet with you right here, right now.

Love,

Jessica

ABOUT THE AUTHOR

Jessica Alyse is a Louisiana girl with a heart for Texas. She is a member of the American Christian Fiction Writers. She has a passion for Jesus, romance, and storytelling, and writes Christian love stories with a touch of humor for hopeless romantics looking for a little bit of charm and a whole lot of Jesus. When she's not writing, you can find her reading, dreaming about the day her stories are adapted into movies, or in the event of a baseball game, cheering for the Houston Astros.

JessAlyse.com